THE
SINS
and THE
VIRTUES

LUST

Also by
CHARLOTTE FEATHERSTONE

SINFUL
ADDICTED

And watch for the first novel in Charlotte Featherstone's
new historical romance series

SEDUCTION & SCANDAL

from HQN Books

CHARLOTTE FEATHERSTONE

THE
SINS
and THE
VIRTUES
LUST

Spice

Spice

LUST

ISBN-13: 978-0-373-60552-1

Recycling programs
for this product may
not exist in your area.

Copyright © 2011 by Charlotte Featherstone

For questions and comments about the quality of this book
please contact us at Customer_eCare@Harlequin.ca.

Spice and the Colophon are trademarks used under license and
registered in Australia, New Zealand, Philippines, United States Patent and
Trademark Office and in other countries.

www.Spice-Books.com

Printed in U.S.A.

To Grannie MacAlpine,
whose stories of the dark and mysterious Fey did not have the intended effect.
I wasn't scared in the least that a Faery would come and pluck me out of bed
because I was up after I had been safely tucked in. I was entranced.
And inspired! Thank you for those stories,
and for shaping my love of Faeries, and faerytales.

The Curse of the Unseelie Court

IT IS SAID THAT THE FEY HAVE ALWAYS LIVED amongst mortals, their world lying parallel to ours. They live in two courts; the good faeries belong to the Seelie Court, where gaiety and light reign. Opposite to the Seelie Fey are the Dark Fey, those who live in the Unseelie Court, or the unholy court as it is known. These dark faeries are mysterious and sensual, well versed in pleasures of the flesh. It is said that to look upon them and their beauty is to be drawn into their erotic, voluptuous world, and once there, your fate is sealed, your body and will no longer your own.

And this is precisely what happened once, long, long ago, to a beautiful queen of the Seelie Court, who had the misfortune to catch the eye of the Dark Fey king.

Immediately, the king was besotted with the queen, driven to possess her at all costs. Queen Aine was all the king could think about, but Aine spurned him, forcing King Duir to steal her away from her golden court as she slept. Like Persephone taken to the underworld, Duir brought Aine to his dark court, plying her with his erotic skills. The Unseelie king was certain he could win Aine, but the queen despised Duir. Long had she plotted against her captor, vowing to leave the king and his court behind, but Duir kept her prisoner, a concubine for his dark pleasures.

The queen's loathing of the king festered, until she could think of nothing but revenge. Fueled by hatred, Aine searched for a way to break free—all to no avail. Until one day, she was delivered of the king's twin sons. Enraptured by his progeny, and grateful to the queen for giving him such a gift, Duir became less watchful, allowing the queen new freedoms, and it was then that Aine found a way to leave his court.

One night she stole away, taking with her one of her sons, the golden-haired child who was the image of her Seelie self, leaving behind his dark-haired brother who bore his father's resemblance. As she fled, Aine placed a spell on the Unseelie Court, that it whither away, never to thrive again until the Dark Fey could make a woman give herself to him of her own free will. As well, she cursed the sons of Duir's siblings—and any future male children of the king—with each cardinal sin, further destroying her own dark son's chances of finding a virtuous woman who would give herself willingly.

To this day, the queen's spell holds strong. The Unseelie Court is dying. There is but one hope for the court—to find the seven women who represent the virtuous aspects of humanity. Seven women who embody chastity, temperance, charity, diligence, patience, kindness and humility. Women whose very being calls to the sins deeply buried in each prince, sins that are eager to corrupt, through erotic pleasure, their virtues.

If the court is to survive, the fey princes will have to find a way to make the virtues follow them willingly, while satisfying the basic needs of their sins. Sins of which, perhaps, each virtue is ready for a taste.

PROLOGUE

Dear Diary,
Born of a higher power—gifted, favored...cursed. I am all of
these things. It is said that not only my conception, but those of
my sisters as well, was an auspicious event. Like the visit from
the angel Gabriel to Mary, my father was visited in his slumber
from the faery queen, who foretold the coming of our births and
the importance of not only myself, but my three sisters. In his
dreams, it was whispered to him the part we would play in a
world that we had not yet seen—a world, it seems, we will never
really become a part of.

Like the spirit of Christ to the Virgin, the queen infused
within my father the qualities that all humans wished to pos-
sess—attributes that many sought through absolution at church,
and monies given away to pardon them for any trespass. Through
his seed, our virtues were passed on, each daughter possessing the
moralities that would define her—humility, kindness, temperance
and chastity.

We are bound to these virtues as surely as we breathe. They define us, our personalities, our hopes, our desires. They enslave us. Chain us, until the day our purpose in this small, confined world is revealed.

It is our lot in life. Some would say that others have endured far worse than what we have. After all, we were born into the Lennox dynasty—a family whose powers stretch from the southwest of England into the wild beauty of Scotland. A family whose riches have flourished. A family who is revered, and just a touch feared, for the four daughters who were born within minutes of each other.

While some fear that we're witches, others eager to possess wealth and power fear not the mysterious happening of our birth, but the fact that we are beyond possessing. We are made for something else, something beyond the pleasures and ambitions of men.

We are made pure. Righteous. Virtuous. Lonely.

Imagine, as I have, going through life and never experiencing all it has to offer. Imagine what it is to dream—and dread—a future which you know nothing about, because, as my sisters and I know, we were not created for such mundane purposes as tending home and hearth, but for some other mystical, and I fear sinister, reason.

Imagine if you can bear to, never feeling the touch of a man or desire spear your loins. Imagine listening to your friends speak of the beaux they dance with and the shirtless laborers who toil the soil, their perspiration trickling between muscles, a sight that you're afraid you will never understand the power of, or feel your own cheeks heat with a rush of physical longing at such a masculine, virile sight.

Picture, *if you can, never feeling any heat warm your blood when a man's gaze caresses you, lingering on breasts that should make you feel womanly, but instead, from which you feel disconnected. Indifferent. Sexless...*

High and mighty they call me. Frigid. But I am neither of those things. I am Chastity—my name, and my virtue. It is who I am, my entire being. It, I fear, is my prison.

One

"YOUR HIGHNESS, THE TIME HAS COME."

He knew it. Heard the wails for what seemed like days now, the resonance ringing in his ears. Not even here, in his private solar, was he free from the cries that seemed to haunt his court. Another howl, worse than the keening of a banshee, echoed through the castle, whispering through his blood and settling deep within his black soul.

The curse was upon them.

Niall, king of the Unseelie Court, son of Duir and the most powerful of the Dark Fey, stood before the enormous hearth with legs braced wide and hands clasped behind his back. Unblinking, he watched the orange flames engulf a blackened oak log, sending sparks sizzling up the flue and into the chamber. Another female scream rent the air; its chilling sound found its way once more inside him as he fought to show no outward emotion.

"Your Highness—"

"Who is the maid who struggles to bring her child into the world?"

"Gertrude, female of Irian."

Niall shut his eyes against the pain of knowing his cousin would suffer this night. Irian, despite his Elvish blood, or perhaps because of it, was his best warrior at court. It did not matter to Niall that his cousin was a Halfling Fey. Irian was loyal and trustworthy, and like a brother to him. More than the blood brother whom Niall had shared a womb with. Irian's mixed blood had never been of consequence to Niall, until now.

"It was a mistake to allow him within the inner sanctum," the seer of the fey growled. "He has incurred the Mother Creator's wrath, and now we shall all suffer."

Niall held himself still, breathing deep, willing his anger to tether. "It is not the Mother Creator who has cursed us, Gwynad, but *my* mother."

He heard the seer growl behind him. The tip of the old man's yew staff slammed against the gold tiles, but Niall ignored Gwynad's theatrics—no one cowed him, especially this wizened old mage.

"How did the female come to be at our court?" he asked, grasping at anything at all that might tell him she and her babe would be spared from his mother's hatred and the curse that shrouded his court.

Gwynad sighed and rustled forward, his velvet robe whispering against the floor. "The girl was a servant. Irian purchased her from a mortal. Thirty pieces of silver, and a blessing on the mortal's child."

"It seems an even transaction," he grumbled, despite the growing unease in his belly. The woman—Gertrude—had not cried out in the last few minutes.

Gwynad pressed closer, his voice a hushed whisper. "She did not want to come to the Unseelie Court despite Irian's assurance she would be treated like a princess. She tried to persuade the mortal to take her back, but then Irian and his crazed Elvish blood took over and he stole her, carrying her here as though he were god of the underworld and her an innocent maid.

"She was not willing, nor has she softened," Gwynad hissed, reminding Niall, not so subtly, of the curse his mother had placed on his court.

Irian loved the mortal. Niall knew that. But he also knew that Gertrude had never grown to love Irian. They were doomed, as was their babe. As was the Unseelie Court.

Suddenly the door to the solar was thrown wide, the thick oak ratcheting off the wall. Behind him, Niall heard the enraged breathing, smelled the scent of sorrow mixed with the sweet smell of death.

"She's gone."

Two words filled with gut-wrenching agony. Niall closed his eyes against it, steeling himself in opposition to the pain he heard in Irian's voice.

"Damn you, she's gone!"

Slowly Niall turned, bracing himself for what he would face. Draped over Irian's arms was Gertrude, limp and pale—lifeless. She was dressed in a white gown, from the waist down the snowy fabric was coated red. His lover's lifeblood dripped onto Irian's boots and puddled between his feet.

"She will be afforded a fey burial as though she were your wife, Irian. As you are a prince of the Dark Fey, she would have been your princess. She will be buried as such."

Niall looked up into the anguished face of his brother of the heart, willing Irian to look at him, but the warrior was consumed now, and the only thing Irian saw was his dead mate lying in his arms.

"What of the babe?" demanded Gwynad.

Irian growled, took a menacing step toward the seer, but caught Niall's eyes and steadied his raging blood.

"It is a boy. He's…alive. I do not know for how much longer. The mortal midwife says he has been born too early."

"Gwynad," Niall commanded, "fetch a woman to feed the child."

The old man looked at him as though he were mad. "We have not had a child born to this court in years, Your Highness. There is no milk to be had from our women."

"Then you have my permission to steal a wet nurse from the mortal realm."

"And bring more disaster down upon us?" the seer thundered. "Your Highness, I beg you. There can be no more stealing from the mortals. Our court is dying! We must find a way to break your mother's spell—"

"And what do you think I have been doing since I claimed the throne?" Niall roared in frustration. "Sitting on my arse, having a merry party? Is that what you think I do in here all damn day?"

The seer bowed and took a step back. "I know you have been searching for a way—"

"Enough!" Niall barked. "Gwynad, you will order two servants to take milk from the cow Farmer Douglas leaves out in the pasture for us to avail ourselves. I gifted him and his wife with a child through my magic. The cow is a tithe. Go now." He turned his gaze to Irian. "Let us bury her in our way, my friend."

A sob escaped Irian as he looked down into his dead lover's face. "She didn't want that, to stay here with me and our court. She begged me, Niall, as she saw her impending death, to free her. I...promised her I would."

Swallowing hard, Niall watched Irian sink to his knees, weeping over Gertrude's lifeless body. Not for the first time, Niall cursed his mother, the queen of the Seelie Court, for the spell she had cast. He cursed his father for allowing decades to go by without bothering to search for a way to lift the spell. But most of all, he cursed the day his mother had taken his twin and left him at this court to watch his people dwindle and die.

"Irian," he murmured, resting his hand atop his cousin's shoulder. "We *will* avenge her death. I promise you that. I will find a way to break this curse. You will find another woman, Irian—*you will*. And she will want you and desire you as fiercely as you desire her."

Irian looked up at him, his black eyes glowing like onyx through a veil of anguish. "We are all cursed, Niall. The court is dying. Despite the riches we have and the bounty of food in our trenchers and the comforts of our chambers, we are cursed. We have every material thing a fey could desire except the love of a woman and children to see to the survival of our race."

"I will break this damnable curse, Irian. I will do whatever it takes. I vow that."

Irian's face twisted from sorrow to anger. "Who will want us, Niall," he sneered, "when we are condemned by sin?"

Standing in his father's bedchamber, Niall pushed aside the cobwebs that had grown in the years since Duir's death. Inside this room, the secret to lifting the curse was hidden, Niall felt sure of it.

A shiver of abhorrence slithered along his spine as he looked around the untouched chamber. The room was cold and oppressive, like the man who had once occupied it. Despite its warm jewel-colored bed hangings and lavish pillows in velvets and silk, the bed, indeed, the entire room, felt like a tomb. This room had also born witness to the rape of the Seelie queen, as well as the conception of him and his brother and their subsequent births. These walls had witnessed the night his mother had fled the Unseelie Court, taking with her his twin who was the image of her Seelie self, leaving him, the image of his father, to grow up in the care of a man who became nothing short of a raving madman.

In this room was the tainted past, and hidden amongst its dark secrets was the way to end the curse.

He glanced at the massive bed, its ivory sheets twisted

and trailing to the floor, and saw the image of the king, dying. Leaving Niall to rule over a court that had no hope. A court tainted by the sins of his father.

As if whispered through the threadbare bed curtains, he heard the curse murmuring around him, a reminder of what he already knew—the legacy of his mother's wrath. They might as well have been inked onto his skin, for those words and her spell were embedded into every facet of his being.

His mother. He looked to the portrait that hung above his father's bed. Aine was silver haired and violet eyed— he had her eyes. She was from the court of sunlight and gaiety, and his father, from the court of night and carnal sin. Duir's was a world of dark beauty and erotic sensuality, and his mother had been repulsed by it. His father hadn't cared. His lust was too strong, so he had stolen her from her bed while she slept and forced her to accept him. His father, in his misguided Unseelie ignorance believed that he could make her love him through sex.

But his mother had never softened. Just as Gertrude had never softened with Irian.

Aine's hatred and vengeance was complete against the dark court. No mortal or immortal could be brought to the court against their will and made to love a fey. They had to come of their own volition. They had to give their body and soul willingly. And it was for certain that no female would want him, or the other Dark Fey, once they discovered who they really were. Beyond their faery beauty lay the sins of the world. Lust, vanity, envy, gluttony…all seven consumed in each fey prince. Wrath was

Niall's sin, and tonight it was simmering beneath his flesh. He wanted revenge—bloody and merciless—against his mother, his twin and the entire Seelie Court.

"Tell me how," he whispered hoarsely. "How do I make this right?" He hoped the spirits, either malicious or benign, who haunted this chamber would hear him. "Tell me how to lift this bloody curse and save my court from this black spot."

A whisper, barely audible, brushed past him. Movement near the bookshelf caught his attention. The fluttering of vellum edged in gold leaf flittered to the floor, making him press closer. By magic, the image of words in the ancient fey tongue appeared before his eyes, giving him hope for the first time since he had assumed the throne of the Unseelie.

Some by sin rise, and some by virtue fall...

Two

Glastonbury, Somerset, England
1789, the Eve of Beltane

THE TOR ROSE ABOVE THE VILLAGE LIKE A MEGA-lithic warrior, glinting in the sunlight. Atop the mysterious mound, like a stone needle penetrating the clouds, towered the remnants of St. Michael's Church. For centuries the villagers had said that Arthur and Guinevere were buried there. But others believed most steadfastly that the faery folk dwelt deep beneath the rippling green grass that resembled layers of plush velvet. It was said that underneath the grass, beneath the tor itself, lay a labyrinth of winding crypts—the magical path to the Faery.

On certain nights of the year, like tonight, the Eve of Beltane, the veil between the immortal and the mortal realm was thinned and the fey and all their beauty and magic walked unknowingly amongst man. But Beltane was not until twilight. Hours away, yet. They were free from the faeries. At least for now.

Casting an admiring glance at the mysterious and striking tor, Chastity, of all people, knew to believe in the tales of the *Daoine Side*. The Faery People.

Drawn to the tor as she was, Chastity gripped the handle of her wicker basket tighter in her gloved hands, as if grounding herself against the luring beauty that tried to bewitch her. The tor, it was believed, was the site of the Unseelie Court—the unholy court of the fey. Dark faeries, the Unseelie were. Enigmatically erotic, haunting, beautiful fey that corrupted a soul with all the unearthly, sinful pleasures that any human could ever desire. The Dark Fey and their wicked enchantments were everything that Chastity stood against. The deep-seated virtue within her balked at everything they were: lustful, tempting creatures who stole virgins away from their beds and ravished them.

She should not be intrigued by the tor, or the tempting idea of a magical netherworld that was the Unseelie Court. She should be repulsed. Terrified for her mortal soul. Yet the only time she ever felt the slightest bit of tingling in her woman's body occurred when her gaze lingered upon the sacred mound. Even now, as she strolled down the high street of Glastonbury with her sisters, her gaze was fixed on the tor. There was the faintest tingling in her body. She felt a touch warm, her thighs quivered slightly. Only the tor and the thought of the Dark Fey made her feel this way. Perhaps she felt the prickling awareness because they represented danger. They were the opposite of her in every way. To her virtue, they were sin incarnate. Yet, she could not discount the way her blood grew warm whenever she thought of them. It was only thus, she thought sadly, with the fey. Mortal men provoked nothing in her but bland conversation and an absurd impulse to hide beneath her cloak of chaste piety.

As if to prove her thoughts, Caleb Graham, a baronet in the village, passed her on the street, shooting her a most amiable, handsome grin.

"Goody day, ladies," he murmured, his voice pleasing in a masculine way. "Lady Chastity," he said as he removed his tricorn hat and bowed before her. "How lovely you look this morning. The walk has added an invigorating glow to your skin."

Nothing. Not even the faintest fluttering in her belly. She had heard the other village girls—most of them older women—talk of Caleb Graham's handsomeness. His desirability. Chastity saw it perfectly well. He was a handsome man, and his broad shoulders and chest belied a virile manliness that attracted the fairer sex. But nothing feminine stirred within her.

"Good day, sir," was all she replied, for she was unable to make any idle or pleasant conversation with the opposite sex, however much she longed to possess the ability.

Chastity could not help but notice that his eyes had darkened as he replaced his hat atop his brown hair. Her aloofness was not what the baron was used to when he chatted with females. But Chastity was not blessed with the gift of artful flirtation. She didn't know how. Didn't understand it. Hers was a purity of the mind, soul and body. A paragon above the temptations of mortal man.

"Shall you attend the green this evening?" Caleb's query was directed at her, while his gaze was firmly fixed upon her ample décolletage, which she discreetly covered with the corner of her silk shawl.

"I am afraid not. Do excuse us, sir, for we must be on our way."

The censure in her voice startled him, causing an expression of maligned vanity to cross his features. "Well, then, good day," he grumbled, and Chastity heard him mutter, "Frigid shrew" beneath his breath as he stabbed the ground with his walking stick and proceeded up the high street.

"Pay him no heed," Prudence whispered next to her. "He doesn't know a thing about you, and his assessment is wrong. Besides, I've heard stories about him. He's not the sort you'd wish to set your heart upon."

With a nod and a sigh, Chastity continued to stroll with her sisters down the cobbled street, taking in the bustling activity of the May Day preparations as she forced the interaction out of her mind. Caleb was handsome, so why couldn't she bear to look at him, much less converse with him? Chastity feared she was the oddest female in Christendom. She most certainly was unlike any of the other young ladies of her acquaintance.

"You have such a way with the opposite sex," her sister Mary chortled. "Would it hurt to bestow a smile upon one?"

Chastity did not take the bait. What did Mary know, she thought savagely. Mary didn't realize the mental anguish Chastity suffered, the pain that came from knowing she wasn't like other women. How would Mary feel if she were to discover that the desires of man and woman would never be hers to experience?

"Come, Chastity, you could have offered him a bit of encouragement. Caleb Graham has been hungering for you for a year, at least. Give the poor fellow a smile, or heaven forbid, a dance at the assembly rooms. Who knows, perhaps you might even enjoy shedding your mantle of purity."

"Leave off, Mary," Prudence demanded. "You're just being hurtful and spiteful. Besides, it's not done to stop in the middle of the road and talk to a man. It looks gauche and common, and Chastity was quite right to rebuff the baronet's presumptive behavior."

Mary sent Prudence a horrid glare. "A tip of the hat and a bland 'good day' is presumptive? Dear me, Prudence, you must come down from your tower room and live amongst the real world. I vow, you would have a fit of apoplexy at some of the things that have been whispered to me by the opposite sex."

"Well, then," Mercy said cheerily, changing the course of the conversation. "Shall we stop at the baker's and have a Bakewell tart? I will buy them, for I have brought my pin money."

Chastity glanced at her youngest sister. *Mercy.* The virtue of kindness, trying her utmost to make her sisters the best of friends, not to mention lessening the sting of Baron Graham's painful assessment of Chastity.

"Come," Mercy pleaded, "we shall all have a little sweet for the walk home."

"We really shouldn't dally," Chastity replied. "Although, a quick stop for a tart to eat on the way wouldn't be a bother, would it?"

Prudence, the second eldest, who was always restrained and temperate, declined. "None for me, thank you. But naturally the three of you may indulge."

Chastity nodded in understanding before fixing her gaze on her three sisters. They were paragons. Everyone thought them utterly perfect. Yet each of them knew of the other's desire to be anything but what they were. On the outside, they were ethereal models of the womanly ideal. Inside, they were empty vessels, trapped by the virtues they were born to embrace and embody.

"Well, come along, then," Mercy said as she held her bonnet in place with her hand as a stiff wind gusted up, threatening to take it from her flaxen curls. "My mouth is positively watering at the thought of a tart."

Within minutes they were in the cramped little baker's, inhaling the fresh aroma of pastry and almonds and sweet-cream icing. "Oh, heavenly," Chastity found herself murmuring. Her stomach rumbled in response to the scents. Or perhaps, she thought, glancing over her shoulder at Prue, who waited by the door, it was her sister's long-denied belly she heard. She could see the hunger in Prue's eyes, and Chastity tilted her head, indicating the wooden shelf where countless treats awaited them.

Typical of Prudence, she pinched her lips and shook her head. Denial was all Prue knew.

"There," Mercy announced, passing them each a tart as they stood outside the baker's. She had bought one for Prue, but she refused it, so Mercy handed the tart to a small child who stood beside her mother, who was busy selling irises from a wicker basket.

"Oh, thank you, luv," the woman said gratefully as her daughter reached for the tart and shoved it hungrily into her mouth.

"'Tis no trouble. The eve of May Day," Mercy replied, "is not complete without a Bakewell tart."

As Chastity smiled at the little girl, her gaze caught something radiant in the middle of the road. A man riding a pure white horse that was adorned with a glimmering gold bridle.

He was handsome, more striking than any man she had ever seen. He was tall and fair-haired, and his clothes appeared as though they were spun of gold gossamer threads. His tailoring was richly embroidered, embellished with layers of lace and cloth-covered buttons. He did not resemble a puffed-up peacock like so many gentlemen did in the current fashion. He was every inch a man, a feat nearly impossible to achieve considering his elaborately embroidered frock coat and waistcoat.

As his white horse trotted elegantly by, his eyes caught Chastity's stare. The stranger inclined his head and moved along, forcing Chastity's gaze to follow him as he made his way through the carts and carriages that littered the high street.

Who was he? she wondered, still entranced by the stranger. He didn't live in the village. She would have seen him before now. Heavens, all the village women would have been talking about him. She would have seen him at the assembly rooms, or at a tea or luncheon or *something*.

As he made his way up the steep incline of the road, he glanced back at her once more over his shoulder. He did not stare at her like other men did, with a mixture of intrigue and lust. He was a gentleman. A *polite* gentleman.

But then he was gone, and Chastity realized that she had fallen behind her sisters. Catching up, she stayed to the rear of them, content to eat her tart and contemplate the stranger on horseback. He carried himself as though he was a prince. An ancient prince, she mused, the kind who had also been a knight, leading his men into war.

Fanciful thinking, she reflected. But what more in life did she have to do than think whimsical thoughts as she waited for the future to unfold?

"The village green looks remarkable, does it not?" Mercy said. "I adore Beltane. One day I would love to take part in the festivities. I wish it could be tonight! The weather is very fine and the moon is full."

"I suppose it wouldn't hurt if you had a dance around the maypole," Prudence murmured.

"You know what will happen if I go to the green," Mercy replied as she tied the long pink satin ties of her bonnet. "Everyone will run away as though I have the plague."

No one replied. What could they say? It was the truth. The villagers were superstitious and as a consequence gave the sisters wide berth. The only ones not afraid to speak to them were rogues and rakes who were far too bold and who wanted nothing more than a bit of immoral fun. Which was something that their inherent virtues forbade.

But Mercy, with her virtue of kindness, was more easily forgiving of their lot in life. For her, it was easier to accept. At least, Chastity believed it to be so, for Mercy never complained.

"It is for the best that they are wary," Prudence reminded them. "We aren't like the others. And the fact has never been made more clear than now that we've reached our womanhood."

"Oh, for heaven's sake," admonished Mary, "you make us out to be pariahs. We're not, you know."

Chastity cast a glance to Mary, the eldest of the four, as they walked down the high street. Mary was not like herself, Mercy or Prue. She was altogether different. What virtue Mary possessed had never been very clear. She was far from humble, so the virtue of humility was out; so too was charity, for Mary was notoriously ham-fisted when it came to sharing. Perhaps she was the virtue of diligence? She certainly did have a very great enthusiasm for the opposite sex, and her pursuit of them.

"We *are* pariahs, Mary," Prue's stern voice intruded on Chastity's thoughts. "It is a fact that cannot be denied."

"Well, I have no difficulty whatsoever in finding friends, male or otherwise."

Indeed, she did not. There were always circles of men around Mary for she was the prettiest of them all. Although they had been born within minutes of each other, they all looked different from the other. Mary possessed startling black hair and dark eyes. She was exotic and breathtaking. Chastity could not help but notice just how breathtaking as she walked alongside her. The men, it seemed, preferred Mary's dark looks to Chastity's fair hair and green eyes.

"I fear that you all will die old maids," Mary admonished. "You put too much stock in what you *should* be instead of what you *could* be."

"Have you not listened to anything Father has told us?" Prue asked, censure in her voice.

"I don't believe in Father's absurd stories about a faery queen bequeathing to him daughters who bore the virtues. It's nonsense."

Mary had never been a believer. But then, her sister felt unrestrained joy and mirth. She felt desire when a male caller came to tea, or when a rogue asked her to dance. Mary had experienced things that her other three sisters never had. *Life.*

Perhaps if Mary had been forced to live the life of a true virtue, Chastity mused, she would find herself believing in faery tales—or at the very least the frightening ones.

"If you three would allow yourself to leave the estate, you might find a suitor. It is your eccentric natures that make others suspicious, nothing more. Smile, flirt, flash a bit of ankle or bosom for once, you might be surprised what it will induce."

"You are far too liberal in your dealings with others," Prue cautioned. "It is better to be temperate and even."

"And boring as the devil," Mary returned. It was a direct hit. But Prue bore it well as she always did.

"Come now, we're sisters," Mercy whispered, linking her arms with Prue and Mary. "What is there left, if not kindness between us?"

"I'm only trying to help," Mary sniffed. "For I have no wish to see you all end up as old maids, and I for one will not sit in my tower room becoming one with you. Tonight I am going to the green, and I am having a dance and a meat pie, and I'm going to go a–Maying as all other young ladies do. There is no harm in it, Prudence," Mary snapped, "so you may put away your pinched lips and your disapproving frown. Now, who is coming with me?"

Her question was met with absolute silence.

"As I thought. You three are utterly hopeless."

The twigs cracked beneath the horses' hooves as they emerged from the edge of the woods. Before them, sunlight filtered through the leaves that whispered around them. The hounds they brought sniffed the air, their ears alert, their dark, obsidian eyes watching the humans as they prepared for the Beltane festival.

Niall's words seemed to whisper all around them. *Some by sin rise, and some by virtue fall...*

"Do you believe him? Our king's belief that our curse will end once we find these virtues?"

Thane shrugged at Kian's question as he watched the approach of four women down the path. Niall, while king of the Dark Fey, was also his half brother. As the eldest, Niall had always seemed awe inspiring to Thane, who was younger by five years. He had never had occasion to doubt Niall, nor had his older brother ever been proven wrong. They had very little to go on in regards to the curse, so why not trust in Niall and his vision?

"Seems a great folly to put any stock in the Bard's words," Rinion grumbled. "He's only a human after all."

"Shakespeare," Avery grunted. "I only cared for *A Midsummer Night's Dream*. But then, I'm partial to Titania."

"To fucking the mortal actress who plays Titania," Kian corrected.

Thane raised his hand to silence their banter. Pointing to the women, he commanded silence, then waved his hand, concealing their presence with faery glamour. If the women were to look their way, they would see only the iridescent glimmer of a sunbeam sparkling through the trees.

Convinced they could not be seen or heard, Thane turned to his companions. "Niall would not have sent us here if he supposed it was foolishness. Every one hundred years, the virtues are born into the mortal realm. They have been born. And they are of age. Our king believes that this is the only way to break his mother's curse on our court."

"Do you think the time is right?" Avery asked as he reined in his black steed to a halt. The women were close and the faery mount could smell their presence. "It's only been six months since we were here to bury Irian's woman."

"And you stole that maid from the village," Kian snapped.

Damn him, Kian was intent on starting something with Avery. Thane sent his twin a hard glare, which Kian naturally returned.

Like Niall, Thane's twin was a fey prince, possessed with the cardinal sin of envy. Thane could see the jealousy in his brother's eyes as he glared at Avery, who harbored the sin of gluttony. Of the seven of them, Avery and Kian were most opposed. As Envy, Kian coveted everything Avery had. And as the host of gluttony, Avery always had more, acquired more and strove for more, which made Kian's jealousy deepen and simmer. It was a never-ending circle of gluttony and envy, and the inability to ever be satisfied.

Cursed since birth, Thane had always lamented his fate. However, in times like this, he realized that to be consumed by lust was a gift, as opposed to always needing to have what others had, or always needing more. At least lust could be satiated.

"She was a luscious armful, that one," Avery said with a leer as he recalled the maid he had taken from the village. "Many bountiful pleasures to be had in that tasty morsel. I would have shared her, but then she preferred to be devoured whole by someone well versed in pleasure, not jealousy." He laughed, taunting Kian.

Thane brought his horse to stand between them. "Enough. We needn't have dissent between us. We are here for our souls, for the survival of our court. Petty jealousy and taunts have no place now."

Kian glared at him, opened his mouth to say something, but Thane cut his twin off. "We can wait no longer. We must find, and possess, our virtues. Put your considerable skills into seduction, not barbs and insults."

"I feel it's time. It's been six months in Faery, nearly three mortal years since we have seen the virtues," Rinion, the harbinger of vanity announced. "They were nearly grown then. By now they're of a suitable age to seduce. No, I agree with Thane. It's time. As Niall said, we can wait no longer. The curse must be broken. And there is always the chance that our Seelie enemies might also be looking for them. We need to get to them first."

Thane felt his body twitch as the sound of female voices drifted over to them, caressing his skin. His sin, Lust, reared its head, heating his blood. His gaze fixed on the sight of the four young women, dressed in richly embroidered silk gowns, passing them by. He knew instantly who they were. The Lennox girls. *Their virtues.*

Thane had no difficulty in recognizing his virtue. Chastity. The opposite of his sin called to him like gin called to a drunkard. She was a vision as she walked by him, completely unaware of his and the other princes' presence in the woods that ran alongside the path.

It amazed him that a virtue could be a dichotomy. He expected Chastity Lennox to be a pinched-faced maid in a fragile, bony body. But Chastity was not fragile, nor pinched-face. Her face was ethereal, glowing of innocence, but her body... He cast his covetous gaze over her luscious form and felt himself swell. Her body was not chaste in the least. Her curves invited the most licentious of thoughts, the most amoral of all pleasures. What he and his sin could do with that delightful body had him sweating beneath his silk jabot and embroidered waistcoat and jacket.

Chastity Lennox, he realized, was going to be a delicious reward. He could not wait to touch her, to feel her in his arms. He could not wait to corrupt her.

Thane shoved his sin aside. Lust was a separate entity, housed within his body. A knowing need that grew hungry and powerful when aroused. A need that was always desiring sex and pleasure. Anything triggered the sin inside him, a bonny face, ample chest or a coy smile. Hell, a stiff breeze had been known to stir the sin within him.

Most times Thane could subdue it—somewhat. But as a Dark Fey, his natural inclination was toward the pleasures of the flesh. Which, of course, only pleased Lust. Lust very rarely was left to grow hungry and impatient.

But he was now. Yet Thane knew he could not allow his sin to reign. Not yet.

There were times when his sin so took over that Thane was powerless to stop it. When Lust came to the forefront, he was a powerful creature to deny, almost as though he were a separate entity. Most times, he was quiet inside him. Thane was aware of his sin only in thought, and desire. But once his Unseelie blood was heated with need, and Lust was rattling to be set free, absolutely nothing stopped him. Memories tripped through his mind of the debauches in his past. For now, those memories must suffice. Lust would have to learn to feed on them, while Thane wooed the virginal Chastity.

"There they are," Avery murmured as he wet his lips, which were obscenely erotic on a man, let alone a fey. "And every bit more grown-up," he purred as he devoured all of them with his greedy gaze. "Imagine them at court, surrounded by all kinds of decadence. What treasures they will be. I will very much enjoy showing them what pleasure true excess can be."

Lust began to seethe, to pull at him. His sin took umbrage at Avery and his hedonism, that he was entertaining ideas about what it would be like to taste Chastity. Avery was a damn glutton, never satisfied, always craving, always needing more. Thane knew that Chastity would prove a most challenging delight for Avery and his sin.

"Now who bears the green eyes?" Kian asked accusingly.

Thane gave his twin no heed as he attempted to control his thoughts, but when he saw Avery's black irises, which were rimmed in violet, dilate with hunger as his gaze fixed on Chastity, Thane said rather impulsively, "Brothers, I leave you to your virtues."

With a wave of his hand, the veil of glamour dropped. Nudging his mount forward, he walked the animal a few short paces before pulling in beside the Lennox sisters. "Good morn, ladies," he said, trying to resist the urge to grasp Chastity and haul her onto his lap. He could not steal her. Not if he wanted to break the curse. She must come to court of her own free will. She must give herself and her soul up to him, he could not take it from her. Her body was to be his gift, and therefore, he must wait until he was gifted with it.

"Sir, you are not known to us," one of them said through lips that were plump, but pressed tightly together until they were thin and bloodless. Temperance, he thought as he caught her reproving glance as she and her sisters walked by him.

Jumping down from his horse, he took the reins in his gloved hands and followed them. "Then allow me to remedy that," he said as he sketched a graceful bow.

"Come along. *Now,*" she muttered as she ushered the other three women along the path as though she were a mother goose gathering her chicks as a fox approached.

"Prue, for heaven's sake," one of them muttered before stopping and curtsying before him. "Don't be rude." When she glanced up, Thane was struck by the darkness of her eyes and the onyx ringlets that danced in the breeze from beneath her straw bonnet. "I am Mary Lennox," she announced. "And this is my sister Prudence, my other sister Mercy and..." She glanced amongst the straw bonnets and the rippling silk shawls that billowed in the May wind. "And hiding behind them is Chastity."

Their eyes locked, and he was stunned by how alluring Chastity's green gaze was. Thane felt the instant heat of unbridled desire flare inside him. Lust wanted her. *Badly.* He smiled, trying to remember that he was portraying a mortal gentleman. As a fey prince, he took what he wanted. Their court manners were not mortal manners. But if he were to act as a fey now, he would never have a chance to win Chastity, nor experience her surrender.

"I am honored." With a deep bow, he removed his hat and placed it over his heart. "I am Thane."

He did the pretty and pretended he was a gentleman. All to no avail, for Chastity barely glanced at him, and certainly with nothing that could be considered reciprocal desire.

At that precise moment, his faery hound decided to come bounding out of the woods. He was large and strong, and making the most mournful sound Thane had ever heard. Something between a whimper and a snarl.

"Bel, that is enough," he commanded. Pointing to the spot beside his boot, Thane motioned for the dog to sit. But Bel possessed a mind of his own, and instead, began sniffing the women's skirts, shoving his nose up their hems. Lucky beast, he thought with amusement, until he heard the frightened little voice at the back.

"Stay away!" The voice sounded panicky—trembling. It was Chastity's voice.

"Bel," he admonished as he stepped around the women and reached for his pet. Chastity was there, looking up at him with sheer terror in her eyes.

"He's friendly," he said, trying to be soothing. "He's only a pup really, and more curious than anything."

Thane saw her shoulders tremble as she fearfully watched the dog. "I…I don't like beasts."

Thane wondered if he could be classified as a beast. The Dark Fey were certainly known to be beastly in their appetites.

"Bel is such an unusual name for a pet," the one named Mercy said. She held her glove palm out and Bel loped to her side, sniffing and licking the leather.

"It is an old Gaelic name that means the Shining One. He is named after the Celtic sun god of healing."

Mercy bent down and rubbed her hands through Bel's pure white fur. "I am afraid that Chastity is not the animal lover in the family."

That, Thane realized, was going to be a bit of a problem. The fey lived in the woods, surrounded by nature and all its creatures. With Chastity's fear of animals it was going to be very hard to induce her to come and live at his court.

Thinking it best to steer the conversation away from animals, and Chastity's increasing fear of the eagerly sniffing Bel, he asked, "Are you by chance going to the May Day celebration?" He indicated the village green, which was decorated for Beltane. Beyond the green, by the ruins of the ancient abbey was a pile of branches and logs, the beginnings of the traditional Beltane bonfire.

"No, we are not," the one named Prudence announced in a clipped voice. "Now, good day to you, sir."

Thane watched the four young women commence walking along the path. In the distance the tor rose, and at the foot of it was a grand manor home, fit for a duke.

It was the Lennoxes' estate. And Chastity's home. He even knew what bedroom window was hers.

Despite her cold reception, he was not thwarted. Lust knew how to break down any resisting barriers. Thane could almost taste Chastity's surrender on his tongue. Her sexual awakening aroused him, roused a hunger in him that had not been sated by any of his previous conquests. Lust, it seemed, was most eager to corrupt the innocent Chastity, in the most depraved ways. But it was not only his sin that desired her. Thane and his Dark Fey blood wanted her, too.

Allowing his gaze to linger, he followed the prim and beckoning Chastity as she sauntered down the path to her home—to safety. But Chastity Lennox was not safe anywhere from him—from the desire that was growing inside him.

Every one hundred years, seven virtues were born in the mortal realm, he reminded himself. Chastity had been born for him, to sate the sin inside him. She had been created exclusively for his sexual appetites, and the power that she was his, intended solely for him, was a feeling more dominant than orgasm.

Christ, he wanted her. And he would have her, too.

With a cheeky little backward glance, the dark-haired Mary smiled at him over her shoulder and he returned it, thinking of how soon it was going to be that he would see Chastity smile at him like that.

"Do not get any ideas about her," Rinion said as he emerged from the woods and came to stand beside him. "She is mine."

Thane glanced at the fey who harbored Vanity. He was astoundingly handsome. Women fell at his feet. Thane looked back at the dark and exotic Mary, thinking of her and Rinion together. It was good that the lovely little minx was his virtue. She'd give him a hell of a merry chase and Rinion deserved nothing less.

"I have no interest in your virtue, Rinion. I covet my own."

Vanity laughed as he fiddled with his already immaculately tied lace jabot. "And she looked at you with as much lust in her eyes as a man does a used-up whore."

"She's chaste," he replied, finding himself snarling the word.

"Poor you," Rinion murmured before nudging his mount forward. "My virtue is humility. Already, I'm eager to see that saucy wench of mine on her knees. She will submit, I have no doubt, but I wish to see that sparkling, mischievous gleam in her dark eyes as she does so. Now then, I'm off. I have a virtue to corrupt."

Thane pulled the reins of Rinion's horse, bringing the animal up short. "Remember the curse. Seduce them. Corrupt their virtues, but don't force them to follow you to court."

Vanity's brow rose, making him look even more handsome. "That little minx is practically begging for it. I'll have her at court with her thighs spread before midnight."

With a gentle nudge, Rinion moved his mount forward, but not in the direction of the women. Instead, he cantered for the open plain that had once been fenland

and headed for the mansion. Rinion was a fool if he thought to go riding into the gates, proclaiming his stake on the eldest Lennox daughter. It wasn't going to be easy to get within reach of the girls. George Buckman, the Duke of Lennox, was notoriously ham-fisted when it came to anyone coming near his daughters for even a dance, let alone with the thought of courting them.

Behind him, Thane heard the woods rustle, then Avery and Kian flanked his sides. "Next move?"

Thane pulled the black satin tie from his queue and allowed his long black hair to blow in the wind. He listened to the woods, to the creak of the tree limbs and the whisper of the shimmering leaves. Glancing at the tor, he imagined his court that lay beneath the mound, and the winding labyrinths that led to the magical other-world where the Unseelie Court lay, amidst a faery forest and enchanted waters. His was a magical world beneath the ground of the mortal realm. A court that resembled something out of the mortals' Arthurian legends. The court that was so richly and lavishly appointed with gold and marble, silks and velvets. The court that was cursed and dying. The court that so desperately needed these virtues.

"For now we wait," he announced. "And we watch." *And yearn,* he silently added, feeling the burn in his loins and the hunger in his belly.

As he gathered the reins, he turned his mount just in time to see one of them—a faery galloping across the grassy knolls.

Crom.

Avery and Kian stiffened beside him. What was Niall's twin doing out here, and so close to the Lennox estate?

"Bloody hell," Kian hissed, the sound full of spite, "the Seelié want them, too."

THREE

BEHIND HIS ENORMOUS ROCOCO DESK, THE DUKE of Lennox pored over the papers that were spread out before him. He had received them that very morning by messenger, from his man of affairs. Scouring the last statement, the duke sat back in his chair and smiled. All seemed to be in order. His wealth had doubled from last year, making him one of the richest landowners in England. *Bloody faery magic,* he thought, then laughed out loud as he reached for his crystal decanter of fine French brandy. It was illegal, of course—England was at war with France. But there was very little that his money could not secure, smuggled French brandy being one of them.

Pouring the golden liquid into his goblet, he sat back in his chair and smiled with satisfaction. Power, ambition, riches. He had them in spades. At last. And all it had taken was a little pact. A tithe, the faeries called it.

"Your Grace," his duchess murmured as she swished through the opened library door. "The bills have arrived for the girls' trousseaux."

Leaning forward, Lennox waved his duchess into the room, still awed by her dazzling beauty after all these years of marriage. "And what has their trousseaux set me back?"

"An enormous amount," she said with a smile as he captured her hand in his and brushed his lips along her fingers. She blushed. As pretty still as the day he had first laid eyes on her. He had wanted her so much. Still did. Nothing would have stopped him from possessing her. In fact, nothing had. There had been one particular hurdle to jump, but nothing too serious.

"The modiste has done an extraordinary job of dressing them," his wife said. "Wait till you see them in their new gowns. Mrs. Hartwell has such a way with color and draping. And the lace," his wife continued, obviously over the moon with pride, "the lace on their cuffs is at least three inches thick, and so finely spun. I can hardly credit how she is able to design such gowns."

He did not want this private moment with his wife spoiled by talk of the village modiste. "Why you did not send for a modiste from London for a proper trousseau, I will never understand," he grumbled, thinking of the woman who ran the only clothing shop in Glastonbury. "You know how I adore my girls, nothing is too good for them. I want them to have the best."

"I like our modest little modiste," his wife replied. "And their gowns look as though they were designed and made in Paris, not Glastonbury. Besides, our modiste is rather gifted."

His brows arched. "In what way?"

"The villagers say she's been blessed by faeries. They say," his wife murmured, leaning into him, "that the reason her gowns are so magnificent and her stitches so delicate, and her lace so beautiful, is that the faeries visit her nightly and fill her orders."

A harrowing thought, indeed.

"They say," his wife continued, whispering in his ear, "that our little village modiste is happy to repay them in their favored currency."

"Carnalities?"

"Honeyed milk."

Patting her rump, Lennox sent his wife a lusty smile. "How little you know of the fey, my dear, for they would much prefer humping to honey."

She blushed at his vulgarity. "What are you working on?" she asked, flipping through the papers that littered his desk.

"Nothing to concern yourself with, my dear," he cajoled. Gathering up the papers, he stacked them away from her reach. His investments were listed there, and some of them were dubious to say the least. He had no wish for his wife to discover how he made his coin. Her Grace might be beyond accepting if she were to learn that the jewels around her throat were paid for by his investment in a notorious bawdy house that catered to humans and fey alike.

"Your Grace…" His butler coughed discreetly from the door. "You have a caller."

"Who is it, Salisbury?" he grumbled, not wanting to be disturbed. His wife was feeling much too fine in his lap, and the thought of the Nymph and the Satyr, the bawdy house and all the erotic, decadent delights to be found there, had him aroused. Suddenly he found himself wondering what it would be like to have his wife and a little fey concubine addressing his needs. He had heard that the fey, particularly the Dark Fey, could fuck like the devil. Perhaps he would make a trip into the city and watch a female fey with her lover from behind the privacy of a peephole. He could put the theory to a test to see if indeed the fey were sexually insatiable. And maybe he'd even have one, too, a little pixie on his cock.

What a delightfully debauched diversion. Perversity was a healthy thing to maintain a man's vigor as he neared the end of his fourth decade, and there was no place on earth more perverse than the Nymph and the Satyr.

"Your Grace?"

"Who is it?" he growled as his palm skimmed his wife's rounded rump.

"He refused to give his name, Your Grace. He said to tell you that the time has come to pay up."

Lennox lost his grip on his wife. All thoughts of nymphs and pixies rousing him to a sexual peak flew out of his head. Bloody hell, he did not wish for Salisbury to say another word. Thankfully, the butler correctly interpreted his hard stare.

"Probably Arawn," he murmured as he patted his

wife's thigh. "Always a prankster, that Arawn. He'll be wanting to take Prue on a ride or some such thing."

"I shall leave you alone then, as you hammer out the details of Arawn's courtship of Prudence," his dutiful wife replied, slipping from his lap and straightening her hooped skirts. "By the by, do inform Lord Arawn that it will not ingratiate him at all to me if I hear of any of my girls being talked of in such a fashion. Paying up refers to commodities, Your Grace. Our daughters are not things to be traded."

"Of course, of course," he said, ushering her along with a wave of his hand. "Wouldn't dream of such a thing." And he wouldn't. By God, he loved his daughters, and only wanted the best for them.

Lennox's gaze followed his wife out of the room before fixing on his butler. Damn it, he knew it wasn't Arawn come to pay a call. He had an idea who the intruder was, and needed a second or two to formulate his plan. His girls, he thought, thinking of them upstairs giggling and laughing as they pored over the boxes of new clothes and petticoats, stockings and ribbons. He must protect them at all costs.

Clearing his throat, he asked, "What manner of man is he, Salisbury?"

The butler frowned. "Rather odd, Your Grace. I've never seen him before. He's tall, fair…a most regal, yet intimidating fellow."

Lennox felt his throat dry up, from relief or apprehension he knew not. "Send him in," he commanded, "and allow no one to disturb us."

As if by magic, the stranger appeared behind the butler, startling the retainer. But Salisbury recovered with aplomb. "His Grace will see you now."

The man breezed in and slammed the library door shut. For long seconds, his penetrating violet eyes stared him down, and Lennox refused to give in to the urge to loosen his jabot.

"George Jasper Buckman, the fifth Duke of Lennox?" the stranger inquired as he took the tapestry chair in front of the wide desk.

"Yes," Lennox replied as sweat began to bead on his forehead.

"Queen Aine has sent me."

He felt his face drain of blood. The man smiled, then reached for the goblet of brandy that Lennox had just poured. Raising the crystal to his lips, he took a sip, his eyes scrutinizing his discomfort.

"Queen Aine?" Lennox asked vaguely.

"You received a gift from my mother, did you not?"

"Did I?" he asked, feigning boredom. "I'm afraid I don't recall being introduced to a Queen Aine."

The man sat forward, his strange eyes darkening. "She found you weeping over the cradle of a deformed, lame little wretch. Your heir, I believe."

Robert. His son. His heir. Aye, he had sired a twisted little thing. Lame, broken. He had wandered into the nursery one night, the night of his son's first birthday and wept as he watched him sleep. The queen had appeared then. The lovely faery queen. She had offered him his greatest wish, a whole son. An heir that could take his rightful place as duke once he departed this world. And she had asked for nothing but a tithe to be paid later on.

It had been twenty-five years since that visit. He had never seen or heard from her again. He had produced the four daughters she had spoken of. They were virtuous girls, just as she had said they would be. He had done everything, and the queen had made Robert strong and handsome—and whole.

"Your heir enjoys a rather rich and healthy life, does he not?" the man asked as he settled into the chair. "I hear he has recently married."

Lennox didn't care for the tone in the man's voice. Hackles raised, he met the stranger's gaze. "State your business."

"It is time the tithe was paid."

"How much?" he asked, reaching into his desk drawer for a bank draft.

The man laughed and crossed his long leg over his knee. "The queen has no need of your mortal money. What she desires are your daughters."

"All of them?" he demanded, his eyes narrowing.

"All four of them."

Reaching for the brandy, Lennox swallowed the contents of the goblet in one swig. Bloody hell, this was going from bad to worse. Never had he thought the queen would demand his daughters. Damn it. He'd already bargained with another of their kind for one of his daughters. That was where his wealth had come from. He wanted the best for his daughters, and before the fey had come, his purse was light, the debts heavy. So, he had made another bargain—one for gold, and his daughter's happiness and comfort.

Christ, he was a man who had been visited by the fey not once, but twice in his lifetime. And both times the blasted creatures had known what he had wanted.

"The queen demands that you take the girls to London. They are not safe here."

"Now, see here," Lennox roared, "I take very good care of my daughters and there is nothing on this green earth that I would allow to harm them."

"You, Your Grace, will have no power to stop the ones who are coming for them."

"Bah," he grumbled, waving off the concern. "There is nothing that wealth and influence cannot buy. My girls are safe here under my protection."

"Others are coming for them. I assure you, they will not be bought off. Your wealth and influence will mean nothing to them. You must take your daughters and leave. At once. Your son and his wife are hosting a ball tonight, are they not?"

Lennox narrowed his eyes, unnerved that this stranger—this...creature could know something so mundane, yet personal, about his son and the masked ball he was giving.

"I am correct, am I not? Your son is having a grand party."

"Now, see here. I'm not packing up the house and leaving for London today. Besides, we won't make it to the ball in time."

"Do you know who I am?" the stranger asked. He appeared bored, but his voice was sharp, full of warning.

"One of *them*," Lennox found himself grumbling as he searched for a way out of this tangle. "Like her."

The stranger smiled. "Indeed. I am Crom, the queen's son."

"It was a pleasure to meet you. Salisbury will see you out."

Two large palms slammed down atop the shiny rosewood, making Lennox nearly jump out of his skin. "Your Grace, you do not amuse me. I am at the length of my patience. You will take your daughters, and you will leave Glastonbury. *Today*."

"We won't make it in time for the ball," he repeated, "and I am not having my family on the roads in the dark of night. Thieves come out when the moon rises in the night sky. Infidels, sir. Highwaymen with whom I do not wish to cross paths. Imagine what the bastards will do if they discover my daughters and wife in the carriage."

"You would risk my temper and my considerable powers to a weak roadside thief?"

Lennox bristled at the dangerous tone. "It cannot be done. Not today."

"I have many powers, and getting you to London before the ball will be no great trial."

"And what do you expect me to tell my wife?"

"Tell her whatever you need to. I don't care. Just take the girls away from here. The others have discovered the presence of your daughters. They will stop at nothing to possess them. They are ruthless. Embittered. Dangerous."

"The others, you say?" he asked, looking once more upon the golden faery that loomed over his desk.

"The Dark Fey."

Lennox felt his face drain of blood for the second time in minutes. Christ, what had he done?

"Pack your things and leave the rest to me. The queen will meet with you four mornings from now in the woods of Richmond Park. Do not fail to arrive, or her gift to your son shall be broken."

"Wait," he called as Crom prepared to leave. "What does she want with my girls?"

"It is none of your concern now. You accepted the gift and now it is time to pay the tithe."

"I…I won't have them hurt, you blackguard. They're innocent young women. Good girls."

"Allow me to allay your fears, Your Grace. They shall be treated like queens. One in particular. Chastity," he said with a sly smile. "She is to be my bride."

"And all my daughters? Are they to be wed?"

"Yes."

"To your kind?"

"Of course."

Lennox swallowed hard. Bloody hell! "All of them?" he asked in a choked voice. His wife would castrate him if she ever discovered that her daughters were wed to the fey as part of a bargain he had made. There had to be a way out.

Crom's eyes took on a cruel expression as if he could

read Lennox's mind. "Yes. All of them are to wed and to reside in the Seelie Court. So you had better find a way to break the vow you gave to my mother's enemy. For no daughter of yours shall be wed to anyone but the men of my court."

"And these Dark Fey, they're coming?" he asked in a strangled whisper.

Crom smiled, a show of cruel mirth. "Even now one approaches. I'll leave you to settle your business with him. I suggest you put an end to your dealings with him. After that, you will depart for London."

Nodding, Lennox fell back against the leather squabs of his chair. His bloody greed was catching up with him now. He had no alternative but to tuck in his tail and run. Perhaps the faery queen would protect his daughters from the damnable bargain he had made three years ago.

Crom vanished, his figure only to be replaced by that of Salisbury. "Your Grace, a Prince Rinion is here. He claims to be well-known to you."

Indeed he was. "Send him in, Salisbury."

The tall, imposing Dark Fey sauntered into the study. His eyes were a startling shade of blue, and his long dark brown hair was worn loose, down to his impressive shoulders. With a smug smile he looked about the room. "How very nicely appointed this library is, Lennox. Much more comfortable than the last time I saw it. I am so glad to see you are enjoying my little gift."

He couldn't speak. God help him, his normally calculating mind was blank. What if this Dark Fey discovered his deceit?

"Do you recall that night we struck our bargain? Riches beyond belief, all in return for the hand of your firstborn daughter."

Lennox swallowed thickly. "Aye. I remember." Three years ago the wretch had presented himself in the back garden, appearing like a fabled magus as he rose from a vapor of fog. His daughters had been dining alfresco beneath a tree, and the beast had not been able to take his eyes off Mary. Darling Mary.

They had been approaching that tender age, when a come-out season and balls were most important. They were already well past the age that most young ladies made their debut, but he hadn't the blunt to provide a season for them. He had wanted to, but he was so heavily in debt. And to give all four of them a season at once was beyond what his pocketbook could allow.

The wretched faery had known his weak spot. His daughters. And coin.

"'Tis Beltane, Lennox. Your daughter is now three and twenty. I want my bride."

"Yes, yes, of course," he murmured as he tried to put aside the memory of their meeting, and the fact that despite his love, he had given one of his daughters away for coin. Of course, he hadn't known what Rinion was then. He'd thought him one of those kind, benevolent faeries, not a member of the Unseelie Court. He'd never have made the bargain if he'd known the bastard was a Dark Fey.

"Tonight. At the end of the Great Hunt. I will claim her then. She is to wear this," he said, waving his hand toward the settee beneath the window. Magically, a sheer gown made of white faery silk and trimmed in silver appeared. Atop it, a silver and crystal mask glittered in the sunlight. "Make certain she is ready to become my bride."

Lennox found himself nodding like a fool. Thankfully the arrogant bastard took no notice of his agitated state before leaving the room.

"Midnight, Lennox," the fey reminded him as he departed, "or I will be forced to come after you."

The library door shut, and Lennox dropped his head into his hands. Christ, what a mess he was in. But there was nothing to be changed now. He'd been crafty in his dealing with the fey, and once the bastard discovered the truth of their bargain, there would be hell to pay.

His mind, which had been blank, suddenly began calculating and figuring. He thought of a way out of this debacle, and knew it would work, for at least as long as it would take him to remove his family to the capital.

"Salisbury!" he roared as he slammed shut a drawer in his desk. "We're leaving for London."

"London, Your Grace?"

"Yes. Within half an hour. Inform my daughters' maids that the girls are to be ready. And take this." He thrust a folded missive into the butler's white gloves. "Have a footman bring this and the clothing on the settee to the seamstress in the village."

God help him, he thought as he gazed out the window, if he and his girls were not long departed before the Dark Fey discovered his deceit.

★ ★ ★

"I don't know why Papa was in such a hurry to leave Glastonbury," Prue muttered, her mouth pursed with distaste. "It's most unseemly. People will talk. And poor Mama—" she sighed "—she was fit to be tied."

"Hmm, he did act as though the devil were on his heels, didn't he?" Mary said as she looked around the crowded ballroom, watching the masked dancers glide through a minuet. "But Mama is a forgiving soul, she has doubtless forgotten all about it by now. Look…" Mary nodded to the corner where her mother was busily chatting with friends. "She seems rather happy, don't you think?"

"I was worried the coachman was going to kill the horses," Mercy added. "I don't think we've ever made it to London so quickly."

"It all seems very indecorous," Prue admonished. "Poor Robert and his wife were astonished to find the entire family standing on their doorstep, hours before their ball. It sent the whole house into a flurry."

"Robert didn't mind," Mercy murmured. "He loves us and was quite happy to see us in the threshold, rumpled from our hasty journey."

With one ear to the conversation, Chastity listened to her sisters chatter on as they stood beside the table housing the punch bowl and champagne. She caught Mary smiling at a masked stranger who had caught her eye. A delicate pink blush painted Mary's already lovely cheeks.

Quizzically, Chastity wondered what it was that caused

such a reaction in her sister. Certainly the stranger was handsome, but nothing out of the ordinary. Nothing that would make *her* blush.

"What do you think?" Mary whispered to her. "He's fascinating, isn't he?"

With a delicate shrug, Chastity studied the man who had started to make his way most diligently to where she and her sisters stood. "How can you tell? His face is covered with a mask. In fact," she said, looking around at the opulent setting of the ballroom, "everyone is masked."

"Yes," Mary said, her voice breathy. "It makes it that much more exciting, does it not? Can you not feel it, Chastity, the excitement heating your blood when your gaze locks on a man?"

Chastity studied the pearl trim on the lace cuff of her sleeve. "No, I cannot."

Her voice was intended to be firm, censoring, but instead Chastity detected a note of bitterness. No, she felt nothing when her gaze skated over the numerous gentlemen who were at the ball. She did not feel warm, or excited, or—

"Look for someone," Mary instructed, "when you find a man that is pleasing to your eye, let your gaze linger. Imagine pulling the mask from his face, slowly revealing his identity. Imagine that you are the only two in the room. Two strangers, eyes locked, skin burning to be touched, lips aching to be kissed."

Mary's voice had dropped to a seductive purr, clearly entranced by the provocative words she used to paint her sensual image. Yet, Chastity had not fallen victim to any warmth or feeling, most especially the awakening of anything amorous.

"Imagine, sister, what it would be like to sample a forbidden taste of sin."

Frowning, Chastity had always believed that sin would taste rather bitter, not the sweet delight Mary made it out to be.

"My lady, will you do me the honor?"

The stranger was reaching for Mary's hand. In her other hand, Mary slowly waved her fan, allowing the lace edge to whisper over her exposed skin, making her heavy perfume rise up and linger between them. The man inhaled delicately, his dark eyes closing behind his mask for the briefest second.

"I would be delighted," Mary said in a sultry voice before snapping her fan closed, allowing the masked gentleman to lead her to the floor.

Prue and Mercy had retreated to the wall, where they were talking with Ruth, their new sister-in-law. Chastity chose to stay where she was, unable to take her eyes off her sister and the man she was dancing with.

Mary's color was high, her lips parted in a coy little smile that Chastity had never perfected—had never bothered to try. The mask she wore gave her some measure of privacy, and she used it to study the couples dancing before her. The wine and champagne was flowing freely, and the hour had grown late. There was a certain lack of inhibition growing amongst the crowd. She could feel it now, like a seductive fog hovering low on the floor before slowly rising and wrapping around them.

She smelled it, the desire in the air. It was thick, drugging in its mixture of sweetness and spice. It clouded her
head, drew her in, made her feel languid and sleepy and
immensely relaxed.

Through the eye slits of her mask, she looked around
the room, waving her lace fan delicately back and forth,
stirring the air in an attempt to clear her head of the
luscious scent that seemed to be floating through the
air. Straight ahead, the French doors were inched open,
and Chastity made her way to them. She needed the air,
which would be fresh and mind clearing.

Checking over her shoulder before she slipped through
the doors, she saw that no one had noticed her, nor would
they notice her exit. It would only be a short reprieve
from the dance, but a most welcome one.

FOUR

QUICKLY, CHASTITY SLIPPED THROUGH THE PARTED
doors and stepped out onto the balcony, which was
shrouded in darkness. To the left of the balustrade was
a boxwood maze, shadowed by the height of looming
oaks and willow trees. Inside the maze there was a bench
where she could sit and rest feet that ached from her delicate dance slippers. She knew she should not be out here,
alone, in the dark, but her head still remained cloudy, and
the lure of a rest in solitude was too great. The exotic
scent still lingered, but her head would begin to clear
when the fresh night air swept over her while she rested
in peace and quiet.

What a queer sensation that had been. She had never
experienced anything like it. It had warmed her body as
nothing ever had, not even champagne. The lingering
heat and the languorous feeling still seemed wrapped
around her, giving her the fanciful taste of what the

enduring effects of sensuality must feel like. Despite the fact she had never experienced any sensual feeling before, Chastity knew that what she had experienced was some unexplained erotic charge in the air. Unsullied or not, she was not a simpleton.

Taking a few calming breaths, she stared up at the sky, watching as the sliver of silver moonlight appeared behind a black cloud. It was the Eve of Beltane, she reminded herself. The night of the Great Hunt, the union between the god and the goddess. Of course there was a carnal element to the evening. Everyone was anticipating the hour of midnight when it would be Beltane, and the frivolities and promiscuous activities of the spring and May Day would be welcomed with eager arms.

Back home in Glastonbury, the Great Hunt would just be beginning, and the bonfire on the village green would be blazing high into the sky. In the woods, men would chase maidens, and beneath the very same sliver of moonlight they would celebrate the rites of spring.

The Great Hunt and all Beltane's festivities were steeped in pagan belief and the old way of the Celts. With the mystery of the tor and its prominent setting in the village it was not hard to feel rather pagan most of the year, but on evenings such as this, everyone threw aside propriety and Christianity to participate in the ideals of growth, sexuality and fecundity, for those three things had long represented the spring.

For centuries, Glastonbury, which had always been known as the Land of the Summer People, had been at the center of Beltane. As a child, her father, who had been raised in the little village, celebrated this very night every year. Every year except this one.

For some reason, her father, who had never been averse to accompanying them to the village on the Eve of Beltane, had acted as though the villagers and the festival were anathema. This year, after promising her and her sisters that they were old enough to witness the Great Hunt, after they had allowed themselves to grow excited about the prospect, he'd denied them.

"You're not going to such a hedonistic display. It's archaic," he had grumbled as he waited for them to cram themselves into the town coach. After the carriage had lurched down the drive, he had refused to speak anymore of it, telling them only what they already knew, that they were off to London, to her brother's ball, and then back to the Lennox town house in Grosvenor Square to spend at least a fortnight.

It all seemed so very strange, especially since her father had always striven to keep them very far removed from the capital. "Nothing but rakes and dowry thieves in London," he had always claimed. So why now had he had a change of heart?

It seemed that their whole life their father had prevented them from being tainted by the sights and sounds—and smells—of London, only to turn around that very morning and all but force them to embrace the city.

Something wasn't right. She sensed it. And that something had to do with her father and his perplexing behavior. Thinking it through, Chastity found herself at a loss to explain it. Perhaps, she thought, taking a deep breath, she couldn't make heads or tails of his behavior because her mind was still clouded by the lingering scent of…of whatever that had been back in the ballroom.

Glancing back at the beckoning maze, Chastity glided to the stairs, the hooped silk skirts of her gown making a soft brushing whisper against the stone. She would find privacy and quiet there in the maze to reflect upon the puzzling events of the day.

Descending the stairs, she trailed her gloved hand along the stone banister, noticing the sparkling moonbeam that widened over the quartz cut stone. The moonbeam became less filtered light, and more like a fine swath of iridescent wetness. Like mist, but it radiated such a dazzling brilliance that Chastity watched it, hypnotized by its beauty, as it seemed to dance in and around the banister as though it were alive.

What folly, she chastened herself. It was a reflection of the rock quartz in the moonlight, nothing else. *And the scent?* her mind whispered to her. *What of that?*

It was back, that lush, exotic blend that reminded her of a faraway place, a spice island, or India perhaps. It was heavy, evocative, almost drugging, yet it made her feel as light as a feather. As if *she* were the one floating, and not the mist particles that glimmered in the moonlight.

Ceo Side, something whispered to her. Faery Mist.

She had heard of it before, the ability of the faeries to come as rain, mist, fog and shadow.

Now she heard it murmured on the wind as her slippers sank into the damp grass. Were the *Daoine Side*—the fairy people—here in the back gardens of her brother's estate? But why here? Why now? For her whole life, her father had talked to her and her sisters about the fey, yet she had never seen them, never perceived that they were somehow truly a part of her life. So why now was she obsessed with the idea of them? Perhaps it really was the champagne making her head fuzzy, and nothing more.

Head heavy, limbs warm, Chastity moved deeper into the darkness of the ten-foot-tall maze. She was breathing heavy, she realized. The lace that held her cameo secure around her throat felt suffocating. Her stays were tight, pushing her breasts higher, making it difficult to get air into her constricted lungs. Her fan dropped to the deep, damp grass as the air grew thicker, began to wrap around her, where it worked its way under her skirt to caress her calves, then thighs. She felt strange, as though she was disembodied. Her mind, always sharp and clear, would not work, and her lungs did not seem able to provide her body with adequate air.

With a gasp, she felt heat slide over her waist, then up to her breasts and, unable to bear it, she tore the lace choker off, flinging it to the ground, gasping to breathe. She was being smothered, but by what or whom, she could not fathom. She was utterly alone—and yet she wasn't.

"A beautiful woman such as you should not be out in the dark, unaccompanied by a gentleman."

Whirling around, Chastity startled when she heard the deep voice behind her. The man's identity was cleverly concealed by an intricate mask made of gold and wire, designed to look like foliage. With his height, and the breadth of his shoulders outlined by the moon, and his long black hair whispering in the slight breeze, he looked like the fabled Oak King come to ravish her.

Unsteadily, she took a step back, coming up against a large birch tree that marked the entrance to the maze. She did not know this man, yet there was something about him that called to her—his voice, perhaps, or maybe the way he stood, so proud, so masculine, so…certain of himself.

"I have frightened you." His accent was thick and alluring as he spoke to her, his voice musical, yet deep and intensely male. "I would not have it so."

"I didn't hear you approach, sir," she said, noticing how the mist had not evaporated, but seemed to draw to him, like a moth to a flame. It was almost as if he was shrouded in it, shimmering in the glow. Chastity stared, frozen, fascinated by the magic of it, lured by the beauty of him.

"Forgive me." He stepped closer to her, the vapor glinting and shifting around him. The scent that made her feel so strange earlier became stronger, heavier. It was a delicious smell, one that made her body tingle with a warmth she could not define.

"Have we met, sir?" she inquired, taking a step back as he approached her. He was now bathed in a shaft of moonlight, the effect quite breathtaking. She saw, even despite the mask he wore, that he studied her from beneath a thick veil of black lashes. His hair was as dark as a raven's feathers, heavy and glistening like spilled ink in the moonlight as it grazed the shoulders of his velvet jacket. A frock coat that Chastity was quite certain required no extra padding.

He let her study him and she half wondered as their gazes met if the man was not fully aware of what his face and his figure must do to the opposite sex. Any sane woman would find this man unavoidably compelling and sensual. Any woman would wish to find herself in his arms, being kissed by his lips and ravished by his elegant, yet extremely masculine, hands.

She was not just any woman. Yet this outsider seemed to have a most disturbing effect on her. He possessed a beauty, a mysterious strangeness that seduced her even as her brain warned her to run, to leave the maze as quickly as she could. But she could not move. Her dance slippers were fixed firmly upon the ground as if they had been glued there.

Do I not tempt you? Are you not thinking, at this very moment, what my body would feel like upon yours?

The words came from nowhere—*no, from him*—despite the fact he had not moved his lips. Did not even smile. Just stood before her, silently allowing her perusal.

Your gaze lingers on my fingers as though you hunger to have them caress you, to slowly pull the tapes of your stays and reveal what has been so meticulously hidden beneath that gown. Despite the mask, I see in your eyes that desire, the burning deep inside to have my hands upon your flesh.

His voice again, beautiful, lyrical. His words luring. Enticing. But still his masculine lips did not move. Her own thoughts, then? she wondered. Was she even capable of conjuring up such base imaginings?

It frightened her to think so. It was impossible to believe that she, an innocent who had never been touched, could consider such things, yet Chastity could not dispel the fact that the stranger had not spoken aloud. Regardless, she heard his deep voice as though the words had been whispered intimately in her ear.

Reaching for her hand, he wrapped his ungloved fingers around her delicate ones, the warmth sending a delightful frisson along her spine.

"You are far too bold, sir," she gasped, flustered when he looked up at her with piercing blue eyes that only seemed to glow as the gold of his mask glinted in the moonlight.

"Is it?" The deepness of his voice caused flutterings in her stomach. "Then let us begin again," he suggested silkily. "An introduction in a private garden while bathed in moonlight is an auspicious event. One must ensure that it is perfect and unforgettable."

Somehow Chastity knew that she would never forget one moment of this meeting.

The mist glittered in the moonlight, outlining his broad shoulders, moving with him as he stepped closer to her. He was otherworldly, breathtaking in his beauty. She would be recalling this moment, the feel of her body tingling and awakening, when she was an old woman sitting by the fire.

"The moonlight becomes you," he said in a voice that was rich and smooth, that seemed to wrap around her.

He reached out and Chastity saw how the glistening mist crystals glittered on his fingers, then wafted over her to her shoulder, where he caught a loose tendril of hair. "You were made to be seen in the dark. You are a perfect angel by sunlight, a tempting goddess by moonlight."

She could hardly think. Was it the scent that surrounded her? The strangeness of the glittering mist and the masked stranger? Or was it that she was breathing too fast? Whatever it was, it was playing havoc with her mind. Had she heard him correctly, that he had seen her in the sunlight? Impossible.

"I don't believe," she said, then licked her lips to moisten them, "that you know who I am. Perhaps you have mistaken me for someone else?"

"No, there is no mistake." The tendril of hair wrapped around his finger and he used it to pull her closer to him. "You call to me. I could find you anywhere, even in the largest crush of people or in the shadows of the Dark Walk in Covent Garden. There isn't a place where you could hide from me."

She should have been terrified by such a statement, yet she was horrified for another reason altogether—her body's quivering response to such knowledge.

"You don't realize it, but your body cries out, and my own answers it. We are destined to be together. Each to complete the other."

His voice dropped to a seductive whisper as his eyes held her transfixed. This conversation was much too intimate for any innocent, let alone a virtue. He had obviously mistaken her for someone of experience and worldliness.

"I must beg you, sir, to release me. You are not known to me, and I am certain that you have mistaken me for your midnight rendezvous."

"Lady Chastity," he purred, drawing out the end of her name. The sound gave her goose bumps and she shivered, her fingers trembling in his.

"Sir?" she murmured, trying unsuccessfully to look away from his mesmerizing beauty. "How..." She licked her lips. "How do you know who I am? We've never met."

"Haven't we?" Turning her palm up, he bared her wrist and traced the delicate blue veins with the tips of his fingers. Together, they watched his graceful finger-tips skate across her smooth skin, and Chastity, unable to control the sensations his touch evoked, whimpered with the need to feel his caress all over her. His lashes lowered and he closed his eyes as if he knew that her whimper was one of desire, not fear.

"What is your title, sir?" He was too richly garbed, and too well-spoken, to be anything other than an aristocrat. But his voice held a slight accent, an exotic-sounding one that was luring and seductive.

"Prince," he murmured.

"A prince, no less," she stammered, knowing she needed to go, but unable to make herself leave his side. "I...I have never met a...a prince."

"How fortunate I am to be your first."

It was a double entendre. She had heard them before

and always recoiled from them. But this one, said in his deep voice, only tempted her further. Made her watch the slow brush of his fingers against the bounding pulse in her wrist and wonder what it would be like to watch his lips graze that very same spot, or other more intimate places on her body.

"I am your first prince, but am I the first to touch you like this?" he asked, glancing up from the lush fringe of his lashes, which his mask could not conceal.

"I am a lady, Your Highness," she admonished him, but her voice was breathless, husky, and he smiled, the barest fleeting hint of a self-satisfied grin.

"An extraordinarily lovely lady."

Drawing in a deep breath, he brought his mouth to her skin. She heard as well as felt him sniff delicately. His lips suddenly parted and she saw a glimmer of brilliant white teeth behind his sculpted lips. Slowly, the tip of his tongue crept out from between his lips and her breath caught, freezing in horrified wonder as she watched him.

With exquisite care and reverence he lightly grazed her wrist with the tip of his hot tongue. His lips soon replaced his tongue as he looked up at her. His eyes, Chastity noticed, were now black, as if his pupils had dilated and swallowed the blue iris.

"And what of that, Lady Chastity? Is that the first time a prince, or any man's tongue, has tasted your flesh?"

Like a simpleton, she nodded, unable to do anything more. She should break this trance he held her in, but suddenly she lacked the incredible moral strength it would take. She was weakening, and Lord help her, she didn't want to find her wavering resolve. She wanted more, to discover what he would do to her, how far he would go in this game of seduction.

Watching her, compelling her with those black, fathomless eyes, he drew his tongue across her wrist once more, their gazes locking upon one another, their faces still masked, heightening the charge between them.

"Do not fear me," he whispered as her hand trembled in his. "I would never hurt you. 'Tis only pleasure I seek to give you."

"My God, your voice," she gasped, tugging her fingers out of his hold and backing away. Suddenly she was thrust back to that afternoon, and the vision of a huge white dog and a dark-haired man came rushing back to her. "I...I know you."

"You have mistaken me for another."

"Today, by the woods, back home," she began, stepping back, trying to put a safe distance between them. "You were on horseback and you stopped us on the path. But how could you..."

The sensual haze began to evaporate. How could this man—this stranger—possibly be the one who had found her and her sisters walking that very morning? How could it be that he had come to London? To her brother's ball? But something inside her screamed that it was him, and that she needed to run from him. He was dangerous and not just because he was a threat to her innocence.

He followed her like a tiger stalking its prey. Farther and farther she backed up, until she was deep amongst the trees that stood tall around the garden bench. Surrounding her, the maze rose high, engulfing her and the stranger. Step for step, he followed her, his gaze never leaving her face. The intensity of his stare grew stronger, more bewitching, singeing her flesh until she was hot and struggling to breathe.

"Is that really what you want? What you were feeling just a few seconds ago—the very great desire for me to leave you?"

"Stop it at once, sir," she demanded, although her voice lacked conviction. Behind her brocade stomacher and the tightly laced stays, her breasts inched up, caused by her ragged breathing. Breathing that should have been harsh and rasping owing to fear, not this strange, intoxicating sensation that only could be lust.

"Come to me, Chastity," he coaxed, "I can feel how much you want to, just allow yourself one moment of unguarded pleasure."

Her lips parted as she struggled for air. She heard herself gasping as she cried out, coming up short against the trunk of a tree. With lightning speed he was before her, his arms wrapped around her waist as he pulled her deeper into the maze.

"Stop this," she cried, struggling in his arms—not because she was afraid of him, but because she was afraid of herself and the need that was suddenly ruling her.

"I have spent so long just waiting—watching. You call to me, to the deep-seated hunger inside me. A hunger I would never allow to hurt you, but only wish to share with you."

His words shocked her. The intimacy of them, the honesty made her still in his arms. Pressing her backward over his arm, she felt his solid, flexed muscles beneath her shoulders. His mouth was mere inches away from hers, and his eyes, those intense, mysterious eyes which were still black, held her steady.

He held her thus, bent over his arm, her breasts straining against her formfitting bodice, the mounds of which were in increasing danger of spilling out of her demure square neckline.

Chastity was aware of her body, of how it heated and yearned, her flesh swelling against her stays, the liquefying between her thighs, and all the while he continued to stare down into her upturned face, scrutinizing every inch of her. She wanted to say something, to act as though she were not a naive innocent, but she could not catch her breath or think clearly when she looked into his eyes.

His free hand came up to roam over the contours of her face before trailing down to her jaw. "Never fear me," he whispered at last while tenderly stroking his finger along the pounding pulse at the base of her throat. She didn't cry out as his fingertip glided down toward her décolletage, but swallowed hard.

His eyes seemed to glow even brighter as his gaze dropped to the wild fluttering in her throat, then lower to her breasts, which were now generously spilling out from her stays.

"The way in which the moon plays over your skin beckons me to explore. To touch. To taste."

His fingertips lingered lightly over her pulse and she

heard him growl, the sound of a jungle cat purring in satisfaction. His mouth lowered then stilled, and a cry, not of the jungle cat but that of savage beast, emanated from deep in his throat.

"There can be very great pleasure to be found in darkness. You needn't fear it. But only embrace it."

Closing her eyes, Chastity tilted her head back, savoring the heat coming from his mouth as it washed over her décolletage. She burned, breathless, waiting for something she could not name.

She didn't understand, only knew that this feeling must not leave. She wanted it to consume her. Wanted to fall victim to him. She was not this person, this wanton. She was a virtue, but it seemed her virtue had abandoned her, leaving her as she truly was, a woman yearning to be seduced.

"Yes, yield to me. Let me come to you as I am. Embrace the darkness, the darkness in me, and let me take you...*corrupt you*..."

Breathing hard against Chastity's milk-white throat, Thane endured the pain that pierced him. He was forcing her. It was forbidden. It would only deepen the curse, but by the goddess, he wanted her, wanted to take her without any thought or control and sink himself into her luscious body.

She whimpered, not out of fear, but of feminine arousal, and he decided that perhaps he could still make her want him. He couldn't hide his little growl of victory as he brushed his lips along the full, throbbing vein that ran from her neck to the apex of her breast. Parting his lips, he breathed hotly against her. The mist that was part of him began to float over her, whispering softly, covering her until the little beads of moisture turned to a glistening rivulet of water that trickled between the valley of her generous breasts.

She squirmed in his arms, but it was not an attempt to be free of him. No, she wanted him, like a woman wanted a man. He could smell her arousal, the scent of passion wafting up from beneath her gown. He could smell the rich, heady nectar of her blood through her skin, which was sweetly anointed with the perfume of orange blossoms. Perfume as an aphrodisiac was a poor second, and no match for the power of a woman's blood, heated by lust. But Chastity's innocence mixed with her heavy perfume was as intoxicating as a pint of faery mead.

Staring down at the woman he held in his arms, Thane watched the rise and fall of her breasts. A perverse sense of need, inspired by his sin, made him desire to see his seed trickling between her luscious breasts. He wanted her marked, covered in his scent. Thane wanted her for his.

Wanting to taste her. Needing to rip away the contraption that caged her body from him, he lowered his head, inhaling her musky scent. Thane listened to the erotic cadence of her heart that beat urgently beneath her breast. He wanted to feel that rhythmic pulsing around his cock while he was buried deeply inside her, her virginal quim clamping and throbbing, surrounding his shaft, milking him dry.

He would stay there, just like that, savoring the feel of her body accepting him. He would raise himself above her, blotting out everything but him. She would see only him, above her. Feel only him, deep inside her. And then, when she was focused solely on him, their gazes locked, he would take her. Body and soul. Virtue to his sin.

Their nights would be spent in pleasure. In slow, languorous lovemaking, and frenzied fucking, in which he would feel her sweating against him. She would beg him to stop—only to plead with him to take her once more.

She was still as death in his arms, and he looked up from her overflowing bodice and into her eyes. Was she afraid? Terrified? Did she know what he wanted to do to her? Could she see into his mind, and watch his fantasy of her beneath him, her bottom in his hands, her hips arching to meet his thrust? Did she know how badly he wanted to watch her body open to him? How he wanted to take her to his court and mate with her as a Dark Fey should?

By the goddess, did she know what sort of monster he was? He was Lust. He fucked like an animal. He was insatiable. She could never, in her innocence, understand what he wanted to do to her, or have her do to him.

He should leave her, this innocent little lamb, yet she represented what he so desperately wanted. Something of his own. Not a possession or a thing. But his. His opposing virtue. The woman who was opposite to him in every way. The woman who could help free his court of its curse. The woman who might very well free *him*.

But the sin inside him was raging beneath his skin. His sin wanted to defile her. To take her now, while her large eyes were wide with wonder, and with her body smelling of desire. Lust wanted to fuck her. Thane wanted to… He didn't know. Yes, he wanted to taste her, to feel her hot body surrounding his cock, but he wanted something else. Her to desire him. Him, the prince. The Dark Fey. He did not want her under Lust's hypnotic guise.

"Chastity," he whispered before brushing his mouth along the swell of her breast, tasting mist and the scent of woman on her flesh as he moved his mouth along her. "Let me taste you."

She blinked up at him with her wide eyes and he saw the desire to be desired shining in them. Lowering his mouth to hers, he felt a jolt of excitement rush through his veins. Her lips were soft, pliant beneath his. He pressed another soft kiss to them, and this time he opened his mouth, allowing his heat to envelope her.

Hungrily he pressed up against her, encouraging her to part her lips for him, but she wouldn't, or did not know how to allow him the intimacy. In growing frustration, he cupped her chin with both hands, slipping his tongue effortlessly between her lips. Boldly their tongues touched, stroking each other with increasing fierceness.

She was clutching him to her breasts and he could hear as well as feel her heart steadily beat faster and faster with each stroke of his tongue.

He was suddenly consumed with the need to see her and opened his eyes. Hers were closed, long lashes fluttering against pale, porcelain cheeks. Her fingers were in his hair, tangling and gripping as she purred and moaned and brushed her curved body against the length of his.

Lips parting, he fastened onto the supple flesh of her throat, began to suck, and she crumpled deeper into his arms, unable to stand. He sucked and laved, kissed, then blew hot, moist air over her wet flesh. His tongue and lips explored her throat until he was met with the lace barrier of her bodice, and then, he tore at the buttons, thrusting the bodice wide open until her décolletage was once more bared and he was scraping the tips of his teeth along her skin that was now warm and flushed pink.

The scent of her passion-infused blood was so strong it overtook all his senses. He could no longer hear, could no longer see because of the lust that was blinding him. He could only smell, and the scent only grew stronger until his own body was shrouded with her arousal.

Pushing her breasts up against his mouth, he alternated between kisses and licks, searching for the elusive nipple he knew he would find budded and erect beneath her stays. As he pulled her breasts free of the corset, she fell to her knees before him. When she looked up at him, he saw the ecstasy in her lovely eyes.

Lust like he had never known assailed him and he felt the animal within begin to stir again. He was no longer able to hide his glamour, and Chastity was now fully ensnared by the beauty of the fey. He didn't want to entrance her or trap her. He wanted her to want him of her own free will. But her lush body and innocent mouth made him powerless against his sin. The fey with honor, with good intentions, was unable to sway Lust to give up his hold on Chastity Lennox.

Reaching for her hair, Thane pulled the pins free and shook out the long silky tresses that cascaded down to her waist. He studied her, thinking of her as an ancient pagan goddess with her heavy breasts bared and her head tossed back in an enchanting sexual display of femininity. This, he thought, as he palmed her breasts, was what he desired from his mate. This liberation to feel passion, to indulge in the needs of man and woman. One day, she would agree to come to him, to join him in his court, and there, they would be together, his intended mate. He would spend the night with her, awakening her in the dark with his kisses and the slow languid rhythm of his cock sliding inside her.

Chastity Lennox. His future mate. His virtue. His fantasy. He wanted her, regardless of the consequences.

Her eyelids fluttered closed as his fingers traced the rounded contour of her cheek. Her lips parted on a sigh, and he imagined what it would be like to have her on her knees, waiting for him to slip his cock between her lips.

Yes. Both the fey and Lust in him wanted her just like this, bare breasted with tousled hair and kiss-swollen lips parting, waiting to pleasure him with her lush, innocent mouth.

"Beautiful Chastity," he whispered reverently, allowing himself the forbidden image of her taking his length in her mouth. Her mouth would be hot. Wet. Infinitely exciting.

"Please." The word was whispered so quietly, almost pleadingly. No, he wanted to reply, no, he couldn't stop. But he tilted her chin up and saw the shame in her eyes. Any glimmer of passion and desire was now gone, leaving her staring up at him with such fear, like a lamb going to slaughter.

"Do not look upon me with such horror," he whispered.

"Then leave me be."

Stepping back, he released her. Abandoning her was the most difficult thing he had ever done. Being denied was so shocking, so foreign to him. He found himself off center. His fey glamour had not been subdued. His beauty, he knew, was undeniable, utterly compelling to humans, yet here was this young woman, in the first flush of arousal, denying him and her own sexual needs.

She blinked, the glaze in her eyes clearing as she looked around her surroundings with confusion, then horror. She cried out and covered her breasts with her hands. He didn't want to see shame make her face pale. He didn't want her to hide anything from him, least of all her body. A body that could make the most celebrated courtesan murderous with envy.

He could only imagine the thoughts running through her mind, the indignity her virtue would force her to feel.

"I…" She jumped up, tears trickling down her cheeks. "You have humiliated me, sir."

"No," he said, his voice harsh as he reached for her. "There is no shame in desire."

"There is a very great indignity in animal lusts, my lord. And you, sir, are the worst sort of defiler."

"Does my passion disgust you?" he asked as he captured an errant curl and ran his finger through it, "or is it your response to my lust that mortifies you?"

Her eyes widened, and her mouth parted on a silent word. The ugly creature inside him rose, gnashing its teeth, wanting retribution for her slight. His sin wanted to take her, to ravish her and show her shame, humiliation. And the Dark Fey... He wanted to lash out as well, his pride stinging at her hurtful, if not accurate, assessment of him.

He captured her, brought her up hard against him so that her bare breasts were pressed against his silk waistcoat. She gasped as a button rubbed against her nipple, pebbling it. "You feign innocence so well," he whispered hotly in her ear. "You act as though you're offended, disgraced, ruined, but still your body heats for a touch. Your scent perfumes the air, and I would wager that if I were to search beneath the layers of lace, and innocent white linen of your petticoats, I would find your tight little cunt wet for me."

She slapped him hard across his cheek. "Never."

He smiled and allowed her to walk away, if only for a moment so he could collect what was left of his honorable intentions. "Have you thrown the gauntlet down, Lady Chastity?" he called after her.

"I will never submit to you," she sneered as she righted

her dress. Reaching for her, he brought her up against him, whispering hotly in her ear.

"You will do more than submit, I assure you. When I next have you, you'll beg."

FIVE

"WELL?"

"They have found them."

The smash of a crystal goblet against the gold wall made the handful of pixie handmaidens hovering about the faery queen jump with fear.

"Leave us!" the queen snapped, further frightening the easily agitated pixies. Crom watched the servants file out of his mother's salon. They knew as well as he did that it was never a good thing to invoke the ire of the queen. She was one of the most powerful fey in the world, and she did not suffer setbacks easily. Her thirst for the annihilation of the Unseelie Court kept her strong, focused and easily angered.

She whirled on him, the silver robe she wore over her long gown billowing out like a puff of smoke. Her beautiful features twisted into a mask of horror, anger and perhaps fear. "How can this be? How have the Dark Fey learned of the virtues?"

"I do not know. But I assure you, they have."

"No," she huffed as she paced the perimeter of the gilded room. "No, it is impossible. They could not have discovered that the mortal blood they need to end their curse is that of the virtues. That secret has been safe for two hundred years. *I made it so,*" she seethed. "It is my spell, my curse, and the virtues," she scoffed, now in full-blown anger, "are my creation. *Mine.* Designed for use in *my* court. I control them. I use them. Not," she huffed breathlessly from her tirade, "the Dark Fey."

"Mother, calm yourself," Crom suggested as he reached for the decanter of mead. Pulling the crystal out of his hand, she slammed the decanter back onto the table.

"I want answers, Crom. It is impossible that Niall, or any of the others, could have learned of the virtues and their importance in the curse."

"Perhaps," Crom murmured as his gaze followed her about the room, "you have a spy in your court."

That stopped her cold. She glared over her shoulder, violet eyes glistening with malice. "There is no snitch here."

"Are you certain?"

"Completely. No one would dare defy my orders or betray their queen."

"What of Viviana? She has escaped our court. Perhaps she is aiding your Unseelie son now."

His mother stopped pacing, paused to look out the window and steadied herself, while pondering the thought.

"She is a mortal, born a hundred years ago. Of course, living in our court slows her aging, but once she leaves..." His mother turned to him, her violet gaze now steady and assured. "She's been gone six months, which is three years in the mortal realm. If she's still alive she's an old woman, probably crippled and babbling away. But more likely she's turned to ash and the wind has carried her far away."

His mother was usually right, of course. But in this matter, she wasn't thinking clearly or broadly enough. Viviana was the virtue of diligence. *Persistence.* She had been brought to the Seelie Court with the first seven virtues and mated to a fey who was domineering and harsh. She had not been treated like the other six virtues. No, Crom thought, remembering the painful cries of Viviana as her fey husband mated with her. No, if anyone had the will to see something through, it was her. If anyone had a reason to betray the queen and the court, it was Viviana.

"Absolutely not," his mother murmured. "It is not Viviana. Besides, Sucellos had a firm hand on her. She was submissive and content at last with her lot in life."

No, she hadn't been. His mother was deluding herself if she truly believed it. Sucellos was the fey warrior who ruled over fertility and death. His magic was powerful and dark, and Viviana had feared him, the monster Sucellos was. Twisted by his power in the Seelie Court, and the darkness that seemed to simmer in him, Sucellos was cruel, depraved and commanding. Crom would bet his riches that Sucellos carried inside him the blood of a Dark Fey. A fact that Sucellos was scrupulous about keeping from the queen.

"If not Viviana," he asked, "then who?"

"No one in my court," she firmly replied. Crom flicked a piece of lint from his lace cuff and glanced at her. So blind, he thought wonderingly. When had it been that his mother's desperation for justice had started to overshadow the well-being of her own court? She was consumed by the need to bring the Unseelie to their knees. To see them obliterated. Their destruction was her every waking thought, and no doubt, her nightly dream.

"Perhaps," he suggested carefully, "you underestimate my brother's mental fortitude. He is not a simpleton, but a powerful Unseelie king."

"He is a bastard barbarian," she spat. "Born of that brute who raped me."

"You forget something elemental," Crom said, knowing he was going to enrage her. "Your blood also flows through his veins."

"Do not talk to me of that...that monster," she roared. "He is a Dark Fey, an abomination. I need no reminders that he came from my womb."

"Still, he is your son—with at least half of your powers."

She blanched. The beautiful, imposing queen of the fey actually paled, and Crom hid his grin. He had finally figured out his mother's greatest fear—his twin.

She recovered swiftly and resumed her pacing. "The Dark Fey are stupid creatures. They care more for sex than magic and politics. Their court is a cesspool of carnality, not influence or elegance. They're not capable of unraveling the secret of my spell."

"Regardless, Niall has discovered that the key to releasing his court from its fate is to breed with the virtues and infuse his dying court with the much-needed—and powerful—pure mortal blood."

"They are to be ours!" his mother cried, her hand curling into a small fist. "The first seven came to this court a hundred years ago, and now the time is ripe for the next seven to mate with our princes. It's been arranged. I've chosen well, not only for strength, but for a higher purpose for our court. Each Seelie that I've chosen will enhance the virtue, their offspring will infuse our court with every desirable quality. Those women are to be ours, gifts to my faithful courtiers. I will not allow it, my...creations to be tainted by the touch of a Dark Fey."

"Calm yourself, Mother," Crom drawled. "You forget that to end the curse these virtues must come willingly. Once they are exposed to the sins of the Dark Fey, these innocents will not follow them."

"You do not know the power of the Dark Fey," she murmured, wringing her hands. "Their glamour, it is the most beautiful in the world. Their seduction, the sweetest, most heady arousal you have ever felt. Even as your mind hates them, your body—" she trembled, then steeled herself "—your body desires them, craves them. These women, they may not have a chance to protect themselves if they fall prey to a Dark Fey's glamour."

An interesting and most informative little lesson. Had his mother forgotten that he was also part Dark Fey? His father had been their king. And although he looked like his golden Seelie mother, there were undeniable characteristics within him that were all Unseelie.

"Mother, you worry over naught. I've taken measures to protect the virtues."

His mother sank onto a velvet chair. She looked fatigued and old, almost as old as her two hundred and fifty years. "Tell me."

"They are close at hand and are being guarded by some of my men who are posing as footmen."

His mother brightened. "London?"

Crom smiled. "Indeed. I've warded off the Lennox town house. Naught but mortals shall enter their domain—at least until we have decided what is to be done about my brother and his band of cursed princes."

"I need to speak to Lennox," his mother demanded.

"Four mornings from now," he announced. "It's all arranged. He will meet you at the gates of Richmond Park. I assumed that would be beneficial to you, since the park incorporates your court. You will be safe on your warded ground if the Dark Fey decide to follow Lennox."

His mother's smile widened, making her expression beam with loveliness. "You are very much my protégé, are you not?"

Crom inclined his head. "You have been both mother and father to me. Naturally, I have followed in your footsteps."

"And what do you want, Crom? I sense that this interest in the virtues is not merely to keep your mama happy and the curse against your bastard brother alive."

Ah, at last they had arrived at the crux of the matter. He needed to be cautious, for his mother was as shrewd as she was beautiful. Every move, every decision was made for the greater good of the Seelie Court. The damn court was all his mother lived for, thrived for. Her vengeance against the Unseelie had never wavered, only grown since she had fled his monster of a father's court a little more than two hundred years before.

In mortal terms, it was an unfathomable length of time for vengeance to perpetuate. In the world of the fey, it was nothing. But Crom felt as though it was aeons. He was tired of it. Sick of being treated as a youngling by his mother. It was time to take over the helm. The Seelie needed a king, and never more so than now, with the Unseelie coming out of their dark court to wreak retribution upon them.

"Crom?" his mother prompted, her voice full of suspicion.

There was no need to rile her, to make her suspect that he planned to throw her over and build a new Seelie Court. No, he needed to play his hand wisely.

"I would request, Mother, that you consider bestowing one of the virtues to me."

"To you?" She laughed as she picked up a silver mirror and gazed into it. "Whatever would you do with a virtue?"

It annoyed him, the way she thought of him as an

ineffective courtier. Well, what did she know? He had been gathering his little mutinous army beneath her nose for the past three years. With the promise of fairness, and a mating with a virtue to strengthen their Seelie powers, the six fey he had chosen to help usurp his mother's throne were more than eager to set his plan into place.

His mother had ruled too long. Her only care was for the utter destruction of the Unseelie Court—a vision he shared. But he had many more ideas of making their court thrive, something his mother had long ago abandoned. There were alliances to be made with other fey in other countries. Fortunes to be created, both with fey and mortals alike. The world was advancing, and more and more the mortals who inhabited the earth failed to believe the stories of the *Daoine Side* the way their ancestors once had. No, times were changing, and if the Seelie were to survive, they must change with it. There were millions of mortals in need of fey gifts, and millions more to use as pawns.

His mother didn't see that. She only saw the destruction of the court that had turned her into an embittered woman.

There was nothing he would have enjoyed more than informing her that her days of ruling the Seelie were numbered. But one thing he had learned being her son was that one needed to be certain that one had the upper hand—fully. Crom was not quite convinced he had that yet. So, he pretended that his motivation was far more benign.

"I would like a wife, Mother. I believe I am entitled

one. And younglings. Wouldn't you enjoy that, playing the part of doting grandmama to lovely little fey-virtue children?"

She waved her pale hand, dismissing him. "Pick one of my ladies-in-waiting, or a courtier's daughter."

"I want a virtue," he said, grinding his teeth together. His mother arched her brow, replaced the mirror atop the table and glared at him.

"And what would you do with a virtue?"

His mother would not believe it if he told her. For three years he had been fantasizing about Chastity Lennox. Her innocence, her purity would be the perfect symbolism for his new court. As queen, she would emulate everything he was trying to achieve. And in bed…he felt himself grow aroused as the image of the voluptuous Chastity Lennox formed in his mind. In bed he could be as wicked as he wanted to with her. She would belong to him— only him. Oh, he kept his Dark Fey blood well hidden from his mother, but the appetite of a virile Dark Fey was there, simmering deep within him. He wanted to dominate the virtuous Chastity, and hide her away in his bedchamber, corrupting her through the night, and purifying her by day.

"Mother?"

"I suppose I can think on it." Which meant she wouldn't give the matter a passing thought.

"After you meet with Lennox?"

"Yes, yes," she replied absently as she reached for the decanter and poured herself some faery mead.

Crom stood and smoothed his waistcoat with his

palm, then he turned and reached for his sword, which was tucked safely away in his scabbard. "Good day, Mother."

There was silence until he reached the door, then her voice called out to him, engaging and lyrical, sweetening the warning in her words. "Do not think to overrule me, Crom. You will not enjoy the effects of losing to me."

Closing the door, Crom pressed his back against the carved wood. It was not going to be easy, but he would do it. He would overthrow his mother, and in the end, he and his faithful men would possess a virtue, and thereby form a new Seelie Court.

"Well?"

Crom watched as a tall, blond warrior emerged from the shadows. "As we suspected. She'll favor her old courtiers with the virtues."

"And the Dark Fey, how did they discover the women?"

"I don't know, and that will pose a threat for us and our plans. We must discover how they learned of it while preventing the virtues from falling into their hands. The Unseelie need all seven women to break the curse on their court. We must prevent any of the women falling into their hands."

"What now, Your Highness?"

"You have ingratiated yourself in Lennox's household?"

Arawn smiled. "Yes. I told him I was sent by Queen Aine. He believed it. The poor sod is terrified of the queen's wrath and the subsequent repercussions, should he disagree. He believes that the queen sent me to take his daughter as part of the tithe he owes."

"Then it is all arranged?"

Arawn nodded. "I am to court Prudence, the virtue of temperance and restraint."

Crom smiled, satisfied with the progress Arawn had made. "Good. Get me an introduction to Chastity—and be quick about it."

"Someone has warded off the town house," Thane spat, his blood boiling with rage.

"That would be my bastard brother, Crom. No doubt acting on orders from the queen," Niall murmured as he leaned against the trunk of an ancient oak tree in Hyde Park.

"Then they know we're after the virtues," Kian replied as he gazed between the trees limbs. It was late afternoon and the sun was moving west, its rays dappling between the leaves. Numerous carriages littered the park, and Thane and his friends took care to appear as though they were naught but gentlemen, out for a ride during the fashionable hour. Amidst the green foliage they blended in. They were fey after all, nature was their home. They were as comfortable in the woods as they were beneath the stars and moon. As Dark Fey, night was more to their liking. With the sun setting, their powers—and their glamour—began to awaken. But with their fey blood stirring, so were their sins.

"Now, with the Seelie following our footsteps," Kian

continued, "it won't be easy getting them to our court, especially since we cannot just carry them off to ours."

"Use your glamour," Niall grumbled, "but only to gain their notice. We must work quickly if we're to secure them. Our counterparts will have no compunction about using their magic to seduce the women. We must do everything in our power to prevent that."

"Against the Seelie?" Avery said with a laugh. "Those pious fey won't even know how to go about a proper seduction. I will have my virtue bedded and enthralled by the time they seek an introduction."

Niall flashed Avery a wide grin. "Your prowess is legendary, my friend, but remember the curse. They must come willingly to you and to our court. You cannot use magic to sway them."

"I require only the magic in my hands," Avery said with a leer.

"Getting them to our court is only half the battle, I think," the king murmured. "It's keeping them there. They will be leaving the only life they've ever known. Their families, friends—their mortality. It will be a most difficult challenge."

"What of the other three virtues?" Kian asked. "Lennox daughters are four, chastity, temperance, kindness and humility. Where are diligence, charity and faith?"

"I am making inquiries," Niall pronounced as he tracked the path of a bluebird flying from tree to tree. "We cannot be too careful. Who knows how many other fey courts pay allegiance to my mother? There could be others after the women, as well."

"What do you suggest?" Thane asked, feeling restless and angry. He did not like the idea of Chastity being protected by any other than himself. Most especially a Seelie Fey. If it was indeed Crom who had warded Lennox's house as Niall suspected, then Thane was all the more enraged. He despised the king's half brother, and the thought of him taking Chastity made his blood boil. There was no way Thane was going to allow a Seelie to claim his virtue. *His...*

Unable to stop himself, Thane relived those moments in the maze, and the hunger he had experienced then only felt more gnawing. Nothing assuaged it. He wanted his virtue. He had tried last night to gain entrance into her room. That was when he discovered the town house had been warded off. He had been unable to break the complicated enchantment, and the failure of that only furthered the deepening rage inside him. He wanted Chastity, and he wanted her now.

"Have you tried more traditional methods to gain entry into the home?" Niall asked. "An introduction perhaps or a call?"

Thane glared at his king. Fortunately, they were half brothers, and Niall tolerated far more insolence from him than from others at his court. "What do you think I am? Of course I've already seen that I've been introduced." Hell, he had not been able to get the introduction out of his head. He hadn't meant for it to happen like that, but she had looked so damn good standing there in the maze, and he wanted her, had to struggle with Lust to keep from ravishing her.

"And?" Niall prompted

Thane frowned, remembering how she had run from him. "She will not see me."

Niall stared at him with a look of amusement. "A bit more of a challenge than you first thought?"

"Yes," he hissed, "but that wouldn't be the case if some Seelie infidel hadn't seen to keeping her from me. I'm certain the servants are Seelie that have been planted in the house specifically to hamper our ability to get to the women. They're using their glamour. It won't be easy when our magic is evenly matched."

"Might I suggest, then, that you find other ways?"

"I've tried. The windows are sealed shut by magic. I came as fog and mist, even rain, and could not make my way in."

"Then try harder," Niall commanded. "Our court deserves to have your tenacity in this matter."

Thane heard himself growl. Tenacious he was, but he had lost his way, forgetting that he needed Chastity for the survival of his court, and not just to satisfy the ache in his loins.

The need to feel her once more in his arms outweighed his true purpose here in the mortal realm.

"Avery, what did you find out about Lennox?" Niall asked.

The biggest of the fey, Avery stood well over six feet, with shoulders the width of a giant oak. A true glutton, Avery was the furthest thing from a fat, lazy lord. But his need for more—of everything—fired a compulsion to experience anything that might satiate his senses. Leave it to Niall to exploit Avery's sin. The fey would stop at nothing until he was satisfied that he had "consumed" all the *on dits* there were to be had about the Duke of Lennox.

"It seems the duke, while always appearing to be financially respectable, came into a rather large amount of money three years ago. His peers describe him as having the devil's own luck for investing. A luck, I might add, that was only just average—until three years ago."

Niall's eyes flashed. "It appears that Lennox must have found the goose that lays the golden egg."

Nodding, Avery continued. "Everything he touches turns to gold. He's become more than rich. He's powerful, and there isn't a man about London who would not give his firstborn for the chance to partake in an investment scheme with him."

"What are his investments?" Kian grumbled. Already Thane saw his twin's sin color his blue eyes green. Envy...a horrid sin to be saddled with.

Shrugging, Avery leaned back against the trunk of a tree. "The usual. Land and properties. A speculation consortium to develop the plot of land behind Grosvenor Square, a factory up north that is building some locomotive engine propelled by steam. His interests and investments are varied. But," Avery said with a leer, "there's one venture he keeps silent about."

"Oh?" Niall asked, his interest piqued.

"The flesh trade," Avery answered. "I discovered that

fact last night while feeding my sin. You know nymphs, they can never keep their mouths shut—a blessing that," Avery said with a smile.

Thane's eyes flared wide. "The Nymph and the Satyr?"

Avery nodded. "The bloody bastard is a silent partner. He knows about us. At the very least, he knows the fey exist."

"It seems the duke is well accustomed to doing business with the fey," Niall said thoughtfully as he gazed up at the sky.

"The Seelie Fey," Kian spat. "Lennox is in league with them."

Niall turned to Thane's twin and smiled. "Then let us acquaint him with how the Unseelie do business. Meet me two nights from now at the Nymph and the Satyr, and we will see what inducement we can provide to entice His Grace to allow the three of you to call upon his lovely daughters."

"I cannot wait two nights," Thane grumbled rather impulsively. Hell, he needed to gain control of himself. What was this madness that was invading his thoughts? She was a woman. A means to end a curse.

"My brother is anxious to get his cock wet." Kian laughed, but Thane saw the jealousy in his eyes. "And who wouldn't be with that luscious morsel? I'll wager there is enough of her to share, brother."

Control. It was Envy talking, not Kian—not his twin. Rage—and jealousy—suddenly consumed Thane. Was this what Kian had to deal with? Was this truly what his twin's sin felt like, this all-consuming malevolence? This compulsion to take, to hoarde, regardless of what pain it might cause others?

The thought of sharing Chastity with anyone was enough to make him as violent as his king—who was ruled by the sin of wrath.

Avery, the gluttonous bastard, shared Kian's view. "Aye, curved and full, as is my preference. I could show her a thing or two that Lust couldn't. For starters, never to settle for one dish when there is an entire buffet waiting to be sampled."

Thane's sword was out of his scabbard and the glistening tip pointing to Avery's Adam's apple before Thane could reason out his actions. The faery metal sang as it swooped through the air and glimmered as the steel pricked fey flesh. "If you so much as look at her, I will skewer you."

Another sword tip landed atop Thane's, which forced his hand lower and away from Avery's throat. "There is no need to kill one another," Niall muttered. "There is a woman for each of us."

"But one is not enough," Avery replied. The leer that was so often present in his gaze was gone, replaced by fear. Not alarm elicited from Thane's sword, but another fear. The type that was soul-deep and haunting.

"Perhaps we may find our sins vanquished once we have the virtues," Niall suggested. "Mayhap what torments us now no longer will. Maybe all of us will be free."

Avery closed his eyes as he rested his head against the

tree trunk. "I cannot even imagine it, what it will be like. I have never dared to dream of it."

"Neither have I," Kian murmured.

"None of us have, but the future is in sight," Niall reminded them. "We have found four of our virtues. Now we must find a way to possess them. And without the use of faery magic, that means we must work together, opposing sins and all."

Nodding, Avery and Kian agreed. Thane noticed his sword was pointed at the level of Avery's heart. Inside, jealousy and an impassioned desire to protect Chastity still ate at him, but he nodded, allowing the sword to fall away.

"Two nights from now, at the Nymph and the Satyr," Niall reminded them.

"My informant tells me that Lennox never avails himself of the wares," Avery replied. "His business dealings with the house are through his solicitor and man of affairs."

"I will bring him," Niall assured. "Just make certain the three of you are there. And where is Rinion?" Niall demanded.

"Probably lost in the reflection of a looking glass, marveling at his own beauty."

Niall grinned at Kian's obvious envy of Rinion's legendary beauty. "Vanity does enjoy looking at himself. But find him."

"I believe that Vanity has already found his virtue. He made it very clear that he intended to wed and bed her on the Eve of Beltane."

Niall frowned. "He was not at court when I left this morning."

"Have you seen his virtue, Your Highness?" Avery asked. "I think you haven't, for if you had you would realize that Rinion most likely has her locked away in his room. She's quite a beauty, and Rinion was like a stallion on the scent of a mare."

Laughing, Niall sheathed his sword. "Then we are fortunate. Rinion has secured us our first virtue."

Kian's eyes flashed with resentment. "I'll be next."

No, Thane thought. I will. Chastity was nearly in his grasp. He could feel it.

"I cannot linger," Niall announced. "I'm going north, where I've heard some reports of women who may be the last of the seven we are searching for. Do as you must, but remember not to enchant them or force them."

Thane watched as Avery, Kian and Niall left the woods. Climbing atop his horse, Thane nudged his mount forward, then began to canter through the paths of Hyde Park while Bel loped beside him. After a few short minutes, he found himself across the road from Chastity Lennox's town house.

There he would wait. If he could not go to her, he would have to find a way for her to come to him.

It was a fine evening for a stroll in the gardens. The air was fresh and the sun was setting in a most marvelous display of fuchsia and orange. Picking a handful of lily of the valley, Chastity inhaled the heady scent. She had always enjoyed the smell of flowers and grass. Her

family liked to tease her about her sensitive nose, claiming she was like a bloodhound. She supposed there was
some truth in that. Her olfactory sense was rather height-
ened and developed, so sensitive that she could detect the
subtle differences between base, middle and top notes in
a perfume or a decadent dish laced with herbs and cream.
Even now, she could decipher the difference between the
sweet perfume of the lily she held in her hand and the
delicately soft essence of the lilacs that were in bloom at
the back of the garden.

Strolling through the herbal garden that had been allowed to grow out of control, Chastity mentally made
a list of things that needed to be done. The trees and
plants seemed to be in decent health, but the herbs had
grown woody and coarse, requiring a heavy hand with
the pruning. She had been a small child the last time she
was in London, and in this garden. While her sisters had
preferred the formal ornamental gardens at the side of the
yard, Chastity had always preferred the kitchen garden.
She used to come out with Cook and the housekeeper,
Mrs. Badderly, and help them cut herbs and flowers. The
garden had always held a mystical charm that Chastity
found intriguing. There was no formality here, no rules.
The flowers and herbs grew alongside each other, their
borders not defined into perfect manicured squares like
those of the ornamental garden. She had spent many an
afternoon here, chasing butterflies and frolicking with
Cook's assistant.

But then she and her sisters had gone away. She had
often thought about this little copse at the back of the

house, and the hours she had spent running free. It was such a shame that her favorite spot had been neglected, allowed to whither into wildness.

If they were going to be spending any time in London, Chastity would need to see to this garden. Not only because herbs and flowers interested her, but because she needed something to take her mind off last night in the maze and the dark-haired stranger. He hadn't said his name. She knew only that he was a prince, and that he had spoken to her most scandalously, and she had allowed it. Truth be told, she had *reveled* in his words, in the way his breath was hot against her throat and his hard body pressed into her soft one.

After coming in from the maze, she had been disoriented, her head heavy and foggy with the lingering effects of his seduction and the heady scent that had preceded his arrival. Thank heavens Mercy had found her and pulled her into an empty salon where she had immediately set Chastity's hair and gown to rights. Mercy, in her kindness, had not questioned Chastity's crumpled state, but her worried expression had told Chastity how dreadful she really looked.

She complained of a headache and a desire to leave the ball, so her father had promptly loaded her and her sisters into the carriage and taken them home. Mary had been livid, of course, but Prue and Mercy had seemed to understand. Once home, Chastity had fallen onto her bed and slept as though she had been drugged. Her sleep had not been peaceful, but clouded with visions and dreams of a masked stranger with blue eyes and black hair. A stranger whose voice seemed to constantly whisper to her.... *Let me in....*

Even now she heard it, murmuring to her from across the stone fence at the back of the garden. She didn't know how to resist it, only knew that she must. It was a trial, she realized. A test of her strength, her virtue. And sometimes, especially in the dark while she was alone in her bed at night, she feared that she would fail it. Her virtue, she knew, was slowly being stripped from her, and she was helpless to impede it.

Stopping to inspect a row of peonies and their swelling buds, Chastity noticed a footprint in the dirt. It was large, pointed at the toes. The imprint, she was certain, was that of a boot, a pair of Hessians.

It was a strange place for a footprint to be. Perhaps if her father had been a big man, or if they had a gardener, she would have thought nothing of it, but her father wasn't tall enough to have a foot of this size, and with their arrival in London only a few days ago, a gardener had not yet been installed. It could not belong to her brother, Robert, either. For Robert had not come to call on them.

Intrigued, Chastity followed the footprints, noticing how they seemed to lead away from the garden and the house. Which was even more bizarre because there was nothing back there but the stone fence that enclosed the garden. Beyond their yard was a small thick brush that was slated to be razed to make way for another square of fashionable town houses.

Where did the footsteps lead? she wondered, clutching

the posy tightly in her hand. The trail abruptly stopped at a wall covered in ivy at the back of the garden. By now, the sun was slipping quickly beneath the horizon, making way for the moon to creep up into the evening sky. It was rather dark back in the corner, what with the ivy and the shadow of the house and the tops of the trees that loomed over the garden wall. She really should return to the house, but she ignored the self-protective instinct.

Dropping to her knees, Chastity saw that the ground was disturbed, as if something had been slid against it. But what? There wasn't a gate in the garden, not that she could recall anyway. But there was a footprint there...

Perhaps the man had scaled the garden wall and dropped to the other side? But what would someone be doing in their yard? A footpad? A housebreaker? Fear skittered through her, making her thoughts race. But then the breeze blew, taking the long, loose tendrils of ivy, scraping them against the stone, revealing a fleeting glance of a rusted piece of metal. A latch? A gate?

She thrust aside the ivy, revealing a long-neglected garden gate in the faint glow of dusk. She had never known of a gate, but as she reached for the rusted latch a deep-rooted memory sprung forth.

"Oh, don't be going through that gate, miss," Cook's assistant had said in her thick Yorkshire accent. "The faeries will take ye and carry ye off and we'll never see 'ide nor 'air of ye again."

A little tremor fluttered in her stomach as she recalled that day, saw her own chubby little fist grasping the latch.

She had been six and adventuresome—full of harmless mischief, her father had always said. The assistant, whose name Chastity could not quite recall, had been a superstitious young lady. But then, the country folk from the north typically were. Alas, however, those from Glastonbury could hardly be called any different—for she believed in the fey, too.

"Do you believe in faeries?" she remembered asking the young woman as she pulled Chastity away from the gate.

"Aye, I do. And you should, too."

"Are faeries good?"

"No, miss. Not all. Some faeries... Well, some faeries are full of mischief and darkness."

"Darkness?" Chastity had asked, perplexed. The young woman had flushed then, and checked over her shoulder to locate the cook, who was busily snipping away at a sprig of rosemary.

"Aye, darkness. But the kind of dark that ye dunna need to know about yet. But rest assured, the Dark Faeries, they will corrupt you they will, by tempting you with all sorts of wicked delights."

Chastity in her innocence hadn't known what the servant meant by that, but now she did. She believed in faeries, and knew that there were beautiful, sensual fey out there that could tempt even a nun to commit any kind of sin.

And tonight, in the darkening of the twilight sky, she was no longer six. And there was no one to warn her away from the gate and remind her that not all faeries were good and benevolent. Whatever lay beyond this garden gate was far more powerful than a memory from her childhood, for it pulled her forth, making her forget that it was growing dark and she should be inside.

Dropping the bouquet of lilies, Chastity used both hands to tug at the latch, which seemed to be rusted shut. But that was impossible! The footprints had led her there. In fact, they seemed to disappear beneath the gate. Someone had been in the garden, and that someone had opened this very gate and stepped through.

Chastity tugged one last time. With a groan the ancient hinges gave way, allowing her to open the gate far enough to slide through sideways. As she was squeezing through the opening, her gown caught on a rusty nail, which snagged the hem and tore through her stocking, also tearing at the skin of her ankle.

But Chastity barely felt any pain. She could only look around in awe at the magical land before her. A forest. An enchanted forest, it seemed, for everything was beyond beautiful—and glistening. She had never seen anything so lovely. And the scents… She inhaled deeply, discerning a mixture of florals and heavy spice. The perfumed air was a dichotomy of light fragrance and heavy, drugging aromas.

Standing by a copse of ancient oaks and rowan trees was a dark-haired man atop a black horse. Beside him, a large white hound with black eyes stared back at her, as if he and his master had been awaiting her arrival.

A gust of wind came up, making her skirts billow around her feet. The wind carried the scent of blood that she felt seeping into her shoe over to the beast and the man. The animal whimpered and lowered to his haunches, as if frenzied by the metallic tang of blood. The man's blue eyes suddenly darkened with a hunger that frightened her.

She turned to run, every instinct warned her to, but the gate suddenly slammed closed, pushing her all the way through and into the forest that now surrounded her. The dog whimpered again, and slowly Chastity turned, her back pressed against the gate as she watched the animal's ears fall flat against its large head. Mentally she prepared herself for the attack, for the dog was now whimpering a series of low howls, its black eyes fixed on the small maroon puddle at her foot.

The man nudged his mount forward, coming into view beneath the moonlight. The same man from the path in Glastonbury. The mysterious and seductive stranger who had been the focus of her nightly dreams. The very one who made her think illicit thoughts, made her want, deep in the night, when she was alone and her body was aching.

"No," she whispered, her eyes widening in alarm. He smiled, even as she reached behind her back, her fingers trembling as she attempted to find the latch. Frantically she endeavored to open the gate, but to no avail.

"Chastity Lennox," he drawled in that hypnotic, seductive voice. "I have been waiting for you."

Six

THE SCENT OF BLOOD—CHASTITY'S BLOOD—
slammed into Thane, sending Lust to the deepest part
of his soul. Strange, when Lust was hungry, needing
to be satiated, almost nothing had the power to make
him retreat. But the smell and sight of her bleeding sent
Thane's cardinal sin running, freeing him to slide from
his horse and go to her. Bel immediately loped beside
him, just as eager to reach Chastity.

With her back firmly pressed against the garden gate,
Chastity seemed to pale even more as she watched their
approach. Thane suspected her pallor was not from blood
loss, but trepidation of both Bel and himself.

Recalling her fear of animals, Thane sternly ordered
Bel to heel where he was. The insolent pup made a snarl
of complaint, but with a well-placed glare, Bel wisely
chose to listen to his master.

"Come, sit down." Reaching for her hand, Thane

gently guided her to a stone bench beneath a weeping willow. Trembling beside him, Chastity, wide-eyed, followed him, her gaze never leaving Bel. "He won't eat you, if that is what you fear."

She did not smile at his jest, indeed she trembled even more as he assisted her to the bench. When she sat down, he saw her wince, and he bent to his knees, carefully slipping the shoe from her right foot.

"Don't," she squeaked. He tried again, but she moved her foot before putting space between them. "It's naught but a scratch and it isn't proper for you to see my... limb."

He'd be seeing a damn bit more than her foot, he thought—and soon. But he needed to remember that she was a lady, and ladies didn't allow gentlemen, known or unknown, to touch them. Anywhere. Not even something as innocuous as a foot. And this particular lady, he reminded himself, was more than just a highborn lady of the ton. She was a paragon of virtue.

"You're hurt and bleeding," he replied softly. "Allow me to help you."

Her gaze caught his, and he saw how wary she was. "I will just go back through the gate and to the house. My maid will have a look at it."

"Why? When I am right here and ready to assist you?"

Her chin lifted, sending him an impertinent glare. "Because you are not known to me, sir, and you make too many presumptions with my person."

"We were introduced the other day. Have you for-gotten?"

The way his voice dropped reminded her of the sensual stranger in the maze. She knew then they were one and the same. Heat came to her cheeks as she recalled the scene in the maze, his face against her breasts, his tongue curling around her nipple. Oh, how she wanted that again. But even more, she wanted to stay and enjoy his company. To discover who he was. What he wanted with her. Perhaps, even to be courted by him. In the middle of the night she had allowed herself that fanciful turn of mind, but that was in the night, this was another matter. She absolutely could not allow herself to stay here.

"My name is Thane," he reminded her, drawing her out of her thoughts. "You were with your sisters."

"That was not an introduction, sir. We are still not known to one another, and therefore, this—" she glanced around at the garden that surrounded them "—this secluded spot we now find ourselves in is most danger-ous. Now, then, excuse me."

As she slipped her foot from his palm, Thane watched her attempt to stand. Her balance was off because of the pain in her ankle—the pain that was very much evident on her face. But like a proud, determined little solider, she took one step, and then another, hobbling her way back to the gate to the place where he could not follow.

He knew he wasn't supposed to do this, but he had no choice. Standing up, Thane caught her, turning her so that he could place his hands on either side of her face, forcing her to look at him. Then, slowly, he lowered his mouth to her ear, brushing his lips along her hair. Gods, she smelled so good. So right. Never had a woman's scent—fey or mortal—aroused such a deep-seated hunger inside him. He wanted her. With a blinding intensity that he could not resist. Even now he pulled her closer, trying to rub up against her, to weaken her defenses.

"Release me," she gasped.

No, he couldn't. Even if he wished to, his movements were no longer his own. Lust was beginning to rule him now, to become separate from the fey. "Chastity," he murmured as his mouth descended to her neck. "You know not how you tempt me."

"Release me at once, sir!"

The shrillness of her voice cut through the haze of lust that not only clouded his vision but his judgment, as well. He knew not how to soften her, to make her desire him. He had never met a woman he could not seduce. Until her.

"Please."

Her plea effectively sliced through his conscience. "Forgive me." Reluctantly he moved away from her. Once he was at a safe-enough distance away from her, he cleared his throat. "There is no need to run from me. Tell me what I can do to help you."

"Allow me to return to my garden."

Anything but that. She had been here with him for too short a time. He had wasted these moments alone with her by making her frightened of him. He was at an utter loss as to how to go about lessening her fears. How to change that wariness into a burning passion for him.

No woman had ever been able—or willing—to resist his erotic charms. This woman, who did not appear to desire him at all, was a complete novelty to him. But Thane could say with all honesty that he had never wanted a woman as much as he wanted Chastity Lennox. The thought of her leaving him now gave him a panicked feeling. Him, the fey who had no shortage of women vying for his attentions and body. Automatically his fingers reached for her, pulling her lush body close to his.

"My lord," she demanded. "Release me at once. It's most improper to be alone with you, and in the dark no less."

Ignoring her protests, Thane knew what he must do. So he began whispering the ancient enchantment spell into her ear. The moment she went soft beneath his hands, he knew the words had worked their magic.

She was entranced now, but not completely under his spell. He was only temporarily bending the rules, he told himself, not breaking them. He would not use the enchantment to seduce her, even though Lust, and his own body, were crying out for release.

Trying to think of something other than sex, Thane reached for her hand. "Let us see the damage, shall we?" he suggested as he helped her to the bench. Carefully she sat down, her hands folded demurely in her lap—a movement he knew came instinctively to her.

Bel chose that moment to shove his muzzle between Thane's shoulder and Chastity's stockinged foot which was now stained red. "Not yet," he told his hound. Obediently, Bel sat on his haunches and waited.

"He means you no harm," Thane murmured as he gently turned her foot inward to examine what he hoped was only a scratch on her ankle. "He remembers you, that is all, and is eager to make friends with you."

Her lovely green gaze turned to him, and the full impact of her stare focused on him made Lust begin to rear up again. The enchantment spell had taken some of the fear and apprehension from her eyes, leaving them wide and lustrous—dreamy. It made him think of how she would look after he kissed her, or teased her skin with his tongue. Which made him think of his current position between her thighs—which of course made him think of sliding the layers of taffeta and linen up higher, revealing her quim, which would be at a perfect level for tasting.

He wanted that, to debauch her with his mouth, to feel her fingers gripping at his hair, her hips calling to him in the ancient female rhythm begging him for more.

No matter how much he wanted that, Thane could not allow his sin to become the stronger entity. Chastity was vulnerable like this, under this light enchantment he had placed her in. He had only done it in case he needed magic to mend her flesh, or dull her pain—and to ease her fear of Bel. He did not enchant her to take advantage of her. But Lust would not give a damn about that. Lust had no honor. No feeling other than euphoria. Lust, Thane was afraid, had gotten him into all kinds of moral entanglements—all of them affecting his own honor and soul, not Lust's.

But Thane had honor. Dignity. And seducing Chastity

under the guise of magic was not honorable. Besides, he wanted her to desire *him*. No woman really ever had. They'd only cried out for Lust, but never, he thought, for the fey prince.

What would it be like, he wondered to have a woman desire him solely for himself? What would it be like to have *this* woman? To have more than just sex with her? He'd never experienced that, an emotional attachment with his liaisons. He was suddenly parched for it, friendship and love. Quiet conversation while she lay in his arms. What would it be like to touch without intent to fuck, but rather to simply feel her skin, to bring her close to his body, to absorb her into his soul.

Gripping her ankle, he looked down at his fingers, which were holding her foot while he tried to forget what he had just admitted to himself. Lust and Thane were synonymous. Never to be separated. Chastity would have to accept both. And…he would have to share her with Lust, no matter how much he coveted her for himself. Would Lust want those tender, intimate moments that Thane did? Would he even allow it?

Tongue thick in his mouth, Thane noticed that his heart suddenly felt strange, as if it were not beating properly. He must not dwell on things that could not be changed, he told himself. Chastity was to be brought to his world for the good of his court. She was therefore not, in essence, completely his. But God help him, he wanted her to be his—all his.

Quickly he stole another glance at her, his body tingling with desire. She was so perfect to him. A surprisingly lovely dichotomy of angel and devil. Her body, he thought as his gaze raked over her bodice, was pure sin. Designed for the carnal appetites of men—and fey.

She caught his stare, and the forthrightness of her gaze made him cringe. He was completely certain that during her perusal of him Chastity Lennox had not experienced one libidinous thought of him—of them—locked in carnalities.

He truly needed to think of something other than her lovely breasts, and the filmy fichu that had come loose from her bodice. Beneath the expensive lace the cleft of her décolletage beckoned, and he was so close to answering the call. With any other female it would be so easy, but with this one...

"Tell me, why do you fear animals?"

Her gaze slid from his face to fix on Bel. The dog pressed in, making her shudder and reach for his shoulder, where she clutched the velvet of his frock coat, making the pounding of his heart beat harder in his chest. Did she not understand the torment she put him through when she touched him like that? Her scent...he was going mad from it. What was it? he wondered as he discreetly inhaled. Angel Water...the perfume was all the rage after all. Every fashionable lady in London was daubing her bosom with the mixture of orange flower, rose and myrtle water. It was a scent used to entice the male sex, an aphrodisiac made to incite the deepest of sexual appetites, but never had the perfume had such an effect on him. Perhaps it was because he had never encountered its heady scent mixed with the fascinating aroma of innocence. It called to him, begging him to corrupt her in all the ways he knew how.

Fingers on his shoulder dragged his thoughts away. He really was nothing but a beast. A creature controlled by base thoughts and sin. Would he ever be able to give Chastity a semblance of a normal life—a mortal life? Or would it only be about sex and pleasure? In the years since his sin had grown in strength, it had overtaken him, leaving him unaware of who he truly was.

He had never cared before, but now, strangely, thoughts that were utterly foreign to him began to invade his conscience. He barely knew this woman, yet he desired a deep and abiding connection with her. One that was, yes, sexual. But a bond that was also based on friendship. Closeness. Contentment. He didn't know when it had happened, but he wanted more. Not just a bed partner but a mate.

"Sir?"

Shaking his head, he realized that he had been looking up into her face. Staring at her. Dreaming of all the things he wanted with her, and not one of his thoughts had been for his dying court or the damnable spell that cursed his kind. He was forgetting his purpose here in the mortal realm.

"You were saying?" he said, making pretense of studying her ankle.

"You asked me about my fear of dogs."

"So I did."

He felt a shudder run through her, and then her fingers

moved from his shoulder, only to graze the strands of his hair that had blown free of his queue. It was his turn to shudder at the innocent contact. Thankfully, she was entranced, and unaware of his wayward thoughts or desires. Had he not entranced her, he would not have had this time with her, unguarded and vulnerable.

"When I was a child, a dog…of this size knocked me down. He…bit my arm, then began to drag me by my leg. I'm certain he intended to tear me apart."

Bel's tongue was lolling to the side as he panted. When he licked his lips, Chastity made a small whimpering sound and pressed closer to him, clutching him as if he were her savior.

"I…I can still feel its teeth tearing into my flesh."

"Shh," Thane whispered. "You need not recall such a painful memory." He reached for her face, and she surprised—and delighted—him by placing her cheek into his palm. The enchantment, he reminded himself. This was not the real Chastity, this was one who was bespelled.

"Sometimes I awake in the night, screaming, remembering what it was like to feel its teeth in my skin, my body being dragged away."

"You are safe here with me, Chastity. I will not allow anything to harm you. Not even your nightmares."

Skimming his fingers along her cheek, Thane absorbed the feel of her petal-soft skin, imagining what it would be like to experience her curved body pressed against his. It would be thoroughly arousing. But would it be as satisfying as this very moment, with her clinging to him and him protecting her from a frightening past?

Women had sought him out for pleasure, but never for sanctuary. He had never been called upon to protect a mortal woman—to keep them safe. To hold them till the storm of fear had passed.

As Chastity looked down into his face, her fingers still clutching steadfastly to his shoulders, Thane wanted more than a sexual connection with her. He wanted her trust. To be the embodiment of a knight in shining armor. It was ridiculous, but he wanted something more out of his union with his virtue.

Breaking the spell of her eyes, Thane examined her foot and concentrated on what he was supposed to be doing. "I vow to you, Chastity, on my honor, that Bel will not hurt you—ever."

The white stocking was saturated, torn at the ankle with a fresh trail of blood flowing from beneath the tattered silk. With trembling hands, Thane slid his palm up higher on her calf, knowing the stocking needed to come off. The wind blew up, carrying the metallic tang of blood on the air, which made Bel whimper, which made Chastity jump and squeak.

"Be easy, *muirneach*." The whispered endearment slipped effortlessly from his tongue.

"I don't like the way he is looking at me, as though I were a nice juicy lamb chop."

Despite the gnawing tension he felt, Thane could not help but smile and laugh at her jest. "How did you know that lamb is his favorite?"

She watched Bel warily. "He seems the sort of beast who delights in consuming the most innocent of creatures."

She had more to worry about from him than Bel, if her fear ran to beasts who consumed the innocent. When he looked up at her, she was watching him, as if she knew of the beast that lurked inside him, the animal that wanted to lower her to the ground and lift her skirts and plunge inside her. It was like that, when Lust was starved. He gave no thought to pleasure or seduction, only the feeling of ecstasy—his own.

Thane didn't want that for this innocent woman sitting before him. He wanted her to be writhing with desire, flushed with sexual arousal. He wanted her first time to be decadent, consuming. In Lust's famished state, there would be no lazy caresses and kisses. No slow seduction. It would be carnal. *Fucking.* Her first time would be base and animalistic. Not beautiful, as he so wanted it to be for her.

No, he could not be the beast with Chastity.

"Do you trust me, *muirneach?*"

Her head cocked to the side, and the moonlight glowed around her hair, giving her the appearance of a celestial virgin, which, of course, she was. While he awaited her answer he studied her expression, watched her gently arched brows pucker with concern.

"I know I should not trust you, but I cannot help it. Something deep inside me tells me that I can. That I ought to. There is a voice there—" She stopped, shook her head and glanced away.

"What does the voice say?" he asked as he slid his palm up behind her knee. Her breath hitched, the sound a punch to his midsection.

"The voice," she whispered, "it speaks of strange feelings. It tells me to crave things that I know are sinful and wanton, and not what I should feel. But my mind tells me that trusting you is folly. That you are not what you appear to be."

His nerves sharpened. What could she know of him? He had taken great pains to hide his fey glamour. To appear as nothing other than a titled gentleman. "Who am I, then?"

Her gaze flickered to his. "You are the masked stranger from the other night."

Closing her eyes, she sniffed delicately at the air. "I smell you—everywhere. The scent is dark and seductive, arousing, yet drugging. I feel awakened, yet asleep. It lures me, rouses that voice so deep inside me. It was the same that night, too. I was aware of the same scent, and then you appeared."

Hands shaking, Thane slid his palms higher, to her knee, where he felt the satin of her garter brush his fingertips. He was now the one to be entranced. He was charmed by the blissful expression on her face, aroused by her words.

"There is an erotic masculinity to the fragrance, calling to a place inside me that I didn't know existed. A place I fear because I cannot understand it." He watched her inhale deeply of the air. "I remember the scent so well. It is the same now, as it was when it wrapped around me in the maze. Notes of sandalwood and frankincense, mixed with the faintest scent of cedarwood and jasmine. It is the scent of night and moonlight, of forest and forbidden, decadent lands. Even now I can feel it enveloping me."

Mesmerized by her words, he slid his palms up her thigh and pulled the ties on her satin-ribbon garter, feeling it unravel in his hand. The next time, he would untie it with his teeth and nip at the ivory flesh above her stocking. But for now, he could do little more than listen to her words, and wonder if somewhere inside her, Chastity longed for pleasure. If she realized how deeply she could connect with her sexual nature, if she would but allow him close to her.

"It was you last night in the maze, wasn't it?" she asked.

Memories of them together, and what he had done to her, must have surfaced, for the pale skin above her bodice began pinkening, giving him a glimpse of what she would look like when flushed with sexual need. He, himself, was now fully ensnared, and Lust…he was practically salivating at the thought of tearing into her skin and sinking himself deep within her quim. But Lust could not appreciate the beauty of her virginity. The significance of it. Lust could only be ruled by his urges, and breaking the barrier is all he would do. Lust, Thane knew, would not take care of her, would not wait to feel the petals of her sex moisten and blossom, unfurling for him beneath his touch. It was Thane and his Dark Fey need to arouse and pleasure that would see to that. It was Thane that would make their first coupling beautiful and sublime—passionate. So damn impassioned that she would think never to spurn him, to live without him. And then, she would agree to follow him to Faery, to his court of voluptuous pleasures.

"Thane?" Her voice was so soft, a bit husky with wariness, and perhaps desire. "That is your name, isn't it? You were the one in the maze."

She was fully beneath the charm of his spell now. He could do anything he wanted with her and it ate at him, sapping his strength, giving Lust the edge over his iron self-control.

His hands shook and he glanced at Bel, trying to take stock in something other than the idea of pressing himself atop Chastity. He would ruin it all, destroy her innocence and faith if he were to allow Lust to rule him. He had not waited behind this gate for a day only to destroy it with his unbridled desire for the woman before him.

When he had discovered the gate, he'd also learned that it was the only place on the grounds or the house that was not warded by the Seelie. Whether they had not known the gate existed, or whether they thought it insignificant, did not matter. Thane had used the fact to his advantage, warding this forested patch to his benefit. Then, with his magic, he'd turned what had been an uninspiring view into the image of the land that surrounded the Unseelie Court. By day, it was a lovely quiet spot full of solitude and trees and a trickling stream. At night, it became a decadent pleasure garden. Even now the vista was changing, the night-blooming flowers opening, releasing their heady perfume.

He had no idea that Chastity would be so responsive to the garden, to the fragrance of not only the flowers, but his body. He was aroused by the notion, intrigued that an innocent could be so open to the seduction of scent.

"It was you that night, wasn't it?" she asked again, cutting into his musings.

She was under his spell. Anything he told her, he could wipe it away, make her forget if he needed to. "Aye, it was me."

"You ravished me."

No, he had merely toyed with her.

Swallowing hard, he focused on her cut foot, not seduction. She was under the influence of magic. It was dishonorable to act upon what was so obviously innocent sexual curiosity.

But honor only got him so much. It would not do anything for his cock, which was now hard and demanding. Just a glimpse, a touch…

Raising her skirt, she protested, but he quietly shushed her. "It's okay," he whispered. "You'll like this."

Skimming his hand up her thigh, he made small circles there, watched her expression, her wide eyes, the way her tongue came out and moistened her bottom lip. He let his thumb pass over her sex, and she squirmed, her bottom coming closer to his searching hand. "That's it," he encouraged. "Part your legs for me."

Under his enchantment she obeyed, and lifted her skirts, revealing her quim, the blond thatch that shielded her center. Parting her, he traced her slick sex, bringing the wetness on his fingers. Drawing back, he saw the moisture on his fingers, and heeding Lust's beckoning pleas, he brought them to his mouth and licked them clean, tasting her.

A startled sound escaped her, and he smiled wickedly. "Lie back and let me put my mouth to you."

Struggling with what she should do and what she wanted, Thane watched Chastity break for him. With a triumphant smile he lowered his mouth to her sex, and brushed his tongue along her. She cried out, grasped his hair as he teased her. His tongue circling her clitoris, he felt her fingers tug tighter, her hips searching, begging for more. So quickly she began to shake. Exploding beneath his mouth. So soon...he could hardly believe it, she was an innocent, yet she shuddered in orgasm.

Excitement made Lust eager. He could take her like this. Lust wanted that, but Thane didn't. She was under his enchantment, and he wanted her free of any magic when she gave herself to him.

Turning away was the hardest thing he'd ever done. Lust protested violently, but he ignored him. Pulling the stocking from her leg, he tossed it aside and lifted her foot. In the moonlight he could see that the skin was torn—but not horribly so. With a nod to Bel, he allowed the animal to come close. First he sniffed the wound, then, with his long tongue he began to carefully lick the cut. Bel was not just any dog. He was a faery hound, and a healer. It was what he was meant to do.

With a squeak, Chastity seemed to come out of her trance. The sensuality and the afterglow of orgasm he had seen in her eyes was gone, replaced with horror and fear.

"Shh." Thane silenced her protests. "He has the ability to heal."

Chastity watched in fascination as Bel licked at her injury, which seemed to heal before their very eyes. When he was done there was nothing more than a pink scrape-mark on her ankle.

When their eyes met, Chastity pulled her foot from his hand and jumped up from the bench. "What are you?" she cried.

The languid feeling that cloaked her vanished, and Chastity was left horrified by the evidence that was strewn around her. Her shoe and stocking were scattered upon the grass, and her fichu was half hanging out of her bodice, revealing the swells of her breasts in the low-cut gown.

The man—Thane—had been perched between her thighs, the hem of her skirts raised to her calves. Even as she took in the scene around her, her words came rushing back. Such personal, intimate thoughts, and she had said them out loud. Had admitted to this stranger something that she had not even allowed herself to admit to.

Rising to his full height, he towered above her, watching her with his strange blue eyes. Eyes that a woman could drown in. Eyes that promised pleasure and seduction.

"Oh, God," she whispered as her fingers trembled over her mouth. "What are you?"

"A man."

She shook her head, her hair spilling from her pins. "No, you can't be. You aren't a man."

Chastity somehow suddenly knew what he was. A fey. A Dark Fey. Those beautifully seductive creatures whose sole purpose was to entice. Defile. Deflower. What had she done by walking through the gate? What sort of enchantment had he put her under?

His hand reached out to hers, but she jumped back. Frightened to touch him. Horrified that the voice deep inside her pleaded with her to allow it.

"You're not a man."

His eyes narrowed and he folded his arms across the considerable breadth of his chest. "If I am not a man, what then do you propose I am?"

"Fey."

The word hung heavy and quiet between them. His gaze darkened even further, becoming a thundercloud of swirling tempests.

"I am Thane," he said again. This time his voice brooked no argument.

"A prince of the fey." She stepped back from him, attempting to put as much distance between them as possible. "You're a Dark Fey."

Deep inside she knew she was right. He was a member of the notorious Unseelie Court. Everything screamed it to be true. Every instinct she possessed warned her to run from this creature and hide before he could carry her off into the night. For that was his intent.

Lifting her skirts, she ran blindly into the shadows,

making her way to the gate, but she was stopped, lifted high off the ground and brought up hard against a body that felt like granite. "What do you want from me?" she cried, terrified of what he would do to her.

Pressing her up against him, he turned her in his arms until her breasts were crushed against his chest. "I want everything," he whispered in her ear. "Your heart, your body. The very essence of your soul."

"No!" she cried, fearing he would throw her to the ground and take her right there.

"You're mine. Created solely for me." The words were deep and dark in her ear. "I will have you. Take you. But I will not throw you down on the ground," he said, his voice growing seductive as wisps of hot breath caressed her ear. "I don't want you quick. I want you long—slow and languid. I want to take my time when I lure you. Defile you. Deflower you."

Struggling in his hold, she punched at him, frightened of his masculinity and the fact he knew her thoughts.

"Soon, Chastity. Soon I will come to you and you will be mine. But this is not how I want it. I do not want you fighting me. I want you—"

Begging me... His words in the maze came back to her, and she saw how he smiled. He could hear her thoughts!

"Soon, *muirneach,* you will come to me, but not now. This has been an ugly scene, and I would not have you remember this moment. This is not how it will be between us."

"I will never forget it," she said with scorn. But he waved his hand over her face and whispered in her ear.

"The only thing you will remember is that moment when you were intoxicated by my scent, when you wanted something more. When you wanted to be anything— *anyone*—else besides chaste and innocent."

The bluster went out of her and she softened. No longer fighting him, she felt herself clinging to him. "Chaste is what I am. *Who I am.*"

"No, it is what you've been told to be. It is not who you are. I promise you," he said hotly in her ear. "I will show you who you truly are. Deep inside, where that voice is trying to be heard. I will answer that voice, give it what it wants, and in the end you will be reborn into what you truly are. *Mine.*"

$\mathcal{S}$EVEN

"DID YOU HEAR? I AM TO HAVE A GENTLEMAN caller this afternoon."

From a distance Chastity heard the voice, drawing her away from a garden bench that was surrounded by trees and flowers and the presence of a mystifying stranger.

"Chastity?"

Do not awake yet...

The other voice was deeper; velvety and luring, beckoning her to stay. She wanted to...wanted to lie down upon the thick carpet of grass and run her hands through the long blades and feel the sun upon her face.

Do not leave...not yet...

Early-morning sunlight streamed in through the lace curtains. The heat from the rays was glorious and, sleepily, Chastity lifted her face to the sunlight, basking in the spring warmth and the smell of trees in bloom and the freshness of grass.

Till tonight then.

The voice faded, as did the image of a garden at night recessing, only to reveal the morning sunlight. There truly was nothing as remarkable as spring, when the world awoke from months of slumber.

"Did you hear me, sleepyhead?" Prue asked peevishly. "I am a bundle of nerves, and you're lazing about like a fat kitten."

Groggy, Chastity forced her eyelids open. She was no longer in a garden, but her room, her dream wafting away like smoke.

With a groan, she came awake. She did feel remarkably lethargic this morning. Normally she jumped right out of bed, eager to begin the day. But this morning she wished she could curl up under the blankets and return to the dream she had been having.

"Chastity, for the love of God, you're not going to fall asleep on me, are you? I need you."

"No," she murmured, struggling to keep her eyes from closing. "Of course not, Prue." But sleep beckoned her, along with the elusive memory of a magnificent forest, resplendent with exotic flowers, and the heady aromas of some numinous land.

The onslaught of the scent that had been present that night in the maze suddenly came back to her. In her dream, she had been held in the arms of *someone* who possessed that erotic scent.

If only she could get back to that dream, she might discover his identity. In her sleep she could pull that golden mask from his face and reveal his identity. She would know the true face of the man who had come to her in the maze, and in last night's dream.

"What in the world is wrong with you?" Prue asked with concern.

"I'm tired, that's all." But Chastity knew something else was wrong. She had never felt this way before, had never had these thoughts, and certainly she had never experienced such dreams as these.

Strange, everything had started to change that morning in Glastonbury when she and her sisters had been taking a stroll. First, she had seen the golden-haired man atop his horse, and then another man, dark as sin. And then, their hasty departure to London.

No, nothing was as it should be—as her life usually was.

"How can you be so sleepy? You went to bed before ten o'clock last night."

Had she? Her body felt as though it was much, much later. When she had ventured into the garden it had been before twilight. The sky had been pink with the setting sun. But upon her return, the moon had been high and the sky drenched in black velvet. Yet she had the feeling that she had not been gone long, otherwise her mother would have been worried, would have commented to her about the length of time she had been strolling the paths. But Mama had said nothing. In fact, it was as though Mama hadn't realized that she'd even left the salon.

The garden… Chastity struggled to recall her walk through the paths, but could bring to mind nothing. Her memories seemed to stop after the moment she picked a posy of lily of the valley. What had happened to make her forget?

"What is this?" Prue asked, reaching for Chastity's hand, which was hidden beneath her pillow.

Chastity watched as Prue pulled a pressed flower from the palm of Chastity's hand. As her fingers uncurled, the most alluring scent wafted up, dragging her back to a fuzzy recollection of a man whispering into her ear before pressing a flower into her hand.

I will answer that voice, give it what it wants, and in the end you will be reborn into what you truly are. Mine.

The jasmine dropped from her fingers, landing on the blue satin coverlet where Prue picked it up and examined it.

"'Tis night-blooming jasmine, is it not?"

Chastity nodded, trying not to stare at the flower in Prue's hand, or recall the words that suddenly filled her thoughts. Had she heard them in her dream? It had to be, but the memory was too visceral for a mere dream.

She could actually recall the heaviness of his body pressed against hers, the warmth of his breath caressing her ear, the tremor of fear and excitement as he whispered those words to her.

Was it possible for a dream to be that real?

"Wherever did you find this?" Prue asked. "The garden is terribly overgrown. I can't imagine that something as delicate as this could survive."

No, it couldn't, Chastity mused. The climate was too harsh here for jasmine to grow. It needed a hothouse or an orangery. Jasmine was notoriously fragile. So where had she gotten it?

"What does your herbal say of jasmine?" Prue asked as she sniffed delicately at the tiny buds. "My, it's intoxicating, isn't it?" she whispered, sniffing once more at the delicate little blooms. "The scent quite goes to your head."

Indeed it did. Chastity knew about many flowers, and she knew that jasmine was purported to turn even the most pious of women into wantons, and men…it turned the opposite sex into slavering beasts. Culpeper's herbal said that dreams in which jasmine appears are lucky for lovers. Had she dreamed of jasmine?

Gently, she took the flower from Prue and set it on the commode beside her bed. She would think on its appearance later, once her head was cleared. It was only a dream, she reminded herself. But never had her dreams been so vivid, so…sensual. Never had she dreamed of a man, a small voice inside reminded her, but she ignored it. That voice, she realized, was becoming louder, more insistent to be heard. She mustn't let it win out over good reason, and above all, her chasteness.

"You said something about a caller?"

Flushing, Prue began to nibble on her lower lip as she nodded. "Mama came to me this morning. Papa has arranged it. A Lord Arawn. He's from the north."

Chastity frowned. "For what purpose?"

Prue glared at her. "You know what for."

"No." Chastity felt her cheeks drain of blood. "He has not arranged a marriage for you." Chastity suddenly felt the fear of losing her sister. All four of them were inseparable. To have Prudence taken away...she couldn't bear the thought of it.

Terror clouded Prue's blue eyes. "I do not know about marriage," she whispered anxiously, "but Mama told me that I am to join them for tea this afternoon in the salon, and that I am to have a gentleman caller, so I am to wear my best day dress. Oh, Chastity," Prue cried, clutching at her sister's hand. "I am afraid of men. I...I don't know what to say to them. I'm...I'm not Mary. I don't converse easily, and I'm so...restrained."

"Prue," Chastity asked with a small laugh, "what are you trying to say?"

"What if he doesn't like me?" Prue blurted out as she clung tightly to Chastity.

"Prudence, you're being silly."

Gazing up from their locked hands, Chastity saw the glimmer of tears in her sister's eyes. "It is no secret that men find me boring and insufferably proper. 'Cold and indifferent,' I have heard them whisper about me. But I do not know how to be anything other than what I am. I cannot be fun and light like Mary. Or smile and be benevolent like Mercy."

Chastity squeezed her sister's hand. "I am not so sure that Mary is like us—a virtue. She is very different in her thoughts and manners. I have often wondered how she can be one of us."

"I have often questioned the same thing, but we were conceived at the same time, born minutes apart. How can she not be?"

"I do not know. I only know what I feel. Oh, Prue," Chastity whispered, flinging her arms around her older sister, hugging her tightly. "You're beautiful just the way you are."

"You have to say that. We're sisters."

"I have to say no such thing. I speak the truth. Always. You know that."

"What am I to do?" Prudence asked. "I...I...I..." She paused, and Chastity knew that Prudence was trying to speak her innermost secrets.

"It's all right, Prue. I won't tell a soul."

"I want to make him like me," she gasped. "I want to have a man look at me and...and desire me. I wish to be like any other woman, courted and loved."

Yes. Chastity knew the pain of that confession. She had admitted the same thing to herself—finally. But she had not realized that her sister felt the same way, too. The discontent that had been steadily eating away at her was gnawing at Prue, as well. She wondered if Mercy and Mary also suffered.

"Just once," Prue murmured, "I would like to be... normal."

"Oh, Prue." Chastity was unable to find the right words to ease her sister's worries. How could she, when she felt the same thing, feared the same things? Finally she said, "It will happen. We will have a normal life. The life of a woman."

But they weren't customary. None of them were. They were destined for something other than a life for a lady of good breeding.

"We have a higher purpose," Chastity reminded her. "In time, we will learn what this purpose is. If this man is your destiny, then it will be all right, won't it?"

Prudence had always believed, as Chastity had, that their lives and destiny were not theirs. That their path had been preordained from the moment of their conception. If they were to believe what they had been told, and Chastity did, they were infused with the power of the fey. And where there were faeries concerned, nothing was normal, or as it should be.

Nothing was ordinary now. It was as if, on the Eve of Beltane while strolling through Glastonbury, they had been drawn from a long slumber. Awakened by seemingly innocuous events—the dark beautiful stranger who spoke to them on the path, the gorgeous golden god riding atop his horse. All very innocuous proceedings that had the veneer of innocence, but Chastity knew that if that veneer was rubbed away, it would unveil something completely different.

Everything had changed that day. Therefore there was only one conclusion—the actions that had unfolded were by no means happenstance. She and her sisters had been awakened that day by something they could not name.

"You know that our lives are not our own," Chastity reminded her. "We belong to the fey."

"Perhaps they have forgotten us," Prudence said as she pulled away from Chastity's embrace. "The faeries, that is."

Glancing at the sprig of jasmine, Chastity felt a little tremor race down her spine. "Perhaps," she answered, but she didn't believe so. While she couldn't remember a large chunk of last night, she knew that something had happened. One simply did not forget hours at a time, or awake with flowers beneath their pillows.

A click of her chamber door drew Chastity's gaze away from the flower. With a bright smile, her mother peeked around the door.

"Good morning, Mama," Chastity said.

"Ah, good, you're awake. I assume Prudence informed you of her good news?"

Chastity shared a look with her sister. "She has."

"Well, you have cause to celebrate, too, my dear, for Lord Arawn is bringing with him a friend. You are to wear your best dress also and join us for tea."

Swallowing hard, Chastity looked between her mother and sister. What was she to say? There was no avoiding it. Her mother appeared determined to foist her and Prudence upon any willing man who came to tea.

"But, first, I think we will go to Bond Street this morning," her mother said to no one in particular. "The day is fine for shopping. Come along, girls. Your maids are waiting to attend you."

Clutching hands, Prudence sent her a pained look of sympathy. "We'll talk later," she whispered before slipping from the bed and heading to the door.

Annie, her maid, breezed in after Prudence left, carrying a freshly laundered stack of stays and petticoats. "'Tis a fine day, miss," she said cheerily. "I hear Her Grace is taking you shopping."

"It would appear so." She had never been shopping in London, and on Bond Street no less.

"Shall you wear the green silk and velvet walking dress then, miss? It goes lovely with your coloring."

"That will be perfect, Annie."

As she was shoving back the bedcovers, Annie turned in time to see her with her night rail to her knees. "Oh, miss, you've done something to your ankle."

Glancing at her foot, Chastity saw the long pink mark. It was wide, like a gash, but the skin was pink, as though it was nearly healed. It hadn't been there yesterday.

Annie bent down and picked up her foot, examining it. "It's not a rash. It looks though like it was a big gash."

Suddenly an image of a man crouched on his knees, his shoulders pressed between her thighs, his hand sliding up her skirt, inundated her and she jumped up out of the bed.

"What's wrong, miss?"

"Nothing," she said hurriedly as she reached for her wrapper. "I should not keep Mama waiting, is all."

Something most definitely was not right. Everything inside her whispered that the life she had always known was about to change.

I will show you who you truly are…

The memory echoed deep in her soul, and when she sat down upon her dressing chair she saw in the mirror before her her image. And behind her shoulder, in the mirror's reflection, she saw the fleeting reflection of a dark-haired man, a gold mask glimmering in the brilliant morning sunshine.

"Miss?" Annie asked. "Shall I begin brushing out your hair?"

"Please," she murmured, watching the mirror for another glimpse of the stranger. But he never reappeared, and Chastity blamed her overwrought nerves for seeing it in the first place.

Being a paragon was stifling at best, but it was made all the more bearable by indulging in one simple vice. As the perfumery bells tinkled, signaling her arrival, Chastity secretly smiled. This was the only time she ever felt truly alive—as though her body was awakening. Except for two nights ago, when she had found herself in the arms of a masked stranger, her breasts bared and her blood pounding.

But she refused to recall that almost addictive sensation of desire. It was over. The black-haired stranger was gone, nothing but a figment of her mind, and last night, her dream. She had seen his fleeting image that morning in her looking glass; however, it was nothing but a folly. Just a fanciful girl thinking of the impossible.

In truth, she should be scandalized by what the rogue had done to her in the maze, and how she had allowed him to do it. As Annie had brushed her hair, remnants of her dream came back to her...

She'd entered the house from the garden and had immediately gone to her chamber, where Annie had been turning down the bed. After getting into her night rail, Chastity had slipped swiftly into sleep, and promptly her subconscious had plunged her into a dreamworld.

Even now her cheeks flushed as she lost the battle to push the memories of that vision out of her mind. At first she had been horrified to recall the memory of her body pressed up against another's. A man whose own body was hard and hot against hers. She had let her midnight dream lover touch her and whisper words into her ear that still had the ability, even now, hours after awakening, to make her body tremble.

In her dream, she had asked for a kiss. A simple one, but he refused her, and Chastity had feared that she would awaken before she could feel his lips upon hers.

Please, she pleaded, afraid to open her eyes and have her dream vanish in the darkness. *Kiss me,* she asked over and over, but he only traced her face and the shape of her mouth with his fingertip. *I won't be able to stop at a kiss,* he replied, his voice deep and husky, calling to her womanly needs—needs she had only just discovered she had. *One kiss,* she pleaded, touching her pursed lips to his throat. *Just one, please...*

One kiss, he'd replied, lowering his face to hers so that his breath whispered against her upturned face. *Open for me, Chastity, for I want all of you in this kiss,* and then he pressed his mouth against hers, kissing her softly, reverently, until she moaned and touched her tongue to his. He deepened the embrace, bruising her lips and clinging to her, kissing her hungrily, devouring her mouth, stroking her tongue with his as he pushed her deeper into the mattress so that she found herself beneath him. Wantonly she kissed him back, clutching at him, as if he would turn to vapor in her arms. In her innocence, she was wild, untutored, but she gave herself up to the heady pleasure with abandon.

Beautiful Chastity, he murmured against her as he nudged her head back, seeking her throat and unlacing the demure silk ties that held her nightgown together. *I ache for you. I ache to be inside you.*

She had pleaded with him in her dream, nearly begged him to show her passion, but he had refused. And then she had fully awakened to the brilliant sunlit morning, aching to return to him.

Good God, what was happening to her?

The memories of the dream and the hypnotic scent, she had no difficulty in recalling. But the events in the garden, the minutes or hours that had elapsed between discovering the gate and returning to the salon, were frustratingly blank. What had happened in that interval? How had she received the mark on her ankle? Try as she might, she could not recall any of it.

"May I help you, miss?"

Chastity glanced up to see the perfumer studying her. His powdered wig, which at one time had been white, was yellowing, and sat upon his head askew. His eyes, which were bright and cunning, fixed on her. Good Lord! She was standing in the middle of London's most famous perfumery and she was woolgathering about an indecent dream she'd had. What must he think of her?

With a flush she nodded and gripped the strings of her beaded reticule tighter. "I am just browsing, thank you."

"There is much in my little shop to tempt a lady."

"Indeed, I've never seen a perfumery that could rival this one."

The little old man beamed with pride, then, with a curt nod he moved away, down to where a group of fashionable women were congregated near the back of the store.

With a deep breath, Chastity looked about the elegant shop, which was decorated in the heavy rococo fashion. Gilt and pale cream tones filled the large space. Mirrored shelves offset the glimmer of the exquisite rows of perfume bottle and atomizers, creating a dazzling display of sparkles and glimmer.

Excitement lanced through her. She had never seen anything so superb. The small perfumery in Glastonbury certainly was nothing like this.

Vice. This was hers. The desire she had begun to crave with the stranger in her dream was something she absolutely could not indulge in. This vice, however, was utterly harmless. She need not feel guilty about this one, simple pleasure. This one was perfectly safe.

The aromas hit her, filling her nostrils with thrilling temptations. She could spend hours here, breathing in the intoxicating scents. She loved perfume, and the pretty bottles that went along with the feminine luxury.

In every facet of her life, she was a paragon. But in this one thing, she allowed herself one weakness. Perfume.

Strolling along the marble floors, she watched the gathered women, resplendent in their fashionable clothes, sniffing an assortment of aromas. Chastity found herself wondering if the women were out merely to be seen, or if they too held the same sort of appreciation as she.

Stopping before a crystal-encrusted bottle, Chastity pulled the topper out and held the tip to her nose. The heavy floral notes of rose dripped from the pointed tip. She loved the smell of roses. But then, what woman didn't?

Rose was an interesting flower, she thought as she watched a clear drop of essence fall back into the bottle. A famous and favored scent, the rose was a symbol of love and devotion. But its bouquet, heady and heavy, had a deeper connotation. One of sensuality and eroticism. In ancient Rome, a rose fastened to the ceiling told visitors and revelers that anything happening in the room should not be spoken outside it. Which meant, of course, that sinful things were happening within those walls. *Carnally* sinful, she reminded herself.

Yes, the rose was sensually evocative—to both sexes.

"Beautiful," she murmured as she inhaled the perfume once more.

"There cannot be a perfume here to match the natural radiance of your beauty, or your own natural scent."

Startled by the deep voice that seemed to be addressing her, Chastity glanced to her right, and saw a tall man standing beside her. He was looking down into a glass case that bore lockets filled with perfumed creams. His black hair was tied back in a queue and his profile was both masculine yet beautiful.

Slowly he raised his gaze to her and she was pinned by

beautiful blue eyes. Removing his tricorn hat, he bowed elegantly before her. "My lady."

She gasped, instantly recalling the man standing before her.

"Perhaps you remember our meeting in Glastonbury, Lady Lennox? I am Thane."

"I do not know you, sir," she snapped. Heart racing, she turned away from him and walked to another section of the store, where more customers were gathered. The perfumer was eagerly unveiling his newest creation, and she pressed in, trying to lose herself in the small huddle.

She was being utterly rude, she knew, but she could not help it. She had seen that man before, and not just in Glastonbury, but in the maze and, God help her, last night in her dreams.

Good God, what was happening to her? Perhaps she really was going insane after all. It was all too much. The strangers. The dreams. The lapses in memory. It was as if she was the victim of a cruel spell. A faery spell? she wondered.

"I will not give up until you at least say hello."

The deep timbre of his voice washed over her and she closed her eyes, steeling herself against the way his voice made her weak and warm. He was standing too close; the heat from his chest burned into her back through the thin pelisse she wore.

A matron glanced at her from beneath the wide brim of her bonnet, then her stare darted to the man who was standing behind Chastity. His position, pressed into her, was too close to be considered civilized. Even if they were husband and wife, his proximity to her person was positively indecent.

"Let us try again. Good day, my lady," he murmured next to her ear. The whispering caress of his voice made her shiver before she steeled herself.

"Hello," she grumbled, hoping it would satisfy him and he would move along, but it only made him chuckle.

"You wish me far away, do you not?"

"You are not known to me, sir. It is not done to converse with someone you do not know."

"I am trying to remedy that, but you're proving most difficult."

"I must leave," she muttered. Slipping the strings of her reticule onto her wrist, she tried to gently push her way out from the crowd, but he followed her, like a black cloud looming over her head.

"Not yet."

"I do not even know you, sir," she snapped. But images of Glastonbury, the maze, trickled through her mind, replaced by the fleeting image…the figure of this very same man awaiting her beyond the garden gate.

She gasped, straightening her spine. The memories were foggy, disjointed, but she recalled a garden bench, and a man bent on the ground—between her thighs. Struggling, she tried to pull at the memory and bring it forth. Had it really happened, or was it only part of a dream?

"There is no use running or feigning our lack of acquaintance. For I will only pursue you," he whispered, breaking into her thoughts. "I will hound you until you allow me to call upon you."

"That is impossible," she scoffed as she extricated herself from the crowd and made her way to the door of the perfumery. Oh, where was Prudence when she needed her? Next door, at the bookseller's, she thought peevishly. Oh, why had she ventured in here, without even a maid or a footman?

This was too much. She was out of her element, afraid not only of him, but herself. She was a paragon, she reminded herself. Born to a higher standard. She was not a dockside doxy.

Reaching for her wrist, he grasped her, stopping her with the barest pressure of his fingers.

"Am I so terrible to converse with that the thought of having me for tea makes you tremble?"

No, she was quivering for quite another reason. Good Lord, he was spectacularly handsome. In the sunlight that filtered through the window, his eyes appeared to be the most brilliant shade of blue. Offset with black lashes, his gaze was penetrating and intense, and it made the fine hairs on the back of her neck stand to full attention. Good heavens, she had been in the maze with this man, her breasts bared, her lips swollen from his kiss. For what purpose had he left Glastonbury to pursue her in London? Desire was one thing, but to come all this way to kiss her? There were any number of women who would fall at his feet for a chance to be seduced by him, so why had he chosen to mark her for his games?

Barely able to focus on the conversation, Chastity felt

trapped in his gaze, her body no longer her own. "You must release me, sir," she found herself murmuring, "for I am not able to speak with you."

"Why?"

"I am promised to another." Technically, it was not a lie. She was promised. She just didn't know to whom, and if he would be man or fey. Besides, she would have said anything to get away from him. She was not herself in his presence. She would do, say anything to put space between them, to deter him from his ardent pursuit.

His fingers squeezed hard against her wrist. "Who is he?" he demanded.

Thankfully she was spared from having to answer by the perfumer. "Does the lady wish to have a signature scent?" he asked, his shrewd gaze volleying between them.

"No," Chastity answered.

"Yes," Thane replied at the same time. "The lady does wish to have something created especially for her."

The perfumer's eyes lit with excitement—and greed. "Of course, signature perfumes can be rather expensive to make and—"

"Cost is no matter," Thane drawled as he reached for her reticule and slowly slipped the strings from her wrist. Carefully he set it aside and placed the bag on the counter.

"Does the lady know what flowers she prefers?"

Thane cocked a brow in question as he lifted her hand in his and began to slowly unfasten the buttons of her leather glove.

"Floral? Citrus?" the elderly shopkeeper asked as he reached below and lifted three glass jars onto the counter.

Swallowing hard, Chastity watched in fascination as Thane slowly pulled her glove from her fingers and placed it atop her reticule.

The perfumer was watching them intently. "Does the gentleman have a preference as to what sort of perfume the lady should have?"

"He does indeed," Thane murmured as he brushed the tips of his long fingers along the inside of her wrist. The sensation went straight to her womb and the tips of her breasts. What was he doing to her? Why was she feeling this way?

Despite knowing that they were causing a scene, that everyone was watching them, Chastity could not break the spell of this moment. He seemed to know it, too, because he smiled wickedly as he lowered his mouth to her wrist. And she was helpless to do anything but allow it.

I am promised to another.
Like hell.

Thane barely controlled the instinct to lift her into his arms and carry her out of the store. Promised to another man? A mortal, who was no match for him? A Seelie Fey? Never. Whatever she had been told, whatever she thought, Chastity Lennox was his and he protected what was his.

As she looked up at him, her green eyes watching him

warily from beneath the brim of her bonnet, Thane felt the consuming need to make her his. Damn the curse and his court, he would make her his.

Even now, Lust was barely tethered inside him. *Ravish her* was all he could hear pounding in his ears. Damn it, his hand was shaking as he held her wrist in his palm. He wanted her so badly. Too much, he told himself.

Watching his fingers gliding against her skin, which was so white and pure, made him feel like the filthiest of beasts. But he could not help himself. Could not stop. This moment was too much. The feel of her skin, so supple and soft like a rose petal, made him think of things he shouldn't.

The warmth of her pulse fluttered against the pad of his thumb and he felt the erratic beat. Her frantic pulse excited him, called to him, and he could not stop himself from lowering his mouth and nose to her wrist and inhaling deeply. He closed his eyes against the onslaught of desire that rushed through him like a drug.

"My lord?" the perfumer inquired.

"Warm, heady," he murmured as he traced the fine blue veins beneath her skin. "Something to bring out the subtle essence of her skin. Eroticism blended with innocence."

"Notes of neroli, perhaps," the perfumer murmured. "As an aromatic, it is as seductive as it is sedative." Turning, the old man lifted a glass jar from a shelf and reached for a medicine dropper.

"As well as something to heighten the senses," Thane suggested. "Perhaps a combination of scents that transports one from the cerebral plane to that of the subconscious."

"An aphrodisiac perfume," the man said with a grin as he put a few drops into a brown glass bottle. "Perhaps a gift for your new bride? Or something to be enjoyed on your wedding night?"

Thane met Chastity's gaze. He wondered if she saw feral hunger in his eyes. A wedding night with Chastity. He wouldn't endure the wait. "Yes. A gift for the lady."

"I cannot accept it."

So proud. So demure, he thought as he drew tiny circles over her pulse. Untouched—except by him. Her chasteness at once frustrated him, yet intrigued him. The primitive male within him gloried in her virginal state, for she would belong to him only. He would mold her body to fit only him.

"You know I can't accept a gift," she whispered as their eyes met. "You place my name and that of my family's in jeopardy, sir."

Where she was going—to his court—she would not need her name or her reputation. She would be revered as his princess, adored as a virtue and savior of his people. "Please put the perfume in a special bottle for the lady," Thane ordered. "I believe she is especially fond of the blue-and-gold atomizer."

Chastity's eyes widened as her gaze darted to the ornate atomizer then back to him. *Yes.* He could read her thoughts, but only when they were deeply connected like this. Touching was simply not enough. Their connection needed more. Perhaps it was when their gazes were locked like this? Or maybe it was when his heartbeat seemed to synchronize with hers.

Whatever it was, it had happened last night in the garden. He had been able to hear her thoughts, read her body and learn of the deep desire that was hidden within her. A desire he wasn't sure she realized yet.

And that same bond they had shared in the garden had lingered long enough for him to enter her dreams—where she had asked him to kiss her.

Yet she was to be given to another? Not fucking likely. She was intended for him in all ways. *His.* Not some bastard Seelie Fey or incompetent mortal. No other man would have this connection, no male ever could. And he intended to make certain it was impossible. Perhaps he should give her back her memories of the garden. Let her remember how he had skimmed his fingertips along the petals of her sex, how she had watched him lick the wetness off his fingers. He would like to see the expression that would cross her face as she recalled the way he had slowly lowered his head between her thighs and parted her folds with his tongue. But then, he reminded himself, she would recall the moment when her intuition had ruined all. When she had realized he was something other than he claimed. She would remember that he was fey, and this moment would be ruined, too. It was too soon for her to know. He needed to hide what he was from her just a bit longer, until she was sexually ensnared, or better yet, until her heart was engaged, and she trusted him fully.

No, he decided, he could not give her back those memories.

"Sir, you know that this...is quite beyond the pale," she whispered softly. "We do not even know each other."

"Indulge me," he murmured as his thumb rubbed higher, disappearing beneath the sleeve of her light green pelisse. "No one has to know. It will be our secret." Like last night in the garden. The memories of that, the taste of her, aroused him, made Lust restless inside him.

"How can it be a secret when even now everyone is gawking at us?"

"Believe me, I can make them forget they ever saw us here. Take this small gift as a token of my desire to... court you."

Her eyes flared wide. "You cannot. That is, I'm already promised—"

"To whom?"

He watched her swallow, followed the delicate movement of her throat. He wanted to kiss her there, inhale her scent as her body warmed. "My father, he has promised us to someone."

To the faery queen.

Her thoughts echoed inside his head, and he stepped closer, forcing her gaze up to his. "I will fight for you, Chastity Lennox. Believe that."

"You don't even know me," she replied, her voice hitching.

Taking her hand, he placed it alongside his face. It felt so right, her skin on his, her flesh pressing into his. "I know that your body and soul are crying out to break free of the virtue that imprisons you. I know that my own body and soul is trying to desperately answer."

Her face flamed with embarrassment, but her eyes glistened with womanly desire. "There is no sense in fighting, my lord, for it is hopeless for me to change who, and what, I am."

"Take the perfume," he whispered, attempting to tighten his hold on her hand, but she slid her palm from his cheek, leaving him bereft of her touch.

"You try to tempt me with things I cannot accept."

"Is it so very wrong to be tempted by me?"

She glanced away, her lashes flickering and lowering. "You know it is." *You are a paragon, a virtue. Intended for something altogether different.*

Thane felt her resolve as he heard her words to herself, reminding that quiet voice inside her that she would not—could not—follow where it yearned to go.

She would not invite him in. Even though she might want to, she clutched her virtue tightly to her body.

"May I call upon you?" he asked, struggling to keep his sin in check. Lust had been finished with this conversation long ago. He was ready to carry her like a sack of flour over his shoulder and bring her to court, resisting or not. Lust wanted inside her, but Thane wanted more. Thane wanted that deep connection, to feel them joined more than physically.

"Chastity?" he asked again, capturing her gaze. "May I? Allow me to prove myself. That I am worthy of you."

She would not look at him, but instead focused on the cobalt-blue atomizer and the amber liquid that was trickling into the bottle. "My life, my destiny is not my own. I cannot change that fact. So, no, you may not call. And please," she whispered, finally looking at him with her honest eyes. "Please do not speak with me again. Let us pretend we have never before met."

A sense of finality hovered between them, and for the first time ever in his existence, Thane experienced an onslaught of panic. She was slipping through his fingers before he had even had a chance with her. How was he to claim her if he could not enter her house? If she would not even speak with him? How was he to seduce someone who appeared to be truly above temptation?

And then he had it. The way into Chastity's home— and her body.

"I will leave you in peace on one condition."

"And that is?"

He handed her the atomizer and pressed it into her hand. "You must accept my gift."

Her gaze slipped to the bottle then back to him. "You promise never to speak with me again?"

"I promise to leave you in peace, how about that?"

She studied him, as if knowing that his answer was a play on words. He had no intention of leaving her be, but he did have every intention of seducing her into a peaceful sensuality that would make her beg for more.

"I will accept it," she said at last.

With a smile he knew was wolfish, Thane tipped his hat to her and sketched a bow. "Then I bid you goodbye."

Placing a few banknotes on the counter, he paid for

the perfume, then promptly left her, walking to the door, into the bright beams of sun that shone through the transom windows. If he could not court her the mortal way, then he would do so in the manner of the Dark Fey. He had discovered Chastity's greatest weakness. He would become the intoxicating essence of her deepest, most forbidden desire.

Before anyone could see—or notice—he turned into particles of mist and wafted on the sunbeams over to where the perfumer was removing the stopper on the perfume bottle.

"Gently now," the perfumer was advising Chastity as she bent over the bottle. "A delicate sniff and only a droplet or two is what is needed. This is a most hypnotic creation," he warned.

Wafting down into the bottle, Thane became the very thing Chastity most coveted.

"Oh, my," she whispered as she took in his scent mixed with neroli and rose—and him. "It's beautiful. But quite drugging, isn't it?"

"Aye, it is. A love potion, all right," the old man said with a smile in his voice.

A perfume as an aphrodisiac, Thane mused. He'd never done or thought of becoming such a thing before, but if it afforded him the opportunity to be smeared all over Chastity's body, then who was he to complain? And besides, it allowed him into her home despite the Seelie wards and guards. And he would be in her bedroom. And there was no place he wanted to be more than in Chastity Lennox's bed, covering her body.

EIGHT

NERVOUSLY, CHASTITY SIPPED AT HER TEA, CAREful to ensure that her gaze did not linger on the man seated across from her. He was tall, but not nearly as tall as Thane. He was not as broad, either, but lithe, like a sleek cat. His tawny-colored hair reached his shoulders, the long golden locks tied back in a simple queue. If not for his eyes, which were a lovely and exotic shade of violet, he would have resembled a regal lion. However, with those eyes, he appeared much more than animal— but otherworldly.

And when he smiled, Chastity heard Mary suck in her breath. Admittedly, their visitor was very handsome. But Chastity did not lose her breath the way her sister did. She did not feel warmth, low in her belly, in the place that was never, ever mentioned. Yet, she had felt that warmth and a curious tingling deep inside that morning at the perfumery, when Thane had been there.

She had relived that conversation, those moments when he had touched her, lighting a fire beneath her skin and tissues till it heated her blood. Standing there, gazing up into his beautiful face and eyes—eyes that reflected an enthralling darkness, it had taken every ounce of her steely resolve to deny him. It had been the only thing to do, the voice of reason consoled her. It was right to leave him. But her body continued to disagree. Her body knew what it wanted—Thane's touch. Which frightened her because the touch of a man's hands on her body was something she had never desired before. And that she should want something from only one specific person puzzled—and horrified—her.

How bizarre this whole thing was. How strange her response to him. She had been most imprudent in her honesty and openness. The furthest thing from chaste. But there was something about him that invited ease, that begged to be told her secrets. She should fear that knowledge. Instead, she secretly yearned for more, to be freed of the heavy burden that had suddenly claimed her these past days. Never had the virtue she harbored within her been this choking and oppressive. All her life, she had coexisted with her virtue, and now it seemed that she was struggling to break free of the only existence she had ever known.

"Smile," Mary murmured as she reached for her teacup. "He's watching you."

"Maybe it's you he's gazing at?" Chastity retorted, immediately sobering as her mother gently shook her head, reprimanding them for whispering between themselves.

Both she and Mary shared the settee while Mama and Papa occupied the wingback chairs, which left Mama free to watch her daughters. Poor Prudence had been left to share the other settee with Lord Arawn, who possessed the same golden beauty as the man who introduced himself as Crom.

No title. No salutation. Just Crom.

The golden giant who had been riding his horse in Glastonbury now stood by the window, cutting a fine form that was outlined to his advantage by the sun. It seemed to suit him, Chastity thought as she carefully studied him. The sun appeared to be drawn to him, the way moonlight had been drawn to Thane when she had dreamed of him.

Darkness and light…strange that the darkness seemed to draw her. She should fear the black, and embrace the light. But there was something about the moon, and the earth, how it came alive amidst shadows and mist that beckoned her. There was beauty to be found in darkness.

"'Tis very lovely weather we're having," her mother exclaimed as she poured more steaming tea into the fragile gilded Limoges cup.

"It is rather fine," Lord Arawn acknowledged as he accepted the tea from her mother. "A ride in the park would be quite fitting for weather as fine as this."

Chastity saw how Prue's fingers whitened around the handle of her delicate cup. Poor Prue. Chastity completely sympathized with her. Since the gentlemen had arrived a half hour past, the conversation had been painstakingly cordial and...unbearable. Between herself and Prue, the air was thick, like the butter covering the currant scones that sat on the table before them. Idle conversation with the opposite sex was not one of their talents—for either of them.

Between the two of them they hadn't said more than a half-dozen words. Thank heavens for Mary. Her sister loved to make conversation, and even more so when the opposite sex was present.

"I do love riding in Hyde Park," Mary prattled on. "The fashionable hour is filled with many delights, is it not?"

Lord Arawn nodded and glanced at Prue, who was struggling to swallow her tea. Crom, who was still standing by the window, smiled, making Mary's breath hitch yet again. Chastity reached for a thin slice of lemon loaf. It was rather unfortunate, for Crom did not make her breathless. She had found him rather lovely to gaze upon that morning in Glastonbury, but her memory of him had paled and faded the moment she had come across Thane, whose sensuality and air of danger she could not seem to forget.

"Do you care for riding, Lady Chastity?" Crom asked.

The small wedge of cake lodged in her throat and she smiled benignly as she tried to make it go down.

"Chastity is terrified of beasts," Mary answered for her. "But myself, I am rather drawn to them."

Chastity glared at her sister. Mary's voice had dropped to a seductive purr. The double entendre was obviously not lost on Crom.

"You must be careful with beasts, Lady Mary, for they have a habit of occasionally biting."

Mary smiled artfully. "I am not afraid of the occasional little bite."

"Mary," Chastity hissed quietly to her sister as her father began to chat to the men of horses and conveyances. "You're being far too forward."

"It's called artful flirtation, sister," Mary replied. "You should learn it."

"I have no wish to."

Mary arched her brow in annoyance. "That beautiful specimen of a man is here to see you, and you're acting as though he were a leper."

Chastity lowered her gaze to her hands, which were folded primly in her lap. "I am not as bold as you."

"No, you're a frightened little mouse," Mary teased. "Trying to blend into the woodwork, but the truth is, he has not taken his gaze from you since he prowled into the salon."

Chastity dared a glance at the man and held her breath when she discovered he was staring at her. He *was* very handsome. *But not as handsome as Thane,* the voice intruded.

"Perhaps, Lady Chastity, you would do me the honor of accompanying me on a ride in the park tomorrow afternoon?"

"Splendid idea," Lord Arawn announced as he looked to Prue. "Why don't we make it a foursome."

"Impossible," her father said with a scowl. "We…have plans tomorrow afternoon." As if seeking her support, their father glanced at her mother.

"It is true, I'm afraid. Lady Sefton's garden party."

"The next afternoon, then. Your Grace?" Arawn directed his gaze to their father. "I trust you have no objection?"

Her father flushed and shifted his position uncomfortably on the chair as his gaze shifted between the two men. "None at all," he murmured.

Suddenly Chastity felt as though she had been sold. There was something in her father's eyes that alerted Chastity to the fact that something monumental had been asked, and answered.

"Well, then, we should be on our way," Crom announced, straightening away from the window. "Lady Chastity," he murmured as he reached for her hand. "It has been a pleasure. I very much look forward to our ride."

Bowing over her hand, he pressed her fingers lightly in his. He frowned, then met her gaze. "Your perfume… it is rather…exotic."

Flushing, Chastity pulled her hand out from his grasp. "A signature scent," she replied as she located the beautiful little atomizer that sat upon the mantel of the hearth. She had been in the midst of showing it to Prue and Mary when their guests arrived. So she had placed it on the mantel, safely out of reach.

"What a lovely surprise," Crom murmured. "An innocent maid with a penchant for the more…amorous scents." Chastity felt her face flame and her eyes grow wide. "Angel Water would become you much better," he said, straightening from her. "For you are as heavenly to behold as a cherub."

With a smile, Chastity accepted his compliment. It felt false, she realized, leaving her flat and slightly cold. Thane had not been artful in his speech. He had been bold, and…common, and it had inflamed her. Had made her desire him, despite her virtue, despite all the warnings that ran in her head.

Chastity followed both Lord Arawn and Crom with her gaze as they left the room. A footman reached for the handle and shut the door with a quiet click. Immediately, the entire room let out a collective sigh.

"Well, I think that went very well," her mother said with a smile. "Don't you, Lennox?"

"Mmm," her father mumbled as he stared at the highly glossed surface of his boot. "You are a better judge of these matters than I. I will defer to your superior knowledge."

"Then I account this first meeting a success. Both Crom and his lordship were quite smitten with our girls."

"Well, one of your girls wasn't quite as smitten," Mary teased. "Chastity barely glanced at the man."

"*I* am rather taken with Lord Arawn," came a quiet voice from the other side of the room.

Prudence. Chastity shot her sister a secretive smile.

One that said they would talk later. But her mother, clearly beside herself with the idea of marrying off a daughter, plagued Prue with questions, until their father was forced to jump from his chair and prowl about the room.

"The truth is, m'dear," he growled, "I'm not settled on the idea of those two courting my daughters."

Her mother's alarmed gaze followed the purposeful path her father was making through the salon. "But you said they are of good families and income."

"Yes, yes," her father muttered, "I daren't say otherwise."

"Papa, what do you mean?" Chastity asked. She was alarmed by her father's nervous behavior.

"Nothing," he grumbled. Suddenly he smoothed his hand down his brocade waistcoat, his long fingers lingering over the pocket. "I have a meeting tonight, m'dear. Business, I'm afraid. We will discuss this matter later. When my head is clear."

Rising from her chair, their mother nodded. "Of course. Come along, girls. Your father wishes to be alone, I think."

Lennox watched his family saunter out of the salon before he allowed himself to collapse onto a chair. *Christ above.* What had he done? Making deals with both faery courts? Had he truly believed that he would get away with it?

Damn it, what was to be done? The Seelie wanted his daughters, and now it seemed so, too, did the Dark Fey.

Palming the pocket of his vest, Lennox felt the folded missive. He was to meet with the Dark Fey that evening at, of all damn places, the Nymph and the Satyr. It was time to pay the tithe, the summons said. But he couldn't. That particular prize had already been given to the Seelie.

But who posed the greatest threat? he wondered. The Dark Fey or the Seelie? That answer, he would find out tonight. And God help his daughters, he thought, if they were to become the concubines of the Unseelie Court.

Rising from the chair, he strolled to the window and watched as the two Seelie Fey rode their elegant mounts out of the courtyard. The air seemed to still crackle with the remnants of their magical presence. He had felt that energy before, when the queen had come upon him that fateful night in the nursery.

Damn it, what was he to do? He was to meet with the queen in the morning. He knew what she would say. What she would want from him. And he knew the consequences of denying her. His clandestine transaction with her had miraculously been kept a secret. Robert's slow recovery from his deformity had been met with scientific marvel, not skepticism or suspicion. His wife had been so overwhelmed with happiness and gratitude that she had not asked how such a miracle came to be. No one knew. Only he and the faery queen.

But if his secret was found out, it would be bloody disastrous. He would lose everything. His position in society, his fortune, his friends. And possibly even his wife. Not to mention his son, whose handsome face and fine body would be reduced to a withered cripple. And his daughters…he wasn't man enough at the moment to think of them. He'd been selfish in his desires and now his girls would pay the price.

Contemplating all he had to lose, Lennox knew instinctively who the greatest threat was. Reaching into his pocket, he pulled the missive free and tore it up.

He would ignore it, he decided. Let the Unseelie come to him if they wanted their tithe so badly.

The Unseelie were here. Crom had smelled them, the spicy notes of male Unseelie flesh. It had covered Chastity's wrist. As he looked into her eyes, he'd seen nothing but wariness. She didn't know of the Dark Fey, or realize that she had come into contact with one—close contact, he reminded himself.

"You are thinking?" Arawn said as he reached for the reins of his mount. "Your frown tells me that you don't like something."

Crom swiftly mounted his stallion. "Did you sense something in the house?"

"No, why?"

"I smelled the Dark Fey."

"Impossible, you warded the house yourself. There is no possible way that our enemies could have broken through your protection spells."

"Nevertheless, I sensed their presence. Ensure you keep your eyes open," he commanded the footman, who was a Seelie from his court. "And keep His Grace's daughters in your sight. I don't like this. The Unseelie are more powerful than we thought. Our magic might very well be an even match."

"If that is the case, then we must move swiftly."

"Indeed." Nudging his horse forward, Crom cantered down the drive. "I will not have my plans to rule the Seelie Court thwarted by my twin and his cursed brethren."

The warm water trickled over her back. With a sigh, Chastity lowered her head to her bent knees and allowed her maid to gently scrub her back.

"How was your day of shopping, miss?" Annie asked.

Chastity moaned as Annie washed along her spine. She was particularly sensitive there. "Too hard?" her maid asked.

"No, it feels so delightful."

From the corner of her eye, she saw Annie nod, then reach for the soap. Lathering up the cloth, Annie proceeded to wash her back once more.

"Tell me of your day, miss. You've not been out of Glastonbury. How our little town must pale when compared to London. What sights you must have come across."

"Next time I shall take you with me," Chastity murmured. "I daresay you will find it most amusing. I never dreamed there were so many stores in London."

"Lady Mary certainly seemed to enjoy herself. The footmen were stumbling up the stairs while trying to carrying her boxes."

"Hmm, restraint has never been my sister's forte," Chastity said wryly, while thinking of the numerous boxes Mary had packed into their carriage. Of course, Prue had allowed herself one indulgence. A book. A novel, of all things. Prue was nothing if not practical, and the new fashion for novels with romance and passion in them was the furthest thing from sensible.

No wonder her sister had tried to hide it from them. But Mary had pulled it out of Prue's reticule, and had teased her mercilessly about it after they had left their father in the salon.

"That lovely perfume bottle was your only purchase, miss?"

Chastity raised her head and glanced at the dressing table. The atomizer looked stunning on the mirrored tray that held her other perfumes. But nothing she owned was as beautiful and ornate as the bottle she had been given that very morning.

"Yes," she whispered, watching as the glow from the hearth flickered along the delicate crystal, making it radiant in the softly shadowed room.

Since placing it on her dressing table, she had not been able to keep her gaze from straying to it. It was so beautiful, how could one not stare at it? But Chastity had a feeling that it was not only the gems that encrusted it that caught her fancy, but that it had been given to her by a man. It was her little secret, and she clutched the fact to her breast.

She knew she would think of the man who had gifted her with it as she daubed the perfume onto her skin. He'd vowed to leave her in peace, to cease his attentions, and thus put a halt to her inappropriate dreams. She had felt relief then, but now she felt bereft, morose at the thought of not seeing him again, or speaking with him.

For a paragon of chasteness, she certainly was acting the part of the wanton.

"Now then, shall we wash your hair tonight, miss?"

Annie's voice pulled her thoughts to the present. "Thank you, no. I am tired tonight. I'd like to retire early, I think."

"Very good, my lady."

Unwrapping a long bathing sheet, Annie held it out to her. Rising from the water, Chastity stepped from the copper tub and wrapped the sheeting around her. Instantly, the soft linen molded to her damp body. She saw in the full-length looking glass the outline of her breasts and belly as the linen absorbed the bathwater. Her breasts were full and heavy, the nipples pebbled. But not from the cold, but rather the thought of appearing like this before Thane.

Would he approve of her form? Chastity had always thought her body possessed a vulgar display of sensual curves. Her breasts were far too large, and her hips too full and rounded. Hers was a body belonging to a harlot, not a virtue.

A faint flush covered her throat and neck as she studied her reflection in the looking glass. If she had any sort of decency and modesty, she would cease staring at her almost-naked form. Yet she could not look away. She had never truly gazed upon her nakedness. Had always been too ashamed of the voluptuousness of it, of how it seemed to beckon men and their leers. She had never taken pleasure in her shape.

With a flush, Chastity glanced away from the image she saw. A true paragon would not have studied herself. A true innocent would not have wondered what it would be like to stand naked before this very mirror and imagine what it would be like to watch a man's hand caressing her body, discovering her, as she had never allowed herself to do.

"Miss?"

Shaking away the fantasy, Chastity turned away from the mirror. "That will be all for tonight. Thank you, Annie."

With a polite bob, Annie cleared out the bath things. "I shall send the footmen up in half an hour to remove the tub, miss."

"That will be fine," she answered as she made her way to the bed, where Annie had laid out her new night rail and wrapper. Mama had purchased it for her, and Chastity found herself eager to get into it. Never had she seen so many layers of satin and lace ruffles. The gown resembled the illustrations in books about faery tales. She was going to be the faery princess in this gown.

The thought struck her odd, and she smiled as she dropped the sheeting to the floor and slipped into the night rail. Not a faery-tale princess, but a fey princess, she thought, amazed how natural it sounded. Almost as if it were an everyday occurrence to believe in faeries. Instinctively, she had always known that her future lay with the fey. She did not understand how she could realize such a fact, let alone accept it. But she did.

And that had been the reason she had told Thane that she was promised to another. In her heart, she knew she was. Her path lay with the fey.

Most women her age would be horrified by the prospect of believing that the fey existed, but Chastity had been raised knowing that the faeries had come to her father. It was a secret that she and her sisters had kept with him. They were not to tell Mama. Why he had told them, Chastity could never understand, but he had trusted them with his secret. Perhaps he thought that if they believed in the faeries, if they knew that at some point in their lives the fey might come for them, they would be less shocked, less frightened.

And perhaps he was right. Because Chastity had known the minute that Crom and Arawn had entered their salon that they were not mere mortal men. They were fey. Beautiful, golden faeries.

That was the reason for Papa's restlessness, his barely concealed anxiousness. Mama had sensed it, but she had interpreted it as a natural inclination for a man to protect his daughters from men who would court them. But she and Prue knew differently.

"May I come in?"

Chastity was slipping into her robe when Prudence peeked around her chamber door. "Yes. I'm finished with my bath."

Prudence flew into the room, wearing a similar gown and wrapper. They smiled when they saw each other.

"Well, Mama did always enjoy dressing the four of us alike."

"Yes, well, I thought that stopped when we turned sixteen," Chastity said with a laugh.

"I suppose she thinks this is her last opportunity."

Chastity saw the twinkling in Prue's eye swiftly fade. "What is it, Prue?"

"I'm afraid, Chastity. Father has not said anything, but you and I both know that Crom and Arawn are not mere gentlemen."

Nodding, Chastity motioned to the bed, where they sat down upon the sage cream-silk counterpane. "My feelings have not changed from this afternoon when we spoke. I still believe that they are fey."

"And we're to…marry them?" Prudence asked with a gulp.

"I truly have no idea. But why would they call and ask to take us driving if not to court us?"

"What do you think they truly want with us? I mean, aren't there faery women to marry?"

Shrugging, Chastity picked at the crème satin ribbon that ran through the lace cuff of her sleeve. "I do not know. All I know is that we must speak to Father. We must learn more about what they want with us."

Prudence made a scoffing noise. "He won't talk of it. I'm certain. I attempted to this evening, after supper, but he flatly ignored me and shut himself in his study. I don't like this, Chastity. Something feels wrong."

"Are you only just beginning to realize that?" she asked, shocked by her sister's naiveté. "I have always thought our lives rather strange. Think on it, Prue. Four girls conceived simultaneously? A visit from the faery queen who foretells of four daughters who will possess virtues? For what purpose are we paragons? Humanity? Or fey?"

Prudence glanced away. "I've tried not to think of such things, to be truthful. I tried to believe that Papa only told us stories about the queen's visit to make us smile. I pretended that he liked to think of us as special, so he told us fantastical tales about our importance—and the faeries."

"I wish I could have consoled myself with those thoughts, but I have only come to dread the truth of what our future holds. I believe, Prudence, that the faery queen will come and take us. That we are, in essence, her creation."

"How can that be?" Prue cried. "It's not possible."

"What is *im*possible where the fey are concerned?"

A sense of defeat stole over her sister, and Chastity watched as Prue's shoulders sagged. "I'm afraid, Chastity, because I fear that I rather liked Arawn. I am afraid that my attraction still stands if he be man or faery."

Chastity clutched Prue's cold, trembling fingers in her hands. "You don't have to apologize for your feelings."

Prue shook her head and smiled sadly. "The first time I feel attraction, and the slightest bit of liberty with a man, and he turns out to be a fantastical, magical creature."

"It does sound rather odd, doesn't it?" Chastity laughed.

"But have we not always been considered odd?"

"Indeed we have."

"And you?" Prue asked. "How did you feel about the one named Crom? Mary has not ceased prattling about him. Even Mercy became a bit short with her this evening for carrying on in such a way. You can only remark upon a man's beauty for so long before it becomes tedious."

Glancing down at their entwined fingers, Chastity strove to find the right answer. Yes, Crom was handsome and refined. He was very gentlemanlike. But he did not make her blood quicken in the same way it had that morning, when Thane had looked at her, or when she remembered the stranger in the maze. Those memories made her blood boil and the space between her thighs hot and sticky.

"He is very handsome," she began, "but...I do not know..."

"I understand," Prudence murmured, now consoling her. "It is very difficult to let go of what we are in order to be courted. It goes against everything we are. *Who* we are."

Yes. Except it had been all too easy to forget who and what she was when she had been with Thane.

Why, dear God, did every thought and feeling come back to him?

Because you're mine.

She heard the words in a whisper and glanced to the perfume bottle. Its beauty enthralled her and its contents lured her as if it contained a magic enchantment. There was no denying that she could not resist peeking at the bottle that sat atop her dressing table.

"Perhaps all will seem much clearer in the morning," Prue suggested as she rose from the bed. "Sleep tight, and pleasant dreams."

"Prue," she called after her sister. "What if...that is to say, what if we don't have a choice about who we are to wed?"

Prudence tilted her head and studied her. "Papa won't force us to marry someone we do not want to."

"What if *he* has no choice," she whispered, giving voice to her fears. "That is the way of the fey. Gifts come with conditions, and sometimes, faery gifts can be more curse than reward."

"What are you saying?"

She didn't know, really. She just knew that inside she was confused. All her life she had lived as a paragon. Not only was she chaste and completely innocent, she was obedient, she never questioned, never rebelled. But now a seed of discontent was growing inside her. She hadn't been able to put Thane out of her mind, nor had she given a proper thought to Crom, other than to wish him away.

In her heart, she could not be happy with Crom. Her body, she knew, had already given itself away to the touch of another man.

"Chastity," Prudence asked quietly, "do you fear the marriage bed, is that it?"

"Yes," she admitted, but more important, she feared what it would make of her. She knew no other form of herself beyond her chasteness. Who would she be when she was no longer virginal?

"One can still be pure and innocent, sister," Prue murmured, "even after one has lain with one's husband."

Nodding, Chastity knew her sister was right. But could one still be innocent after experiencing the pleasures of the flesh that were more...ribald? Would she still be chaste if she were a willing participant in such pleasures? She didn't believe so. To remain a paragon—the only thing she had ever known—was to bear the attentions of her future husband. To allow him to copulate with her. She would provide no hysterics. No crying or pleading. She would lay beneath him and tolerate his attentions. It was for the begetting of children. It was not sinful then. It was only sinful when the actions between two people were wild and wanton. For pleasure instead of purpose.

Duty. It would be her responsibility to procreate, and to raise chaste, virtuous daughters and strong, noble sons.

"You're thinking too much," Prue admonished. "You're frowning and you'll get terrible lines around your mouth and eyes if you continue this way."

Smiling weakly, Chastity chased her thoughts away. "Thank you for the talk, Prue."

"I'll see you on the morrow. Sleep well."

Now, alone in her room, Chastity made her way to her dressing table. She needed comfort. The only thing that truly did soothe her. Reaching for the bottle, she pulled the stopper free and inhaled the seductive perfume.

This was her forbidden desire. The only indulgence she allowed herself.

Slowly, she trailed the crystal tip from down her neck, savoring the cool glide of the perfumed droplet.

Yes, put me all over you.

She heard Thane's voice in her head as she brushed the crystal along her skin, daubing her body with the perfume. How wicked and sinful to think of such things. To think of him. But she was helpless to stop the words. They came, despite her resolve not to hear them.

Her mind's warning was not heeded. Her body now felt warm, and her head swam with fleeting images of Thane and vignettes of her dream, as if the perfume was starting to drug her.

Let me become part of you. Cover you. Feel me.

"Yes." One word of acquiescence. Acceptance.

NINE

WRAPPING HIMSELF AROUND HER, THANE MAR-veled at the feel of her. Even through the heavy layers of her night rail and robe, he was acutely aware of the outline of her body—very generous breasts, full hips, lush thighs. A body suited to his taste—a body that Lust wished to sink into and possess.

Enveloping Chastity with his scent, he felt a primitive satisfaction, knowing he was marking her. Soon, he would mark her with his essence—inside and out. She would smell of him—the erotic incense of the Dark Fey, along with the musky sex of Lust.

Even now he felt Lust push forward, insisting on sharing her with him. How could he not? Lust had been starved for too long, deprived of any sexual play. But sex with this woman would be like nothing Lust had ever experienced—or Thane for that matter. She was so pure and innocent. An intoxicating experience for someone as corrupt as he.

Lust wanted her, too. The unsullied, chaste Chastity. He wanted to play with her, to teach her all the depraved sexual acts his sin lusted for.

Instinctively, the Dark Fey in Thane reared its head, struggling with Lust. In all his other conquests, he had allowed Lust to win over—to overtake the dark, sexual needs of his Unseelie blood. It had been easy. A matter of no consequence, for he felt only desire for the women he had bedded, not this all-consuming compulsion to protect and possess.

But tonight, Thane felt as though he was fighting for his life and that of Chastity's precious mortal soul. To allow Lust to win would mean that he would have to give Chastity over to his sin.

He couldn't. Everything Unseelie inside him roared in protest. Chastity was his and no one else's. When he had seen Crom in the salon, courting her, he had nearly revealed himself. Crom wanted her.

The dominance of his blood sprang forth, forcing Lust to retreat. But then he was left with his Unseelie self, hot-blooded, dominant, aching for Chastity to yield to him. To thwart Crom and steal her away to his court.

As he watched his body shroud hers, he studied her response to the perfume that was his very essence. She was aroused. The pale skin above her throat was flushed red with sexual arousal.

"Do you wish me to come to you?" he asked while her skin absorbed him, and he sensed that profound connection with her. He experienced the pulsation of her heart within his body, heard her breathing, experienced the little tremor of excitement as it raced through her blood, only to feel the way her nipples beaded, and her core pulsed in anticipation.

Stilling, he concentrated on her, absorbed her entire being into his, as she had done with the perfume. And finally he heard it, a small little whisper, barely audible, despite the quiet.

"Yes."

"Who do you want to come to you?"

The secret voice she buried so deeply answered his silent question with a flicker of images; him as the masked stranger in the maze, followed by Thane in the garden, then back to the masked stranger. Chastity's mind volleyed between the two until the images morphed into one, that of the masked stranger stripping himself of his disguise, only to reveal Thane's image.

He knew what she wanted. Knew who the voice inside her desired. *The Dark Faery.* The dangerous, prevailing side to the man she had met in the perfumery.

With Lust banished for now, Thane allowed his body to come together. No longer perfume, he changed to mist, then smoke, slowly and sensuously unraveling himself from around her waist and hips before sliding along her thighs.

He heard her inner cry of protest that he was leaving her, but he quieted her alarm and stood behind her. He was, at that moment, his true self. A Dark Fey prince whose glamour was not disguised or diminished.

As much as he desired to see Chastity yield, to watch her shed her mantle of virtue, the need for her to know who it was she belonged to was stronger.

"See me."

Slowly her eyes opened and she gasped at the image that met her. In the long looking glass she was standing barefoot, clad in her virginal white lace and ruffles, while behind her, all darkness of hair and eyes, stood his Unseelie form.

He towered over her, dwarfing her with his height and the bulk of his body, which was clothed in the way of a mortal gentleman. He felt and heard that voice tremble inside her, replaced the rational voice she allowed to govern unchecked. *He could break me, hurt me...dominate me.*

"Not break. Not hurt," he murmured as he raised a hand to her cheek and smoothed his fingers down its softness, "but dominate, yes. Master you? Yes. Make you yield to what you want, make you surrender to who you truly are? *Yes.*"

Bending his head, he brushed his face against the crook of her neck, taking every nuance of her humanity— body, mind and spirit—into his own. "You have a friend inside," he murmured darkly, "a friend who shows me everything you try so desperately to hide."

"No."

"I have already heard that voice, crying to break free. Trying to allow you to experience one simple pleasure— like that kiss you asked for in your dream."

Her eyes pressed shut, and he thought for certain she

would deny it, but she softened with resolve, and pressed her head against his. "I'm frightened."

"Not of me." He inhaled her scent, warmed by the heat of her rushing blood as he skimmed his fingertip down her quivering throat. "But of what you truly desire."

She shook her head in protest, but he pulled her to him, reached for her unbound hair and gently clutched it in his hand. "Do not be afraid of desire. Lust is a powerful thing. Consuming. Elating. *Freeing*."

He watched her eyelids close, her lashes fluttered as her head tipped back, exposing the long, smooth column of her throat, which he wanted to kiss and lick. Lave and most definitely nibble at. "Have you ever wanted to be free, Chastity?"

"None of us are free. We are bound by society's rules, and the dictates of our sex. Women are slaves to men. Men are slaves to money, power and position."

Her words pierced through his thoughts. Indeed, both mortals and fey were indentured chattel. He and the other Unseelie princes were more so than any other Dark Fey. He was a slave to Lust. A disciple, compelled to follow and kneel beneath the very great desires of his ever-present voracious sin.

This mortal, he thought, watching her, was going to break him.

"I am imprisoned by chains I cannot shed," she said.

"It is your fears that bind you," he replied in a hushed whisper. "You allow your virtue to keep you prisoner because it is easier to hide behind it than to accept your wish to submit to your desires."

She gasped, a sound of shock. He had hit on something. A secret fear she kept hidden. "Ah, I see that I am right. You have wondered what it would be like not to think. To only feel. To experience."

"No, that's not true."

"Have you ever thought of what it would be like to yield? To lay down at someone's feet and give yourself over to them?"

Her body went soft, the scent of her quim perfumed the air, and he knew then that Chastity Lennox secretly yearned to be taken. With that knowledge, Lust all but overtook him, desiring to dominate her. The Dark Fey in him wished to see Chastity submit to him. He would make her surrender so stunning, so beautiful and intense, that she would never think to leave him.

"This is truly not happening. You are only a dream. A figment of my imagination," she admonished, struggling against her inner feelings.

"But am I who you want?" he asked softly, allowing his breath to whisper past her ear. Inside him, he felt her response, felt desire pool between her thighs, where it mixed with his own need, and the swell of his cock.

Slowly her lashes raised, revealing her eyes, which were now the color of green grass—the very same color of the grass he would lay her in while he lifted her gown and put his lips to her cunt.

His fantasy flashed through not only his mind, but hers, and he saw her version of him, with his dark head buried between white thighs and her hands ruthlessly pulling at his hair.

"Yes, you want me there, but this image behind you—open your eyes and see—does the image of the man you see now, is he who you want?"

Quieting his mind, he listened for Chastity's thoughts, her fears, her possible repulsion of him. There was silence—for so long he thought he would never hear her. Then it came. A quiet voice, laced with innocent wonder and alluring huskiness.

So beautiful. So dark. He calls to me, and my body wants nothing more than to answer. A…a… She could not finish the thought, so he aided her.

"A Dark Fey."

Her eyes widened in shock, but her body trembled with yearning.

"There is a whole new world out there, Chastity, a land of decadent pleasures. A court filled with bliss and passion. Allow me to show it to you."

Thane felt the inner struggle, the fear tearing at her. So strong. Her virtue ran true and deep.

"Submit," he whispered as he nuzzled her neck and pressed his aroused body against hers. "Surrender to me. Give me pleasure by allowing me to show you my world."

"This is not real," she said in a voice that was trying to be firm, but fell short. "You are not real."

Thane allowed his hands to leave his sides and cup her breasts from behind. As the heat from his palms permeated the silk, he heard her gasp. Felt the tingling of her nipples as their connection intensified. "Is this not real?" he asked. "The hardening of your nipples and the swelling of your breasts?" Gently, he pulled at her nipples through her night rail, making a rhythm that was slow and arousing, matching the cadence his mouth would make as he suckled her.

She whimpered, her legs weakened and he pressed against her, holding her upright. "You have enchanted me with your faery magic."

"No," he said darkly. "You have enchanted me. You are all I can think of. Thoughts of you consume me."

"What are you doing to me?" she whispered brokenly.

"Awakening you."

Smoothing his palms along her breasts, he soothed the hardened flesh, trying to stave off the desire to rip the gown from her body and reveal her naked form to his hungering gaze.

"You will come to me," he demanded as he clutched her chin in his hand and lifted her face to his. "In your dreams you will allow me in. You will deny me nothing. You will submit to me and my desires."

Her gaze flickered, wavered, but he held her firmly in his grasp. "And I will pleasure you, Chastity Lennox, like no man, or other fey, could."

"What is a dream but a hopeless wish?" she whispered brokenly. "For I have dreamed for so long things that can never be."

He softened against her, and brushed his mouth softly against her lips. "Never hopeless, *muirneach*."

Her gaze flickered to his, and he saw great sorrow mix

with retreating passion. "I can promise you my dreams, but never my waking moments."

"I will take that promise—for now," he added. "To bed. To sleep. Only to come to me and my court."

Dear Diary

Something is happening to me. I am changing. I can sense it, the woman I was is slowing being taken from me, replaced with a woman I do not know. A woman I cannot understand.

As I look about my room, my gaze always returns to my dressing table, and the assortment of beautiful bottles that litter the mirrored tray. The bottles are all different, all decorated with gilt and gems, and inside, a myriad of scents are concealed. But there is one bottle that always draws my eye. It is blue and gold and, inside, the perfume is clear, like the crystal of a bead of water. It sparkles in the sunlight, and against the orange flicker of the hearth at night, it glows bright and enticing—beckoning me to cover my body with its crystal liquid. I resist, for I derive far too much pleasure in dipping my fingers into that bottle and touching my skin.

Even now the bottle calls to me, as though it were alive. Its voice is dark and compelling, and when I close my eyes, and shut out the world, I can still hear the bottle calling, but this time the voice is more seductive. It whispers to me to do very wicked things. Sinful things. And my body... Oh, my body wants to obey that voice, but I cannot.

I am a virtue. An innocent. But perhaps I am not. Perhaps I am just an ordinary woman. And that frightens me more than these feelings of lust. I have always known who I am. What

I was destined for, but to discover that maybe I was wrong…
That the person I thought I knew had never really existed…

Who am I? I question myself. The silence answers me, and
it terrifies me.

She did not dream last night. Chastity did not know
why, but felt slightly bereft by the fact. She had wanted
to dream, to return to that moment when she had stood
in front of her looking glass and imagined that Thane
was standing behind her.

Foolish though she was, she pretended it was real.
Pretended that Thane had truly come to her. A dream.
A hopeless wish…

He had been a Dark Fey in her daydream. She did not
know what that meant. Was it a deep-seated longing,
finally breaking free, or was it a secret fear, or a method
for her mind to come to terms with what her future held?
Surely it was aberrant to dream of sexual pleasures—with
any man—let alone a dark and commanding faery.

"Come and see the lotus flowers," Mercy called from
her shady spot by the pond. "Lady Sefton says that they
were shipped to her in a crate from India from the Brit-
ish East India Company. They're a marvel," Mercy said
with a smile. "I've never seen anything so strange yet so
beautiful."

Wrapping her woolen shawl around her shoulders,
Chastity fell into step beside Prudence who shrouded
them from the afternoon sun with a parasol. "You're very
quiet today," her sister commented. "Did you not sleep
well?"

"I am in a contemplative sort of mind today, I'm afraid."

Prudence nodded and studied their youngest sister. "Mercy seems oblivious to what is going on. I wonder at her naiveté."

"She copes with it the only way she knows how. By constantly wearing a smile. It is just another mask she wears. Different from ours, but its purpose is the same."

"I hope for her sake that the fey have not made a mark for her. She's a far too gentle and trusting soul."

Smiling, Chastity thought about what Prudence was saying. "I don't know. I think Mercy could prove quite tenacious if the provocation was strong enough." Chastity glanced at her elder sister. "You're talking of the fey today as if you have somehow come to accept the truth throughout the night."

Prudence's fair skin blushed pink. "I did. It was somewhere around three and four in the morning as I was tossing and turning, unable to stop thinking of the golden man who was sitting so close beside me on the settee." Prue stopped and placed a gloved hand on Chastity's forearm. "It's blasphemous, isn't it, to believe in the fey. *To actually desire an alliance with them.*"

"There are many who have committed greater sins, Prue. For this, for longing for a man who makes you *feel*, well, I believe you'll be spared purgatory."

Prudence glanced at her, was about to say something in response, but held her tongue as they came to stand beside their sister. "Gorgeous, aren't they?" Mercy asked, pointing to the white flower.

"Indeed they are. Do they smell nice?" Chastity asked.

Scooping up a flower, Mercy held out her palm to Chastity, who inhaled delicately. "Floral. Pretty. But there is a spice to it."

Mercy colored delicately. "I heard Lord Ashcrombe telling Lady Sefton that the lotus bloom is compared to a woman's most intimate parts for the way the petals unfurl, and it's sweet but spicy scent."

Prudence snorted, and Chastity inhaled the bloom again while she said, "Lord Ashcrombe is desiring an affair with Lady Sefton. He would tell her anything she wanted to hear."

Shrugging, Mercy plucked the bloom from Chastity's hand and let it slip back into the pond. "I thought it a beautiful analogy, actually."

"I've never been one to compare my intimate parts," Prue said on a chuckle. "But then, being the virtue of temperance and restraint, I have given very little thought to anything that could be construed as…licentious."

Mercy turned to look at them. "Do you really think that wrong?"

"Yes, I do," Prue whispered. "A man should not even know what a woman's parts look like. If he were at all a gentleman, he would see to his needs in the dark, as is proper. He most certainly should not go about gazing at flowers and thinking of intimacies."

Mercy shrugged, allowing Prue's censure to run off her

like water off a duck. "Ah, well, I could stay by this little pond forever. I find it so tranquil. The water is so clear and still that you can see your reflection perfectly."

"Do you not think you've stayed here long enough, Mercy?" Prudence asked with reproach in her voice. "People will start to talk about your not socializing."

"I only wanted a few minutes alone with my thoughts. I'm tired of small talk."

"And smiling and being kind," Chastity finished for her.

Slowly Mercy nodded as she untied her bonnet strings and pulled her hat from her golden hair, only to lay it on the grass beside her. "Remember in the books Mama would read to us at bedtime? The ones filled with faery tales and romance? Do you recall how one of the stories spoke of a magical pond that when one gazed deeply into the water, one could see the reflection of the person they were to marry? No? Well, I do, and I have sat here all this time, gazing at the water, and I've seen nothing. Naught but my own smiling reflection, and it's left me feeling...empty, I'm afraid."

"Oh, Mercy," Chastity whispered. "I understand completely."

Her sister's eyes started to glisten. "Something so strange is happening. I've felt it ever since Beltane. Have you?"

She nodded. "I've felt it, as well."

"I'm trying to be understanding with Papa, but he's been so...evasive. I've asked about the fey, and the faery queen, and he will not talk of it. Yet I cannot help but believe it has something to do with them. You know, Beltane is the time of year that the fey are known to walk freely amongst mortals. Do you think we can actually feel their presence amongst us? Is that the mysterious change we feel coming upon us?"

"I believe so." Chastity swallowed hard. "Have you seen one?" she asked.

Mercy shook her head. "Other than the two who came to tea yesterday."

"So you know."

"Of course." Mercy's lovely eyes turned cold. "I'm the virtue of kindness, not idiocy."

Smiling, Chastity let her gaze drift over the fine lawns and gardens of Lord and Lady Sefton's grand Elizabethan home. She had always thought Mercy, in her kindness, naive and blind to the darkness of men. This show of backbone made her feel so much better. She had always worried that Mercy would be taken for granted by some unscrupulous man who would leave her broken and dispirited. Because of her kindness, Prue and she had shielded their youngest sister, oftentimes forgetting that she was only ten minutes younger.

"Those two who came to call are from the Seelie Court," Mercy said. "The Unseelie Court are more apt to move beneath the light of the moon."

"And how do you know so much?" Prue asked.

"Because it's my most favorite topic," Mercy said on a sigh. "I adore the fey."

"The Unseelie," Chastity said, steering the conversation back. "What did you mean by they move through the night?"

Mercy contemplated her. "They are the Dark Fey, followers of pleasures and sin. Naturally their guiding star is the moon. Their element the darker forces, mist, fog, rain and shadows. They seduce and entice their victims in the darkness."

Mist? Glistening mist? she wanted to ask. Oh, Lord, she truly had encountered one of them—the Dark Fey—that night in the maze. Thane…

"The fey are incredibly beautiful creatures," Mercy continued, warming to her subject, "but the Dark Fey are by far the more beautiful. Theirs is a sensual voluptuousness. Even their voices are deep and seductive. They live for pleasure, for the thrill of seductions. Their needs are dark, commanding. They say," Mercy whispered conspiratorially, "that the Dark Fey are very dominant in their desires and that there is no greater pleasure than for a woman to submit herself to them."

"Oh," Chastity whispered as her hand flew to her heart. If Mercy was intending to frighten her, she was doing a poor job of it. For Chastity was utterly intrigued. Dark and commanding. Beautiful and compelling. That was Thane.

"Well, I cannot imagine such heathen wantonness," Prue scoffed. "If we're to be given up to the fey I'm grateful that it is to the Seelie Court. Sunlight and joy seems much more enjoyable then being dragged to the underworld and ravished."

Chastity didn't think so. She would much rather be

ravished than revered. As she admitted the fact, her virtue rose within her, chastising her for such thoughts.

"Good afternoon, ladies."

The three of them turned their heads to the sound of the deep voice coming from beyond the trees to their right. As if by magic, Arawn and Crom appeared. Chastity heard the soft intake of Prue's breath. She waited for the same response and felt nothing as her gaze skimmed over Crom.

Today he was dressed in black britches, tall boots and a blue overcoat with a matching waistcoat made of silk and embellished with gold thread. It was a very rich, very elegant outfit, but somehow she found herself comparing it to the black jacket and silver waistcoat that Thane had worn yesterday. She found Crom's lacking. As her gaze skimmed the tall length of him, she realized that his hands did not look half as exciting from beneath his lace cuffs as Thane's. His hands had been very masculine, despite the lace resting against them. His fingers were long, elegant, but possessed of strength and an aura of authority. Even the ring he wore was black and shining. A mixture of onyx and moonstone. It hadn't looked effeminate or foppish. Not that Crom did look foppish, but when compared to Thane, he came across as somewhat lacking.

"A glorious day for a stroll, wouldn't you say," Arawn announced as they came to stand before them. "We could not stay away, knowing you were here."

Studying them silently from beneath her bonnet brim, Chastity could not help but wonder how…ordinary they were. It almost made her wish to believe that they were mere mortals. But once one looked up into their faces, once one's eyes took in the extraordinary handsomeness, it was impossible to believe that such beauty could belong to a man. No, they were fey posing as gentlemen.

She wondered at their ruse. Did they think that she and her sisters would run in fear of them? How long did they intend to pretend they were something they were not? Till they were safely wed? Till they had them secured in their court?

"Shall we, then?" Arawn inquired as he held out his arm to Prue. "I see two benches beneath those enormous willow trees that we could stroll to. And as they are in full view of the other guests, it wouldn't be considered improper or risqué."

Chastity could almost hear the rapid firing of Prue's heart. Her sister was infatuated. She wanted this stroll with her golden fey. However, Chastity wished for nothing more than to sit by this pond, reflecting. But reflection would only make her dwell on Thane. Was he a man as he would have her think, or was he something else. One of them, or...a Dark Fey?

If she refused to join them on their stroll, she knew that Prudence would not accept Arawn's arm. Her virtue would forbid it. Would ruin this moment for the notoriously even-tempered and restrained Prudence. But her mind was warring against it. She needed to sit and think. To recall every second of her meeting with Thane for any clue of what he truly was.

"Miss Lennox?" Crom murmured, holding out his

arm to her. Gazing up at him, Chastity forced herself to paint a false smile on her face.

"A short stroll seems very nice. Mercy?" she asked, looking down at where her sister sat in the grass, her linen skirts spread full around her. "Will you not join us?"

"Thank you, but no. This spot has too great a hold of me, I'm afraid."

Chastity looked up at her companion to see the relief that washed across his face.

She didn't want to be alone with him. She knew that much. But she didn't want to ruin her sister's afternoon, either.

Ahead of them, Arawn and Prue were leisurely strolling. Chastity placed her hand over Crom's forearm and allowed him to steer her toward the white bench.

In silence they walked, until he cleared his throat and looked upon her. "I hope you do not feel put-upon, Miss Lennox. My friend and I petitioned Lady Sefton for an invitation right after we left your house yesterday."

"Not at all, my lord. I do hope I did not give you the impression that either I or my sister are put out." Although, she had to admit, she was rather put out. Now, she was going to have to spend time with him. She would much rather be unguarded and at ease with her sisters.

Glancing in Lady Sefton's direction, she saw her flittering like a butterfly. She was rather busy flirting with Lord Ashcrombe, who was a notorious libertine. Chastity could only guess what faery gift they had offered to induce the notoriously selective lady to give up two invitations to her coveted garden party.

"You look very lovely in that shade of blue. Ethereal, even," Crom said.

The compliment grated on her nerves. Especially the thought of being ethereal. She was not an angel, nor did she wish to be. She was a virtue, and neither did she wish to be that, either. His compliment was benign. Uninspired. She had heard that, about her beauty, many times, and she was rather tired of it. How she would have much rather heard something else, about her mind, or her intelligence. Something. Anything more substantial then a comment about her looks.

"You are very quiet this afternoon, my lady. As much as you were yesterday."

"I am not skilled at conversing with ease with the opposite sex." It was best to stay with the truth. He was a fey. She didn't know if they could discern truth or lies, and she didn't feel like discovering the fact this afternoon.

"You are a very pure spirit," he whispered, "both in thought and deed. I am not deterred, for I know what appears as aloofness is really an innate sense of decorum."

And disinterest. He stopped them in the clearing between the pond and the bench. Taking her hand off his arm, he brought her gloved fingers to his mouth. His gaze held hers while he pressed his lips chastely against her fingers. "I won't be deterred. And I'm not put off by your innocence and modesty. In fact, I'm rather drawn to it. What man would not wish to have a paragon for a wife?"

Her heart suddenly constricted, missing a beat entirely.

She did not want to be his or anyone's paragon. She wanted to be a wife, a woman, not some model of virtue to be put up on a pedestal and stared at.

"What is the saying?" he asked, his violet eyes shining. "Ah, yes, who can find a virtuous woman? For her price is far above rubies."

She smiled, not knowing what else to do. There was a price to be paid. She instinctively knew that. But what she was growing to fear was that she and her sisters were the cost.

Still holding her hand, Crom brushed his thumb across her knuckles. "I hope I have not been too bold in my suit. It is not my wish to frighten you, but only to make my intentions known. I would like to court you, Miss Lennox."

And this was the price. Her hand to this fey. Prue's hand to Arawn. But in repayment for what? she wondered.

"Of course," she said, bowing into a polite curtsy. What else was she to say?

"Excellent." He flashed a brilliant smile, then motioned to where Prue was sitting on a bench, and Arawn was standing beside her. They were deep in conversation.

"I sense that there is something on your mind," Crom said.

"No, nothing."

"You know what I am."

Chastity looked up sharply. "I beg your pardon?"

"You know I'm a fey."

She swallowed hard. There was no point in denying it. "Yes. I know."

He sat down beside her and gazed straight ahead. "It makes matters much easier, doesn't it? There is nothing to hide."

She could only nod. How strange it was to talk to a faery. "I must caution you that while my intentions are most honorable, others of my kind are not so principled."

"What do you mean?"

"The Dark Fey, my opposite. They are unscrupulous. They take mortals, trusting and innocent, like yourself, and ruin you."

"You're warning me."

"Yes. You must be careful."

"If it makes matters easier between us, I have not come across these Dark Fey you speak of."

"But you will." He reached for her hand. "I know they will come for you."

She thought of Thane—why, she didn't know. Perhaps it was because she thought of the way he had made her feel while in the perfumery. Warm and fuzzy, with the very great desire to see him again. She never felt this for Crom. Never had the butterflies, or the urge to feel his touch.

"You will come to me if any of the Dark Fey come to you."

She didn't understand his warning, the importance of the Dark Fey. But she nodded her agreement, if only to put an end to their intimate tête-á-tête.

"Of course, I shall inform you at once, if I ever come across one."

"You make a jest of my warning, but soon you will understand."

She was about to ask why the fey were all of a sudden in her and her sisters' existence, when Prue and Arawn came up to them.

"We are raising suspicion."

Chastity saw that Lady Sefton's guests were taking a great interest them, and not the lavish luncheon the servants had brought out.

"Well, then, shall we? I have no wish to put a black spot on your reputation," Crom said.

No, indeed, she thought sourly. He wanted her virtuous. Spotless. *Perfect*. Chastity knew what he wanted of her.

She had always hated her virtue. But never more than now as she looked down the long road of her future path. It was cold. Filled with duty and expectations. She would never break free of the morality that chained her. Would never be allowed to break the bonds. She was horrified by what she knew would be her life. And she felt reckless. Wild. Inside, she revolted. She wanted at least one moment of excitement. One wild interlude of abandon. Like last evening, she had stared deeply into her looking glass and imagined Thane's hands all over body.

That had been wicked. Wild. Wanton. And she so desperately wanted to find that woman again. Somewhere deep inside her, that woman was locked tightly away. But Thane had found her. Had used the key to unlock her. But he was not here. She had sent him away. And now she was utterly imprisoned.

TEN

ABOVE THE TREETOPS, THANE AND KIAN hovered. He was mist, his preferred form when not in his own skin. Kian was shadow.

He saw his twin hanging between the leafy canopy of two ancient oaks. He was not completely gray, but a mixture of black and green. A clear sign that his sin was ruling him.

Thane knew what had prompted the beast. It was the same as what had awakened his. The Lennox girls, talking to two Seelie Fey.

The site of Chastity's hand on Crom's arm infuriated him. Made him want to lash out and pull her to him. But his sin could not rule. Lust must be shoved aside and fed later. He must learn, for the sake of the other princes and their dying court, what deviousness the Seelie were up to.

Beside him, he felt Kian stir, saw the shadow move

and grow ominous. He hoped that his twin could control Envy. It would not do to engage the Seelie. Especially Crom, Niall's twin. Their king was powerful, and Thane believed that his brother was, as well.

No, their war could not be brought out now. Not in front of the mortals, or the Lennox girls.

"I think a storm approaches," the one named Prue remarked as she looked up into the trees where he and Kian lurked. "That shadow is rather dark. There must be a thundercloud forming behind the trees."

When the Seelie glanced up, Thane was relieved that they paid little attention. They had no idea that their dark counterparts where there, listening to them. Fortunate for them, the Seelie magic did not enable them to shift their shape. That was a dark power, and one he and the other princes reveled in. In their altered shapes, the Seelie were as ignorant to their presence as the mortals. But Crom was part Unseelie, Thane reminded himself, and none of them truly knew what Crom was capable of.

"Oh, indeed," Chastity murmured as she glanced up at them. "That cloud is rather menacing. I've never seen green before in a cloud."

Thane was about to remind Kian of their mission, to warn him to control the jealousy he felt, when his twin suddenly left the safety of the trees, only to spread in a wide arc across the open expanse of grass to a pond. And to the form of a woman whose fingers were grazing the still waters.

Thane supposed he could not fault his brother for

wanting to meet his virtue. Thane wanted to meet with his, too, and ravish her on the forest floor.

"I suppose," the other fey, who Thane did not know, murmured, "we must be on our way. We've occupied your time for far too long. I see a few knowing glances being cast our way."

"Of course."

"Tomorrow then?" Crom asked. "We shall pick you up at five for the fashionable hour in Hyde Park."

Prudence seemed all enthusiasm. Chastity, however, was anything but.

"Good day to you," Crom murmured in a silky voice that was designed to enthrall. "I shall be counting the minutes until tomorrow."

Thane wanted to choke the bastard, or better yet, run him right through with his sword. But the Seelie would hear the singing of the faery blade slicing through the air. It would alert him to their presence, which was counterproductive. But it would be damn satisfying to watch the golden bastard die by his blade.

As the Seelie left them, Prudence and Chastity were left alone on the bench. Thane knew he should follow the Seelie, to learn of their plans, but he could not force himself to leave. He was above Chastity, and he wanted to drink her in. To use these minutes to settle the tumultuous feelings that ripped through him at the sight of her with his enemy. Any other man with her would have angered him, but the sight of a Seelie touching her sent him into a blind rage.

"I believe I will take a stroll amongst Lady Sefton's

lavender garden. Will you join me?" Chastity asked her sister.

"No, I'm afraid I see Mercy with a stranger. I think I shall go and rescue her. Enjoy your walk."

This was the moment he had been waiting for. A chance to come to her. Would she welcome him? Or would she remind him of his vow to leave her be?

As mist, he followed her to a secluded path, and slowly allowed the iridescent droplets to form into his shape. He would have much preferred to come to her in the moonlight, but the daylight would have to do.

Who said that one must be seduced by the light of the moon only?

Mercy watched as her pale fingers glided through the still waters. Her gaze was still fixed on the elegant, yet strangely formed, lotus flower. Her sisters had thought it a strange thing. Had thought her little story behind the flower even more bizarre.

Perhaps it was really herself that was odd. For she had warmed to the story, her insides doing a strange flipping sensation. But it was not only her belly that had reacted. But her breasts and her own intimate parts, as well.

Sighing, she enjoyed the warm breeze as it ruffled through her hair. She was hot, sitting in the sun with her heavy afternoon gown and the layers of petticoats beneath the full skirts. How she wished she could lie in the grass in only her chemise, feeling the wind caress her body.

Wicked and wanton thoughts. She had many of them,

but she kept them well hidden from her sisters. Mary had little time for her. And Prudence and Chastity would not understand. As the virtues of temperance and chastity, their thoughts were pure and innocent. They would be appalled to know that Mercy harbored fantasies that no lady of breeding should even know about, let alone dream of.

The heat and the sun were suddenly blocked by the passing of a large cloud. Mercy tracked its progress over the grass, and then as it drifted over her. She took respite in its coolness, in the way it blanketed her. She followed the path of shadow as it snaked its way across the pond. Gazing at the water, she gasped as she saw the image of a man reflected in the water.

Her head came up and she squinted as sunbeams outlined the breadth of the stranger's shoulders. He was bathed in shadows and sunlight, the effect breathtaking.

"One must be careful when one gazes into the still waters, for it is said that the image you see is that of your future."

Mercy's attention drifted to the water. She saw the outline of the man. Then the image was replaced with a man who was bent on his haunches, staring at her from across the small, ornamental pond.

He was stunning. Breathtaking. His eyes were blue, the color of ice, his hair long and black and silky as it blew in the breeze. He was well muscled. Despite his frock coat, Mercy knew that his shoulders and chest were broad and that beneath his linen shirt, and the lace jabot he wore, his skin would be smooth and warm, and infinitely seductive.

"I am Kian."

"Mercy," she replied. Swallowing hard, she forced her gaze away from him. She was being too bold in her perusal, but she could not stop looking at him.

"Kindness," he whispered. Their eyes locked, and Mercy felt a jolt of some foreign, but not unwelcome, sensation pierce her. "I could use some of you," he said thoughtfully as his cool gaze devoured her. "Most definitely I could use you."

He rose and walked around the pond, perusing her body as he came to stand beside her. "The milk of human kindness, how sweet the taste."

He actually licked his lips and Mercy shivered, her core heating and wetting. Then he lowered himself until they were eye to eye.

"I believe I could drink you dry."

Her heart was beating too fast. She couldn't catch her breath. And when his hand came out and his fingers trailed along her cheek, she closed her eyes, marveling at the sensations his touch induced.

"Look upon me," he whispered, and she did, allowing her lashes to flutter and her eyelids to slowly open. "The water doesn't lie. I am your future. Your destiny lies with me."

She nodded, blindly accepting his words. She could hardly process what he was saying. All she could think of was how astonishingly perfect he was. No man could be this beautiful, this sensual and engaging. As she looked deeply into his eyes, she knew him for what he was.

A fey. An Unseelie. A creature of darkness whose intrinsic ability to seduce and entice called to any woman who crossed their path. If his looks were not enough to disclose what he was, his words were. So darkly direct and erotic. She knew what he had meant by drinking her dry, and suddenly she felt like offering herself up to him.

"Mercy." He murmured her name like a caress as it whispered against her ear. "I shall show you none as I pursue you. I will spare none to any of your other suitors. I *will* possess you."

She swallowed hard, and his finger left her cheek, only to trail down the column of her throat.

"You know what I am. I can see it in your eyes."

"I do. That is, I know."

"And do you fear it? Fear me?"

"No." Her answer had been quick and utterly truthful. All her life she had been told stories of the fey. She had been fascinated by them, by their power and their beauty. But nothing had captivated her fancy like the Unseelie. She'd always wanted to see one. To gaze into their eyes knowing what sort of sensual creatures they were purported to be. And she was elated to discover that none of it had been exaggerated. For the fey who stood before her was not only beautiful but dangerous, as well. There was a barely controlled darkness about him. She felt it. It seethed from him. Yet his touch was gentle.

"Let me in," he whispered, "and I vow to show you

pleasure you could never dream of. Come to my world, and you will never want for anything."

"And what will I have to trade for this...gift?" She knew no faery gift came free. There was always a tithe to be paid.

"You will leave this world and come to mine."

"I cannot," she replied. "To live in your world is to give up my life. My family. My sisters. I cannot, for one night of forbidden pleasures, toss away everything. I thank you for the offer."

"One night?" His grin was slow and sensual. Heart-stopping. "Oh, no, I will show you no clemency in that, either. I will have you over and over, until the nights melt with the days and you are no longer cognizant of time or place. You will know only me. The pleasure of our bed. The hours of endless ecstasy."

Said like that, how could she resist? But one glance at Prue charging across the grass, preparing to defend her honor, was all it took. "You will only take from me, leaving me an empty husk. Your pleasure comes with a price that is too steep for me to pay."

His blue eyes turned to a most astonishing shade of green. The color of jade. "We're not done, Mercy Lennox. No, indeed, your path with me has just begun."

Mercy watched as he stepped back. Shadow engulfed him, and she saw how he stared at her. She shivered. He was far too dangerous. She could never manage him. The thought thrilled yet frightened her.

"We will meet again," he said, "and when we do, I

will show you no leniency. No kindness. Only a single-minded pursuit. I *will* have you."

Mercy hoped with everything in her heart that this particular fey was true to his word. She was already thinking of the next time their paths would cross.

Chastity strolled along the manicured paths of Lady Sefton's perennial beds, fanning herself against the heat of the afternoon sun. She had left her bonnet on the bench, and now regretted it. The sun was much too bright. She could feel the warm beams on her face. Mama would be livid with her if she allowed herself to burn. It was gauche to have tanned skin. Pale and flawless was the mark of exceptional beauty.

She should go back and retrieve it, but she had no wish to leave the path or to make idle conversation. So, instead, she strolled on, enjoying her solitude.

The garden was hot and sticky, the paths full of elegantly dressed couples—the cream of London society, all turned out for the Seftons' annual garden party. The scent of roses and lavender assailed her senses, and she stopped to inhale the heady fragrance of a blush-pink damask rose. Smoothing her finger over the velvety petals, Chastity flushed, remembering her fantasy of Thane, and the way his fingertips had felt very much like the petals, soft and velvety, as they brushed her skin.

Chastity shivered despite the warmth of the air. She'd acted wanton last night—more than wanton, she'd been sinful. What had provoked her to feel herself in such a manner, and to fantasize that it had been Thane's hands

touching her and not her own? She still couldn't fathom what had made her do it.

Feeling restless and just a touch unsteady, Chastity slipped behind an enormous oak tree, resting against its cool, rough trunk. Why was it that Thane was the only man to arouse her thus? What was it about his wickedness that called to her carefully suppressed wantonness? Closing her eyes, Chastity let herself relive those moments in her bedroom. She had wanted more. Was prepared to think of the whole thing. But how could an innocent such as she be so in tune with her body? How could she dream of something she had never experienced? she wondered, continuing to fan herself, letting her fingertips graze the exposed skin of her breasts.

The sound of gravel crunching alerted Chastity that the couples were making their way back to the lawn for tea and cakes. Relieved to be truly alone at last, Chastity let her fingers move the air before her, cooling her neck and bosom.

A twig snapped, and her eyes flew open, greeting the dark blue eyes of Thane.

"Sir," she huffed, blushing furiously, her skin instantly aflame·with prickles of heat, of awareness.

"Good afternoon, Miss Lennox."

Her body came alive at the sound of his voice. And the scent that suddenly surrounded them. It seemed to follow them wherever he went, and it had the strangest effect upon her. Thane... She was at once elated and dismayed by his appearance.

"Are you enjoying yourself?"

She flushed. Had he seen the way she had allowed her fingertips to caress the swells of her breasts? Could he read her thoughts—the thoughts she had been having about him? She was mortified by the very idea.

"Chastity?"

"Sir?" she whispered, unable to meet his gaze.

"Are you enjoying the party?"

"Oh. Yes," she said, blathering on like a simpleton. "It's very lovely, but then Lord and Lady Sefton's gardens are renowned for their beauty."

"And their frivolity," he replied.

She could not answer that. It was far too bold. Even though Chastity knew there were many shenanigans that went on in the gardens during the annual party.

"How are you acquainted with the Seftons?" she asked.

"Old friends. And you?"

"Oh, my parents and brother are close friends. I've never actually been to their party, this year is the first, but I've lived vicariously through my brother's reports in his letters home."

"And why have you never been?" he asked, taking a step closer to her.

"My sisters and I are content to stay in Glastonbury. This is our first time in London in well over a decade."

"Content," he repeated, his voice dropping to a purr. His exotic accent made her light-headed. She was acting like a silly green girl, but she could not help it. He affected her that much.

"Are you really? Content that is."

She felt herself bristle at his thinly veiled assumption that she was anything but. "Of course," she said haughtily.

"Forgive me if I spoke out of turn. But you must allow me my opinion. And my belief is, you're the furthest thing from satisfied. You yearn for something other than this life you're leading."

"I am very contented, sir."

"Are you? Really?"

She nodded and took a step back. He was closing in on her, and she felt cornered. Afraid of her response, which was not fear, but an overwhelming desire. This man did not think angelic when he looked at her. He would not put her on a pedestal and worship her like a sainted female. He would demand more of her. Would make her look deeply inside. Would force her to accept what she found there. He had the courage to see all of her, not just the virtuous wrapping that everyone else saw.

"Why are you here, all alone?"

"I do not mind the solitude."

"You hide from yourself."

She flinched as he touched her. It was only a slight grazing of his fingertips against her cheek, but the intimacy shocked her. The response from her body startled her.

"You've never been touched," he murmured. He took another step to her. They were now toe-to-toe. Her back was still pressed against the trunk of the tree, and Thane's tall body blocked out the small amount of sunlight that filtered through the leaves. His fingertips found her cheek again, but this time, he bent his head and softly inhaled the patch of skin behind her ear. Tilting his head, he moved lower, to the skin on her neck, where her pulse throbbed. He inhaled... She heard the soft intake of air. It was followed by the delicate brush of his fingers. Then his mouth was moving lower, to the place where her breasts where pushed together and up. To the décolletage that was above her tight-fitting bodice. He inhaled there. A deep, masculine purr broke the silence.

"The perfume is so right for you. I can imagine you seated at your dressing table, anointing this perfect flesh with it."

Oh, God, could he see inside her mind? Did he see that she had dreamed of him touching her?

"I want to touch you," he murmured, as if indeed, he could hear her thoughts. "You must know that. You must sense how much I want that."

She did. She wanted it, too. But she couldn't give in. But the way his breath caressed her skin, moistening it, the way his lips were just a hairbreadth from kissing her breasts, made her weak. Her resolve was slipping.

"Sir, you mustn't," she said on a hiss as he trailed his fingertips along the tops of her breasts. His tongue came out then, licking the skin as it pressed against the edge of her bodice. She gasped, and pressed herself farther against the tree.

"Why mustn't I?" he asked as his large palms circled her ribs, then moved slowly upward till he was cupping her in his hands. "You want me to. Do not deny it."

She tried to, but her moan made any protest seem utterly ridiculous. So she used another tack to rebuff him.
"You promised you would leave me be."

"No," he said darkly as he lowered his mouth to the
quivering mound of her breast. "I told you I would leave
you in peace. Which I will."

Pulling at the bodice, he lowered it an inch, the pale
flesh spilling out from behind her corset and the tight
stomacher. His mouth moved to the spot where he began
to draw the swell of her breast into his mouth. He sucked,
the sensation going straight to the tips of her breasts and
her womb.

He sucked harder, bit down, then soothed the little
sting with a slow glide of his tongue.

"I can smell your desire. Taste it."

She shook her head, denying his words, but he bit
down teasingly, making her draw in a sharp breath. Chastity's lips parted on a silent breath as he traced his fingers
along the edge of her bodice, and then boldly slid his
fingertips up between her breasts. Her breathing became
rapid, her breasts were heaving, begging to be freed from
the confines of her bodice.

She had never taken any pleasure in her breasts
before. Yet now she was acutely aware of them. How
sensitive they were. How they made her feel exquisitely
feminine.

As if aware of her torture, Thane pulled one sleeve of
her sky-blue muslin gown along her shoulder, revealing
her plain white stays. The crest of her breast was bruised
and he circled the mark with the tip of his finger, his

eyes darkening to near black as he focused on his brand. Then he reached for her, and tugged at the corset till her breast sprang free, and she was mortified by it, the white skin stark in the daylight. Her nipple long, pointed, arching up to his mouth. He stared at her, and she closed her eyes, cringing in her embarrassment and, dare she admit, longing.

Without a sound he circled her nipple with his thumb. Her eyes flew open, and she saw his gaze searching her face. Chastity felt a disconcerting urge to shut her eyes against his experienced gaze, but somehow she knew he didn't want that. He wanted to see the desire in her eyes, to see what effect he was having on her. And she wanted to give him this.

He traced the underside of her breast, his finger softly and almost imperceptibly grazed her skin, swelling her breast further, making her thrust forward in order to feel more of his hand against her. Finally, he tore his eyes from hers and stared at her erect nipple. Chastity stiffened as he went to his knees. Wetness pooled between her thighs, waiting for him to touch her—with his hands, his mouth, with whatever he would. Expertly he slipped the taut pink tip between his lips.

"Thane," she whimpered, her hands fisting in the folds of her skirts. She dare not touch him. He pulled away, and with one last longing look at her, he lifted his gaze to her face. Capturing her cheeks in his palms, he lowered his mouth to hers, kissing her softly. It was a kiss that lured, coaxed. She had no knowledge of how to return it, but Thane didn't seem to care.

He showed her, with his mouth, how it slanted over hers. His tongue swept against her lips, and she mewled shamelessly in his arms. Then he opened her mouth, slid his tongue inside and devoured her.

He was holding her, thank heavens, because she could barely feel her knees. She was floating. And when Thane moved his palm down her chest to cup and squeeze her breasts, she wrapped her sinful body around his, forgetting who she was.

Tugging at her nipple, he tweaked it, soothed it, and she gasped, cried out as he left her mouth and pulled her other breast free of her stays. She was bared to him, reminding her of how she had been that night in the maze with the stranger who could only be a Dark Fey.

Sliding his body along hers, Thane clutched her breasts, pressed them together and brushed his face along them. Her back arched and she moaned, the sound so wanton. He sucked her hard and, unable to resist, Chastity fisted her hands through his hair, holding him to her as he ate her.

Oh, God, she had never felt anything so exquisite. She had no idea how much pleasure she could take in having her breasts played with. How responsive they could be—how sexual.

Abruptly, she was bereft of his mouth and hands. "Someone comes." Deftly he helped her right herself as she stood lost in a mass of confusion and longing. When she was presentable, he clutched her face and kissed her hard.

"You might believe this is all about seduction, but it

is not. I want you—all of you. I want to be inside you. To learn you. But I also want to sit in the quiet and talk with you. Laugh with you. I want to lie in bed at night and feel you against me, listen to you breathe, glide my hands through your hair and watch you sleep. I want years of growing old with you and thousands of nights beneath the moonlight. You must sense that there is more here than simple pleasure. Believe it."

He pulled away, and she reached for him, fearing to be left alone.

"We will meet again—soon."

And then he was gone. Leaving Chastity alone, shaking and anything but in peace.

ELEVEN

Oh, Diary, until I saw him again, I didn't realize how much I needed to see him. He makes me feel alive, womanly. Makes me forget what I am, who I ought to be.

I thought I wanted him far away, but now I know that I want nothing more than to have him at my side. To be alone with him. I want what he can give. Pleasure. But there is more there. There is a yearning for friendship. Courtship.

For the first time ever, I yearn to see a man. I long to have my dreams come true.

Thane is that man. The one to awaken me. I would risk anything to be with him. The virtue inside me screams in outrage, but I will not listen. My path is with Thane. I sense that. I will go to him in the garden and discover what it is to be touched and loved. My lover awaits me.

RUBBING HER HANDS DOWN HER ARMS, CHASTITY walked away from the stone wall that was draped in ivy.

She had come to the garden promptly upon her return from the Seftons'. Driven to this place, she could not understand the call, nor could she comprehend why the gate, which had opened before, now would not. Perhaps it hadn't really. Maybe it was just another dream, a fantastical memory that had never really taken place. She had been having many of those lately. But that afternoon in the Seftons' garden had not been a dream, or a fantasy. It had been real.

As if to confirm the fact, her finger brushed against the skin of her bosom. She had seen Thane's mark, the one that had been left by his mouth. She could still feel the silk of his hair running between her fingers, the heat of his breath, the press of his body against hers.

It had been impassioned. Madness. Addicting.

"What are you doing out here?" her father asked, pulling her out of her musings. He was standing behind her, his hands fisted on his hips. His expression was one of concern. "You're supposed to be napping before the masquerade tonight."

"I was not sleepy," she replied, shrugging gently. She saw his gaze pass over her shoulder to the patch of ivy that had been disturbed. Did Papa know of the gate? When his eyes narrowed, then turned on her, she suspected he did indeed know of it.

"The point of lying down," he said, "is to restore your energy for the dancing. It doesn't matter if you are tired or not. You're supposed to be resting."

She wasn't a three-year-old. She did not require naps to put her in good humor. Besides, her mind was restless, unable to stop focusing on the events with Thane. Her body was also agitated. It craved more. Needed more.

"Off you go." The order was followed by a wave of his hand. "And mind that you do not come out here alone again."

She stopped, turned back to look at him. "Why, Papa?"

"It's not safe."

Her father was not himself. She saw it in his eyes. Suspicion. Fear. His body was tense, and she could see the way his jaw tightened as he surveyed the grounds.

"What is it, Papa? I know something is worrying you."

When he looked at her, Chastity saw just how affected he truly was. "Do you recall my stories of the faery queen?" he asked quietly.

"Of course."

"Do you believe them, or do you think I only made them up to entertain you and your sisters?"

Stepping closer to him, she touched his arm, offering him comfort. "I believe, Papa. I've always believed."

"Good." He nodded and gazed up at the horizon. "The fey are very real, my dear. Very real."

"And they are here, are they not?"

He turned swiftly and clutched her by her elbows. "Have they come to you?"

"You know they have. Crom and Arawn are fey. You cannot hide that fact from us. We knew, almost immediately."

His hold loosened and he pressed his eyes shut. "Aye. They're fey."

"And they're here for us, are they not? To take us away to their court?"

Her father hugged her tightly. "The faery queen demands it. But I've a meeting with her on the morrow, and I will bargain with her. I'll not see my daughters wed to any fey."

Fear suddenly gripped her. "What did she gift you with, Papa?"

His fingers wrapped around her shoulders and he pressed her close, kissing her temple. "That is not for you to worry about."

"And the fey, should I worry about them?"

He smiled. "No. You should not. I can manage them. After my meeting, I will call you and your sisters to my study and discuss matters with you. But for now, I would ask that you keep this to yourself. There is no need to worry your sisters—or yourself. No one will be leaving this house."

"Mama?" she asked, swallowing hard. The color drained from her father's face, and Chastity knew that her mother had no knowledge.

"Your mother..." he began, "she doesn't know. Doesn't believe."

"Papa," Chastity whispered as she reached for his sleeve. "What will you tell your wife when her daughters are taken by the fey?"

"You won't be, by God," he thundered. "I'll offer the queen something else. Anything else. But I swear to you,

I'll not let you go. Not one of you. Now then," her father grumbled as he kissed her cheek. "Off you go. There is naught to worry about."

Chastity was reluctant to leave. There was more to this than her father was sharing. If only he would allow them in. If he would share what he knew of what would become of them. But his expression was resolute, and she knew that no amount of pleading would make him change his mind. He was intent on keeping them ignorant, and confusion swept through her that he could be so blasé about it. This was her future, her sisters' as well, and their father was intent on shielding them from it. They would have to live it, would have to discover it on their own, and silently she fumed at the injustice of it. Females really were just the chattel of men.

And the fey? As Chastity left her father standing in the garden, she knew he could not manage anything about them, or their world. The fey were powerful. Much more than mere mortals. If her father had accepted a gift from their queen, then he was obligated to pay the tithe. That was basic faery lore. The fey did not give their gifts away for free.

And if she and her sisters were the tithe, then there was no help for them. They would belong to the fey. Would be taken to Faery. The only question remained was which court. The Seelie or the Unseelie?

Taking the side entrance, Chastity climbed the back staircase that led to her chamber. She was lost in thought and worry, and did not hear the door beside her groan on its hinges.

"In here."

Someone grabbed her arm and dragged her into a room. She glared at her sister. "Mercy, for heaven's sake, you frightened me half to death."

"Shh, keep your voice down. Mother thinks we're napping."

"And why aren't you?"

Mercy snorted. "I could ask the same of you."

"What is it you want?"

"I saw one. Today. At the Seftons' pond."

"Saw what?"

Mercy pressed in and lowered her voice. "A Dark Fey."

Chastity reeled back. "No!"

Mercy shook her and pulled her deeper into the room. "He was the most beautiful creature I ever saw. Even more so than the Seelie Fey who have come to call on you and Prue."

"What did he want?"

Mercy's light blue eyes widened. "Me."

"Oh, dear God," Chastity whispered. This was a nightmare. Papa should be informed. What would he do if both courts desired them? Suddenly she felt ill with the thought that perhaps her father had made bargains with both courts.

But would he do that? She had always thought her father honorable and upright. His life wanted nothing. What could he possibly desire that he did not already possess?

"He said he was coming for me," Mercy babbled

excitedly. "Oh, Chastity, I could barely breathe. The Dark Fey...well..." Mercy nervously licked her lips. "They've long since captivated me."

"Their attentions are not honorable. You know that," she said. Was Thane a Dark Fey, too? Strange how the thought was not shocking to her. Part of her had known all along that he was otherworldly. That erotic, compelling scent seemed to follow him wherever he went, and the way the light seemed to glow around him, made her think of glimmering mist crystals.

"Chastity?" Mercy asked, pulling her from her thoughts. "Have you seen one also?"

"No," she lied. She was not ready for her sister to know about Thane.

"He said he would come for me," Mercy said. "Do you think it will be tonight, at the masquerade?"

"You must take every care," she cautioned her sister. "These Dark Fey are most dangerous. You cannot give yourself up to them. You simply cannot, Mercy."

"You're right, of course. It's just that, well, it was rather thrilling to have someone so...intent."

"You're too kind, Mercy. You put too much faith in people's goodness."

"I won't underestimate him."

Chastity followed Mercy from the room in time to see her sister leave via the servants' stairs. Running to the window, she waited until she saw Mercy exit the house. Crossing the lawn, her sister paused by the fountain and peered into its clear depths. A shadow of cloud covered her sister's back, and all Chastity could think of was how she had seen that particular shadow twice that day.

Kian allowed his shadowed form to engulf his virtue. Mercy, the embodiment of kindness, was bent over, gazing into the crystal waters of a fountain. Was she looking for her mystery man? he wondered. Would she wait there patiently until he showed himself?

Above her, he allowed himself to study her form. She was not normally the type he was drawn to. Envy was his sin. He was naturally drawn to the more experienced type of woman who enjoyed the darker aspects of passion. He needed that to assuage his sin, and give himself respite from the aching pain that Envy tortured him with. But there was something in Mercy that the Unseelie male in him liked. Perhaps it was her kindness. Maybe it was the fact that she was pretty, with her blond hair and blue eyes. Or maybe it was her luscious figure that aroused him. She certainly had an abundance of charms in that regard. In fact, all four of the Lennox sisters were blessed with bodies designed to incite every possible sin.

Maybe it was just the simple fact that she was his. His to possess and claim. His to take to his court. His to hide from the prying eyes of others.

He thought of hiding her away, and Envy seemed to shrink back. He thought of her with another, like the Seelie bastards that had been hovering around her and her sisters at the garden party, and Envy reared its head, making his body shake.

He did not like himself when his sin was loose. He

was cruel. Overbearing. Jealousy caused him to do many foolish things. He could not bear to think of himself hurting this innocent lamb.

"Kian."

He heard his name, whispered in her voice, and his sin slowly retreated, allowing him to see her through his own eyes and not the green haze of envy.

Slowly he regained his form and, coming behind her, he peered over her shoulder. She gasped and whirled around when she saw his reflection in the water peering back at her.

"How did you find me?"

He touched her cheek, caught the loose curls that blew in the breeze. "I could find you anywhere."

She smiled, a fine blush crested against her cheek. If she had been any other woman, he would have caught her up in his arms and carried her to a private place where he could lay her out and feast on her.

From within the house, he heard the pounding of feet. His acute hearing sensed that he'd tripped the wards that the Seelie had set for his kind. He would stay and fight, if he could. At least now he knew where the wards were weak. They were strongest closest to the house. The gardens, while protected, were weaker, allowing him a few minutes with his virtue.

"I must go."

"Don't."

He reached for her and brought her body up tight against his. A possessive warmth invaded his blood and he caught her lips hard with his. She didn't know how to kiss, and the fact strangely pleased.

"Where will you be tonight?"

"At a masquerade. The Carmichaels' in Berkeley Square."

He kissed her again, just as the Seelie were about to open the door. "Expect me."

And then he was gone, turning to shadow. He watched Mercy's face break into a smile just as the Seelie guards, posing as footmen, burst out the door.

"I will wait for you," she whispered.

Rising from the bath, Chastity took the toweling from her maid. Refusing Annie's help, Chastity dried her body.

Inexplicably she wanted Annie to leave. Why, she didn't know.

"That will be all."

"Miss?" Annie asked, perplexed.

"I would like a few minutes alone, please. I will call when I am ready for you."

Chastity could see that her maid wished to inquire further, but she did not. With a little bob, Annie left her alone.

The door clicked shut, and Chastity dropped the toweling and walked to a chair that sat in the corner of the room, then dragged it across the width of the chamber.

Beside her was the dressing table, and atop the mirrored tray was the blue-and-gold atomizer that she had not been able to stop gazing upon. It was as if it had a life of its own, speaking to her through the clear fluid it housed. It made her think strange thoughts. Do strange things...

Reaching for the bottle, she held it in her palm, feeling how warm it was in her hand. Had the fire warmed it? Was the source of heat from the perfume itself?

Look upon yourself.

Naked, Chastity lowered herself onto the chair before the full-length looking glass. She had never gazed at her unclothed body, but something—or someone—had whispered the thought into her head.

Unable to stop her body, she found herself seated, the image staring back at her so foreign, yet evocative. She could not look away, nor ignore the warmth in her palm where the perfume bottle rested.

Cover your body with me. It was that voice again, the voice that sent fluttering in her belly. The voice she could not deny. Thane.

Please, it begged.

Pulling the glass stopper from the bottle, Chastity dipped the pointed crystal into the clear liquid and inhaled the scent. It seemed to change from day to day, one time smelling of delicate florals and other times spicy. Tonight in particular it was a heady mixture of jasmine, neroli and rose, heated with the masculine scents of amber, musk and myrrh. It was a seductive concoction, sedative, yet arousing.

Inhaling the scent, Chastity felt herself grow languid, her mind a pleasant haze, while she felt her body waken.

Of its own volition her hand moved to her throat where the wet crystal tip kissed her skin. Her hand was shaking, and she watched a teardrop of liquid fall from the stopper and splash against the curve of her breast, only to trickle down over the peak—the same breast that bore the mark from Thane's mouth.

Capturing the drop back onto the tip, Chastity watched as she slowly circled the outline of her pink areola, remembering the way Thane had touched her. The pleasure was unimaginable as she watched her own hand against her skin, the pale areola and nipple glistening wet as the perfume coated her skin.

Like that of a lover's tongue...

The image came to her unbidden, a startling vision that was somehow pulled out of the place where she had so carefully and deeply buried it. She blinked through the haze of sensuality that bathed her. The image remained the same. Thane was standing behind her, the black-haired stranger from the maze. He wore the same gold-wired mask as he had that night in the maze, but this time, he was dressed only in black britches and a white linen shirt that was opened, revealing part of his chest. Stepping close to her, he wrapped his long fingers around her chair, letting the lace from the cuff of his shirtsleeve caress her bare shoulder.

Tilting her head back, Chastity closed her eyes and savored the feel of his lips brushing the tender skin beneath her ear. His breath was warm against her, making her shiver. His lips, so strong and masculine, yet supple, felt like a whisper of a rose petal gliding against her. And his scent... Dear God, that scent. It was a powerful elixir. All male and dark and mysterious. Chastity secretly took in his essence. Frankincense and amber, that deeply masculine scent of secrecy and the exotic. He had smelled the same that night in the maze, and its effects on her now were no less than it had been then.

She had the irrational urge to cloak herself with his body, mixing his scent with hers. She was utterly intoxicated by the aromas surrounding her and the sight of his dark head moving languidly down her shoulder.

One hand had left the back of the chair and now rested on her shoulder. His cuff covered her breast, but she could feel the sensitizing scrape of the lace against her nipple, which beaded with every brush of fabric.

He nipped her neck, then her collarbone as his hand on her shoulder steadied her. Bent over her as he was, she felt cocooned in his beauty and the heavy cloud of sensuality that shimmered around her.

Her gaze caught the reflection of the mirror, and she was struck mute by the erotic image of herself naked on the chair, with this stranger fully dressed behind her.

His hand on her shoulder was strong, manly, contrasting in a pleasing dichotomy against the thick lace cuff that lingered over her breast. The gold of his mask glittered against the paleness of her skin and the brief glimpse of his mouth against her upper arm, which was so perilously close to her breast, made her unable to take her gaze away from the mirror and the debauchery that was taking place in its reflection.

"Not debauchery," he whispered against her as his hand

squeezed her shoulder before sliding slowly over to her throat, "but seduction."

How her body responded to his voice. That one word and the passion and the wickedness she heard in it. Seduction...

Her fingers reached for his mask, and he allowed her to pull it free. His lids opened, revealing brilliant blue eyes, and a face that was so beautiful. A face that was becoming everything to her.

"Thane," she whispered.

He smiled, and gently took the perfume stopper from her hand and trailed it across her breast, lingering briefly before flicking at her nipple. She gasped, and he steadied her, his mouth now so close to hers.

"Shh," he murmured as he flicked her nipple against the stopper's cool tip. "We wouldn't want anyone to hear your cries and find you in this position, would we?"

Their gazes met in the mirror and she saw the wicked gleam in his vibrant blue eyes.

"I'm dreaming."

"If you'd like to believe that."

"Even in my dreams I cannot fully shed this mantle of virtue." Embarrassment suddenly pushed through the heavy cloud of lust that fogged her mind, but he wrapped an arm around her waist, keeping her in the chair.

"You blush, not with arousal, but shame. There is no shame in desire, Chastity. The only shame is in denying yourself of the pleasure, and me the rapture of watching you come."

Her body ignited with his words, and again he touched

her, not with his hands, but with the tip of the perfume stopper. Seeing his intent, Chastity tried to move, to put an end to this strange daydream, but he refused to let her go and instead moved his hand lower, down between the valley of her breasts to her belly where he circled her navel. Mortified, Chastity watched as her thighs spread of their own accord, revealing everything to him.

He purred his encouragement, "Yes, like that." His scent was once again wrapping around her, making her thoughts and body heavy. When he trailed his tongue along her throat, in time to the downward scrape of crystal, she writhed, lifting her hips in wanton invitation.

"Put your legs over the arm of the chair."

Oh, she couldn't. But she was obeying him even as she fought his command. "You've enchanted me."

"Perhaps," he whispered. His gaze strayed to the mirror. He studied her, how open she was. He watched his hand descend lower. Moving in and rubbing through her curls in a slow, circular motion. His fingers, which had been brushing the side of her breast, now cupped it. His head bent farther over her as he lifted her breast to his lowering mouth.

"No!" she gasped and squirmed simultaneously as his hot tongue laved her nipple and the cool crystal parted her sex.

This was wrong. So very immoral that she should be taking pleasure in this. But ooh, how good it felt as he took her nipple between his lips and tugged, suckling her. Between her thighs, his hand moved down, then up, stroking and parting the glistening folds of her sex, not with the pointed tip of the stopper, but with the rounded, bulbous head.

She was shaking now, needing to cry out, not in fear or shock, but with passion that was building, with the burning between her thighs that needed a release of some sort.

She could not stop watching his slow seduction of her body. It was an erotic thing to witness, and she spread her legs wider, encouraged by his animal-like growl. He bit down on her nipple as he slipped the rounded crystal inside her. Her moan filled the room and she watched as she raised her bottom off the chair, angling her hips upward, encouraging him to do more. To go deeper.

"Innocent, virtuous Chastity," he whispered as he watched with her in the mirror, "would you give it to me, your most prized possession?"

She knew what he wanted, but she could not agree to it, not when he was no longer inside her. He was teasing her, going back to those light, inflaming caresses. The strokes that merely fanned the flames, not banked them.

"More," she whispered, her gaze at last meeting his. He watched her and she felt that hungry gaze devour her. "Please," she begged.

Reaching between her thighs, she clutched at his wrist, pushing his hand more firmly between her splayed legs. Her back was arched, and her nipples peaked as her heavy breasts swayed to the rhythm of her hips. A rhythm so primitive and natural that Chastity had not been able to fight the instinctive urge.

Faster her hips worked as she rubbed herself against his hand and the cold crystal. He was watching her face, reaching for her breast as she arched. Her lips parted, a scream so close to the surface, but he captured them with his mouth, slipping his tongue inside to touch hers. Reaching an arm up behind her, she clutched at his shirt, fisting the fabric in her hand as the pressure in her womb built higher and higher. It was almost pain, this bursting sensation. She didn't know what to do, how to find it, but then she heard his words—"Let it come to you"—and she understood, slowed her frantic hips, allowing herself to be guided by his rhythm. And oh, God, it was bliss.

Her breathing became short, rasping pants, and she released his shirt, only to run her fingers through his hair. His scent washed over her and she cried out, coming apart then as she continued to press down against his hand.

She couldn't breathe, couldn't stop moving. He pleasured her until she thought she would die, until she was shaking, completely unashamed that she was naked and exposed before a mirror. He whispered to her, words she could not understand. She only understood the need to keep going. To feel more of him. It was unthinkable that she, a heavenly virtue, could know that there was more to this. How did she know that beneath his britches he would be hard and throbbing? That having him thrust deep inside her would give her the relief she sought?

"I want more," she whispered, tugging him closer.

"So do I, love," he whispered back. "But not yet."

"Please," she implored, and she saw how his eyes darkened.

"Do not beg me. I…cannot resist that."

"Then don't. Don't end this. Not now when I need to feel you deep inside me."

Swiftly his warmth was gone, leaving her chilled. His scent, which drove her to the brink of sexual madness, was replaced by the languid, haunting scent of her perfume. She came to, dazed, aghast at what she saw in the mirror.

A flush of pink skin marred her cheeks and throat. The tops of her breasts, too. She was spread out, her sex shimmering, her curls wet. Her left arm was bent over her head, her fingers clutching the back of the dressing table chair. Between her thighs, her other hand was hidden, and inside her…the crystal bottle stopper.

With a shriek, she pulled it out and flung the crystal onto the carpet. Whatever had possessed her to…defile herself in such a fashion, and to…to dream of *him* as she did so?

Racing to her bed, she covered herself in her dressing gown, hiding her shame. What had possessed her? She had not been able to resist the lure. And yet, it had been a dream. No. She had been awake, but in some altered state. A fantasy. Yes. That was what it had been.

Even now her entire body trembled. She wanted more, despite knowing it was wrong and sinful. But she couldn't lie to herself. She needed more, more of the dark pleasures he had shown her. Could one become a habitué of such dark erotic arts? Was that it? Had he bewitched her when he'd touched her in the garden?

For that is when she had begun to yearn and dream.

Begun to want the very thing that was opposite to her in every way. Thane. There was no denying that her subconscious knew who—what—he was. He was a Dark Fey, with a very skilled hand and mouth.

Casting a glance in the mirror, she allowed herself to recall what she had seen in the mirror. She did not hide from the memory, but embraced it. Tonight, she was a changed woman, for tonight, she'd craved the opposite of her entire being. Tonight, she had craved Lust.

Twelve

THE CLACKING OF THE HORSES HOOVES ALONG the cobbles echoed through the quiet Mayfair streets. Normally at this time of night, the streets were bustling with carriages, conveying the elite to balls and soirees and musicales. It was strange for it to be so quiet—sparse. In fact, Chastity knew that there were at least four balls going on this evening, for they had received invitations to all of them. Yet one peek out the carriage window would deem otherwise. It was utterly silent. Eerily so.

Glancing up at the black velvet sky, she noticed the moon, which was waxing in fullness and slowly being obstructed by a series of inky-black clouds. Soon what little light the lanterns afforded the street would be dimmed as the moonlight was all but blocked. Chastity shivered. She would not want to be caught on these streets in the forbidden darkness. Even if it was Mayfair. Suddenly she longed for the safe and subdued evenings she and her sisters had enjoyed in Glastonbury. There was something not quite right about this night. The awareness of that thought prickled her skin and raced down her spine. *Unnatural* was the word that consistently flickered through her thoughts.

The carriage swayed and the rhythmic motion lulled her, attempted to soothe her still-frazzled nerves as she watched the cloud cover the moon. She had still not been able to remove the image that had greeted her in the mirror earlier this evening. Even when she opened her eyes to see herself dressed in her costume for the masquerade she did not see the water nymph she was supposed to represent. Rather, she saw her body naked, spread, and the crystal stopper buried inside her.

Her face flamed hot, and she was glad of the dark shadows outside that shielded her shame from her family. What madness had overtaken her? What had possessed her to do such a thing? *Unnatural...*

Again she heard the whispered word, and in response clutched her reticule even tighter in her gloved hands. In the darkness outside, a thick vapor of fog suddenly rolled in, rising and falling like a current of air, thickening, then thinning, growing opaque and smokelike, resembling tendrils of incense, then solid, impenetrable, consuming.

"Damn strange fog," her father growled. "I detest coming to London because of it."

Prue and Mercy gazed out their windows as Chastity caught the worried look in her father's eyes. Mary and their mother had taken the carriage ahead of them. The

Carmichaels were old friends of her mother, and Mary had wanted to arrive early to lend them support in any way she could. Her father despised masquerades and desired to leave later. As Mary loved balls, and the three of them felt like misfits at them, they had naturally agreed to accompany their father.

"It's quite mesmerizing, isn't it?" Mercy whispered as she peered intently out the window. "Almost like a living thing, the way it moves and shifts its shape."

"You've been reading too many Minerva novels, Mercy," Prue admonished. "They've filled your head with nonsense."

Casting another glance out the window, Chastity wasn't so certain that Prue was correct. The fog did seem to take on a form all its own. And what was even more perplexing was that it seemed to shroud their carriage—and nothing else.

"Why are we turning?" Prue asked, alarm in her voice. "The streetlights are gone, and the road is narrowing. This is not the way to Berkeley Square and the Carmichaels'."

Their father grumbled and reached for his walking stick, which he rapped forcefully against the roof. "You there," he yelled at the coachman. "You've taken a wrong turn."

But the carriage did not stop, and when their father stood up to open the door, he found it quite firmly shut. Any attempt to open it was futile.

"Papa," Prue gasped as she reached for Mercy. "What is going on?"

"The damn coachman is drunk," he roared. "And he's taking us east."

The east end of London held nothing but beggars, whores and thieves—and cutthroats, her father had always told them. Obviously her sisters recalled the same thing, for they gasped and held on to each other.

The carriage continued, picking up speed, and outside, the fog followed, thickening, engulfing the carriage until all they could see was the fog through the windows. Not even the fading yellow of lanterns could be made out through the dense curtain of gray.

Sharply the carriage tilted to the left and turned, coming to an abrupt stop, which made them lurch forward on the bench.

"Wait till I get my bloody hands on him," her father roared as he reached for the handle. But the door opened, nearly sending him tumbling out of the carriage.

"I wait for no man," came the deep voice from the darkness. The fog evaporated and standing in its retreating midst was a giant of a man with dark, shoulder-length hair. His shoulders were as wide as boulders, his legs braced apart as his violet eyes narrowed, piercing her father with a look of hauteur and disgust.

And then he shifted his gaze to the interior of the coach, letting it roam leisurely over Chastity and her sisters. His hand came up, and the words he spoke next were foreign, but so sweetly intoxicating that Chastity could not blink. Could not look away. She was pinned to the bench, as were Prue and Mercy.

"Take them inside, and remember the curse. I will deal with Lennox."

And then, as if she were outside her body, she felt herself lifted, light and airy, as if she were floating, and carried in someone's arms. Not merely anyone's, she thought as she closed her eyes and inhaled the familiar scent. But Thane's.

Oh, God, she was with the Dark Fey. And so were her sisters. And her father...

"Safe," came the whispered voice. "But he cannot take a gift from the fey and not expect to pay."

She swallowed hard, and kept her eyes closed, for she suddenly had no wish to see what lay in her future.

"They haven't arrived, and Lorne, the one planted as lead footman says they left an hour ago."

Crom glared at Arawn. "The streets are riddled with carriages. Is it possible that they are merely stuck in the middle?"

"I sent Lorne to look for them. He hasn't seen their carriage. The mother and the eldest daughter went on ahead. They're here. But Lennox and the other three girls are not."

Purple mist gathered at the corner of his vision as Crom struggled to control the considerable rage that was beginning to storm inside him.

"Check the house, then. Maybe they've retired to a salon where the ladies go to refresh themselves."

"I already have," Arawn growled. "And they are not here."

Crom swore, and two startled matrons gave him wide berth as they walked by holding their demimasks by a long handle. "Where could they have been taken?"

Arawn's blue eyes darkened. "To their court. Where else?"

Crom was nearly snorting in outrage at the thought of Chastity being defiled by an Unseelie pig, and in their court of filth and debauchery at that. The Unseelie would know pain and suffering if they defiled his future mate.

"I can sense that Prudence is…" Arawn closed his eyes, searching for a connection with his intended mate. "She is striving to maintain a semblance of calm, but she's frightened."

"Where is she?" Crom demanded.

"I do not know. I can only sense her emotions. She has not become aware of me—of my powers. She will not understand how to use any link or bond that might be forming between us. It's too soon."

The crystal champagne flute he held in his hand snapped, then shattered into a million shards. It glistened like diamonds against the black marble floor. "I will kill my brother," Crom seethed.

"There is no other way but to go after them."

"Not yet. It is too soon, and we do not yet know if they have a full understanding of the curse. Plus, there is the queen to consider. If we go to their court raising hell, she will become suspicious. She thinks me an ineffectual dilettante. I wish to keep up the facade for as long as possible."

"Surely you are not suggesting that we wait? Your Highness, the Unseelie princes are unscrupulous. They will defile these virtues. Then they will no longer be of any use to us or our court."

"I am well acquainted with the Dark Fey, Arawn," he growled. Gods, his dark blood was trying to take over as they spoke. "What we need is another way."

And then, someone came into view and made him think of a new, very useful plan. Mary, the eldest Lennox girl, flitted nearby, and he watched her, the way she handled her admirers. She flirted like the most experienced little tart, and suddenly he knew. He felt what needed to be done.

"Handle the mother. Find out her husband's plans for this evening. I will take Mary in hand and come up with something that will ensure our suit."

Arawn sent him a sideways glance. "Is that wise, Your Highness? The eldest is not to be trusted."

"All is fair in love and war. Is that not the correct saying, Arawn?"

"Indeed."

"Then I am declaring war."

Stepping over the glass, he made his way to Mary, who was laughing with a group of young men hanging on to her every word. "Good evening," he murmured next to her ear. When she looked up at him, her breath caught and he scented her desire as it perfumed the air. *Excellent,* he mused. She was exactly what he needed.

Prudence glared at the beast who sat like a king behind a table laden with so much food she thought she might have stumbled back in time to the reign of Henry VIII. The wooden trestle table groaned beneath the heavy silver platters that held haunches of beef and venison, as well as a roast suckling pig with an apple in its mouth. Footed bowls spilling over with fruit interspersed the meat platters. Tankards of ale and golden goblets of wine flowed freely, and buxom women flitted about, serving him while they flashed him scandalous expanses of their décolletage.

The man who commanded everyone's attention was huge. An immovable object with wide-set shoulders and thick arms. Even his hands were enormous she noticed as he lifted his gold goblet to his mouth. But his fingers were not thick like those of a laborer, but long and tapered. Elegant. A complete dichotomy for a man of his burly strength and size.

He reminded her of an ancient invader, huge and hulking, using brute strength to send his opponents into submission. He would be a beast of a man if it were not for the mop of black curling hair that fell forward over his eyes. No, that hair was the sort a brooding poet would sport. Something sensual and passionate. No barbarian would have hair like that. *And those lips*. Never had she seen such a sensual mouth. His lips were full, but still masculine. The dusting of black beard, which would look vulgar on any other man, actually made him look all the more appealing.

Good heavens, he was a sensual, wicked beast!

"Look your fill," the creature murmured, his voice as

sweet and rich as syllabub sauce. And his lusty grin when he said it was sinful—and pleasurable.

Prue was certain her face flamed red at the barbarian's insinuation. "I'm sure I don't know what you mean," she replied tartly.

He smiled and drained his goblet. His head was tilted back, exposing the thick cords in his throat, and Prue watched him eagerly drink down the entire contents in one swallow. Never had she seen such a vulgar display. Never had she been so engrossed in the workings of a man's throat and the movement of his Adam's apple.

With a *thunk,* he set the goblet down and shoved his chair back. His legs were spread, and the black leather riding britches he wore were pulled snugly over his massive thighs...and other parts, as well.

Flushing, Prudence glanced away. She could not look at him like that, with his lace jabot untied and lying on either side of his opened shirt. A shirt that was unbuttoned and opened to his waist, exposing a vast amount of dark, male skin, hairless and bronzed.

"Shall you not look, my lady?" he beckoned softly. "I like the feel of your eyes on me."

"Cover yourself, sir," she demanded. "It's most unseemly."

"Ah, the lady is Temperance, indeed," the brute murmured huskily.

Prue stiffened and forced herself to glare at him. "My name is Prudence Lennox and I wish to know what place this is and why we have been brought here."

The barbarian stood and Prue craned her neck to look

up at him. His dark eyes were staring at her, taking in every aspect of her face and figure.

"You're a bit bony, aren't ya?"

She gasped, insulted to her core. "I beg your pardon, sir?"

His insolent gaze raked her one more time from head to toe. "You're not built like your sisters. A pity that. I rather fancied a plump little morsel trying to temper her desires for all things forbidden. I rather enjoyed the luscious visuals of that dichotomy, a voluptuous woman constrained by temperance and restraint, giving in to both." His gaze flicked over her hungrily. "A lovely sight to be sure."

"Now, sir," Mercy said as she came to stand protectively before Prue, "that is most unseemly behavior for a gentleman. A gentleman does not talk about a lady's figure in mixed company. Besides," Mercy said with a coy smile, "my sister prefers tight lacing, that is all."

The brute's eyes lit with something that Prue could only describe as fire. "Does she now? So what's beneath that dress is pressed in and tightened and squished like a sausage?"

"Enough," came a deep voice. From the shadows rose another giant. He had black hair, which he wore long and tied back in a queue. His eyes were a lovely shade of blue, and his voice was deep and rich and accented. One that Prue could not place.

"Kian," Mercy breathed beside her.

"You know this man?" Prue gaped at her sister, but

then she too recalled the man. He had been at the pond that very afternoon during the Seftons' garden party.

"Mercy," he murmured as he strolled out from beneath the shadows and around the table. "I told you to expect me."

"Where are we?" Prue demanded. "And where have you taken my father and Chastity?"

The one name Kian answered. "Your father is with Niall, our…" He paused, sent a look to the barbarian who was still behind the table, before focusing once more on them. "Niall, our leader. Chastity, on the other hand, is somewhere in the building."

"And what is this building?"

"The Nymph and the Satyr," answered the beast. "And it's a bawdy house, for your edification."

This time Prue lost all restraint and shrieked, which made the tall barbarian laugh. Good heavens, a brothel. And those women…she sent a fleeting glance at the women who were now wrapping themselves around the barbarian's big body. They weren't amorous serving girls, they were…whores.

"Shall I ring for a vinaigrette or smelling salts, Lady Prudence," the brute inquired with too much amusement. "You look about ready to faint."

"I am no wilting flower," she sniffed as she straightened her spine. His eyes lit with fire once more.

"I can see that. And I can see a whole lot more when you puff your chest out like that."

"You, sir, are beyond redemption. You're a reprobate."

The beast had the audacity to laugh. He seemed to enjoy her discomfiture. "Before the night is through, lady, you will come to be intimately acquainted with what it truly means to be beyond redemption."

Prue silently fumed, but let his comment go unanswered. She had more important things to think of, and one of them was Mercy, who was sliding her gloved hand into the palm of Kian.

"Come," Kian murmured to Mercy as he enveloped her hand. "Follow me."

"Don't you dare," Prue seethed as she reached for Mercy's wrist. "We're finding Father and getting the blazes out of his house of ill repute."

"You will stay here, if you know what's good for you," Kian said darkly. "There are many out there in the other rooms who would find you enjoyable."

"I will not stay with this...this rude, arrogant... *barbarian*."

Kian shrugged. "Then you may take your chances with the animals out in the salons."

She gasped. Good Lord, what was happening? It was like a nightmare, a never-ending cycle of horror from which she could not wake up.

"Avery will see you safe."

"And well fed," the brute added with a leer.

Prue narrowed her gaze as Kian pulled Mercy close to him. As her sister brushed by, Mercy whispered very quietly, "Do not take any food they offer," and then she was swept away from her, leaving Prue alone with the barbarian.

"Come," he commanded in a gruff voice. But Prue folded her arms over her breasts and held her ground. Her resolve suddenly melted like a cube of sugar in hot tea when the barbarian began to speak. This time his voice was much more compelling and hauntingly beautiful, and she obeyed him despite not understanding a word he said.

Blinking, she found herself standing beside him. He was looking down at her, smiling wickedly. "Sit," he ordered, "and let me feast."

Niall watched the mortal man as he sat in the wing-back chair, perspiring. He could smell the bitter stench of anxiety and fear. Saw the way his blue eyes blazed with terror, the way his gaze cast about the chamber as if searching for a way out. *Good.* The human should fear him.

"My girls," the man began as his trembling hands clutched the silver chalice of mead. "Are they safe?"

With a slow nod, Niall told the mortal he had naught to fear. His daughters would be treasured. They were the means to the survival of his court. With their mortal blood that ran pure with virtue, this man's daughters would make the Unseelie Court thrive and flourish once again.

"I don't understand the meaning of this, abducting me and my daughters—"

"Your daughters are safe, and are now in the hands of those who would guard them with their lives."

Lennox leaned forward and glared at him. "Who are you, sir?"

Niall allowed the man to see him for what he was. A Dark Fey. His glamour was dropped, revealing him in his fey form, which he knew glistened like diamonds. His violet eyes shone, and his hair grew longer, flowing past his shoulders. He no longer appeared as "just" a human.

The man recoiled, striving to put as much distance between them as possible. "God help me, my daughters," he mumbled and crossed himself.

"They are safe—enough," Niall taunted and laughed when the duke paled even more.

Replacing his glamour, Niall hid his fey beauty. But beneath the fey and the glamour his sin began to pace. Wrath was eager for retribution against Lennox and his virtuous counterparts. He thought of Irian, back at court, nursing his wounded heart. Irian was dying. Grief stricken. Heartbroken. The will to live was gone, and not even the fey had the power to survive a wounded spirit. Irian had not even held his son, nor looked at him. Even the wet nurse that Kian and Avery had provided for Irian and his son had not been enough to give him some kind of hope. *Irian wanted to die.* And it was all because of his mother's curse. His mother's hatred for him and his father.

Niall would have rather borne her curse and her hatred if she would have spared the innocents of his court. But his mother, while beautiful and a Seelie, had never been kind or gracious. When she sought to destroy his father, she decided to obliterate anything and everything that was connected to him. And if that meant the lives of innocent fey, their only trespass being they were Dark Fey, then so be it. His mother cared for nothing else but her festering hatred.

"Tell me what you want," the duke said, pulling Niall from thoughts of his court and his dying friend. It didn't help that Irian was possessed by the sin of sloth. It made it more difficult to convince Irian that he needed to get out of his chamber and attend to his life. Sloth took perverse pleasure in the grieving Irian.

"What is it I want?" Niall asked. "One thing. The survival of my court. It's dying."

"What am I to do about it?" the duke gasped. "I have no magic. No power to give you such a thing."

"Do you not?" Niall questioned. "No magic? I doubt that. You own this house, do you not?" Niall asked as he took a seat opposite Lennox. The fire cracked beside them, and the man visibly jumped, then took a large swallow from his cup.

"Aye, what of it?"

"It was purchased with money that was procured via a gift from my brethren. Is that not correct?"

Lennox took another sip and slowly nodded. Niall smiled. The enchantment had started. One could not accept food or drink from the fey and not become en- thralled by them. It was one of two of their most basic spells to beguile humans. Offering food was a way to gain a certain amount of power over the humans. In this case, Niall had bespelled the honeyed mead that Lennox was drinking. Niall's spell had been a suggestion spell. Soon Lennox's only wish would be to please the Dark Fey. It would be so strong that it would only take one whispered word and he would do whatever was asked of him.

"Aye, I'm part owner of the house," Lennox murmured before he took another small sip from the chalice.

"And the money. It came from a gift. Did it not?"

"Aye. The fey came to me and visited. They know your deepest desires. They know how to lure."

Yes. They did. Even now Niall could feel Lennox in his grasp. He wondered how the other princes were doing with their virtues. Was their success as easy as his?

"So, you know then, that we exist? You believe?"

"Aye, I know of the fey." Lennox licked his lip where a drop of mead had rested. "And I curse the lot of ye."

"Why?" Niall asked, smiling. "Was our gift not to your liking?"

It was Lennox's turn to narrow his gaze. "Our gift? I've never seen you before, sir."

"I believe you met my mother. The Seelie queen."

Lennox's pale eyes bugged out of his head. Niall knew that the human could not believe his eyes. The queen was beauty and light. He was darkness and sin.

"Tell me, what did my mother offer you?"

Lennox put his chalice aside and watched him as Niall rose from his chair and began to pace. Wrath was eating away at him, whispering to him to take Lennox's sweating throat between his hands and choke the information he wanted out of him. But Niall was the king of the Unseelie. He had honor. He could ferret out the information he wanted by being a fey, not a beast.

"Do you not know? Crom did."

Niall froze. "Crom has been to see you?"

Lennox frowned. "Yes. He is the one who ordered me to London. He said…the Dark Fey were coming after my girls."

They were indeed, but it was too soon to reveal that. "Crom is my twin. We're estranged."

"Aye." Lennox looked him over. "As opposite as day and night you are."

"Let us get to the heart of it, Lennox." Niall stiffened and looked down his nose at the man. "My mother granted you a gift, and in return she will have requested payment. What is it?"

Lennox resisted. Niall glanced at the chalice. It was still full, and the duke had only taken two small sips. But he tried the spell nevertheless. *Tell me what I want to know,* he silently commanded.

Then the duke's lips began to move, even as his fingers curled into the worn leather arms of the chairs. His eyes were wide as saucers as he struggled fruitlessly to hold his tongue. But the spell had him now. His words were no longer his to hide.

"My heir, she gave him a new body. A whole, hearty one. And in return she told me that I would sire daughters embodied by the virtues. And then, just a few days ago, Crom came to me, saying that the queen wants my girls. They're to go to her court."

Niall smiled in triumph. He had unlocked the key to

his mother's spell. The secret of making his court thrive once again did lie with the virtues. Now the only question that remained was if they were required to have all the virtues, or merely one to break the curse. Perhaps Lennox knew, so Niall compelled him to answer.

"I don't know anything else about it," Lennox was saying. "I...I have a meeting with the queen, tomorrow morning. P'raps then she'll tell me."

"Where is the meeting?"

"Richmond Park."

Of course. A large part of the royal park was enclosed within her court. She would never dare venture out of the Seelie wards for fear that he and the others were lurking about. No doubt Crom had already told her of their arrival.

"You will meet with her," Niall ordered Lennox as he passed the mortal the chalice one again. "And you will find out as much information as you can about your daughters. What purpose they are to have for the Seelie Court, and if she requires all of your daughters, or just one in particular. Ask her about the curse on the Unseelie Court and see what she will tell you. And then, you will return to me—here, that evening, and inform me of what you've learned. And you will bring your daughters with you."

Lennox began to shake his head, and Niall dropped his glamour. This time it was not the Dark Fey that greeted the duke, but Wrath. "You *will* bring your daughters."

It was the only way. He needed his princes to forge an alliance with the Lennox girls. They couldn't be forced, and with the Seelie around, it was unlikely that they would have any reasonable time to spend with the women. Here, in the Nymph and Satyr, there would be ample time to seduce and entice—uninterrupted. He had already taken precautions by warding off the brothel with magic. No Seelie could enter.

"Your daughters belong to the Dark Fey now, Lennox, regardless of what my mother says. Remember that. Your first obligation is to us."

The man began to nod in earnest as he drank quickly of the cup. "Now," Niall murmured, "you are very tired. You will sleep here."

"My girls," Lennox murmured as the empty chalice slipped from his fingers. His eyes were already closing, even as he once more whispered, "My girls…"

"Will be safe tonight," Niall whispered. As safe as they could be in the company of Dark Fey ruled by cardinal sins.

Thirteen

MERCY WATCHED AS KIAN LOWERED HIS TALL body into a chair. They were in a private chamber with a large bed that had bloodred velvet coverings and a hearth that blazed and crackled. Beside Kian was a table filled with wine and nuts and honeyed figs. He selected a fig and she saw how the golden honey ran down his fingers. His blue eyes caught hers, and he offered her a taste of the decadent treats.

"No, thank you," she said as she shook her head. He shrugged and popped the fig into his mouth.

"Delicious," he said after he swallowed. He reached for another one and studied it in his hands. "Are you not hungry?"

She'd give her front teeth for a taste of that fig from his fingers, but Mercy knew she couldn't. "No, I'm not hungry."

His gaze flickered to hers. "The look in your eyes says something else."

With his elegant fingers he motioned to the bowl laden with fruit, and the silver salver that contained prawns and oysters and a glass bowl of nuts. "Perhaps something else is more to your liking?"

"No, I don't believe so."

He sat back in his chair, spreading his thighs as he slouched deeply into the leather. Mercy was hypnotized by the wicked pose. Gracefully he picked up a brown square and bit into it, then held it out to her. "Chocolate?"

Her mouth was watering and her damnable stomach did protest. She was hungry. Had actually eaten very little because she wanted to look her best in her new gown— and because she had desired tight lacing this evening, to look as slim and trim as possible—for him.

"Come, have a taste," he murmured, holding it out to her. "It's the most decadent little treat."

Fisting her hands in her silk skirt, Mercy strove for composure. "You know I cannot accept anything to eat or drink from you."

Kian had devoured the chocolate and was in the process of picking up another fig when he glanced at her. "Oh? And why is that?"

"Because."

Slowly, he licked the honey from his finger before popping the entire morsel into his mouth. The sight made Mercy's stomach flutter wildly.

"Because why?"

"Because you are a fey—a Dark Fey—and to accept food or drink from you will allow you to enchant me."

He smiled, his blue eyes darkening to a deep midnight blue. "And here I thought it was because they were aphrodisiacs."

She blushed and fidgeted with her skirts. He was teasing her and she did not know how to respond. That afternoon he had been intent. Controlled. She had been able to understand him—respond to him. But this light, devil-may-care teasing was so foreign to her. She didn't know if she liked it. She certainly didn't know how to match him.

Slouching farther into his chair, his thighs spread farther, revealing the thick outline of his muscular thighs. The black satin pulled and stretched at the seams, and it took everything inside her to glance away.

"Tell me your name."

"Mercy."

"Your full name."

"I cannot."

"Because I am a fey?" he asked with amusement as he picked another fig from the bowl.

Her eyes flickered to his face. "Yes. To tell a faery your full name is to give him tremendous power over you. It makes your magic much easier to cast upon me. Besides, the fey have been known to steal the names of mortals, making it impossible for humans to find their way home again."

"Tremendous power over you?" he murmured thoughtfully as his gaze leisurely skated along her body. "How interesting."

"I cannot give in to you, no matter how beautiful you are."

"Beautiful." He huffed the word as he studied the flames in the hearth. "If you look deep beneath the glamour, you will not find beauty—or kindness."

"I will find an Unseelie Fey," she whispered. "I know. Almost from the first second I knew what you were."

He lifted his gaze to hers. "And yet you did not run from me. Why?"

"I've always been interested in the fey—the Dark Fey most especially."

He sat back, still slouching in his chair, and studied her for long moments. Mercy fought with herself to stay calm. To not fidget and act nervous beneath his scrutiny.

"There were Seelie there with you this afternoon." She nodded, and his fingers curled into fists. "Why were they there?"

"To court my sisters."

His gaze flashed to hers. "And you?"

"No."

His eyes seemed to change color, and Mercy wondered if it was only a trick of the firelight.

"They will not have you," he said softly. "None of you. But you most of all."

She shivered. The intensity was back. She heard it in his voice, saw it in the way he held his body, and her own body seemed to respond to it—the darkness in him. The dominance she sensed he held deeply hidden.

"Come, Mercy, and sit on my lap."

She wanted to. So much. But she knew better than to do such a thing. She was weak now. She couldn't allow herself to give in to her virtue and be kind to him. To be kind would be her downfall.

"I must leave," she murmured, but when she turned she felt his hand wrap around her wrist and halt her. He had risen from his chair and his chest pressed hotly into her back.

"No mercy," he whispered into her ear, his breath warm and moist against her. "No kindness, no leniency."

She remembered. The same rush of excitement lanced through her as it had that afternoon when he had said the same words.

"Mercy," he whispered hotly into her ear. "Show me a very great kindness and remove your dress."

Her body thrilled at the suggestion, but her mind warred against such indecorous behavior. "Why?"

When she tilted her head to look at him, his eyes were no longer blue, but a swirling tempest of blue-green, like the churning sea.

"Why?" he asked, his mouth lowering to hers. "Because I wish to return your kindness with one of mine. My hands on your body. My flesh inside your body."

She whimpered, unable to hide the small sound when his fingers began unfastening the buttons of her gown.

"No mercy," he murmured as his lips caressed the swells of her breasts. "No leniency." His tongue ran along the quivering flesh and she moaned, clasping his dark head to her chest.

"Please," she moaned. And he laughed, a musical and magical sound as he pulled her close.

"No mercy, remember?" And then he vanished, leaving her alone, her heart pounding, her blood quickening in her veins. And breasts...good God, her breasts were aching for his touch.

No mercy, or kindness, she thought savagely. He'd left her in a state of innocent agony.

Thane slid onto the bed alongside Chastity. Her spine, elegantly curved, faced him. He was in her dream now. He hadn't intended for it to be so, but the act of carrying her into the house, of feeling her frantically beating heart pounding against his chest while he attempted to soothe her fears had forged the bond between them. He could hear her thoughts. Feel her body, her breath inside him. He was part of her, and for as long as she was, he felt her humanity. It warmed him. Made him feel invincible.

When he had brought her to the room, she was asleep in his arms, his spell having worked to ease her fears. He had placed her on the bed, and sat on the chair, watching her sleep. And then, he had found himself being pulled to her, dragged into her dream of them on a bed. Their bodies naked, his hands covering her.

If he were honorable he would have severed the bond, allowing her privacy in her sleep. If Lust wasn't so damn starved he might have found the power to do so. But his sin needed to feed, and the Dark Fey in him needed to pleasure. And she was here. Wanting him in her dream, her thoughts. Her fantasies were visceral and real. He felt her need inside him.

He wanted her, that was true. But he wanted her awake. Looking at him. Not through a dream or a veil of sexual fantasy. But through her own eyes. But he would take what he could get. Chastity's willing exuberance, in the confines of her dreams.

Thane knew she believed that her dreams, while far from innocent, were really harmless. In dreams, nothing was real. But what Chastity did not realize was that in her dreams of them, everything was real—and irrevocable. He was really present inside her mind, her thoughts. He experienced everything the same as if she were awake. And so did she.

As he was pulled deeper into her subconscious, he could not help but wish for things to be different. For her to be lucid, gazing up at him between locks of golden hair. He wanted to talk, to discover her, to forge a friendship with her. But he would be lying if he didn't want this, too. This opportunity to be with her—unguarded—in her dreams.

She was so beautiful. A voluptuous, enticing beauty who had the ability to make his jaded, sinful heart beat not only with desire and lust, but longing and hope, as well.

Sighing, she snuggled farther onto her side, inching closer to the edge of the bed, instinctively seeking the warmth of the firelight as his magic removed her gown, corset and stays and layers of petticoats. She was naked, her skin white as a lily, and he saw how his hand trembled, itching to touch her.

She sighed again as the heat of the fire kissed the front of her body, and she scooted closer, seeking more. Thane followed her, letting his fingers flick the ends of her hair over her shoulder before sliding his fingertips down her neck and along her shoulder blade.

"Mmm," she purred appreciatively. "That feels wonderful." His fingers were at her waist, and the urge to cup her heart-shaped ass called to him. "Your fingers feel so beautiful. Your touch is magic to me."

She was dreaming. He knew that. But something made him think that these thoughts were really true. They were the feelings she kept hidden beneath her piety and innocence. This, he thought, watching her, was the real Chastity. The way she was when unencumbered by her virtue. He remembered her earlier that evening, when he had been part of the perfume and she had anointed him on her body. She had been willing—wanton, allowing him all kinds of indiscretions. How easily she had taken the rounded bulb of the perfume bottle into her tight sheath. How arousing it had been to watch and think of her taking his cock the same way.

One day she would. And he would watch, the same way he had that afternoon.

No, the Chastity who came to him in her dreams was willing to explore the acts of man and woman. As if to confirm it, she brushed her bottom against him and purred, *please*...

There was something that stopped him from rushing

forward, something that made him wish to take his time, to pleasure her as he knew he could. He decided then that he would use his fingers along her skin to awaken her to him. To arouse and satisfy. And perhaps, he might show her a few of his fantasies, as well. The dream Chastity would be receptive. And maybe these stolen, forbidden moments might soften her to him. Perhaps in her waking mind she would allow him to make love to her in the same manner she begged for in her dreams.

"Thane," she murmured, sliding her plump bottom along the bed till it rested in the juncture of his thighs. "Touch me."

And he did. Running the tips of his fingers along her neck and shoulders and down the length of her arms. He swept his fingers featherlight along her back, delighting in her moans and the gooseflesh that arose on her pale skin.

Each time he came a little closer to the swell of her breast, a little lower along her hip, letting a finger trace a small portion of one shapely cheek of her bottom until she became more restless.

He teased her with each stroke until she positioned herself onto her back, provoking him to touch her where she wanted—but where she would not ask him to. He purposely traced the edge of her breast, smiling as she arched her back, grazing her impudent pink nipple against his knuckle. He slid his hand away, letting it rest against her hip. She sighed and raised her leg, bending it so that it was draped over his thighs, exposing her mound of golden curls.

"Please," she whimpered, her voice husky with need, the gooseflesh spreading along her belly and thighs, crinkling her areolae and filling her nipples with blood so that they were no longer a light pink but a dark rose.

"Are you not satisfied?" he asked against her ear, his fingers tracing over her knee before slowly and lightly gliding up the inside of her thigh, stopping just before her wet curls. She arched against his hand and he slid his fingers away from her, fearing that if he touched her all would be lost. But the image of his hand with the crystal perfume stopper came rushing back. He had been aroused by it, teasing her with the cool crystal. He wanted his fingers inside her, pumping, filling her.

"Thane." His name was a plea for surcease. "Please."

"Pleasure yourself," he suggested, placing her hand on her breast. "Learn your body and give it the pleasure it craves."

"I can't—it isn't—"

"Show me how to pleasure you."

Her cheeks turned a hot pink. "You already know."

"I want to watch you," he crooned against her temple, his fingers once again soothing her into restless longing. "Take your breasts and your nipples between your fingers and show me what you would have me do to you."

She cupped them in her hands, bringing the peaks together, her thumbs coaxing her nipples into strained pebbles. Her eyes were tightly shut, but he watched as her lips parted on a silent pant.

"How does it feel?" A husky moan was all she managed. Thane smiled as she worked her breasts faster, harder, between her hands, his own need stirring unruly between them as he thought about sliding his cock between them.

"Now put your hand on your mound."

He saw the hesitation in her face, heard her hushed breathing, but she let him take her hand in his, and together they placed their fingers on her wet lips. His cock leaped at the provocative sight of his long fingers lying atop hers, her fingers buried between her folds, stroking and probing and swirling around in her glistening honey.

The urge to take and plunder, to bury his mouth inside her, to taste what had been denied him thus far, coursed violently through him. She was writhing now, her hips arching slowly, seductively, as her finger swirled around her glistening sex. "So damn beautiful," he growled against her throat, his gaze fixated on her alabaster fingers immersed in pink silk.

"You're watching?" she panted between breaths.

His belly tightened as memories of the afternoon flooded his brain, and he stroked himself, unable to bear the torment of not being touched. Lust wanted release. He wanted release. He prayed that soon Chastity would shed her virtue and come to him, prepared to give and take. To share the pleasures of their bodies together.

"Does watching bring you pleasure?"

"Yes," he moaned. *And dreaming. And fantasizing of you.* All of it brought him pleasure.

Thane gripped his cock, pumping his hand up and down, watching her pleasure herself, reveling in his own self-pleasuring. He'd never tossed off before anyone before, preferring his conquests to do the task for him. But there was something about stroking himself before Chastity that stirred his senses. Something that heated his blood and made his cock throb painfully, knowing she was watching and listening to his sounds of pleasure.

"Thane," she huffed, spiraling toward her climax. "Have you…have you ever done that and thought of me?"

"Yes," he gritted between his teeth, his hand now furiously pumping up and down, watching her escalate her own passion. Memories of the way he'd spied on her soaping her breasts in the bath, remembrances of the way he'd freed himself, coming in his hand as he watched her lather her sex, sprung into his head, making him feel hotter and more sexually needy than he had in years. Even Lust was purring in satisfaction at this innocent bit of play.

"Chastity," he whispered, working himself into complete abandon. "Tell me," he growled, looking into her face, seeing her teetering on the edge of her climax. "Have you ever wanted to reach between your legs and pleasure yourself, pretending it was my fingers giving you release?"

"*Yes!*" she cried, her hips bucking wildly, her breathing coming in short rasps. He growled, reaching for her, pumping himself onto her lush bottom, then sinking back onto the bed with Chastity in his arms, the scent of their arousal mingling together in the quiet room.

"When you yearn to feel me touch you, you'll now be

able to give yourself pleasure, will you not?" She shyly
nodded, burying her face into the crook of his neck.
"Chastity?"

"Hmm," she purred, sounding very close to sleep.

"When you next see me, your body will respond to
me. I won't even have to touch you in order for you to
feel the need."

When no response came, Thane peeked down at the
angelic sleeping face of Chastity. Her blond curls fanned
over his chest. He liked the contrast of it, liked the possessive way her hair covered him. Feeling more content
and satiated than he had in a long while, Thane reached
for the silk coverlet and covered them, drifting off to
peaceful slumber with the woman he never thought he'd
have, lying gloriously naked beside him.

FOURTEEN

CHASTITY CAME AWAKE WITH A START. HER HAIR was loose from its pins, hanging down around her shoulders and before her eyes. Her breathing was hurried as she took in the strange chamber.

Brushing her hair back from her face, she gazed around the unfamiliar room with wide eyes. She was in bed, the gray silk blanket that had been covering her slipped down, revealing the light green frock she had worn for the masquerade. *She was still dressed.* Her sigh of relief whispered through the room.

Remnants of a dream flittered back and she covered her face with her hands in an attempt to smother the scandalous dream away. In her dream she had been with Thane, and she had…pleasured herself. Oh, God, she was ashamed of herself. She was even more mortified to discover the truth on her fingers. She could smell her sex lingering on her skin. Which meant that while sleeping she had acted out those immoral thoughts and wishes.

Only a dream, she reminded herself. She was not, in fact, ruined. But she had entered this room with Thane. He had carried her in his arms, spoken to her in a soft, musical voice that had lulled her to sleep.

And then what? He had brought her here. But where was she exactly? she wondered as her attention turned to the large hearth where a fire blazed. The flickering flames cast eerie shadows on the wall, and Chastity gripped the blanket tighter, pulling it around her shoulders. The only light in the chamber came from the hearth, and narrowing her gaze, Chastity searched through the room. She felt someone's presence, but she saw no one. There was nothing present but a large wardrobe that was carved with flowers and vines, and a painted table that housed a silver decanter and goblet.

It was quiet. Unnervingly so. She could make out no noises from the hall outside the room, or from the streets outside the large window. But there *was* a peculiar scent in the air. Her perfume mixed with... She inhaled softly. Musk? It was a male scent. Strong. Virile. And it was definitely mixed with her perfume.

Following her nose, she slowly slid from the bed. Her gown, she noticed, had been twisted to her knees while she slept. It fell to her feet—which were devoid of her slippers—in a soft swish. She felt languid, her limbs weak and relaxed. In fact, there was a strange sense of euphoria that warmed her blood as she walked slowly around the huge bed, which was lavishly draped in dove-gray silk.

"Hello?" she asked, her voice hoarse and unsure, revealing how frightened she was. "Is there anyone here?"

Something behind her made a noise, and she whirled around to see a man lounging in a chair, his long legs spread, his fingers steepled together and pressed against his mouth.

In the firelight, she saw the glimmer of gold, and he leaned forward, out of the shadows, revealing the gilt mask he wore. Slowly, his hand left the arm of the chair, his fingers grasping the edge of the mask. Breathlessly, Chastity watched as the mask was slowly lifted from his face.

"Thane!"

His eyes were dark, not the blue they had been in the perfumery. His body was tense, like a predator waiting to pounce on unsuspecting prey. He was dangerous. The man from the maze. Not Thane, the man in the perfumery.

Carelessly he tossed the mask to the floor, watching her response, drinking her in. His gaze covered her body numerous times, before settling briefly on the curve of her breasts.

"It was you all along," she said on a rushed breath, finally fitting the pieces together. "You're a Dark Fey."

"Yes. Crom told you, didn't he?"

"Yes."

"To turn you from me." The statement was cold. Hard. His eyes glittered. "Did you believe him? His stories about us?"

"He told me nothing more than to beware of the Unseelie."

Surprise flickered in his eyes. "Did he? And that was all?"

"I told you it was. He said your kind were danger-ous."

"Of course he did. No doubt he left out the stories about himself. Did he try to persuade you that I would hurt you?"

Nodding, she glanced away. She thought of the night in the maze, the times in her bedroom when he had touched her. She hadn't feared him. Hadn't felt anything but excitement and pleasure.

Their gazes met, and the hunger she saw in his eyes frightened her. Was he recalling that night in the maze as well, when she was bared to him? For it was all she could think of. Yet he had deceived her—from the very beginning. Crom was not wrong in that. Thane had lied to her, but why?

"Why?" she asked on a confused whisper. "Out of all the women in the world, why did you choose this mortal?"

"Because fate drove me to you."

He watched her response with his unblinking gaze. *Fate.* Was he her fate? She knew now, unequivocally, *what* he was. But she did not understand who he was to be to her.

"What do you want from me?"

"You don't know? Crom did not tell you?"

She swallowed hard. She did know what he wanted. What did any Dark Fey desire?

"Every one hundred years, seven women are born who possess the virtues."

She paled and tried to back away, but his gaze held her steady—pinned to the spot on the floor before him.

"You are the virtue of chastity. And I am here to claim you as mine."

And why was it so important to him? What did it matter to him? Was it merely her virtue that interested him? Her chasteness called to the base Unseelie needs inside him. Was that it? Was she merely something to corrupt?

His lashes lowered, hiding the expression of his eyes. Somehow she knew he heard her silent question, and he refused to answer her. But she knew it anyway. It was not her he desired. But her virtue.

"You are wrong. It may have been your virtue that called to me, but it has always just been you that has brought me back—time and time again."

She could not allow herself to weaken. She couldn't. Even though she felt her body softening, her resolve wavering.

"Have you stolen me from my family, then, and taken me to your court?" she asked, trying to be brave.

His lips curved in amusement. "No. Not yet."

She didn't know whether to be relived or alarmed by his response. "Not yet" implied that he would. The thought of being separated from her family made her ill.

"You are still safely in London. Your father is with my

king, and your sisters are with my brethren. Unharmed, of course."

He slouched farther into his chair, his pose at once indolent yet arousing. She could not cease staring at him. At how beautiful he was. How alluring and sensual. He seemed to know her thoughts, for he spread his body out farther, allowing her an unobstructed view of him.

"You do not seem overly distressed to learn that I am a Dark Faery."

Cocking her head, she stared at him. "I should have known. Your beauty, your gracefulness, it belies anything human. But you are not golden, you are dark, comfortable amongst shadows and at home in the night."

"No doubt you have heard stories of us—many of which are exaggerated—"

"Crom says that the Unseelie destroy," she blurted out. "That you're not to be trusted. That the Dark Fey only want to seduce, then discard."

His beautiful face twisted into a mask of rage. "That Seelie bastard would say anything to get you away from me and my court. Has it ever crossed your mind that he's lying to you?"

No. It hadn't. She had taken everything for the truth. Seelie were the good fey. They were golden and lively, and truth was their domain. The Dark Fey were sensual, debauched fey, delighting in war and games and darkness. Sin and lies were the foundation of their court. Crom had no reason to lie.

"It is not only the Unseelie who destroy," he said quietly. "There can be cruelty in the light. Danger in the sun. Hatred masked as joy and gaiety. Never underestimate the sinister beauty of the Seelie."

She could not refute his claims. There had always been something about Crom that had not sat well with her. A smoothness that was artificial. A coolness that was reflected in his eyes.

In Thane's eyes she saw heat. Desire. And an openness she had never witnessed in Crom's violet eyes.

"I will not hurt you," he whispered, his voice harsh in the quiet. "You can sense that much, can't you?"

"I do not trust myself to believe anything that you are," she replied quietly. "You've proven that I am a poor judge, that I'm not as chaste as a virtue ought to be. No, I cannot trust myself to believe in anything that you might profess…"

"Because I am a Dark Fey," he finished for her.

She could not look away from him. His beauty was otherworldly, but he looked so much like a man. With Crom, she had known he was a Seelie. But Thane…no, she could not quite believe it. Perhaps it was because he had made her body respond as a woman's does to a handsome man. A *human,* she corrected. Thane was fey. Not human. And therefore her arousal for him was an abomination.

This was the Dark Fey Crom had warned her about at the Seftons'. He'd somehow known about Thane. Were the Dark Fey truly as dangerous as Crom had led her to believe? Would Thane truly hurt her as Crom had suggested?

What motive did the Seelie have to lure her from

Thane? Jealousy? Of course that was it. He wanted her for his own court. But he didn't want her. The woman she was becoming. He wanted her virtue, wanted to place her on a pedestal.

"You're curious," he stated flatly. "Please. Inspect me. See for yourself if I am not just like any other male."

She flushed and looked away. "Of course I am not curious." She could not trust herself. Even though she did have the very great desire to inspect him, she could not risk being close to him. Touching him. He was far more dangerous to her than Crom and the other Seelie ever could be. She had begun to pin her hopes on him, to open her heart to him, only to discover his deceit. She'd been betrayed.

"No? Are you not wondering, even now, what the difference is between a fey male and mortal man?"

She was, but how did he know?

"Turn your eyes upon me."

It was a command that brooked no opposition. She did the unthinkable. Straightened her body until she was looking fully upon him. When he had her full attention, he pulled the lace jabot from around his throat and draped it over the arm of the chair. Then his long fingers began working on the buttons of his shirt, which he opened to his navel.

"You are not a man," Chastity breathed, trying to remind herself of that fact that this was a dangerous faery sitting before her. One she could not trust. One she must escape from.

"Am I not?" he purred, then he tugged the shirt out

from his britches, pulling the white linen over his head. Chastity gasped at the sight before her. The width of his chest, the bulge of muscle in his arms.

Behind him the moon shone through the window, and his body seemed to absorb the moonbeams that glimmered through the filth-covered panes of glass. The effect was stunning.

"That night in the maze, when I had my hands on you, and my mouth on your breast, did I not feel like a man? Did you not yearn for me like a woman does a man?"

She would not answer him. Couldn't.

"And the other times, when I was with you. Did I not make you feel pleasure?"

"Yes," she whispered, ashamed of her actions and what she had allowed herself to believe. "I am asking myself why you did it."

"Because I desire you." His eyes never left her face.

"It was for your own amusement, then? Corrupt the virtuous Chastity and laugh at her when she succumbs?"

"Nothing like that," he growled. "My desire was never feigned. My interest never fleeting. I want you. In my world. As my mate."

"So you saw me in Glastonbury and that was it? You decided you love me?"

She saw the flicker of wariness in his eyes. Then they narrowed. "I desired you. Wanted you in my bed, beneath me. To assume I loved you then would be an insult to us both. I have never loved a woman, not a fey...or a mortal."

Something in her splintered. While she had desired

him, she realized now that she had also cared for him. The first stirring of love had been blooming inside her, and he had felt lust. Nothing more.

"I know what you're thinking."

She sniffed, stiffening her posture. "No, you do not."

"If I were to confess my love right now, you would ridicule me. Deride me. I know you would not believe me."

"Lust and love are two very different things."

"Believe me, no one knows that more than I. Come, trust me. Regardless of what Crom says, or what your heart is telling you, you can believe in that. I would never, ever willingly hurt you."

"You already have."

Cocking his head to the side, he studied her. "Then allow me to make amends."

He sat back in the chair, opening his arms, allowing her to study him fully. She found herself mesmerized by his fey glamour, and helplessly, she stepped forward, till her gown brushed his silk-covered knees and she could smell the bared skin of his chest. He smelled of her perfume and of the woods at night. He compelled her... enthralled her...

"You made me want you," she accused. "You used your faery magic to make me desire you."

"No, I did not work a spell to enchant you. You came to me of your own volition. And every time after that, it was your will that brought me to you."

"You deceived me," she whispered, unable to blink

or tear her gaze from him. She was hurting. She did not want what she had felt, this newfound desire, the sense of freedom and liberation to give in to her buried needs to have been based on magic. She had wanted more. Something real.

"No, I did not."

"Then I have deceived myself into believing that you are something that you aren't."

"You knew me as a man. I am built just like a man, Chastity. See for yourself."

Her gaze slipped down as she heard the fastening of his britches. Slowly he opened the flap, and she pressed her eyes shut, hiding the vision. "Please don't."

"Such innocence," he whispered. "I wonder at it, even though I have seen you naked. Have felt your breasts and the honey of your quim."

"No."

"Yes."

He sat forward and skimmed his finger down the filmy skirts of her gown. "You are only afraid to admit the truth to yourself. It is easier to deny what you want because I am a fey. You hide behind that truth because you do not have to accept that you have been tempted by something you cannot understand. That someone has broken past your defenses, your virtue, to glimpse the woman beneath the innocent veneer—and that someone was a faery."

She shook her head, refusing to believe him.

"But what are dreams?" he murmured quietly, sending her skin prickling in awareness. "What of that voice inside you? The one that speaks to you, the one that I answer? What man could know of that? No, it has taken a fey to finally awaken you, to make you respond. You could never have done so with a mortal man."

"They were only silly dreams," she said, denying everything he was saying.

"Were they really? Close your eyes," he commanded.

Suddenly memories of a garden came rushing back. Thane was there, so was a dog. He was between her legs, touching her... Oh, God, his lips were moving over her, and she felt it, the heat and moistness of his tongue, the feel of him probing, circling, the exquisite pleasure that shot through her body.

"You remember now?" he asked. "Was that only a dream?"

"Why now?" she cried on a broken sob. Why now were these thoughts coming back to her?

"Because I have given you back the memories." She watched as he sat back in his chair, studying her. "It was not the right time to reveal myself, then. You were afraid of what was inside you. You feared me. And I never wanted your fear. Only your passion."

"You stole my memories."

His eyes darkened and he lowered his lashes, shielding them from her. "You were not yet ready for the truth."

"I'm not now, either," she hissed. "I don't understand any of this."

"There is nothing to understand. It is simple. You belong to me."

"No, I don't."

"You belong to the fey."

"Perhaps," she retorted, intending to wound and hurt the way she was at that very moment. "But not to the Unseelie."

She turned to walk away, but he reached for her, his eyes black and glistening as he grasped her wrist, pulling her closer so that she was caged between his thighs. "You claim to know me so very well, but do you even know who you really are?" he whispered silkily in her ear.

"Of course I do. I am Chastity Ann Lennox," she snapped as she tried to free herself from his hold. But then the strangest noise came from him. It was part growl, part purr, and she stilled, forced her gaze to meet his.

"You should not have told me, *muirneach,* for I cannot control what I am."

Something grave had happened between them. She felt it. Her body giving way, her thoughts swaying and leaving her. She was no longer in control.

"Neither am I," he whispered as he pulled her closer, his mouth brushing along her jaw. "I am ruled by my Unseelie blood, by the power you have just handed me. By the si—" He stopped, breathed heavily against her. "By the dark need inside me."

"The dreams, they were real," she whispered, giving voice to her fears as she tried to make sense of everything. "Everything was true. You used your fey magic to come to me, to enter my dreams."

"Yes. But not without your help. Without that little

voice inside you giving you the thoughts, I would not have been able to."

"You forced me."

"No, never." His lips brushed her jaw, across her ear. "You let me in. Accepted me. You listened to the voice inside you. It told you that you wanted me. Wanted to let go of the virtue. Even now that voice speaks to you."

"It's your magic making me believe it."

"No, it is not. It is your true self."

"Please," she whispered desperately, "release your hold on me."

"I cannot. My body burns for a taste of you. My blood…it courses through me, seeking what has been denied me."

Struggling in his hold, Chastity tried ineffectively to free herself. But Thane was too strong and determined to keep her where he wanted her.

"You fear me, but I am the same as I always was. Before you knew who I really am, there was no fear. Come," he encouraged. Reaching for her hand, he drew her closer and forced her palm onto his chest. "Discover that there is nothing so terrible about me."

"Everything about you is otherworldly. How could you believe that I could look at you, touch you, and think you simply a man?"

His eyes shuttered, and she felt his heart thump slow and steady beneath her palm. "Then if you cannot think of me as a man, discover me as a fey."

Thane watched with hooded eyes as Chastity's gaze roved over his body. Allowing his fey glamour full rein, he sat back in his chair, capturing Chastity's hips with his thighs. His body burned. His sin was so close to coming out and claiming her.

But this moment was crucial. He knew that. This was the moment when Chastity would either accept him for what he was, or run from him. Either way she would be his. He already had power over her. She had given him her name. That alone could compel her to do his wishes. But he did not want spells and magic. He wanted her desire to be her own. He knew he was keeping things from her. But he would tell her later. After he had made love to her. After he had made her see that his desire was real, and that beneath the passion there was the first stirring of love.

He'd never thought to have it. But there it was, lurking deep inside him. Somehow it was happening. He was falling in love with Chastity.

Slowly her palm moved over his chest, and the smell of her skin, the scent of her sex covering her fingers coated him. He had come to her as an essence in a bottle, but he much preferred this, her perfume covering him.

He said nothing, just allowed his head to tip back against the chair and permitted her hand to discover him. Gods, her hands felt good, and his heart sped up, his body heating. This night was so important—for both of them. He couldn't allow his sin, or anything else, to botch it up.

"You're warm," she murmured. "Your flesh is much hotter than ours."

Yes. They were warmer blooded, the fey, than mortals. Especially the Unseelie.

"Your heart. It beats so slowly."

His was beating much faster than normal as her fingers crept up to his neck. Gods, her scent. He wanted to reach out and lick her fingers. To taste her.

"Your skin. It's…incandescent."

"The moonlight," he murmured as he closed his eyes. "Nighttime is our element. Our powers are at their strongest and our true glamour is revealed in its glow."

Trembling fingers moved over his chin, her fingertips grazed his lips and he could not resist the lure of brushing his tongue along her fingertips, tasting her sex on her own fingers. Imagining what it would be like to part her and swipe his tongue along the pink silk of her quim.

She gasped, surprised, but she did not pull away. Instead, she continued her study of him, and he allowed it. Allowed himself the pleasure of sitting back and enjoying her touch, which burned into him. Lust for the moment was satisfied. Purring inside him, but soon his sin would deprive him of this simple pleasure. It would want more, would want her complete surrender. Thane wanted that, too, but the sin in him wanted to go about it in a different manner. The Dark Fey in him wanted to seduce, to have her utterly consumed with him before he claimed. Lust wanted only to fuck.

All night he had been battling his sin, and he was winning. But for how much longer, he had no idea.

Her fingertips grazed over his lashes, then moved up to his forehead and over to his hair. The feel of her fingernails scraping his scalp, raking through his hair, was heaven, and he could not hide the purr of satisfaction. His skin tightened in goose bumps at the feel her fingers tightening...holding.

The bond between them was established once more, and he was pulled into her. He could see in her mind her desires. But he wanted her to see his. His mouth on her, his face buried in her cunt as she raked her fingers through his hair, holding him to her. He wanted to sit in his chair and have her come to him, to lie down naked at his feet in surrender. Yes, he wanted that from her. Her complete submission.

"Don't," he whispered, his voice broken and hoarse. Her fingers were gently sliding down to his ears. He could not have that. But she gave no heed to his warning and ran her fingertip along the curved tip of his ear.

He groaned, his cock stiffening even more and shoving free his britches. No place on a fey's body was more highly sensitive than their ears. While the Unseelie's ears were not long, they were gently pointed, and his ears were as sensitive and responsive as that of a clitoris on a woman.

When she stroked them again, he cracked opened his eyes, seeing the rapt attention she focused on his ears.

He was going to come if she continued touching them, and he thought how wonderful it would be to come like this, with her fingers outlining his ear, her pointed tongue licking up the shell.

And then she did, moving forward and brushing his hair back, exposing his left ear. Bending forward, she inhaled him, heard her purr of satisfaction as she ran her nose up his neck, and over to his jaw, to his ear. Christ, it was like waiting to have his cock touched. And may the gods help him if he were to discover what it would be like to have his cock in her hand, and his ear beneath her tongue.

Lust roared through him, and he gripped the chair tight as her tongue delicately came out and ran the length of his ear to the pointed tip. His cock throbbed, filling, and suddenly his thighs clamped tightly around her, capturing her.

He ignored her weak protest and snaked his arms around her middle, bringing her flush with his chest, a chest that felt firm and warm beneath his clothing. Then he released one arm and threaded his fingers through hers, holding their entwined hands against her side, while his other hand trailed down her throat to her décolletage and down over her breasts.

"You are playing with fire, little mortal," he said, his voice harsh and full of sexual desire. "Never toy with a fey's ears unless you are prepared to suffer the consequences."

She met his gaze. "Perhaps I am."

Chastity watched as Thane's eyes darkened. Her gaze flitted from his eyes, which changed color almost constantly, to the gently pointed ears. Placing her fingertip to one, he growled, then pulled her to him.

He cupped her breast, brought her closer, and she felt his breath hot beneath her ear, smelled the perfume of him, spice and claret, beneath her nose. His thumb slid over her nipple, which hardened painfully beneath her silk gown, and he chuckled deep in his throat when she whimpered and squirmed against him.

"Fair is fair, *muirneach*," he whispered. "You play with my ears, and I will play with what fascinates me—your tits."

She gasped at his crudeness, at the way it aroused her. At how she wanted more. To hear more. To feel more.

"I know this is something you desire," he whispered as his finger slid away from her breast and skated down her belly. "You want to know what it is to feel passion. You want the feel of a man's hands on you. You want to know what it is like to have me big and hard inside you. Have I gotten it all correct, Chastity? Have I left out any parts?" His fingers were now at the junction of her thighs and he was stroking his fingertips against the curls that lay beneath her gown.

Her stomach coiled and tightened and she felt her blood thrum heavy in her veins. He was in her mind, hearing her thoughts, repeating them to her word for word.

"I want to take you, fuck you, have you writhing beneath me. Then I want to love you, to feel you clinging to me, begging me to give you release. And then I want to hold you. To kiss you in the dark and watch you fall asleep. And then I will wake you by sliding down your body and lapping at you, waking you with my mouth."

She was in his mind now. Hearing his desires. She gasped, made breathless by the picture he was painting for her. It was not only his words she heard through their connection, but she saw the images he saw. The picture of her, naked, thighs splayed, Thane's shoulders between her legs as he covered her sex with his mouth. She saw, too, how her fingertips toyed with his ears.

"Do I frighten you with my passion, Chastity?" he asked as he leaned forward and kissed her throat. "Or does what you see in my mind excite you?"

She moaned and her legs weakened when he pressed his lips, then his tongue, to her neck. In a warm, wet slide he trailed his tongue down her throat, to her breasts.

"Excites you, doesn't it? I can tell by the way you tremble against me. It is not a shiver of fear, but of desire, a yearning for more. You want to discover the mysteries between men and women. You want to learn why women will risk all to meet their lovers. Why you would risk everything you are for just a little, forbidden taste of what this fey could give you."

"Yes," she hissed when she felt his fingers expertly reach for the edge of her bodice. Slowly he inched it down until her breasts were nearly spilling out of her gown. She arched her back when his nails caressed her breasts, scant inches from her nipples. "Show me," she gasped.

"Are you wet?" he asked, his lips brushing her ear as he whispered the words. His finger traced her jaw. "If I were to touch you, to spread your legs and feel you, would you be ready to come for me?"

She pressed against him, unable to talk or think. How could she when he was even now lowering her bodice so that her breasts were exposed? With his thumb and forefinger, he gently rolled her nipple, and automatically she reached for his wrist, knowing she should stop this. But he refused her and instead brought her hand to his britches and pressed it against the bulge behind the flap.

"Take my cock in your hand, Chastity, and pleasure me." With ruthless determination he curled her fingers around his thickness and pressed himself into her hand. "Play with me, Chastity."

She did not know what to do, other than to slide her fingers along the satiny skin. She was startled by the feel of him. How hard, yet how soft the skin was. She could barely wrap her fingers around him, he was so thick.

She must have been doing an admirable job, for he groaned and thrust his hips forward, sliding his erection up the length of her palm. Closing her eyes, she let her head rest against his, her breath near his ear. His whole body tensed, then his mouth was everywhere, on her throat, the tops of her breasts, her lips. His hands were roaming the contour of her figure and his fingers cupped and stroked every inch of her burning skin. Her heart was pounding so fast she felt light-headed and yet she could not stop what was happening even if she desired to. This passion, the feel of him surrounding her, the intimacy of his tongue in her mouth as he possessed her lips was nothing she thought ever to experience. It was heaven, bliss, an erotic sensation she could easily find herself addicted to.

Fisting her hand in his silky hair, she brought him closer, seeking his heat and his tongue dancing with hers.

He growled and brought his hand up to her throat. His thumb rubbed the pulsating vein in her neck, lulling her into a dreamlike state. He kissed her into a stupor, and mindlessly she moved her fingers until she was teasing him with just a little graze of her finger over the tip of his ear.

Tearing his mouth from hers, he thrust his hips forward again and she curled her fingers tighter around his erection. Sliding her hand down, then up, she pleasured him, listening to his sucking breaths, feeling the tightening of his body, forgetting that she had no experience in pleasing a man—or fey.

He reached between their bodies and placed his hand atop hers, showing her how to hold him and stroke him. When he increased the rhythm of her strokes, his voice was a ragged rasp. She trembled when she felt his breath against her ear.

He was hard, the tip of his phallus was thick and throbbing. He groaned when she swirled her finger along the wet tip of him, and the sound made her feel bold. She wanted to please him, to discover what he desired.

"Slide your hand down me," he rasped against her neck. "Let me feel your fingers around me, stroking me."

She did what he asked, sliding her hand up and down, feeling him thicken and lengthen within her fingers. With a hissing breath, he reached for her skirts and gathered the filmy fabric in his hands, raising it until she could feel his hands grazing her thighs.

Lost to the passion inside her, Chastity did not allow

herself to think, to feel guilt, to remind herself that she was supposed to be virtuous and chaste, for she wanted to be anyone else tonight. Anyone but a virtue.

Gripping him firmer, she boldly cupped the soft sac of skin between his legs at the same time he ripped her petticoats. He stroked her sex and she froze at the intimacy of it, but as soon as she felt him part her and his finger stroke the sensitive nub, she moaned and writhed against his hand.

"See how you play with fire?"

She moaned, wanted more, her whole body quivering.

"This is what I feel when you touch my ears. When you breathe against them—put your tongue to them."

The sensation was mind-numbing. Thought shattering. *More*...was the only word she could find.

"Spread your legs for me—wide." Not waiting for her to comply, he lifted her leg so that her foot rested on the arm of the chair.

"What are you doing?" she cried, steadying herself by holding on to his shoulders.

"Tasting you." Then his hot tongue raked along her folds. "Teasing you, like you teased me." He blew against her, then lashed his tongue once more, parting her folds. "You're so aroused, I want to taste it," he murmured. She whimpered in shame and pleasure.

"Hold your skirts," he demanded, shoving a fistful of taffeta in her hands. Before she knew his intent, he spread her sex with his fingers and circled her opening with his tongue. "I am so eager to put my cock in here." His voice was full of passion and it made her knees weak. "Would you like that, Chastity? My cock in here, pounding into you."

"Yes," she cried, feeling her body coil tightly. And then he was circling the nubbin of flesh with his tongue, flicking it so that she was gripping his hair and thrusting her hips in a rhythm he matched with his mouth.

He rubbed her with his mouth, his lips and nose, and she cried out, her fingers lacing tightly in his hair. And then, to give him some of the pleasure he was giving her, she brushed her thumbs along both his ears, and he growled, burying his face between her legs as he ravished her with his mouth.

With a keening cry, she straightened, her body tense, her eyes tightly shut. She didn't think she could bear such pleasure, but then he lowered her leg and stood, bringing his mouth down hard on hers, stifling her cries, while his fingers thrust into her, filling her full, stroking the last of her climax from her body.

She collapsed against him, and he held her tight. She was completed, but he was starving. His black blood needing her. Lust was ready to toss her onto the floor and take her.

He knew he was too weak to resist. He could no longer defy his Unseelie desires, and Lust's need.

She'd given him her name, he had power over her, and he used it. Just this once, he told himself. Silently, he commanded her to waken, to fight the languid feeling in her body, and instead feel the aching emptiness inside her.

"Thane," she moaned, brushing restless against him. "Please, I need…"

"I know what you need."

Thane couldn't help but growl when he felt Chastity's beautiful tits graze his chin. He was delighting in stroking the vein of her neck with his tongue, and she was delighting in torturing him with her pert nipples, teasing him into suckling her. But he would resist—ignore—the predator within that was clamoring to devour the delightful morsel in his arms.

It wasn't enough to fling her onto her back and embed himself within her. It might have satisfied his craving if she'd been one of the courtesans or opera dancers he frequented. But this was Chastity—the woman he wanted above all others, the woman he had to seduce, to make understand that what she thought was truly him couldn't be further from the truth.

He wanted to awaken her, to make her mindless with need, to slowly satisfy her. He didn't want their first time to be a quick rut—and by the way his cock was swelling and filling, he knew it would be too quick. No, he wanted the awakening of Chastity to be slow and sensual. He wanted to feel her tight against him, then slowly stretch to accommodate him. Unfortunately, if she didn't quit writhing in his arms, brushing her tits against his face and rubbing her mound against his trousers, he was going to grab her hips and take her in an act of raw possession.

The vision took hold, and in an impulsive but highly satisfying act, he took her breasts in his hands, pushing

them together and burying his face between them, inhaling the sweet and innocent floral scent of her while
nuzzling her skin, his thumbs coaxing her nipples to
harden further for him.

The sound was a guttural cry from deep in her throat.
The need, the desire he heard pushed him on, and he
squeezed, then tugged and pinched at her nipples, while
his mouth continued to suck the milky flesh of her
breasts. Her fingers were on his shoulders, tightening,
biting as he took one straining nipple into his mouth, sip-
ping it between his lips before suckling, pulling the flesh
into his mouth, drinking in her passion with increasing
need. She moaned, and rubbed her curls along him while
he sucked, his other hand kneading a path down to her
belly.

She arched beautifully into his mouth as he increased
his suckling, his tongue flicking out to soothe and lave
the reddened nipple. When he grasped it between his
teeth and gently bit, she shivered, her stomach delightfully quivering beneath his fingers. He'd never felt that
before—the quivering of a woman as desire and need
swept through her. He'd been aware of the need in his
conquests from the tightening of their breasts, the scent
and wetness of their arousal, but he'd never taken the
time to study them, to run his fingers along their bodies
and discover where else they might feel desire.

"Oh, God," Chastity moaned, unable to stem the shaking of her limbs as his fingers swept over her belly and
along her sides. If he would only touch her *there.* If she
could just feel his fingers buried deep within her she

could be rid of this escalating desire, a pleasure almost painful in its intensity. Fool that she was, she wanted him. Her body ached for him, her heart pleaded with her mind to give him another chance. *Let him prove himself,* it whispered.

Gooseflesh flickered down her spine and along her bottom as Thane's wickedly sensual fingers swept down her back, tickling her buttocks and trailing down the backs of her thighs.

"Touch me, Thane…like before," she whispered, frantic to feel his fingers in her wetness.

"I'm not sure what you mean." He brought her breasts together again, his eyes challenging her—daring her to say the words.

"Please," she whimpered, silently telling him by rubbing her wet curls against him. "You know where."

He tickled her then, his fingers slowly grazing the top of her mound, his fingers curling in her hair, tempting her, making her wish to beg for his touch. Chastity felt the warmth pool as he slid one finger along her wetness. He parted her, slipping one finger, then another deep within her.

"Do you know what you do to me?" Thane asked, meeting her eyes through the fringe of his sable lashes. "So pure and innocent to look at, but I get one hand on you and you're wanton and hot. You're every man's fantasy, Chastity."

"Every man? But you're a fey."

He groaned, probing her deeper. "Come for me, Chastity. It's been too long since I had you, since I felt you on my hand."

Gods, it wasn't supposed to be happening this way, Thane thought through the thick cloud of lust. Her deflowering was supposed to be gentle, romantic, soft as a dove's feather. He was supposed to take her into the bath, kiss her, stroke her, murmur words of love before laying her on the bed and slowly, carefully sliding inside her. It damn well wasn't part of his plan to have her straddling him, his cock in her hand, poised at her entrance, her tits bobbing in his mouth.

This was Lust, trying to take over. He couldn't allow it.

"Mmm, Thane," she purred against him, her lips pouting in ecstasy, her fingers running wildly through his hair, her hips moving up and down to the rhythm of his fingers. "This feels so good—so right." She sighed.

But he didn't want to take her like this. He didn't know what the hell he wanted. He wanted her to ride him, he wanted to watch her bend before him as he slid into her in an act of raw possession, he wanted to make love to her, watching the wonder in her eyes, to hear her guttural cries of release when he fucked her soundly, pumping himself into her, making her realize that she was his, and only his.

God, he wanted so much. Slow and loving—hard and needy. He desired it all, everything she would give him. Hell, he hadn't shown her a fraction of what he wanted to do. He'd planned to lick her, to taste her and pleasure her with his mouth, to lap her as he made her come. He wanted to watch her learn him, to see her luscious mouth around his cock before he claimed her body. And yet, he could think of nothing more than making her his before anything could happen to stop it.

"Thane," she cried, surprised to find herself on her back with him bent between her legs. He'd at least made it to the bed. Lust had wanted her on the floor.

"I told you that I'd make you mine. You understand what that will mean, don't you, Chastity?"

"That I will no longer be a virgin."

"No, that you will belong to me—only me."

Chastity gasped, then moaned, feeling the unforgiving hardness of him slide into her body. Slowly, inexorably penetrating her. His breathing was harsh, short pants, almost groans escaping his lips as he filled her.

"You're so wonderfully snug."

"You feel…" Chastity squirmed beneath his weight, delighting in his husky moan. "You feel rather large." She skimmed her hands over Thane's muscled back and down to his bottom, which was rock hard between her thighs. Instinctively she put her legs around his waist, letting him go deeper, penetrating her farther.

"Beautiful," he whispered, straightening from her and cupping her bottom in his hands, his gaze trained on where their bodies were joined. He stroked her a few times, letting her stretch, letting her grow wetter around him, all the while watching as he filled her.

"Chastity?" he asked, his voice horse. "I want you to look at me as I make you mine."

She met his gaze, her heart skipping a beat as she

watched every muscle in his chest and arms taut with tension—with virile strength. His eyes were a deep dark blue, and his lips were furled in a devastating grin. With one quick, deep thrust he impaled her, quickly moaning then covering her with his body, slowly moving, allowing her to accustom herself to his size and the feel of him moving atop her.

The pain wasn't as bad as she'd feared. It was a brief pinching, burning sensation before quickly giving way to a delicious feeling of being consumed by her beautiful Dark Fey.

"Move with me," he encouraged, taking her hands in his and raising them above her head so that he covered the whole length of her body, his chest rubbing against her breasts, tickling and sensitizing her nipples. The bed creaked, and Thane's breathing was sharper, harsher then she'd ever heard. With every stroke he thrust deeper inside her, making her moan as she matched his rhythm. Suddenly his body shook and he cried out her name before shuddering atop her.

"I did not love you that day in Glastonbury," he whispered, "but I can say that I love you now." She tried to speak, but he covered her lips with his fingers. "When you leave here tonight, you will not go to the masquerade as planned. You will feign a headache, and return to your home. And then," he whispered, "you will cover your body with perfume, and lie in your bed awaiting me. I will come to you. Have you. Claim you."

FIFTEEN

CROM STUDIED THE WOMAN IN THE SHADOWED hall. Mary Lennox was a sensual creature who called to his baser desires. On the outside he was very much a Seelie Fey. On the inside, however, he was his dark counterpart. There was no denying that his father's blood ran inside him. Thick. Black. Hot.

Coyly, Mary looked up at him, her long, lush black lashes batting ingenuously. Behind the long lashes were dark blue eyes that were shining with anything but innocence.

She was completely different from her sisters. Nothing at all like them. He wondered if she knew it. If it bothered her. As she pressed back against the wall, deeper into the shadows where the darkness engulfed her, he knew that it didn't. She was what she was. Her own woman.

"To what do I owe the pleasure?" she murmured,

and the not-so-subtle huskiness of her voice called to his cock.

"Your sister. Where is she?"

She frowned, then brightened, pushing toward him with her voluptuous body. "Have you lost her already?"

He couldn't think when her breasts grazed his chest. He wanted to rut with her. Wanted to fuck her senseless, but he wanted Chastity more. Needed the virtues in his court—much more than he wanted Mary. But he was angry. Worried that his Unseelie enemies had gotten to her first, despite his careful warding and the spies he had planted in their home. Chastity and her sisters should have arrived at the masquerade.

"Do you really think that my sister can satisfy you?" Mary purred as she ran her palms up the breadth of his chest. "She's a frightened little kitten who would faint at the thoughts that are running through your mind at this very moment."

Carelessly, he tossed out his plans and reached for her, wrapped his arm around her waist and pushed her back to the wall. "But you are not a kitten," he said, cupping her lush breast in his palm. "You're a lynx with an appetite for prey."

She smiled and allowed her hand to move down his chest, to cup his cock. "Just a certain type of kill."

"You're not like them," he murmured. "Not one bit."

She laughed, her voice tinkling in the dark. "Lord, I hope not. Those pious, boring sisters of mine. They are imprisoned by what they think they ought to be. I, on the other hand, long ago shed those chains that bound me."

"You know what I am. What I want."

She moved her body sinuously up against him. "A beautiful, golden fey," she murmured, "who has a taste for mortal sins."

"I want your sister."

"Mmm," she murmured, "but you want to fuck me."

He slammed her up against the wall, his cock pressing between the juncture of her thighs. "Yes."

"Then let us make a deal," she murmured, cupping him. "You give me what I want. And I will give you what you want."

He pulled at her bodice, but she stopped him. "As gorgeous as you are, you're not what I want."

Crom froze and glared at her. *The little cock tease.*

"Give me my fey prince and I will ensure that Chastity will be yours."

Crom's instinct was to snuff the life out of her, but then, his calculating Seelie mind began to shake free of the lust his Unseelie blood had used to cloud his judgment.

"You have one minute to explain yourself."

She smiled, his cock still in her hand. Still hard. Still wanting to climb inside her and pound into her.

"You know that I am different from my sisters."

He nodded. The truth was in her eyes. There was no innocence there. Only feminine calculation.

"I've known it for years. I am not one of them. Not a

virtue. But I want what is mine. I am promised to a fey prince named Rinion, and I want him."

"I know of no prince by such a name."

That was the truth. There was no fey at court called by such a name. But the Unseelie Court…that was entirely possible.

"I saw him. Speaking with my father. He bequeathed to my father riches, and in return he wanted me."

"Then why are you not in his bed," he inquired, "and instead in a dark corner with me?"

Her beautiful eyes turned mutinous. "That is something I would like to know. I should have been his at Beltane. But Father took us away, and he has not come to claim me. I thought perhaps he would come with you, but it is apparent that he did not."

"You want your fey prince and in return for my securing him for you, you will ensure that Chastity will be mine."

"I will do more than ensure it," she whispered. "I will deliver her naked to you, if that is what you desire."

He did. Naked and on her knees. A supplicant. *His.*

"Very well. But I will need one more assurance on your part."

"Yes?"

"Once you are in Rinion's bed, you will become my spy at his court. You will report to me anything you might see or hear."

"Just get me my prince, and I will be anything you want."

"We have an accord," he said with satisfaction.

"My father owns a bawdy house," she said. "A silent part owner, of course, but an owner nonetheless. He was to meet with someone there tonight."

"And how do you know this?" he asked suspiciously.

"I make it my business to know." Her eyes flashed. "Father was careless with his correspondence. I found the missive balled up."

"You're a resourceful little thing."

"I will be of use to you once you place me in the Unseelie Court. I assure you I have many skills that will be rather useful."

"I am sure. But back to this house?"

"The Nymph and the Satyr."

She squeezed him—hard, then released him and slid out from beneath him. He watched her go, smiling to himself.

He had achieved much more than he thought he would. He would have Mary's assistance with Chastity, but more than that, he would have a spy at his brother's court. But there was one troubling matter that he would need to think upon. Mary Lennox was not a virtue. So where was Lennox hiding the fourth?

Outside the bawdy house, Thane carefully lifted Chastity into the carriage. Niall had placed her and Lennox, along with her sisters, under a light sleeping spell. It would be gone by the time they reached their home.

He didn't want to give her up. His time with her had been too short. He'd left things unfinished. They needed to talk. He needed to tell her of her purpose. To convince her that what they had was real.

Slamming the carriage door shut, Avery snapped the reins. He would take them home safely. Kian was back inside, locked in his room. His sin was eating at him, and he did not trust himself to say goodbye.

"You look forlorn."

Thane glanced at Niall. "I cannot help but sense that something ominous draws near."

"She will come to our court, have no fear."

"I haven't told her how we need her. She'll be upset when she learns of it, and I fear that Crom will tell her before I can. Surprisingly, he hasn't already."

"That is because he needs her, too, and he does not wish her to know it. He's playing the same game as us, wooing her to his court."

"I'm not playing at it," Thane said. Niall stepped back and studied him.

"Hundreds of years old and you've never felt this way about any woman. A few days with this one little mortal and you are swept away."

Thane blushed, thankful for the darkness of the alley. Niall was right. How had it happened so soon?

"I hope it happens for me the same way." Niall chuckled. "Now, back to the house. We have work to do. A trap to set for the Seelie."

Thane watched as Niall stepped into the shadows, and reentered the bawdy house. He had no wish to go back there. He wanted to go to Chastity. To take her in his arms and assure her that everything was going to be all right.

Grudgingly he followed his king back to the house. Then he smelled it, the cloying stench of Seelie.

"Show yourself, Crom," he ordered as he drew his sword from his scabbard. The faery metal sang in the quiet as he slowly turned around. "I know you're here."

A rat scurrying along the slime-coated cobbles drew his gaze to a darkened corner where a drunken sailor, passed out, was propped up in an alcove. Able to see the most trivial detail in the dark, Thane scanned the blackness for the Seelie bastard.

There was no visible sign of his enemy.

Besides being devoid of Crom, the alley was utterly silent, as if every creature of the night were holding its breath, waiting for the confrontation they felt building in the thick air.

The Seelie was near, he felt him, concealed amongst the sifting shadows and the dark outlines of the ramshackle homes of Spitalfields.

"I know you're here, Crom," he repeated, circling around, searching through the murkiness of the poorly lit alley. "I can smell you. Coward." He snapped when there was no answer.

Suddenly, something reached out from the darkness and thrust him against the wall. A hand clasped around his neck and tightened, squeezing and crushing the bones of his throat.

"Here I am," a voice hissed in his ear. Tightening his fingers around his throat, Crom pressed closer and growled low in his ear. "You didn't think you were the only one who could use magic to change your shape, did you?"

Thane struggled to breathe, but Crom held on tighter. "While you were murmuring in her ear, *Prince Thane*," he mocked, "did you happen to whisper the reason you need her so badly?"

The bastard. He was going to go to Chastity. His resolve flared, despite the hold on his throat and lack of oxygen. Fingers searching, Thane reached for his belt and the small dirk he kept hidden there. Crom was still seething, still choking him, but Thane managed to pull the dirk free. With the hilt in his hand, he brought his arm up, arching outward, and swiped through the darkness, hoping to connect with Crom. The roar of pain echoing off the walls told him he had.

Crom's golden form appeared, hunched over, blood dripping down his arm. Thane wasted no time, and confronted the bastard.

"You'll leave her alone, if you want to live."

With a laugh, Crom straightened and engaged him with his own sword. They parried, thrust and the anger and fear that ruled him swiftly overpowered Crom. With a shove, he threw Crom against the wall and placed the edge of his sword to his throat.

"She's mine," he said harshly. *"Mine."*

"Let us see, Unseelie bastard."

And then Crom was gone. Vanished into the night, and no doubt to Chastity's house.

Changing his shape, he turned into mist and headed for

Mayfair. He could not let Crom convince Chastity that he cared nothing for her. The Seelie would try to make her believe that Thane was out to use her. Perhaps in the beginning he was. But after tonight, he knew differently. The court might need her, but he needed her more.

chaperone, then we will be forced to cancel the entire outing."

Chastity rested a reassuring hand on Prue's leg. "Of course it will be fine if Mary accompanies us. We will take the town coach, and no one will be able to see if we have brought our maids or our sister."

"I wanted to take the varouche," her sister replied sourly. "It's going to be a lovely day."

"Girls…" Their mother sighed. "Please. No more bickering. You will take the town coach and go with Mary, or you will not go at all." She sighed again, let her head fall into her palm. "My word, I'm exhausted. I can't explain it."

Mercy caught their gaze from across the table and mouthed the words *faery sleep* to them.

Strange. Only Mama and Papa seemed to be affected. The footman who was busy bringing silver dishes of bacon and eggs seemed rather awake and alert. And Mary did as well, and she had not been with them last night. *With the Dark Fey,* her mind whispered.

"Well, then, it is all settled," Mary announced. "I will take my sisters on a ride in Hyde Park with Lord Arawn and Crom."

"And I will take to my bed," their mother murmured, rising from her chair.

"After you, m'dear."

Chastity watched the retreating backs of her parents, her brow puckered in a frown. Something was wrong.

"Well, wasn't that convenient?" Mary smiled, one that

Sixteen

I hear him, Diary, begging entrance. As I look up I see the mist on the window and know it is him. He has come, but I dare not let him in. I do not understand myself. What have I done? I've given myself, everything I am to him. Everything I believed myself to be is gone. I no longer know who—or what I am—save for a ruined woman.

My lover is a Dark Fey. Who wants me for what purpose? I dare not believe in his love. I dare not allow him in because I will only succumb. My head and body war with my heart. They want things that I cannot give in to. Not yet. There is more here than I understand. A reason why two rival courts would fight over me—a virgin mortal of no consequence.

He is gone now, and as I look to the window, I'm hollow. Empty. I am in love with a Dark Fey who cannot be trusted. I am ruined. Alone. Miserable. Love is not anything like I thought it would be. It is painful, frightening, and I would give anything to have never set eyes upon him or Crom. Indeed, I wish I could take everything back and be as I once was, but then I'm left feeling even more miserable, because that would mean that I would never have felt passion.

Everything always comes back to that. To desire, to Thane. To his purpose in my life. And mine in his. Am I something to amuse him? Can I trust him?

Not tonight. But perhaps tomorrow when I can think clearly, when the scent of him is washed from body, and the memory of his body inside me is not so achingly familiar.

THANE HAD NOT ATTEMPTED TO COME BACK to her last night. She had slept fitfully, instinctively awaiting his arrival, but he had not come. And she had not dreamed of him. This morning as she spread jam on her toast, she recalled the events in the room with Thane. She had given him her virginity—a foolish thing to do—yet she could not stop thinking of it, or cease her body's clamor for more.

After their interlude, she had found herself coming to in their carriage. Prudence, Mercy and her father had been there, all four of them fast asleep. They awoke from their faery sleep bewitched.

Their father had been most perplexed, recalling very little of the events. But Chastity and her sisters recalled much more. Each of them had been taken to private chambers and introduced to a fey. Mercy had met with Kian, and Prue had met with a man called Avery—one she despised openly. Thane, of course, had been waiting for her.

Her mother had no recollection of them not arriving

at the ball. It was as if she remembered nothing p[...] terday afternoon. Mary, on the other hand, seem[...] recall perfectly. She kept sending her and Prue cr[...] glances. Strangely, she held her tongue.

"Pass the tea," her father grumbled. "My head ache[...] he mumbled as he rubbed a thumb over his eye. "P'ra[...] another cup will fix it."

"I'm so sleepy," her mother said around a yawn. "I vow I shall have to return to bed after breakfast."

"I'll be joining you," Papa mumbled before pouring himself another steaming cup of tea.

"But who will chaperone us on our ride with Lord Arawn?" Prue asked. Her eyes were wide and frightened, as if she feared not being able to see the golden Seelie.

"Your sister Mary can."

Mary's eyes lit up. "Of course, Papa."

Chastity didn't believe it was at all proper. Mary was only a few minutes older then the rest of them. She was hardly a spinster.

"Do you think that is at all proper, Papa?" Prue admonished.

"It's that, or cancel the appointment," he said impatiently. "And I'm inclined to send our regrets and be done with it."

"No!" Prue gasped. "No, you can't."

"I can do anything I damn well please," her father growled, then immediately softened. "Prue, dearest. My apologies. But you must understand that your mother and I are under the weather today, and if Mary does not

didn't quite reach her eyes. "They certainly know how to get what they want."

"Who?" Chastity asked.

"Why, the fey, of course," her sister replied. "Now, if you will excuse me, I have a letter to write."

Mary departed the room, leaving her three sisters behind. "You may be excused," Chastity said to the two footmen who stood sentry at the dining room door.

Obeying her, the men took their leave. Now she was all alone with her sisters. "What the devil is going on here?" she demanded.

"Faery sleep," Mercy said as she lifted her teacup to her mouth. "It's a common enough spell in the fey arsenal."

"You cannot mean that they have sprinkled pixie dust over Mama's and Papa's heads," Prue snorted. "For heaven's sake. Mama, thank the Lord, was not in that den of iniquity last night. She could not possibly be under their spell."

"What makes you think this is an *Unseelie* spell?"

Prue visibly started, then narrowed her gaze upon Mercy. "Because the Dark Fey are cunning, immoral tricksters, that's why, and because we were forced into their brothel and made to spend hours with them, for their own amusement, and at the expense of our good names and reputations. Not to mention that of Papa's."

"From my reading, that is not how the spell works. A fey must have either physical contact with the person they are putting under their spell, or be given that person's full name. Since none of the Dark Fey have even laid eyes on our mother, it's impossible for them to be at the source of this."

Chastity flicked her gaze to Mercy's. "The Seelie then."

She nodded. "They have the same magical powers as their dark brethren. And they are not above using it to gain what they want."

"And that's why Mary isn't affected, because the Seelie want us—the virtues."

"I will not believe this," Prue snapped, tossing her napkin aside and hastily shoving back her chair. "I won't believe it of them. The Seelie are from the golden court, and those monsters we encountered last night are from the dark court. If there is any malicious spell casting going on, it's their doing, not Arawn's—I mean, the Seelie's."

Prue's face was splotched red. "Everything is so unbelievably strange. I cannot believe I am standing here debating which faery court has bespelled our house. I should not even believe in faeries."

"Prue," Mercy called as their sister stamped out of the breakfast room. "Please don't be angry with me."

"And why are you always so nice?" Prue lashed out as she whirled around to confront them. "Why can't you see that the Dark Fey will ruin us? They will destroy everything we are."

"That is my gift. Kindness. I do see the good in them. They could have whisked us off to their court last night, but they didn't."

"I wonder why. Surely it is not because they possess

morals, Mercy. It is because it did not suit them. Why? I have no idea. But I will not stop till I understand why they want us. There is something going on here, something much stranger than us, and the fact that we are to belong to the fey. Can you not feel it? Of course not," Prue scoffed, "because you are always trying to be kind and understanding. To search for the good. Well, I am telling you, Mercy Lennox, there is nothing good about the Dark Fey."

The door banged shut, emphasizing Prudence's departure. Prudence, who had neither tempered nor restrained her vitriol.

"It's not them," Mercy murmured as she cast her gaze out the window. "I felt the good in him last night. There is good. He could have ravished me, but he didn't. I even would have let him, and sadly, wish he had tried."

Smiling, Chastity reached for her sister's hand. "There is no need to explain yourself. I believe you. Prudence, on the other hand, cannot see past Lord Arawn. She is smitten, you see, and wants to believe that the Seelie are righteous and virtuous—like us."

"They will prove themselves," Mercy murmured. "I know they will."

Mercy rose and left Chastity to her thoughts. Thane was a Dark Fey. There was no disguising how opposite he was in looks and manner to Crom. But despite his Unseelie blood, he had never hurt her, endangered her, forced her to do anything she had not wanted—at least on some conscious level—to experience. But his silence had hurt her. She still sensed that there was more going on than what Thane had told her. He'd wanted her to believe that he neglected to tell her who and what he was because he'd been afraid that she would not accept him. But Chastity knew differently. There was a reason he was so driven to seduce her. It lay beyond his Unseelie desires.

"My lady?"

Chastity's concentration was broken by the arrival of a footman. In his hand was a gold box tied with a black satin ribbon.

He set the box before her. "This just arrived for you."

"Thank you."

Chastity waited for the footman to leave before she reached for the tail of the black ribbon and pulled. The bow unraveled, and she set it aside as she carefully opened the box. Inside, layers of black satin hid its contents.

Her heart was racing as her fingers scraped against a card. Pulling it from the satin, she turned it over to find it blank on either side. Strange. Brushing her thumb over the smooth surface, she gasped, squeaked and smiled all at once as the motion of her thumb caused black ink to appear.

A Dark Fey always bestows a gift unto his lady—normally a mask, to be worn while in the woods. A symbol of his protection and adoration. But I saw this and knew it would speak to you. Wear this, and allow me to adore and protect you.

It was signed *Always, Thane.*

Thrusting her hand back into the box, Chastity pulled

out a silver chain with a black onyx and moonstone pendant hanging from it. The onyx caught the sunbeam, and the stone glistened and glowed, illuminating a little catch at the side.

Not a pendant after all, but a locket.

Prying it open, she revealed a perfumed waxed center. Bringing it to her nose, she inhaled deeply, her blood and body instantly warming to the scent—the essence of Thane. The heady concoction she had smelled in the maze. The one she always detected while in his presence. The very perfume that was even now sitting on her dressing table.

Slipping it over her head, she admired it, the way the pendant dropped low on her bosom. It was a stunning piece of jewelry, but she could not wear it.

You will wear it, and you will think of me.

She heard Thane's command, and found herself with the necklace on. She could not refuse his command, and wondered if this was yet another faery spell.

At precisely half past four, Crom and Lord Arawn arrived at the Lennox home to collect Chastity, Prue and Mary, and the five of them were off by quarter to the hour.

The Seelie were nothing if not punctual, and mindful of such things as polite society. As the horses cantered down the street, Chastity found herself wondering about their court. Would it be full of politics and formalities? Despite it being the court of sunlight and gaiety, would it really be just a somber, stiff affair with a golden veneer?

And the Unseelie Court. Was it really only darkness and sin? Was there more to it than just a place designed for seduction and sensualities?

The horses cantered to the left, and the carriage swayed. So too did the locket that was nestled between her breasts. The air moved, stirring up the scent of the perfume. She had used the wax that afternoon, dipping her finger into it and sliding it along her wrists, behind her ears, down the cleft of her breasts. The heat from her skin had absorbed it and now her flesh shimmered where she had perfumed it. In the sunlight that shone through the carriage window, it reminded her of moonbeams on mist.

Silently, she watched out the window, her gaze averted from Crom, who sat on the bench across from her. He was content enough with her silence, preferring to stare at her instead. She had no idea what his thoughts were, and did not care. She had only agreed to come for Prue's sake, because her sister was so hopelessly ensnared by Arawn's golden beauty. But Chastity was not. She much preferred Thane's dark and mysterious aura. Somehow she had reconciled herself that he was not of her kind. He was a faery, a dark and sensual one. The truth hadn't turned her from him. She feared nothing could. He owned her heart now. In between possessing her mouth and body, he had invaded her soul. In the stolen moments of her dreams, when they had been alone in the garden, she had felt a growing closeness to him. It was desire, yes, but something more. A closeness of spirit. A glimpse of what was just beginning, and what happiness they might find together, despite the fact she was a mortal and he a fey.

Smiling, she thought of that afternoon when she had lain down for a nap, of how they had danced in the garden and the butterflies had flitted around them. She wanted to see his court, to share that with him. She wanted to be part of his life—a frightening but true revelation. Oh, God, she suspected she was already falling in love with him. And there was nothing she could do about it. The only thing she could do was sit in the carriage and think of him, wish he were here with her.

Hyde Park was alive with black lacquered carriages bearing aristocratic crests and elegantly dressed gentlemen riding prime horseflesh. It was the fashionable hour for London's best society. It was the time for the cream of society to see and be seen. She watched the carriages that littered the park avenues, all vying for the best positions. It was like watching the plumage of a bird spreading in an attempt to court a mate. These carriages were all here for one of two things—to court or to gather gossip. It was never simply for pleasure.

There was a sense of forbidden anticipation, a prevailing thought amongst the unmarried women and the courting gentlemen, that the privacy of a carriage ride might just cast enough shadow, or diversion, so that one might steal a kiss, or at the very least, brush hands, without their guardians noticing such wayward behavior.

Chastity averted her gaze from the carriage window and glanced at her sister, who was acting as her companion who was naturally gazing out the other window that overlooked Rotten Row and the numerous gentlemen cantering atop their steeds.

"You are in deep thought," Crom said, breaking the silence between them. Beside her, Prue and Arawn conversed in low tones.

"My pardon. I fear I am not much company or a scintillating conversationalist this afternoon."

"Nonsense. You are obviously consumed with something most pressing. Your brow has been furrowed in concentration since the carriage pulled away from the front of your house."

"Forgive me," she murmured. "I am ruining your drive, aren't I?"

"Of course not. I am just worried for you. You haven't slept much, if the circles beneath your eyes are any indication."

"I have slept well."

"And your dreams?" he asked, his voice dropping low. "Have they been pleasant?"

How impertinent! She would never speak to Crom of her dreams. Would never tell him of Thane, and what they did in the privacy of the dark.

"Obviously my sister is not inclined to share her dreams, my lord," Mary cut in. "She must be persuaded."

Crom glared at Mary, then focused his gaze back on her. "Dreams are very personal things, are they not?"

"They are indeed," Chastity sniffed.

"But best shared, do you agree?"

She stiffened when Crom smiled at her. It was not a

smile of mirth, but one of victory. Mary and Crom shared a glance that Chastity could not interpret.

"I had a dream last night," Crom said as he leaned in and caught her gloved hand in his. "You were dancing with me, and you had a gown on made of gold and silver. You sparkled in the candlelight, just like a queen."

"I believe, sir, that this conversation is best left alone."

Glancing away, Chastity resumed watching the passing carriages. She could not listen to anything more. She would not go to the Seelie Court. She would not attend any further drives or dances with Crom. Not when all she could think about was Thane. Despite everything that had happened and her worries over what he was hiding from her, she wanted him.

Even now, she could sense that he was there with her— *with them*—inside the carriage. She could smell him, and it was not just the perfume. But something stronger. She felt him, his heat along her body.

I will not let you go to him…

Chastity heard his voice in the quiet of her thoughts. How strange it was to be riding in a carriage with flesh-and-blood people while hearing another's voice in her head. Did her sisters know that Thane was speaking to her? Did Crom, or Lord Arawn?

Only you can hear me. Only you know that I am here. Only you know what I am doing.

She shivered, feeling a touch along her neck then behind her ear. It tickled and sensitized her flesh, making her squirm on the carriage bench. Her body was warming, the place between her thighs melting, aching...

She heard Thane laugh low in her ear, felt him kiss her skin and heard him whisper, *Let me seduce you here. Now. The Dark Fey are so very skilled at this.*

Warmth settled along her thigh as she felt him continue to nuzzle her throat. She felt the hem of her gown and the ruffled edge of her petticoats skim over the top of her heeled slippers. Up and up, she felt her skirts being raised. Gasping, she looked down into her lap, fearing she would find her skirts hiked up over her knees. But curiously she found herself in an impeccable state of dress. There was not a wrinkle or a wiggle of linen to give any indication that she was being ravished by an Unseelie faery while sitting in the carriage.

Only you know what I am doing, he murmured, drawing her back to what he was doing with his hands. *It should make you feel wicked and wanton, knowing you are being pleasured so secretly. It should burn you up, knowing you cannot move nor make a sound of pleasure. You will have to be so quiet, so still. You will have to allow me to explore you, and you cannot protest, cannot move away to prevent me from taking what I want.*

Her lips parted on a silent rush of breath and her lashes closed as she felt Thane's hand snake beneath her chemise, only to climb up the length of her thigh. Long fingers pressed between her clenched thighs, and she stole a look at Crom and saw, with great relief, that he had turned his gaze once more to the window.

Spread your pretty thighs for me.

Trying to rein in her breathing, she inched her knees apart. Immediately his hand sunk between her flesh, his palm cupping her.

Already wet, he purred. *How wicked of you to be yearning for this, me fingering you while he sits across from you, ignorant of what is happening.*

Parting her outer lips, Thane caressed her softly and with aching slowness, building her, until she had to move, had to squirm against the velvet squabs of the bench. Stealing another look at Crom, and seeing he was lost in his thoughts, Chastity flexed her hips, forcing Thane to touch her with a firmer, less teasing stroke.

Little innocent Chastity, he breathed. *Tell me you want this, what I am doing to you. That you want this right now.*

I want it, she answered. *I want so much to feel you inside me.*

He sunk his finger deep inside and Chastity had to cover her mouth with her hand to stifle the moan that threatened to escape her. Slowly, he filled her with two fingers, plunging and retreating until she was nearly gasping.

You want to beg for it, don't you? You want to cry out loud for me to finish you.

Please, she begged him, her fingers gripping the soft nap of the velvet upholstered bench. *Please.*

The scent of your cunt fills the carriage, did you know that? He can smell it, your arousal, and the way it perfumes the air. Look at him, Chastity, watching you.

Her head snapped to the right and she saw that Crom

was indeed staring at her intently, his gaze straying over her with a liberality he had never dared before.

It is a pity that you cannot undo the pearl buttons securing the front of your gown. I should like to see his face as you undo your bodice and bare your breasts to him. I should like to see you bare breasted as I have my hand between your thighs. I'd like to watch you cupping them in your hands, bringing them together, offering them up to my mouth.

Her lashes fluttered, threatening to close altogether as she struggled to act as though nothing untoward was happening. Swallowing hard, Chastity fought the image of her hands parting her bodice and freeing her breasts, which were now so swollen and aching from her corset.

He's imagining you naked, spread for him. I can see into his mind, and he's painted you perfectly. But it's me here with you. My essence glistening on your skin.

She cast a glance at her décolletage that was spilling from her bodice. It did indeed still glisten. Moonbeams on mist...

He's wishing his hand was where mine is now. He's wondering what this pink silk would feel like against his fingers. He's wondering how you'd taste against his probing tongue.

She choked a little then and stiffened. Crom's violet eyes darkened, his gaze lowered to her lap where she smoothed her hand along her skirt. *Stop,* she pleaded, reaching for Thane's hand, which she could feel but could not see. *Stop, he knows.*

But he pushed her on, driving her to the brink with his fingers inside her and his thumb circling the bud beneath her hood. She was nearly there, close to release when Thane whispered, *The next time the Seelie bastard takes you driving in the park, I'm going to lift your skirts and taste you. Imagine that, Chastity, my mouth buried between your thighs as you talk to him about the weather and the number of carriages passing by. Imagine me there, pushing you on, tasting, sucking, eating at you as he sits before you, imagining what he will never, ever be able to have.*

Release was upon her. Blood rushed to her cheeks. Her gaze locked with Crom as she felt Thane stroking her to completion. How wicked to know she was being touched in such a way while another sat inches away, completely unaware. Like a wanton, she reveled in the pleasure and saw, in her mind, the image of what she imagined her Dark Fey lover would look like, with his head between her spread thighs, his tongue doing to her what his fingers were doing.

You're coming. I can feel it. You look stunning with your flushed cheeks. He cannot take his eyes from you. Look at him, Chastity, and know who it is pleasuring you.

She did, and found herself smiling wickedly. What sort of fey was this, provoking her to sin?

"I think we had better return home," Crom muttered as she felt herself explode around Thane's fingers. Sagging against the squabs, Chastity took a shaking breath as Crom reached for his hat and placed it on his lap. "The hour grows late. And I fear that—"

The Seelie fears that the scent of your aroused quim is making him descend into madness. Your essence is enough to bring any man—mortal or fey—to his knees, and I, my sweet, am no different.

Half an hour later, the carriage was slowing before their town house. Thane was still with her, holding her. She felt him as if he were actually sitting there beside her. She felt comforted in his arms, as though she was cherished. A comforting warmth stole over her, and she realized now how much he had come to mean to her. In the beginning she had feared him, her attraction to him, she had warned him away. Tried everything in her power to keep him at arm's length, yet he had braved her disapproval, withstood her pleas to leave her be, and instead pursued her. In the end, he had claimed not only her body, but her heart, as well.

Then let me take you away. The words were whispered in her mind. *Let me take you to my court.*

She barely hesitated in her answer. "Yes, take me to your dark court."

Crom watched as the three women climbed the steps of the town house. He was losing. For the first time in his life he felt an uncontrollable rage begin to sweep through him. *Fucking Unseelie bastard!* Somehow Thane had found a way into the carriage. He smelled him. Felt the charge in the carriage as Chastity's body heated, her arousal engulfing the still air. The bastard had been seducing her right beneath his nose and there wasn't a damn thing he could do but watch, and grow hard as she came before his eyes.

She'd hid it remarkably well, but as a fey, he knew.

His senses were keener than those of mortals and he had heard her blood rushing through her veins, the sound of her breathing increase, the way it panted between her lips. He smelled the honey seep from her body.

Damn it! He smashed the wall of the carriage with his balled fist. He would not lose her to the Unseelie swine. And that was exactly what was happening. Thane was going to take her to his court, and she would follow willingly. He couldn't have that. Not only because he wanted Chastity in his bed, but because he couldn't loose her as a virtue. He needed her if he was going to thwart his mother's rule.

There was only one thing to be done, and that was to turn Chastity away from Thane. There was only one way to do that, reveal her true purpose on this earth. It would turn her from him, but then, he had an advantage over the Unseelie. He did not need Chastity's willing acceptance. He could take her, fighting him all the way. Thane had no such luxury. It would be much more difficult for him to convince her to believe his sincerity once Crom had disclosed the purpose of Thane's ardent pursuit.

Chastity was a female, and every female, no matter which species she belonged to, did not wish to be used—especially by a man she believed herself to be in love with.

Chastity's love for his dark counterpart meant nothing to him. He did not need her love. Merely her body and the sons she would give him.

SEVENTEEN

SHE WAS ASLEEP. HE HAD WATCHED HER BATHE and brush her long hair out as she sat in her chemise at her dressing table. Lust had wanted to pick her up and carry her to the bed, sinking himself inside her. Thane had wanted to do the same. Ever since the carriage ride, when she had brought him along after using the perfume in the locket on her body, he had been consumed by the need to claim her.

Crom, that bastard, had leered at her the entire time, and Thane had been able to see inside his mind. See that the Seelie wanted her as badly—and in all the ways—that Thane did.

She was not safe. Not even after he claimed her would she be safe. For the fey were not dissuaded by things like that. Unlike their human counterparts, the fey were not put off by a woman's experience. Frequently they shared their women, so Crom would not be put off the chase simply because Thane had been the one to take Chastity's virginity.

No, the only way she would be truly safe from Crom and the Seelie Court was to come to his court. She had agreed, and he would not linger here, in the mortal realm. He could not risk the chance that she would change her mind.

Standing over her, watching her asleep, with her hand curled beneath her cheek, Thane knew it was the only way. Knew that tonight must be the night.

He knew he should lift her up and carry her away, but Lust was pummeling him relentlessly. One look at her and both fey and sin wanted her.

Pulling back the sheets, he revealed Chastity's pale body in the moonlight. Breasts, round and full, rose and fell with deep breaths as she stirred in her sleep. She was waiting for him. And he could not resist the invitation of her naked body.

Hungrily his gaze raked over Chastity's voluptuous curves, drinking in everything he had longed to see. There was enough moonlight to illuminate her body and the V between her thighs as she spread them for him. He cupped her breast, stroking her nipple and watching as it puckered beneath his thumb. Already painfully aroused, he felt himself swell further, and to relieve a fraction of the ache in his groin, he brushed his cock along her milky-white thigh. None of his suffering was abated, however, and he stroked himself along her smooth skin over and over, watching the tantalizing visual of his flesh atop hers.

She stirred and sighed, coming slowly awake while he fondled her breasts. His gaze slipped to her face and he watched her lips part when he pressed her breasts together. Damn, but he needed to feel those lips on his cock, sucking him in deep.

Raising himself to his knees, he nudged her thighs wider and kneeled between them, resting his weight on his hands. Pressing forward, he trailed his mouth between her breasts, down her belly where he circled her navel with his tongue. Gooseflesh erupted on her skin, fanning out along her midriff. She stretched then reached for him, clutching his hair in her fingers, the tips of her index fingers rubbing his ears. He groaned and brushed his cock against her thighs. Lust was screaming in his head, and his Dark Fey blood was turning black and dangerous.

"Thane," she murmured, opening to him, accepting him. How easily she accepted what he was. But would she still be as accommodating when she discovered what lurked inside him?

Tonguing her belly again he listened for her sighs, felt her hips shift on the bed as she spread her thighs wide.

"Yes," she encouraged, lifting her hips once more. She wanted him there, licking and caressing. And he wanted to taste her. Needed her on his tongue.

Slowly, he lowered his mouth to the curls that were damp. Spreading the soft folds, he raked his tongue up the length of her, waking her fully with his mouth. She was wet and writhing, her fingers curling in his hair while her hips moved in an intoxicating, erotic rhythm against his tongue that was searching and probing.

"Oh, yes…" She sighed, rubbing her sex against him. "Please," she said with a keening cry as she tensed and tightened while he drew out her pleasure. But he stopped his ministrations just before she reached ecstasy. He wanted her wild for him, much more than this. And truth be told, Lust needed his pleasure, too.

Sliding along her body, he licked the valley of her breasts and slid his now-rampant erection between the full mounds. He showed her how to press her breasts together to increase his pleasure and he groaned, watching his cock slide between her breasts.

"Use your tongue and lick the tip of me."

She did not protest or act afraid. Instead, her pink tongue crept out and licked him slowly, teasingly, so that he nudged his cock farther toward her mouth and her eyes widened with shock and perhaps excitement.

"How I've dreamed of this. The most intimate of acts a woman can do for a man."

"Show me what you desire," she whispered, meeting his gaze and flicking her tongue along his erection.

Needing no more encouragement, he moved away from her and brought her to her knees. Kneeling before her, his erection soaring in the air, he entwined his hand in her hair and motioned her forward so that her mouth was poised over the tip of him.

"I want to watch you on your knees before me." And then she slipped the tip of him past her lips and put all of him in her mouth. "God, yes, take all of me."

With gentle pressure of his hands in her hair, he guided her into a rhythm that was painstakingly slow and erotic. He told her how to suck him, how to bring the tip of his cock to her lips without letting him slide out of her mouth. He described how to build his passion slowly with tantalizing glimpses of her tongue curling around his shaft and her hand working the length of him as he watched.

She mastered the skill in minutes and soon he only need groan or fist his fingers in her hair for her to know what he liked.

As she worked her magic on him, he reached for her breasts and filled his hands with them, his fingers becoming more insistent as his desire escalated. Watching her loving him so thoroughly aroused him more than he thought possible. He'd always loved the sensation of a mouth on him, and no woman had so eagerly agreed to pleasure him in such a way as Chastity had. Already he was close to coming, and wanting to draw it out, he moved away from her, settling himself against the headboard and motioning for her to come to him.

When she crawled on her knees to him, he was already gripping his cock in his hand and stroking himself. Damn it all, she was working him up and he needed this release, this climax with her. With a soft purr, she lowered her mouth to his wet tip and he circled her lips with the head of his erection. Her eyelids fluttered closed as her tongue flicked out, as he teased her with his cock, and she moaned, as if she were savoring the taste of him. Slowly her tongue swirled around his shaft until he could not bear it. Pulling out of her mouth, he reached for her and brought her legs around his waist.

"Lean back on your hands and rest your feet on the bed." Parting her thighs he stroked her swollen sex. As she leaned back, her quim was exposed, slick and wet and begging for his cock.

Taking his cock in hand, he rubbed it against her folds, teasing himself by watching and listening to Chastity's escalating pants as he pleasured her. Her hips were rocking as well as her breasts, meeting him stroke for stroke.

Giving in to his desire, he brushed her opening and grinned as she looked up at him through a veil of hair. Teasing her, he traced her slit, watching her passion-glazed eyes widen.

"Please, do it..." She sighed, the sound husky and breathless. Nudging her hips forward, she forced the tip of him inside. She was scalding hot and drenched with arousal.

"What would you like me to do, Chastity?" he asked provocatively, slipping a fraction deeper inside her. She gasped and he watched her toss the hair from her face over her shoulder. He could now see all of her. Full breasts with pink nipples that were pebble hard and lush thighs that were open wide for him, waiting to accept his body.

He reached for her hips and brought her toward him. "Watch as I take you." And only then, when he was assured that she watching him inch inside her, did he take her. Not in one swift movement, but in slow, straight strokes. When he was certain that he had aroused her enough, he looked up from their bodies and commanded that she look at him.

Chastity gasped, then moaned, feeling the unforgiving hardness of Thane slide into her body. Slowly, inexorably penetrating her. *Stretching her.* His breathing was harsh, short pants, almost groans escaping his lips as he filled her.

"Beautiful," he whispered, straightening from her and cupping her bottom in his hands, his gaze trained on where their bodies were joined. He stroked her a few times, letting her stretch, allowing her to grow wetter around him, all the while watching as he filled her fully. Then he thrust into her, a steady rhythm that made her arch, made her cry out.

"Please," she begged, starting to claw at his shoulders. She needed him. More of the pleasure, the fullness of him.

He growled, then said, "I want to take you from behind."

Not giving her a chance to understand what he wanted, he turned her away from him and with a hand on her back he pressed against her, lowering her to the silk counterpane. The deep sound in his throat made her skin tingle and she didn't know what to think. Her bottom was exposed, so was her sex, which was wet and glistening. His large palm was tracing and cupping her. And then she felt his erection slide between the cheeks of her bottom as he slipped into her, filling her so full she could only moan.

"Move against me," he commanded, his fingers pressing into her hips. "Move and let me watch your body take me in."

His body, hard and hot, engulfed her back, and his breathing changed, his voice grew deeper, darker. *Yes,* he said in a growl that washed through her. It was not completely Thane's voice, but something else, something blended with his, but her body responded to it like a fire sweeping through brush. That voice engulfed her, consumed her until she was writhing, flinging her hips back to meet the thrust of Thane's pelvis.

Yes, the voice whispered in her mind. *More, give me more. Ah...* He sighed as his fingers bit into her hips. *Look at your cunt swallowing my cock.*

She went molten then, her body completely his. His harsh breaths mixed with the creak of the bed, and all she could think about was how wonderfully thrilling it was to be with Thane in such a way. She had tasted him, reveled in the way he watched her. He desired her, she knew that now, for he could barely control his strokes. No longer were they smooth and rhythmic, but short irregular stabs that made him groan and grab for her bottom as he impaled himself inside her.

He was wild in his passion and she could not regret anything they had done. She was no longer virtuous and chaste, and the freedom emboldened her. Her heart swelled, as her did her body. She was giving everything to him.

There was a deep growl, followed by the feel of his

body plunging into hers as he forced her down to the bed and drove into her.

Then she felt him, trembling atop her as something hot and pulsing filled her core, warming her to every nerve and fiber of her being.

His voice was back to normal. The remnants of the darkness was still there, but less so. He was breathing hard as he gathered her in his arms.

"What a brute I was to take you like this. I really am just a monster, Chastity."

"Don't say that."

He placed his face alongside her cheek and kissed her. "You don't know what I am," he whispered, "and I hope you never do."

Early-morning fog hovered above the green fields. The sun was just rising, casting brilliant orange and pink above the trees. The fog would burn off soon, but not before he met with the queen.

Reining in his mount, Lennox slid from his black gelding and led the horse into the woods. He sensed the fey surrounding him, and he cursed whatever it was that made him so aware of the damn creatures.

"The Duke of Lennox."

The womanly voice called to him from a group of trees. Narrowing his gaze, he searched fruitlessly through the dense shadows and leaves. And then by magic, she appeared, just as she had twenty-five years ago. Her beauty still breathtaking. Her figure arousing as she walked to him, the long silver flowing robes whispering over her curves, her long pale hair swishing behind her, cascading over her hips.

Aine hadn't aged a day, and suddenly he felt conscious of the twenty-five years his face and body showed.

"We meet again."

He was even more nervous now than back then, when she had first appeared to him. But then, he hadn't been in league with both faery courts, and he hadn't had four daughters to loose.

"My queen," he murmured, bowing low before her.

"My, what pretty manners," she said, her laughter tinkling off the trees. "You always were a flatterer, and if I were not ruined for the company of men, I would have removed you to my court and taken you as my lover."

Swallowing hard, he willed his amorous blood to cool. The thought of lying between her legs was still as pleasurable as it was two decades ago. As much as he desired to know the touch of a fey lover, he had more important things to think on—namely, discovering what he could do for the Unseelie.

Those unscrupulous bastards, he thought, they were the dangerous ones. Crom and his mother he could handle with a deft hand and court manners. But the Dark Fey were beyond that. They wanted his blood, and that of his girls.

The queen's voice broke into his thoughts. "It is time to pay the tithe, Lennox."

"Yes, it is."

Head tilting, the queen studied him. "My son sensed reluctance in you, but I do not."

"I accept your most generous gift, my queen, and as any gentleman of good breeding must do, I must now pay my debt of honor."

"Indeed you must."

He moistened his lips with his tongue. "And how shall I pay you, my queen."

"With your daughters. All four of them. After all, it was our union that brought them into being."

"Union?" he asked.

"My offer of a gift, and your acceptance. It was consummation enough for the creation of four virtues. Your greed and my magic planted the seed for four perfect souls to be created."

He blanched, and the queen noticed. Laughing, she took amusement in his discomfort. "Harsh words, but true. Had you not needed something from me, I would not have found what I needed. Now, I want those girls."

"I love them," he blurted out, as if the queen cared or would be swayed by such feeling.

"I am not completely unmoved by your feelings. I will allow you to visit with them at my court. Your wife, if she can keep her mouth shut about our existence, may come, as well."

"My girls," he whispered, hating to think of them as pawns in the queen's game. "What are they to you?"

"The key to a long-held hatred," she replied. "I assume you've heard, I despise the Dark Fey, and as a consequence I cursed their court. Your daughters could be the key to their salvation. I won't have that. They're needed at my court."

"You will use them."

She shrugged and walked around him. His mount nickered and shifted, nervous around the faery queen. "Women are born to be used by men. Even in my world. It is an inescapable fate. Yes, their virtue is to be used, exploited, but better here, in the arms of a Seelie Fey, than beneath the rutting body of a Dark Fey. At least here, they will be honored. There, in the Unseelie Court, they will be raped. Dishonored. Corrupted."

His knees weakened, and he struggled to stay upright as he gripped the bridle in his hand. The gelding reared his head, not liking the bit pushing down into his mouth.

The bastard had lied to him. The king of the Unseelie had sworn to him that he would protect them. That his daughters would be cherished.

"This curse," Lennox began, "what does it have to do with my daughters?"

"Niall has been very talkative," the queen sneered. "My son is much like his father, he never knows when to shut his mouth."

Lennox watched as the queen's beauty faded, replaced with hatred. "When did he tell you?" she hissed.

"The other night. He commandeered my carriage on the way to a masquerade."

"Bastard! Do not believe him. He's lying."

"Then tell me what I should know. Is there any way they can break this curse and take my daughters?"

The queen paused, watched him carefully, judging

him. Lennox prayed to God that he was deemed trust-worthy.

"Very well, I believe in your love for your offspring, and I find your desire to protect them worthy. The reason the Dark Fey are so desperate for your daughters is be-cause they believe that their virtues will end their suffer-ing. Their court is dying, and to revive it, they must have virtuous, mortal blood. That blood cannot be forced—which, I may assure you, the Dark Fey are exceedingly skilled at. They are also perversely fond of violence and force. But to revive their court, they must woo and love their virtues. They cannot simply take them to their dark court and demand they breed with them."

There was something more. Another piece of the puzzle that was missing. He knew it, but the queen was far too clever to give away too much. She didn't fully trust him.

"Three days, Lennox," she said, her spine stiffening. "I will meet with you here, and your daughters will be at your side, waiting to be given away in marriage. You may stay for the nuptials if you wish."

"And the Dark Fey?" he demanded. "What would you have me do?"

She laughed and stepped away from him. "That is your dilemma. You should not have entered into a contract with them."

"My queen," he pleaded, but she whirled around, and the zinging of metal rushed through the air. Before he could blink, the queen had a sword to his throat.

"I don't give a damn what you tell that bastard son of

mine, for I know he sent you to spy. To learn everything you can about breaking the curse. Well, he won't. You can tell him that. You can also tell him that he won't lay claim to any of the virtues."

Lennox nodded, struggling for air.

"My son appears trustworthy, but let me assure you he is not. He is the very image of his father, the man who raped me and forced his seed upon me. Is that what you want for your own flesh and blood?"

No! God, no, he couldn't bear the idea of any of his daughters suffering beneath some man—or fey.

"Did my son tell you one very important thing?" she whispered, "something that is perhaps even more important than his pathetic, dying court?"

He shook his head, spit flying from his mouth as he struggled to stay focused and conscious.

"He and his six male relations are cursed by the cardinal sins." She laughed as his eyes went wide. "Yes. Sins and virtues. You can imagine what they truly desire, can't you?"

Oh, God, no!

"Seven sins. Seven virtues. Even now, one of them pursues your daughter Chastity. Lust is his sin...imagine what he'll do to her in that dark, sadistic court."

He crumpled to the ground and the queen's laughter tinkled, surrounding him. "Three days, Lennox, or you shall pay dearly."

Eighteen

IT WAS NEARLY DARK. THE MOON WAS SLOWLY being revealed as the sun set below the horizon. Soon he would go to her, taste her once more. One taste had not been enough. Not for Lust, or him. He wanted her, over and over, and as a consequence, he had removed him-self—and Lust—from her. He hadn't trusted himself with her. Lust had been too close, taking over. He couldn't risk bringing her to his court, so he had left her for one more night before he would come and claim her.

He was back at his court. Here he was truly a Dark Fey, and the needs he had been able to bank while in the mortal realm came back, more furious and hungry than ever before.

All of them had returned, needing the court to strengthen their magic. Avery had needed to come back to his women. Kian, to escape the agony of jealousy he felt whenever he thought of Mercy, and himself because he had allowed Lust partial rein when he had taken Chastity.

He still couldn't credit it. How he had allowed his sin to rule. He wished he could lie and blame it on his sin, but Thane couldn't. A part of him had wanted her like that, too.

Beast. Monster. He truly was one.

But he could not get the feel of her out of his mind. He was consumed. Even now he was hard, aching. Lust was screaming at him to take the pixie before him who was stoking the hearth. She was bent over, flaming the embers and adding another log to the fire. It would be so easy to lift her skirt and take her. She had sent him enough coy glances and inviting swishes of her hips to make him believe she wanted him. But he wanted only one woman. But Lust was screaming at him, demanding satisfaction.

Closing his eyes, he leaned back against the pillows on his bed, trying to put the thoughts of Chastity's naked body out of his mind.

"My prince," the pixie whispered next to him, "does your sin need appeasement?"

He swallowed, conflicted by the feelings in his body and the one in his heart. Yes. Lust needed to be sated. If he was, Chastity would be safe from him, and Thane needn't worry overly much about hurting her when he saw her tonight. But the thought of lying with another made him ill. Made his chest hurt. Chastity could never credit it. It was dishonorable. Hurtful. He couldn't spend his existence fearing his sin, and how it would only destroy her.

Could he be faithful to her with Lust ruling him? Would Lust tire of her and find another? Thane knew he would never grow tired of her, but his sin was fickle. Easily aroused, and always looking for another conquest.

Chastity, he knew, was beginning to care for him. He had heard her thoughts while he was inside her. Her body and mind belonged to him, and her heart was swiftly following suit. But she didn't know what he truly was. Cursed. Everyone at court knew. This pixie handmaiden knew he was consumed by Lust. Everyone accepted it— accepted him. But would Chastity when she discovered the truth?

"My prince, Thane," she murmured next to him. "Let me."

"No," he said, trying to force Lust back into place. "Thank you."

She moved away, disappearing into the shadows, and Thane palmed his cock, through his britches, then opened the flap and pulled his cock free. Lust had made him huge, and he watched as his fingers curled around his thick shaft. He'd come two times last night, once inside Chastity, and then after, while lying in bed, he had pulled her toward him, needing her mouth on his cock.

He should have been more then satiated, hell, he should be drained, but he couldn't get the vision of Chastity on her knees, his thighs caging her, his voice, soft and encouraging, instructing her how to suck him.

He groaned, feeling himself thicken even more, and giving into temptation and natural inclination he slowly pumped himself, reliving the vision of Chastity, his hand holding her hair back as he watched her take his cock into her mouth.

She'd looked up at him with her luminous green eyes, the swollen cap of his shaft rubbing against her lips. *Yes,* he'd said, holding his cock so it was erect, directly touching her lips. *Take all of me.*

Lust, white and hot, coursed through him as he recalled the vision of his hands in her hair, guiding her head down to him. He felt the burning heat of her wet mouth engulf him, sucking on him, torturing him in her untutored exuberance as he watched her. He had let her pleasure him for what seemed liked forever. Her touch was gentle, the flicks of her tongue exciting him as he watched the pinkness of it glistening against his flushed cock. Of course he had watched it all. Lust liked to watch.

He'd studied her body, glowing alabaster in the firelight, growing harder as her lush tits swayed with her movements. He hadn't been able to stop himself from running his hand along them, groaning and swelling as they swayed faster, making him think of the way they could capture his cock and the way he could release himself on them, branding them—and her—as his own.

His own hand began to pump furiously with the surging heat in his blood. How damn beautiful she had looked bent before him with his cock in her mouth. He remembered tracing the outline of it along her cheek as it filled her mouth, feeling supreme satisfaction in it. It had been powerful and exciting. She had made him lose all reason, blind to any thought other then pleasure and fulfillment. Surely that had been the reason he'd pulled out of her mouth, only to splash his seed along her breasts, watching and glorying in it. Her eyes had been wide with wonder, and he thought his climax would never end, or that he wouldn't be able to stop coming all over her lush tits.

Release came fast and quick as he recalled the way she had cried out, at the way he'd branded her. Spilling himself onto his abdomen, Thane let himself sink back into slumber.

Soon, when the moon was high in the sky, he would go to her.

Padding quietly across the damp grass, Chastity made her way to the wall, and the garden gate that was hidden behind the ivy. The moon was bright in the sky, giving her ample light to find the rusted latch. As quietly as she could, she pulled the gate open and stepped through, gasping at the sight before her.

"Where am I?" she asked as she saw Thane step out from behind the trees.

"My court," he answered. "A very good replica of it."

The gate closed behind her, and Chastity made her way to Thane. She was nervous. She was not asleep. This was not a dream. In truth, neither had the other ones been dreams. She really was meeting Thane, her faery lover, in this enchanted garden.

And not just any faery, she reminded herself. But a Dark Fey.

"Your hands tremble," he murmured as he caught them in his palms and kissed her fingertips. "You're afraid."

"Only a touch," she whispered as she watched him kiss her knuckles.

"I don't want you even a little bit afraid."

"You're a fey."

He looked up at her with his blue eyes. "And you're a mortal."

"I am sure you have been with mortal women before," she said, hating the feeling the words gave her.

"I have." He looked her steadily in the eye. "But none that I cared so deeply for. None that I wanted to protect and cherish. None that I have brought to my court."

"I…I don't know what to expect. What to think…"

"It is all very new, but we will discuss it after, when we have all the time in the world. When I have you in my court, utterly sated in my bed, we can talk for hours."

"Wait," she whispered, suddenly nervous. "I…need a moment."

Taking her by the hand, he guided her to a patch of grass that was illuminated by the moonlight. Carefully he helped her to sit. When she was comfortable, he lowered his body down to sit beside her.

"I have been waiting so long to see you again," he

whispered, and kissed her brow. "But my memories of last night have kept me occupied."

Chastity flushed. The memories had kept her hot and fevered. The things she had willingly done with him shamed her.

"You must think me wanton," she said, blushing despite the darkness.

"I think you beautiful and the type of bed partner most men can only dream of."

"I was hardly virtuous," she whispered.

"I never wanted you as a virtue," he said as he trailed his fingers down her throat. "I only want you as you are. As you can only be with me."

She swallowed, and he licked her throat, following the movement with the tip of his tongue. "I don't want you lying beneath me, quivering in fear, or still, out of a sense of duty. I do not want what happens between us to be one-sided. I can use my hand on my cock if I desired that. What I want is your participation. Your enjoyment. The two of us together, moving with one another. Taking and giving, Chastity, that is passion and lovemaking."

"I don't know what to be, if not a virtue," she whispered, giving truth to her fears.

"How about just a woman?" he asked, his hand slipping to her ankle, then gliding up toward her knee.

"I don't know how to do that, either."

"Then let me show you," he whispered as he brought her back to his chest.

"Yes. Show me."

"Such smooth, pure skin," he murmured, trailing his

gloved finger along her supple throat to the valley of her breasts. Beneath his finger Thane felt the steady beat of her heart. The erotic cadence throbbed against his finger, drawing him in, sucking him under, until all he could hear was her heart beating in his ears. Until all he could feel was the rhythmic pulsing along every inch of his yearning body as if his flesh were inside her, heating him, as if she were pulsing around his cock.

Pressing closer, he allowed his lips to brush her gently pulsing throat. He smelled her perfume, his essence mixed with flowers. Lust followed then, clouding his vision, making him think of putting her on his lap and sinking deeply into her body.

As if she was aware of his thoughts, she stirred against him, letting out a deep, husky breath that aroused both the sin and the fey in him. His gaze focused on the swell of her breasts and he heard himself say in a voice that was part seducer, part animal, "Beautiful, supple flesh. I want to lick it, suck it. Bite it."

She responded to the fey. To Lust, and his self-control slipped just a bit. The need was so very strong now, he could hardly bear to keep his hands and teeth away from her. The man in him wanted to stretch her wide with his cock, filling her with his flesh, the sin in him wanted to take her, everything—her body, her humanity, her soul—and corrupt her.

She was so close to him…so provocatively draped against him with her head thrown back and her lips parted with slow, soft breaths. He tugged at the buttons securing her bodice and bared the corset she wore beneath. The mounds of her breasts rose and fell above the lace, and he traced his finger along them thinking of what a pretty, delicious picture she made for his dark seduction.

Steadily her pulse increased, the blood rushing through her veins. He could hear it, all that flowing blood filling, pooling beneath her pale skin. He could smell it, the way it made the perfume she wore rise between them.

"Chastity," he growled, pressing his mouth to her throat. A breath parted her lips and her hand came up between them and tugged at her corset, exposing more of her creamy skin. Red swam before him, and all he could see was bloodlust. All he could smell was Chastity in his nostrils—her blood, her sex—the way the two intermingled with her perfume. Everything that made her human. Lust wanted to ruin her. Lust wanted to corrupt the virtue Thane held in his arms.

She arched invitingly forward, giving him a healthy view of her breasts. Pulling the corset off, he tossed it aside and cupped her in his palms. They were swollen with need, the nipples hard and pressing against her chemise and his palms. She asked him with her dreamy eyes to pleasure her. He read the desire in them, and sliding his gaze down the column of her throat, he pressed forward and parted his lips.

He closed his eyes in pleasured agony as his lips met her warm flesh and the steady pounding of her heart pulsated against the sensitive skin of his lips.

I want to drain you.

The words kept tumbling through his mind until he

was shaking with the need to claim her, to take her soul and empty her mortal body—with his magic, with his sin. Like a vampire drinking her blood, he wanted to drain her mortal essence and consume it. To feel her inside him. To know what it was like to be human. To have a soul.

Baring her breast from beneath her chemise, he latched on to her nipple and hungrily took it into his mouth, suckling her. With a keening cry, she clutched his hair, pulling him closer as she writhed against him.

I want to empty you, take from you. Let me...let me...

"Yes," she whispered, pressing against him as she heard his thoughts. "Take from me."

He left her breast and hungrily kissed her mouth. His hand framed her face and he felt his fingers tremble along her warm cheek as he deepened the kiss so that their tongues were mating in the way he wished for their bodies to.

Slowly he brushed his thumb along her temple, enjoying the softness of her skin and the warmth beneath his hand. His other hand played with her breast and nipple until she was moaning and he could smell her arousal drifting up from beneath her skirt and petticoats.

Angling his head, he pressed his face into her throat and kissed the length of the burgeoning vein. The fluttering of her pulse caressed his lips, enticing him to suckle her as he would her nipple or the sensitive folds of her sex.

His mouth became insistent as he sucked and nuzzled, and imagined himself tonguing her sex as he rubbed his engorged cock, still trapped in his trousers, against her lush bottom. She moaned at the feel of him, and he sucked her neck harder and pressed his cock into her, trying to find relief for the ache in his body.

His vision awash with Lust, he continued to suck the thickening vein as his hand found its way beneath her petticoats and to the slick seam of her quim. He parted her and she gasped, tossing her head back against his arm. He wanted to watch her in her passion, but he could not leave her neck...his lips, his tongue could not be parted from her supple flesh, nor could his fingers be denied the feel of her sex clamping around them as he thrust two fingers deep inside her.

Faster and faster, he fingered her until she was spreading her legs wide for more. Three fingers were inside her now, filling her until she could barely gasp, until he felt his fingers were coated with her arousal. Until he could not stand it any longer and brought his glistening fingers to her neck, drawing them down her throat so he could taste—lick—her arousal from her skin that was covered in the perfume, the very essence he had used to enter her world.

Her throat was scented with her sex, and over and over he flicked the tip of his tongue along the musk-scented column as his fingers once more sought the flesh between her legs.

It was the most potent aphrodisiac he had ever known, and when the animal within him could not be tamed any longer, he growled against her.

"Up," he commanded. With a wave of his hand, their

clothes disappeared, becoming mist. She gasped, and looked at him over her shoulder. The wonder in her eyes was arousing.

"Thane?" she asked, her voice concerned for the first time.

She moaned when he fingered her and tried to shift her hips so that he could enter her sheath with his cock. "Not yet, love, but soon."

Chastity cried and whimpered as he sunk his finger deep inside her. She was completely naked, utterly spread out on his lap, like a pagan beneath the moon. She should be absolutely mortified.

"Tell me how much you want this," he murmured as he licked her neck, tasting the wetness of her sex that he'd placed on her skin. "Tell me how you're burning to feel me up inside you."

Chastity couldn't help but lean back against him, hoping he'd give her more of what she needed. "Face me."

She willingly obeyed him, and he surprised her by lifting her onto his thighs, wrapping her legs around his waist. "Look me in the eye and tell me that you want me, your Dark Fey lover," he commanded, cupping her heat with his palm.

"You know I want you," she cried, caging his face in her hands, trailing his lips and chin with soft kisses. "I just want you," she whispered. "My heart belongs to you and I think…I think I love you."

"Do you only think?" he asked darkly. "I already know

that I love you, and I mean to show you. Ride me, Chastity," he moaned, fitting himself inside her, showing her how to move atop him, moving her up and down, the slide fast and urgent. His thighs felt hard and relentless beneath her. His hands at her waist were just as hard, and his lips just as demanding. He was panting against her, urgently pushing up inside, lifting her off his lap. When she felt his hands steal down her buttocks, spreading them, letting his fingers stroke her entrance where he was joined inside her body, Chastity began to tremble. It was so terribly wicked for Thane to want to feel himself inside her as he made love to her—but it was deliciously wicked, Chastity suddenly realized as Thane groaned against her throat while skimming his wet finger around the rim of her while he filled her.

"I love the feel of you stretched with my cock."

Emboldened by his touch, by his low growl, she gave herself permission to love him as her body desired—as he willed it.

"Touch yourself," he mumbled against her lips.

She put her hands on her breasts and cupped them as he had done for her. "Beautiful. Now touch your cunt as I fuck you."

"Thane!" she exclaimed, wanton eagerness making her heart race at the very thought of doing such a thing.

"Put your hands over your mound and pleasure yourself, Chastity. I want to watch."

And she did. Nearly exploding with desire and excitement. It was almost too much, feeling Thane inside her, his fingers teasing the stretched entrance of her body while her fingers furiously worked to pleasure herself. There was nothing soft and romantic about their coupling. It was frantic, furious, hard and unyielding, and Chastity took it all in, reveling in the strength, the raw power of Thane in a full-blooded lust.

With a deep groan, he rocked against her, splashing his seed into her while he buried his face between her breasts, panting harshly against her skin. She cradled him then, rocking slowly against him till his breathing slowed and quieted.

"I should never have done that," he murmured against her. "It was too rough. Too much."

"No," she whispered. "No, it felt wonderful."

Lifting his head from her chest, he looked down at her. "For the first time, I could not hear your thoughts. See inside you. I…wasn't with you, but apart from you."

She shook her head denying it, but he rose from her, untangling his long limbs from hers. "I let…him have you. And I will never forgive myself for that."

"Him, whatever are you talking about?"

"I have to leave."

"But you're taking me with you, right?"

No, he couldn't. Not after this. After discovering how it was not to be with her, to allow Lust to have her.

Thane moved as far away from Chastity as he could. Lust was still blinding him, clouding his thoughts with roars for more. He could not let him have his way.

He made himself think of what he had done to her. The moment he slid inside her, he had waited to feel her response inside him, to feel her euphoria, to hear her thoughts. He had wanted to see inside her, to join with her, but he hadn't. Because it had not been him with her.

"Thane?" she whispered, and he flinched at her touch on his shoulder. "What's wrong?"

He heard the fear in her voice and was helpless to stop it. He would only hurt her more if he continued this way. The court needed her, but he could not subject her to his sin. To the way he must live his life. But most of all, he could not stand to make love to her, and not feel her inside him.

"I've lied to you," he said, steeling himself for her anger. "I pursued you because I must have you. Not because you're lovely and I love you, but because you and your sisters are needed for the survival of my court. The Unseelie are dying, and you and your virtuous mortal blood is the necessary ingredient to break the curse."

He heard her breath catch, and he refused to turn and look at her. Coward that he was, he kept his gaze averted. He had done what he promised never to do. Hurt her.

"I…I don't understand."

"I am not only a Dark Fey. But am consumed by the cardinal sin of lust. I need you—my opposing virtue—to bring you to court. To corrupt you with my body and seed. I need a child from you, to break the curse."

He saw the first tear fall from her eye and splash onto her cheek. And he lost the war with himself. She tried to turn from him, but he captured her in his arms and brought his cheek to hers and caught her tears onto his face, tasting the salt, feeling the warm wetness slide down his face.

"I never wanted to hurt you, to deceive you, but I did. And I can no longer do it."

"You're…a monster," she sobbed. "Lust…? Is that why you wanted me, because your sin needs me?"

"I need you in my court, willingly coming to me. But you won't. And now that I care…now that I love you, I can't let you, because inside I am a monster. I can't be what you want."

The tears fell in earnest and he gathered them onto his face, feeling her pain, absorbing her. "I can't cry. I don't have a soul."

He felt her pain as his flesh took in her tears. "I am doing this to protect you. It's the only way I can. I'll forsake my court for you, for your happiness." *I'll show you my love this way,* he silently added.

"No," she cried, clinging to him, then struggling to break free. "Why have you done this? You've made me want you. You've ruined me, awakened me to new feelings that I never dared to dream about, and now you're going to leave me. Alone. Hurting?"

"I'm not what you need, Chastity. You deserve more than to be used by my court. You deserve more than a fey prince consumed by sin."

"You don't know what I need," she cried, pummeling his chest with her fist. "Up until I met you, *I* didn't even know what I needed."

"It isn't me, *muirneach.* I know that. I'm not the kind of man you need in your life."

"Let me decide. I will do anything. Be anyone, if you will only take me to your court and allow me to be someone else. Someone different from what I am, and what I will always be forced to be."

"You don't understand. I am darker there. Dominant. My sin is always more difficult to control. You wouldn't like me. And I fear showing that side of myself to you."

Her struggles stilled and she gazed up at him, her lashes soaked with tears. "I never knew myself until you came into my life. Perhaps I can show you another side to you—a different side that I see in you. Like the side you knew was in me."

"Chastity," he whispered. "It's not like that."

She clutched him, leaned up and kissed his mouth. "Perhaps I am ready for a taste of sin."

Behind them, the gate crashed open, and Lennox and Crom stood there. Shielding her with his body, Thane protected her from her father who would give her away, and the bastard who would take her.

"Let her go," Crom demanded. "You've got what you want. You've fed your sin. Now leave her."

"No!" Chastity shouted, and Crom glared at her.

"He only wants you to lift his curse. He doesn't truly desire you. It's his sin that wants you. You'll be left at his court. He'll discard you."

Thane felt her indecision. The thoughts that tripped through her mind. He could sense Crom using his magic upon her, making her question her belief in him, a belief that had restored his hope.

"He speaks half truths," Thane said. "I do need you to lift the curse. The whole court does, but I do not know if claiming you will rid me of my sin. It might not. But what is not true is that I will discard you once there. I won't leave you. As long as you'll have me, I'll stay with you."

"My family?" she asked, her resolve wavering. "My sisters? Will I see them again?"

"My brothers pursue them. If they are successful, then you will see them again."

"And if not?" she asked.

"Then they will be part of the Seelie Court and you will not see them ever again."

"No!" she cried, clinging to him. "I can't leave them to the Seelie. My parents—"

"Cannot come where he is going to take you," Crom announced. Holding out his hand, he walked toward them. "If you come with me I will promise that you will have your sisters and parents. You will all live at my court—peacefully."

"He lies."

"I offer you something the Unseelie cannot. Respect. Adoration."

"I don't want to be adored and put on a pedestal. I want a life."

"You won't find that with him."

Thane held on to her tightly. He wanted to take her, to run with her, but he couldn't.

"I don't know," she whispered, and he felt his connection with her slowly pull away. She was pulling away from him, the Seelie magic poisoning her mind against him. She was leaving him, and the bastard Seelie knew it.

Suddenly, his Dark Fey blood exploded and he became mist and took Chastity in his arms and lifted her high into the sky, only to disappear amongst the moon and stars. When he became his fey self, he was in his room at court, and Chastity was lying on the ground, naked, at his feet.

"This is a side of me I didn't want you to see," he growled. She looked up at him through a curtain of blond hair, and his blood sang. "This is the Dark Fey coming out."

He reached for her and brought her up before him.

"Dark. Dominant. Demanding. I never wanted you to bear witness to it, but now you must. It's the only way I can make you stay. Corrupt you. Seduce you, lure you with my dark magic."

"I'm ready," she replied, a measure of defiance in her words and eyes. "Do your worst."

NINETEEN

THANE WAS GONE BEFORE SHE COULD BLINK. HE was mist, and then he was gone. She was left alone in his chamber, a world that was not hers, a place that was utterly foreign to her.

Had he abandoned her? Now that she was here, was he gone, never to be seen again?

No, it was not true. The lingering effects of Crom's voice in her head made her doubt Thane and her own feelings. There had been no doubt there before Crom arrived. There could be none now.

She had spoken the truth. Had wanted to come to the court, and even though he had carried her off, it did not mean she did not want to be there.

"Thane?"

She closed her eyes, tried to quell the shiver of fear. She was alone. She didn't want that. She wanted Thane.

His body loving hers. She wanted to be his in every way possible.

Stilling her mind, she tried to slow her breathing, quiet her thoughts. When they'd made love she had heard him, seen his desires, and she tried now to connect with him.

It wasn't difficult. The image of him came clearly, and what he wanted was whispered in her ear. He was hiding not from her, but from what he truly was. She had hidden her entire life beneath a useless cloak of chasteness. It had enslaved her, but it was Thane who had set her free.

A gilded door drew her attention and she walked to it, opened it and stepped into another room where a fire in a massive hearth roared. In the chair, before the fire, sat Thane.

"You must leave," he said. "I don't trust myself around you. Not yet."

"I trust you."

He groaned, tossed his head back. "Leave, Chastity."

This was the scene she saw in her mind. What he needed—or at least wanted. Submission.

Stepping around the chair, she stood before him, watching as he pleasured himself. He was thick, hard and aroused. He looked different, more wild, less controlled, and this new Thane spoke to her. To the newly discovered side of herself.

Dropping the sheet she had used to wrap around herself, she stood before him, naked, listening to his sharp inhalation of breath, watching as his fist tightened around his staff.

Then, she lay at his feet, just as she saw in his mind.

"No," he whispered, but she knew this was what he wanted. Her to come to him willingly. To accept him as he was.

Thane could not control himself. He wanted her, to show her his love, but that would hold her hostage. She was too new to pleasure. Too innocent to realize that it was not him she wanted, but his sin.

"I love you," she whispered, and she rose to her knees, before him. She watched as he touched himself, and he wished it was her touching him.

"You should not lay yourself at my feet," he warned.

"Why? Will you carry me off to your dark chamber and ravish me?"

"Perhaps."

She smiled and reached out to cover his hand with hers. Carefully, she peeled back his fingers and wrapped her fingers around his cock. "Oh, I do hope so."

"You should be careful what you wish for."

Holding his gaze, she challenged him with her eyes as she lowered her mouth over the head of his cock. It took every bit of strength he had not to thrust deeply inside her.

"Chastity," he moaned, and he reluctantly he reached for her, drawing her closer, thrusting upward. "Ah, yes."

Without so much as a word, he reached for her and guided himself in her mouth, a primal groan, long and deep, came from him, spurring her into recklessness.

There was something about him like this that made
her wish to follow him wherever he would lead. He was
dangerous—virile, utterly male—and it made her aware
of her sexual power.

He groaned again as she took him in her hand and
sucked him, fast, furiously hard. Chastity knew he was
watching—could feel his dark eyes studying her from
behind black lashes, and the knowledge emboldened her,
making her wish to give him a performance he would
never forget.

She felt him swell inside her, felt his fingers shaking
against her jaw and her throat.

Resting his head against the back of the chair, Thane
fought for control, fought to keep his eyes open, watching
Chastity watch him. Was there anything more powerful
to a man—or fey—than to see a beautiful woman on her
knees, his throbbing cock in her mouth, and loving it?
She was loving it, he realized.

"Stop," he commanded, but she continued on, sucking
and laving his cock, until both the Dark Fey and his sin
were purring inside him.

He wanted to come in her mouth, to feel her drinking
him down. She heard him, and sucked harder, giving
him his wish.

He came, filling her, and she swallowed him, her hands
caressing his flesh. She didn't run from him, from his
desires. And when he was done, he was still hard, his
cock still wanting to nudge up inside her.

Wrapping his arm around her waist, he brought her
back against his chest, his hands taking her breasts,

cupping and squeezing, his fingers pinching her nipples, making her wet between her thighs. "You didn't come to the Unseelie Court on your own. The curse won't be lifted, and I don't give a damn," he growled next to her ear. "I'd have taken you kicking and screaming if I had to."

She moaned, feeling his hands on her body, the force of the fey magic in his touch. The magic he no longer hid from her.

"I might have searched you out because of the curse. But you're not here because of it. You're here because I couldn't bear to be parted with you. Because I, a prince of the Dark Fey, is so deeply in love with you, a perfect, virtuous mortal."

She sighed, and he nestled her deeper against him.

"Believe me," he whispered as he rose from the chair and carried her into the next room. Softly he lowered her to the bed and caged her with his arms, his long, hard body.

"I believe you," she whispered back. "I didn't believe in me. In what I could allow myself to feel."

She reached for him, and instead of rubbing his shoulders, she touched his ears, and caressed them, making him shudder. He held himself above her and Chastity watched as he closed his eyes and moaned. Between her thighs, his cock stirred, pressed against her and she opened herself to Thane, to the Dark Fey and the Unseelie Court that would forever be her home.

"Yes, open for me."

Parting her knees, she exposed herself to him. Thane

was mesmerized by the sight of her pink silk, wet with desire, waiting for him.

"Yes," he murmured, his gaze fixed on her sex. And then he filled her in one swift movement, watching as he joined with her. He looked up, and saw that she, too, was watching as she took him in, swallowing his cock in her heated silk.

"Beautiful, isn't it?" he asked, shaking as she caressed the tips of his ears. "We're one, Chastity."

"Yes," she said softly, angling her hips so that she could see more of his penetration.

He hooked her legs over his arms, raising her hips so that she could see all of him as he stroked and filled her.

"I want it faster and harder."

"And so you shall have it as you want it, Chastity," he whispered, filling her as fast and as hard as she would allow.

"Thane!" she cried. His rhythm was pounding, relentless, and she rode it, gripping him with her thighs as he stared down at her. She saw the lust in his eyes, and the love, as well.

Arching beneath him, she brought her arms above her head, let her fingers curl with his as he took her hard, possessively. "I love how you make me feel. What you're making me into."

And she did. She could feel herself changing, becoming someone bold, confident. There had been pleasures of the flesh she had never even heard of, just waiting to be tried, to be experienced. And she would never have had them without Thane. Without her Dark Fey.

"Make me into whatever you want," she begged as release rode upon her. "Please, Thane."

"All right," he whispered, filling her hard, pinning her to the bed beneath them. "I'll make you into what I want you to be—*mine!*"

Her life changed in that moment, claimed by her Dark Fey lover. She was a new woman, in every sense of the word. Sexual. Insatiable.

An hour later, she climbed on top of him, loving him as she wished. He let her do as she pleased, smiling up at her as she learned how to move. When he cupped her breasts, she moaned and he smiled.

"What have I made you into?" he teased. She looked down at him, smiled and caressed his ear.

"You've made me yours. A princess of the Dark Fey Court. A follower of its voluptuous pleasures."

EPILOGUE

Dear Diary,

I have learned through my years as a mortal that change is inevitable. Even for an immortal fey prince, the uncertainty of life is the commodity that binds us together with our existence.

As I reflect upon my life, I have come to a sort of acceptance—to embrace what I once was, and what I am now. Before, I was a virtue. Now, I am a fey princess, bound to the Dark Court. Some would argue that I am no longer alive. That I am cursed. Soulless. Empty. I have given my body and soul to a faery, and therefore, I am nothing—dead.

But if, indeed, I am dead, then I must concede that I am more alive than ever I was. In this life, I am free to be who I am. A woman of noble birth. A woman possessed of a deep well of passion. A woman possessed by Lust.

I remember those minutes, the moments I gave myself to Lust, and committed my virtue to the Unseelie Court; when I gave my soul to my Dark Fey prince. There was no fear, no remorse, only the splendor of passion, the warmth and promise of everlasting pleasure with this man. As my heart slowed, I felt him clutching me, as if silently pleading with me to stay with him, to not change my mind and leave him alone forever.

I watched him take of me—his body loving mine. Never had he made such beautiful love to me. At that moment, I knew that both Lust and Thane were vital to my existence. I felt my soul lift, then suffuse into his body. His beautiful eyes closed in ecstasy at the taste, the intimacy of having me inside him, the sanctity of sheltering my soul for eternity. This image of the man I loved pressed against me was the last my living, mortal eyes saw before I was claimed by him as his eternal bride.

I am enslaved now, but not a prisoner. I have chosen this life willingly, and do not regret it. How could I when I have a man like Thane to tempt me? To care for me? To love me?

I am a virtue. A savior in my new home, for the Unseelie Court is now home. The Dark Fey my family. I have given up my mortal life to become the first of seven women to save a dying court—a court as misunderstood as I once believed I was.

My human family resides "up top" in the mortal realm. I come to them at night, in their dreams, through the magic of my husband. I miss them, especially my sisters whose fates are entwined with mine. I speak to them of the splendor of the court, the pleasures that await them—the princes who desire them. But they are still virtues, and not yet ready to heed the call of desire. But still, their sins await them, ever patient, ever proud. Ever eager to give them a taste of the desires harbored within a Dark Fey. Soon, they will come. They will listen to their hearts, and they will trust as I have trusted. We will be reunited—in this world. I am certain of it.

While my sisters speak to me in their dreams, Mama weeps for me while Papa sits in his study, all alone. He has told Mama of his bargain with the fey, and while she was shocked, heartbroken and outraged, she has begun to slowly accept that we shall meet again. Perhaps it is my nightly visits to her that have helped her accept that her daughters are not cursed, but blessed. We were born to a higher power, a power that is much needed in the Unseelie Court.

I am not angry with Papa. He made his pact with the faery queen out of love. I have come to realize what one will do in the name of love, for I know there is nothing I would not do for Thane.

My heart beats for him. My body burns for his touch. Thane, my Dark Fey prince. My lover. My husband is more than I could ever have hoped for. He has worked tirelessly to bring me happiness. To make my transition from mortal to faery princess as easy as possible. He still feels some measure of guilt for betraying me, even though I have tried to convince him that my heart and soul have always longed for him, to be where he is, whether it be in the mortal realm, or his court. How can he not realize that it was him alone that awakened me? That made me see who I truly was? What woman would not wish to give up everything in order to stay with him? I tell him this, every night, right before he takes me. Sometimes it is Lust who claims my body. Sometimes my Unseelie lover. But it is always beautiful. Always breathtaking. Always love.

My existence was part of a curse, my conception used to thwart this court. All my life I believed my virtue was a higher power, my birth something precious. But it has been a sad truth

*to realize that I was conceived to hurt. To destroy. I was born
to ruin this court, and Thane.*

*For in the weeks here, I have realized that all is not as it
would appear in the mortal realm—or in Faery. Those we
thought we knew, we discover we never really knew at all.
Sometimes it pains us to discover that someone we thought so
highly of is not worthy of our love. Sometimes it gives us relief
to be proved wrong, to be shown the goodness in someone we
feared incapable of anything but destruction.*

*Good and evil, saint and sinner, all relative terms and as
blurred as the many faceted layers of the truth. What is good?
What is evil? I wonder if I shall ever know, shall ever understand
the workings of good and bad. I always thought I did, until that
night when I realized it was possible for good to be bad, and
those who were considered to be evil, to be good.*

*Sin is a pleasure, and sometimes pleasure is a sin—but never
here at the Dark Court. Here, sin is always a pleasure, and I
shall embark to commit it every day of my existence alongside
my fey prince.*

MIDNIGHT. THE GARDEN WAS ENGULFED IN SHADOW.
The air heavy with an impending storm. She had come
again, in her dreams. Chastity. Glowing. Beautiful. *In
love.*

Mary sat on the garden bench, stewing at the memory
of her sister. It had not been a dream. Chastity had really
been there—present in her room. She'd been smiling,
happy, and Mary knew that her sister was lying with a
beautiful faery and enjoying every second of it.

Why? she wondered, not for the first time. Why had

Chastity been first? She cursed Crom for not being able to find her sister in time before she'd been carted off to the Unseelie Court. They had made a bargain, and now she was left here, forced to bear witness to her sister's conjugal bliss.

Angry and jealous, Mary tore the petals off a rose and squeezed the bud tightly in her fist. She would not be left alone.

"You've been betrayed."

Crom's voice came from the shadows, and Mary watched as he appeared, golden and beautiful and virile as he walked toward her.

"You've been robbed of your birthright."

"What do you mean?" she asked, narrowing her gaze. She had not seen Crom in weeks. That he was here now must mean he needed her again. Well, she would not agree to any further alliance with him.

"You were intended for Rinion, the Dark Fey prince possessed of Vanity."

"As I told you."

"Your father made a bargain with him. The hand of his firstborn daughter, for unlimited riches. Beltane was to have been your wedding day."

"Then why I am here?" she snapped. "Why am I still suffering this deplorable existence?"

"Because *you* weren't his firstborn daughter. That honor, my lovely, belongs to the village seamstress's daughter."

"A bastard!" she spat, unable to credit it. "That plain…

daughter of the seamstress, she has the beautiful fey intended for me?"

Crom's eyes glistened. "She does, indeed. And everything he is giving to her, should be yours."

Jumping up, Mary paced before the bench, unconcerned with the fact she was in her nightclothes. Suddenly, she stopped and looked up at the Seelie prince. "What can be done?"

"I am certain that you can have him—but it will cost you. Faery gifts do not come without a tithe."

"Don't I know it," she drawled. "Well, what do you want?"

"Prudence," he promptly replied. "Tonight."

"Why?"

Crom shrugged. "I could not have Chastity. 'Tis a pity, I wanted her not just because she was a virtue, but because I desired her. She is lost now, corrupted by Lust and my dark counterparts. But the other virtues cannot be lost. They cannot be allowed to go to their court. I must possess them if I am to see the Dark Court destroyed."

"And what will I get?" Mary snapped. It was no trial to hand over her sister to Crom. The uptight, spinsterish Prudence actually *wanted* to go their court.

Crom took a step closer and captured her face in his hands. "If you help me obtain your sisters, then I will make certain that Rinion will be yours."

"A Dark Fey, for my sister."

"Precisely."

Crom lowered his head and Mary looked into his

beautiful eyes. "You don't need *me,* do you?" she asked coyly.

"You are not a virtue," he whispered, "but I need you. I think you know just how much."

No, she was not a virtue. She'd always known that. But she wanted what was supposed to be hers. Rinion. But she suddenly found herself curious about what Crom was offering. Men always wanted her, and she wanted them. She could feel how much Crom desired her.

"We'll work together," he murmured as he brushed his thumb over her lips, "and I can show you how to pleasure your Dark lover. I am half Dark Fey, you know, and have more than my share of their desires."

Mary trembled as Crom tore her night rail from her body. She was wet. Aching. She was not virtue. Or a virgin.

"You want this," he asked as he cupped her breasts.

"Yes. I want this bargain. I want you. But most of all, I want what's mine."

"Then you shall have it."

And, heedless of her own betrayal to her sisters, Mary lay down on the grass beneath Crom and allowed his pleasure while she thought of how she would convince Prudence to go with Crom to his court. Thoughts of the Seelie Court soon gave way to images of the decadent Unseelie Court.

Closing her eyes, Mary pictured Rinion, and imagined it was his mouth licking her sex—not Crom's.

"Yes," she cried out, bucking beneath him. Yes…she would have what she was entitled to, even if she had to sell her own mother to the Seelie Fey to get it.

★ ★ ★ ★ ★

ACKNOWLEDGEMENTS

THANK YOU TO KATHLEEN OUDIT, FOR ONCE again spoiling me with a gorgeous cover. It's everything I wanted and more!

And to my fantabulous editor, Susan Swinwood, who most definitely lives up to the adage Patience is a virtue! Thank you for that!

the LOVERS
Eden Bradley

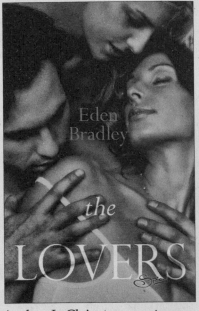

I had long dreamed of having a single experience that would change me forever. Who knew the one to change me would be a woman? But the story doesn't end there. No, that in itself is a whole new beginning.

It seemed ideal—two months at a charming writers' retreat, surrounded by kindred souls. But Bettina Boothe wasn't prepared for just how long eight weeks truly was. Or that in the process she would have to open up and reveal the most secret places in her body and soul.

Fortunately, her fellow authors do not share Bettina's self-consciousness and begin to draw her out of her self-imposed shell. One in particular—Audrey LeClaire—seems to ooze confidence and self-assuredness. Dark and petite, Audrey possesses a potent sensuality that draws the men *and* women in the workshop to her like flies to honey. Bettina is just as vulnerable, finding herself overwhelmed by a very unexpected attraction to Audrey, who makes Bettina her special project.

But when Jack Curran arrives at the retreat, everything changes. Jack is tall, beautiful, masculine. A writer of dark thrillers, he is as mysterious and alluring as his books. He and Audrey are obviously an item, but they eagerly welcome Bettina into their bed. Suddenly Bettina finds herself swept up in a maelstrom of lust, obsession and jealousy, torn between her need for two very different people in a love triangle where she will either be cherished...or consumed.

Available wherever books are sold!

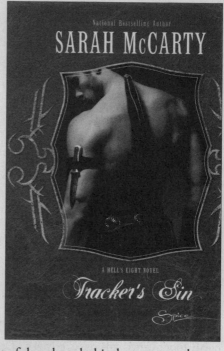

From *USA TODAY* bestselling author

kayla perrin

When money is no object, life truly is cheap.

Their romance was a modern-day fairy tale: handsome older millionaire falls hard for struggling young waitress. Robert swept Elsie off her feet—and into his bed—put a huge diamond on her finger and spirited her away in his private jet destined for happily-ever-after.

Eight years later, Elsie Kolstadt realizes the clock has finally struck midnight. The five-star restaurants, exclusive address and exotic vacations can no longer make up for Robert's obsessive desire to control everything about their life together. From her hair color to her music playlists, Robert has things just the way he wants them. No matter what.

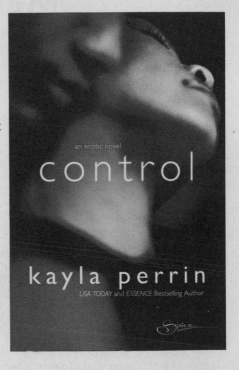

an erotic novel

control

kayla perrin

USA TODAY and ESSENCE Bestselling Author

But it's Robert's ultimate, unforgivable manipulation that finally shocks Elsie into action. Though divorce would strip her of everything, she can't live under Robert's roof any longer. Making her decision easier is Dion Carter, a high-school football coach with a heart of gold and a body of sculpted steel. Suddenly Elsie is deep in a steamy affair that could cost her everything—because Robert will stop at nothing to keep Elsie under his thumb.

control

Available wherever books are sold!

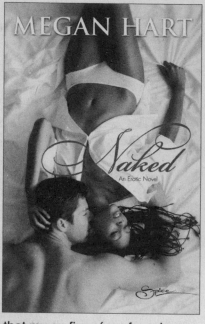

Alison's Wonderland

Alison Tyler

Over the past fifteen years, Alison Tyler has curated some of the genre's most sizzling collections of erotic fiction, proving herself to be the ultimate naughty librarian. With *Alison's Wonderland*, she has compiled a treasury of naughty tales based on fable and fairy tale, myth and legend: some ubiquitous, some obscure—all of them delightfully dirty.

From a perverse prince to a vampire-esque Sleeping Beauty, the stars of these reimagined tales are—like the original protagonists—chafing at unfulfilled desire. From Cinderella to Sisyphus, mermaids to werewolves, this realm of fantasy is limitless and so *very* satisfying.

Penned by such erotica luminaries as Shanna Germain, Rachel Kramer Bussel, N.T. Morley, Elspeth Potter, T.C. Calligari, D.L. King, Portia Da Costa and Tsaurah Litzsky, these bawdy bedtime stories are sure to bring you (and a friend) to your own happily-ever-after.

> "Alison Tyler has introduced readers to some of the hottest contemporary erotica around." —*Clean Sheets*

www.Spice-Books.com

SAT60545TR